The Queen's Huntsman

TANYA ANNE CROSBY

OLIVER-HEBER BOOKS

Published by Oliver Heber Books

0 9 8 7 6 5 4 3 2 1

 Created with Vellum

PRAISE FOR THE GOLDENCHILD PROPHECY

"*The Cornish Princess* is not simply a romantic fantasy. There is nothing simple about it. The characters are complex and do not divulge their thoughts or purpose easily. Crosby has created a balanced, multifaceted genre, one where history's battle cry is tangible while fingers of fable and fantasy pull and tug the unwary."

— *WHISKEY & WIT BOOK REVIEWS*

"Exquisite, lyrical, powerful, and haunting, The Cornish Princess is a heroine for the ages. Gwendolyn of Cornwall's epic journey from the Golden Child of Prophecy to that of a warrior and defender of her people will remain in your heart long after you finish the last page."

— *KIMBERLY CATES, USA TODAY BESTSELLING AUTHOR*

"Holy Cow! This is one of my all-time favorite books I have read this year! Tanya Anne Crosby storytelling ability is absolutely magical and this twisted ending definitely put my stomach in knots that made me totally gasp! An absolute masterpiece!"

— *PURPLE TULIP BOOK REVIEWS*

"A bit of Fae magic, a bit of Arthurian aura... wrap around a nugget of British history that has almost disappeared into the mist of time, to give start to an interesting series that promises to be a classic."

"Crosby created a world I never want to leave. This was the series she was born to write. I am ravenous for the next installment!"

"I've just been inside the mind of a genius. Tanya Anne Crosby is in a class by herself. She creates gorgeous worlds where fact and fiction blend to create a stunning epic. Utterly brilliant."

"A breathtaking true tale with a touch of Celtic magic, brought to life by a soul-stirring storyteller."

"Crosby's characters keep readers engaged..."

SERIES BIBLIOGRAPHY
THE GOLDENCHILD PROPHECY

READER'S GUIDE

Main Characters

Adwen Bryn's uncle, Duke of Durotriges

Albanactus Brother of Locrinus; "founder" of Alba

Baugh Prydein thane, king in the north

Brutus King Brutus; Trojan by birth, "founder" of Britain

Bryn Durotriges Shadow Guard to Gwendolyn

Caradoc Chieftain of the Catuvellauni

King Corineus *[cor-en-ee-us]* vassal of Brutus

Gwendolyn Daughter of King Corineus and Queen Eseld

Queen Eseld Queen consort and princess of Prydein

Kamber Brother of Locrinus; "founder" of Cumbria

Locrinus *[lock-ren-us]* Son of King Brutus of Troy

Málik Danann *[mah-lick dah-nuhn]*

Elowyn Durotriges *[El-oh-win]* Bryn's sister, and
Gwendolyn's dearest friend

Esme Faerie, with unknown allegiance

Estrildis Loc's mistress

Habren Loc's son by Estrildis

Queen Innogen Loc's mother, wife of Brutus

Talwyn Trevena Mester at Arms

Yestin Steward, Trevena

Caledonia (n) Scotland/Scottish

Cymru "Land of friends"

Dryad/Drus Faerie oak spirit

Dumnonia Ancient Cornwall

Ériu [*eh-ru*] Ancient Ireland

Hyperborea Fabled land whence the Tuatha Dé Danann may have come

Loegria Essentially Wales. Old English, meaning "land of foreigners"

Plowonida Ancient London

Pretania Ancient Britain

Prydein Welsh term for the isle of Britain; for The Cornish Princess, specifically Caledonia/Scotland

Sons of Míl Hiberians who conquered the Tuatha Dé Danann and settled Ireland

Tuatha Dé Danann [*too-uh-huh dey -dah-nuhn*] - "Tribe of the gods," ancient race in Irish mythology. Also, *Sidhe* [shē], *Elf, Fae*

Wheals Mines

ysbryd y byd Spirit of the world.

The Four Talismans of the Tuatha Dé Danann

Claímh Solais [*Klau-Solas*] *The sword of light*

Lúin of Celtchar Lugh's spear

Dagda's Cauldron [*DAW-dYAW's Cauldron*]

Lia Fáil [*lee-ah-foyl*] - *The stone of destiny, upon which even Britain's current kings are crowned.*

Awenydds Philosophers, seeking inspiration through bardic arts

Gwyddons/Gwiddons Priest-scientist, believe in divinity of and for all: *gwyddon, male; gwiddon, female*

Druids Priests, teachers, judges

Llanrhos Druids The most ancient order of Druids occupying the area now known as Anglesey

dewinefolk *Witches, faekind*

The seven Prydein tribes

Caledonii Scotland during the Iron Age and Roman eras

Novantae Far northeast of Scotland, including the offshore isles

Selgovae Kirkcudbright and Dumfriesshire, on the southern coast of Scotland

Votadini Southeast Scotland and northeast England

Venicones Fife (now in Scotland) and on both banks of the Tay

Vacomagi Region of Strathspey

Taexali Grampian, small undefended farms and hamlets

Four Tribes of Ancient Wales

Deceangli Far northern Wales

Silures Southeast of Wales; "people of the rocks"

Ordovices Central Wales; area now known as Gwynedd and south Clwyd

Demetae Southeast coast of Wales

Three Tribes of Ancient Cornwall

Dumnonii British Celtic tribe who inhabited Dumnonia, the area now known as Devon and Cornwall

Durotriges Devon and parts of Dorset and Somerset

Dobunni West of England

Remaining tribes of Ancient Britain

Atrebates Far south of England, along what is now the Hampshire and Sussex coastline.

Brigantes Northwest of England; Manchester, Lancashire and part of Yorkshire

Iceni East coast of England; Norfolk

Catuvellauni London, Hertfordshire, Bedfordshire, Buckinghamshire, Cambridgeshire, Oxfordshire, parts of Essex, Northamptonshire

Cantium Far Southeast England, Kent and a small part of Sussex

Parisi North and east Yorkshire

Trinovantes Essex and part of Suffolk

This one I dedicate to my daughter...
And to your daughter.
To all daughters.
Wear your crowns with backs straight and heads tall.
Clutch it fervidly against the coming winds and never
let go.

CHAPTER
ONE

THE SPARROW

"In this world, there is no force equal to the strength of a woman determined to rise."

— W. E. B DU BOIS

M*orning.*
Again.
Another day, the same as any other.

Gwendolyn closed her eyes against the returning sliver of light inching in through the crack in her barricaded window, revealing so little and still too much.

The chamber comprised a rancid bed, a wobbly chair and a crippled bedside table, along with a rusty brazier so full of spent embers she could scarcely imagine it had ever been emptied or cleaned.

Even at this hour, there were armed guards posted outside her door, their eyes darkened with a gloom that must have crept into her own, because she could feel it, even now, stirring like a brume.

Far from being a queen's bower, this was a prison chamber, stinking of piss—some of it her own. Her chamber pot sat near the door, untouched no matter how many times she'd begged for it to be emptied. Not even Ely had permission to do so, although now and again, when no one was looking, she snuck it away, returning it fresh and Gwendolyn felt such pangs of regret over having reduced her dear friend to the duties of a lowly chamber maid.

This was *not* the life she had imagined for herself, nor for Ely, and indeed, unless Gwendolyn were ill, she'd never have been so lazy or rude to burden any of her maids with a chamber pot, only for the sake of avoiding the garderobe.

Gods.

How much loathing could a person endure before the soul turned black as cold embers?

How many tears could a body shed?

How many meals could one refuse before the belly shriveled and the body wasted away?

In the half-light's stillness, Gwendolyn lay curled beneath the stinking furs, with her cheek against the chamber's only luxury, a lavish, wooden pillow—a wedding gift, so Locrinus claimed. Made from polished cedar because the oils in the wood resisted vermin, it was softer and smoother than most headrests, but here and now, mingled with the salt of her tears, the resin caused her cheeks to burn. But wasn't that the reason he'd gifted it to her?

Along with the pillow beneath her cheek, he'd left her Borlewen's blade[1], but she knew why he did not take it: He was ruthless enough to wish her to be re-minded daily of all he had perpetrated against her family... but perhaps more pointedly, all that he could still do.

After all, she still had Ely and Bryn to consider.

Loc was a scourge, a deceiver, murderer, a liar, and thief.

And if all that were not enough, he was a bed-swerver, as well—simply one more thing no one ever bothered to tell her, that he had a lover and child. But he and Estrildis deserved one another—both vindictive and mean—and if Gwendolyn were a betting woman, she'd wager this pillow was her idea. Only a resentful lover would devise something so subtly fiendish.

Although his mother had little feeling for Gwendolyn, she at least understood Gwendolyn's worth. Locrinus still had some need of her, and without Gwendolyn, his crown would be worth less than mud—not that she believed it would stop him from planning her demise, as he had for everyone else she loved.

A soft, keening cry escaped her parched lips, because she couldn't bear to think of it any longer... Her father, her king.

Dead.

Trevena.

Lost.

Borlewen. Cunedda. Lowenna. Jenefer. Briallen.

All dead.

Her mother and Demelza...

Gwendolyn still didn't know where they were. Like Lady Ruan and her husband, there was no word of either, and like Ely, Gwendolyn feared the worst.

However, thanks to Loc's detestable mother, she now knew too much about the Feast of Blades—this was how her wedding had come to be known. With the aid of his two younger brothers, Locrinus had executed every man and woman who'd stood to defend the old kings. The coup began immediately after their departure, at her wedding feast, where many of the guests were not guests at all. They were warriors in disguise, with more than poniards hidden beneath their sleeves. The first dagger found its way into King Brutus's back, and the next came for her father.

Trevena was now occupied by Loegrian forces, all loyal to her husband. Her beloved palace was overrun with his soldiers. The nobles all fled, taking their families with them, and the Druid who'd officiated their marriage ceremony had cursed both their houses and lands, no doubt believing Gwendolyn had had a hand in the coup. But she had not, and by the time her wedding cavalcade arrived in the Loegrian capitol, both dead kings' heads were already displayed atop the city gates, the delicate flesh of their eyes feeding the crows.

Málik, oh Málik! Where have you gone?
Don't think of him, she commanded herself.
Don't think of him.

Because if she did, even for a moment, she would fall to pieces and tomorrow would feel like a burden. Here in this place, she was alone. No matter that Bryn was somewhere in this palace. Gwendolyn seldom saw him, nor had she spoken to him in weeks. She saw Ely every day, but that was not the same. Ely was now obligated to Queen Innogen, forced to share her bed with the Queen Mother's maid, and her attendance upon Gwendolyn was relegated only to the conveyance of meals.

Like a spoilt child, Gwendolyn had once pitied herself for her mother's lack of attentions. She'd struggled with envy because Queen Eseld favored Ely more than she did Gwendolyn. For so long, she had lamented her plight, thinking herself forsaken and alone...

Poor, silly little princess...

Those were a child's laments, and Gwendolyn understood that now... understood because she now knew what loneliness was...

And grief.

And fear.

Each night, she slept with her dagger. Even now, the tapered end lay resting in the smooth wood of her pillow, in the spot her husband's head should have lain.

The violence done to her hair had left her feeling hideous, misused, and vulnerable. But Gwendolyn herself was to blame for that. She'd experienced so much trepidation over marrying Locrinus, and despite that, she'd done nothing to prevent it.

To the contrary, she'd rushed headlong into this accursed union, accepting it as her sworn duty. And worse, her willing participation in this farce—all her public avowals accepting this union—now made good and certain she hadn't any recourse should she choose to contest the marriage. It simply wouldn't matter whether the marriage was never consummated. The Llanrhos Druids would not rule in her favor—not the least of their reasons because she was a woman. But also, not once, but twice, she'd stood before the authorities to give assent—once during her Promise Ceremony and again under the sacred yew, where she took her sacred vows.

For all Gwendolyn knew, the tribes all also believed she'd been a willing participant in Loc's coup. And now... here she was.

The faintest of birdsong persuaded her to reopen

her eyes—a sparrow, its song lovely... persistent and full of promise. Gwendolyn blinked away a tear, listening...

Forsooth. She had never realized how much she adored that sound... till now.

Still in a trance, she watched as the sliver of light from her window lengthened, shining its stingy ray of light on the dagger embedded in her pillow. The pearl in the hilt winked fiercely, and her gaze fixed upon the dragon's eye...

Amidst bushels and bushels of oysters, a simple white pearl was akin to finding gold. Pink was rarer still. Black was extraordinary. Add to that the dragon effigy, without its barbed tongue, and there was only one person to whom the blade could have belonged...

Borlewen.

Last seen in her cousin's possession in Chysauster, along with Gwendolyn's torc, both had been discovered amidst Alderman Aelwin's[2] possessions. That it came to be in Loc's possession said much about his culpability. And regardless, Gwendolyn could not imagine her cousin had gone easily to her fate. She would have fought —much as she'd fought for Gwendolyn and her family.

Outside, the sparrow's song persisted, urging Gwendolyn to rise.

If she lay here much longer, she wasn't sure what would become of her.

Get up, she told herself. *Get up.*

If not for herself, she must find some way to remove Ely and Bryn from this demon's lair. At last, she sat, pulling Borlewen's dagger from the soft wood.

Get up, get up, get out of bed

Let the sparrow's song fill your head.

The song was Ely's, sung to her each morning as she came bouncing into Gwendolyn's room.

Get up, get up, never shall we part.
Let the sunshine fill your heart.

Abandoning the bed, without considering what she would do next, Gwendolyn strode toward the room's only chair, lifting it up and carrying it to the barred window, then climbing atop it. Wedging Borlewen's blade into the crack that had formed between the slats, she wiggled it to widen the rift until, at last, it made room for her fingers.

Outside, the sparrow song continued, so rich with hope, so beautiful. More than anything, Gwendolyn wanted to see it...

In her desperation, she tugged harder, prying one end loose. Then, blinking, she stopped to consider the board...

Despite its brilliant construction, her cousin's dagger would never be suitable for practicing her combat skills. In the absence of her arming sword, she could whittle herself a quarterstaff, and then use it to practice with.

Returning to the task with renewed vigor, Gwendolyn tugged at the wood until it finally came free. Gods knew she might have arrived in this city with fine gowns, ribbons and jewels, yet those were never her usual accoutrements.

Like her father and grandfather before him, she was a warrior to her bones. If these people intended for her to remain abed, weeping evermore, they would be sorely aggrieved.

Hope sprang like a song from a sparrow's beak.

---

1. The blade Locrinus used to shear Gwendolyn's hair. It is also the blade he stole from her cousin, Borlewen. For more information about characters, please see the Reader's Guide.
2. Aelwin is the subject of Gwendolyn's investigation in Book One. He murdered Alderman Brook, poisoning him with prunes.

CHAPTER
TWO

G wendolyn chose her battles carefully, claiming minute victories when she could.

For one, she stopped refusing her meals, as disgusting as they were. It only made Ely worry, and as off-putting as the gruel might be, she needed the sustenance for strength.

As a perk, in graciously accepting her meals, she also discovered that not everyone in this accursed palace was devoted to its new master. Sometimes, she found small gifts on her tray—a slip of golden ribbon tied about her napkin, or a bit of salt hidden beneath the plate.

When she asked about them, Ely said she knew nothing, and Gwendolyn would have sent her to investigate, but Ely was already as skittish as a mouse; she daren't put her in peril.

At one point, when Gwendolyn complained bitterly over the chamber pot, Queen Innogen responded by insisting she was never a prisoner.

"You are *the* queen," she'd said mockingly, and then to the guards. "You must *always* be certain to escort your lady to the garderobe whensoever she wishes. But do not bore her with idle talk." The next was said for Gwendolyn's benefit. "There are some here who wish her ill, and if any harm should come to her, the fault will be yours. I will take a pound of your flesh." The Queen Mother's eyes had fixed upon Gwendolyn though she was speaking to the guards, and the implication was not lost to Gwendolyn. Of course she could visit the garderobe—always in the company of her guards, but at the risk of her losing her life, should she encounter the wrong person— and that person, Gwendolyn suspected, would be Locrinus. He obviously couldn't bear the sight of her. But that was fine; this small modicum of freedom provided her with a sense of place, and her greedy eyes memorized every door she passed, every corner, every turn.

Sometimes, she knowingly got lost, and because her guards were forbidden to speak with her—per- haps because Innogen feared she would ask too many pertinent questions—they were forced to follow, all the while she tested the corridors, poking her head into as many apartments as she dared, always in the guise of searching for the elusive garderobe.

"Not this room," she would say aloud, in a sing- song tone. "Not this one either. Nor this one!" But Gwendolyn knew where the garderobe was, and only once she'd explored as far and wide as she dared, did she ultimately "discover" the proper facility. How- ever, even thereafter, now and again, she pretended to be lost again, hoping to encounter Bryn, but she never did. Wherever his quarters were, they weren't anywhere near hers.

In some ways, the Loegrian palace reminded Gwendolyn of those dark, twisty tunnels beneath her uncle's village in Chysauster, with crude beams bracing the earthen walls—only here the walls were made of wood, with no attention to detail, no carvings along the beams, no tapestries for warmth, very few windows, and no shining cressets for the torches.

All that was missing was a few brown bats and a beetle or two. Though there were plenty of rats, all wise enough to keep to the shadows, but their droppings were visible, regardless.

The floors, too, were crudely done, bare earth between the cracks in loosely placed stone. The result was that no matter how much the floor was swept, there would always be a fine dusting of filth, and sometimes, if one was not careful, it was easy to lose one's balance and trip.

The stables in Trevena were better considered.

And yet, so mean as this palace was, the city itself was meaner—a surprise, considering that Gwendolyn knew Brutus must have harbored a mountain of gold. Trevena alone had contributed so much to his coffers, and despite this, the paucity of his city had been startling. Upon her arrival, she'd found filthy streets, refuse wherever one ventured, excrement as well, and the buildings were timeworn and in need of repairs. They were also constructed too close together. One stray flame might bring down the entire burgh, which could well have been someone's intention, because the ceilings all bore years' worth of soot from overfed peat torches—as dangerous as it was filthy.

Indeed, so much was clear to Gwendolyn after

having seen Loc's abode. Every day of his life he must have begrudged his father's austerity, only now that the city was his, he did nothing to improve it, and more and more, she had a sense that this palace—if it could be called that—was merely a temporary refuge.

In her room, she hid the freshly carved quarter-staff beneath her bed, along with the telltale shavings, certain as she was that no one would notice since her room hadn't likely been swept since Urien's death. And, yes, indeed, it was Urien's room—Gwendolyn's first betrothed, whose death had come so swiftly and mysteriously this past spring.

In a gloating moment, it was none other than Estrildis who revealed the former occupant. So, of course, now the stench made sense.

However, despite her prediction that Gwendolyn would perish the same way he did, Gwendolyn refused to allow her husband's lover to get the best of her, so she said nothing. After all, Demelza used to counsel her that even a fool, in his silence, could be considered wise. And, if that were true, Gwendolyn was oh, so wise.

As for Locrinus, it hadn't taken long for him to grow bored with tormenting her.

Finally, he ceased to visit altogether, not even to delight in her torment, preferring to leave her care to his mother and lover—the former most often, although betimes Estrildis insinuated herself into the cell, if only to posture with one of Gwendolyn's stolen gowns.

Even then, Gwendolyn said nothing.

What should be said? She imagined it was Locrinus himself who'd gifted her possessions to Estrildis, if only to illustrate how insignificant Gwendolyn was—that she was worth less than his lover. He gave Estrildis everything, including Gwendolyn's dowry chest, her arming sword, gowns, jewels, even the extravagant gilded horse she'd received on her wedding day.

Meanwhile, Gwendolyn hadn't been allowed a clean change of clothing, nor a mirror to mend her ruined tresses. The plain shift she now wore she'd received only after the last of Locrinus' visits, when he'd demanded she remove the Prydein gown because it offended his sensibilities. He'd hurled the shift after her and left, and because Gwendolyn didn't wish to argue, she did as he'd bade her, folding her mother's gown and hiding that, too, beneath Urien's bed.

Weeks passed, and no one but Ely even mentioned the missing board in her window.

Even then, it was only to suggest that Gwendolyn might ask for it to be repaired. With summer's end approaching, winter would come sooner than expected, and thereafter, she might prefer the gloom to the bone-shivering chill.

Little did Ely realize Gwendolyn meant to be gone before then.

She only needed to figure out how to make her escape.

If Loc's mother had noticed the broken window, she never once mentioned it—or if she noticed, she wasn't concerned, perhaps with good reason. The window's ledge was too high to climb atop, even with the aid of her rickety chair. Gwendolyn might have pushed the bed over to place the chair atop it, but neither piece of furniture was sturdy enough to sustain her weight, and if she didn't break her neck, or crack her skull, or call in the guards, the practice yard was right below her window—a dusty pavilion, wherein swordplay was too often bloody and cruel.

Bare-chested, with no protection against whetted Loegrian steel, Loc's men all faced one another as though in open battle, and the bloodier it got, the more satisfied Loc appeared.

Each day, when the sound of clashing swords chased away her songbird, Gwendolyn joined her husband's warriors, strengthening her limbs and perfecting her footwork.

In time, her practice sword softened wherever she positioned her hands, all the splinters wearing smooth. Many embedded themselves into the tender flesh of her palms. Undeterred, Gwendolyn pried them all free with her teeth, and then continued practicing till her belly roiled, taking satisfaction in the malaise that accompanied her exhaustion, knowing from experience that it was not an aspect of illness, but a reward for all her hard work.

Today, she felt stronger than she had in months, and that was a good thing, because, last night, she'd overheard the guards speaking of the army's impending departure. To where was not yet disclosed, but she felt certain Locrinus was already preparing to take the army east to take Plowonida as he'd claimed he would on the first night they'd supped together—that city he intended to rename Troia Nova, his new Troy, after his father's birthland.

Regardless of where, if they left before she could find some way to escape, Locrinus would take Bryn with him, and Gwendolyn could not allow Bryn to be embroiled in a war not his own.

Eager to speak to Ely about it, she awoke early, and promptly began her practice, working through her frustrations, eschewing the headdress despite that she knew Ely would be discomfited by the sight of her shorn hair. It couldn't be helped. The scarf was more a hindrance than her plaits ever were, and now that her hair had grown long enough, she could push it behind her ears.

Until now, she'd kept the quarterstaff hidden beneath her bed, leaving her exercise for when she knew the sounds she made would be muffled by the cacophony outside. But it was past time for Ely to know she was preparing—as Loc was preparing—and perhaps to see if there was some way she could get word to Bryn. Together, the three of them must devise a plan.

When eventually Ely arrived with Gwendolyn's tray, she froze, her eyes going wide at the sight of Gwendolyn's make-do sword. Looking like a frightened little rabbit, her gaze slid from the sword to Gwendolyn's sweat-dampened hair, and then her eyes met Gwendolyn's, and she shook her head desperately, opening her mouth to speak. Only after making some panicked sound, she closed it again, rushing over to the bedside table to deposit her tray.

At once, Gwendolyn put down the quarterstaff, leaning it against the wall, but by the time she turned to face Ely, Ely was gone, and no sooner had she departed than Queen Innogen marched through the door, full of gloat and spite. "That poor girl!" she said, glancing after Ely's departure, and her lips turned ever so slightly at one corner.

Gwendolyn braced herself for the woman's careful vitriol.

Hellenes by birth, Loc's beauteous mother was the eldest daughter of King Pandrasus—a man her husband had betrayed. And so it seemed, she was only biding her time to exact revenge on her father's behalf, only waiting for her sons to come of age.

In fact, knowing what Gwendolyn knew now, she profoundly suspected it was Innogen who was the true architect behind the Feast of Blades.

Moreover, though she hadn't proof, in her heart she felt Innogen also slew Urien. It made sense if one considered Urien was not her blood. His mother was Brutus' first wife, who, according to rumors, also died mysteriously, and quite conveniently, leaving Brutus free to wed Innogen.

How familiar that sounded, but Gwendolyn would not wait around to meet the same fate.

"What may I do for you?" she asked evenly, trying not to prick the queen mother's ire. As it was with her son, words were the lady's cruelest weapons. She could wield them as lethally as Gwendolyn could any sword. But, whereas Locrinus was ruled by his spleen, Queen Innogen's wit was quiet and sharp, her reprisals calculated and mean.

"Why should I not wish to visit my beloved daughter?" she asked far too cheerfully, but then her face twisted with a look Gwendolyn interpreted as disgust once she noted Gwendolyn's sudor. "Oh, Gwendolyn!" she exclaimed. "Why must you always be so..." She shook her head, seeking the proper word. "Moist!" She advanced upon Gwendolyn suddenly only to flick a lock of wet hair out of her face. "My dear," she said rather mournfully. "'Tis little wonder my son cannot abide the thought of bedding you." She sighed then, resigned. "Truly, Gwendolyn, wouldn't it seem that a new bride should do all in her power to appeal to her new husband?"

Not this bride.

Gwendolyn swallowed her immediate retort, repulsed by the thought of Locrinus' touch.

And then her gaze fell on the practice sword she'd placed against the wall, and she cursed silently for not having laid it beneath the bed.

"You know," said the Queen Mother in a brighter tone, watching Gwendolyn. "You and I have so much in common—Estrildis, as well."

"Do we?" Gwendolyn asked, crossing her arms, trying to keep her attention off the sword.

"Indeed," said Innogen. "Neither of us could have foreseen our fates—prophecies be damned." She waved a hand dismissively, and then, for a moment, turned to study the tray Ely had brought in, considering it for a long moment before continuing. "You see, Gwendolyn," she said, her gaze shifting once more to Gwendolyn after satisfying her curiosity. "All three of us would be queens without the machinations of men."

"Would we?" asked Gwendolyn, not caring to hear about Loc's beautiful lover—she was hideous where it counted most.

"Did you realize her father was a king as great as yours or mine?" Innogen asked. "'Tis true," she said, when Gwendolyn did not respond immediately. "But, alas, as kings so oft do, he died. In battle with my husband, wouldn't you know? Two years past," she said, then stopped to reconsider, and shrugged. "Mayhap three. The years do fly!"

Not when one was imprisoned and miserable, Gwendolyn thought bitterly. In such case, they crept like a two-legged beetle, dragging its hindquarters.

"Alas, those Huns," she lamented. "They are never quite content to remain where they belong. It was only a matter of time before they set their sights on Pretania. But they made a grave mistake in believing those northern beasts would care to share their lands."

Queen Innogen reached out to pluck a bit of black fur from Gwendolyn's shift, leaving the moment with a pregnant pause, before continuing. "Of course, they drove their army south, where my Alba was camped and there, tried to murder my boy. His father rode to his aid, but not before appealing to *your* father for assistance. Did you know Corineus refused? He claimed it betrayed his treaty with the Prydein." Her eyes flashed with fury, her gaze now spearing Gwendolyn with daggers of hatred, but as quickly as her anger was revealed, it fled, and her voice returned to its usual lilt. "Now I ask you... what good is an alliance if your allies do not rise to your defense?"

Gwendolyn said nothing, uncertain where this discourse was going. It wasn't like Innogen to ramble so much, and Gwendolyn knew she never spoke without intending to make a point.

"That was the first time my Locrinus ever fought beside his father—against Humber. And his daughter —well, he took one look at Estrildis and brought her home."

Gwendolyn squeezed her arms, holding them fast. "So it appears, taking brides from dead kings has become quite the habit for your men," she said, unable to help herself.

For the second time, she wondered why the queen was here—surely not to commiserate, and Gwendolyn didn't need or want a history lesson. There must be another reason, and then she realized suddenly what it could be as the queen's gaze fell once more on the tray at Gwendolyn's bedside.

Did she suspect the gifts?

Did she mean to accuse Ely?

Even knowing that it might expose her make-do sword, Gwendolyn moved between the queen and the tray, prepared to upset the contents if she must. Thereafter, if Innogen wanted proof, she could lick the floor for evidence.

"Of course," she continued, smiling coolly, her gaze shifting from the tray at Gwendolyn's back to meet Gwendolyn's eyes. "Unlike me... unlike you... Estrildis is quite pleased with her lot..." She lifted two fingers, pressing them together. "All but for one small complication."

"Allow me to guess." Gwendolyn lifted her chin. "*I* am the complication?"

Queen Innogen's eyes sparkled, obviously pleased that she had deduced correctly, but how difficult could it be? Her husband and his lover now carried on as though Gwendolyn didn't exist—even so far as installing Estrildis in the queen's rightful apartments, and everybody knew it, though Gwendolyn had only learned as much through Ely.

"I wonder though... have you met my sweet Habren?"

Estrildis' child. Gwendolyn had, but once, and briefly. He was a sweet little boy, fair of hair and temper as well, with a face so pretty he could have been a girl, though he looked too much like his father for Gwendolyn to consider him beautiful.

The queen's countenance softened as she spoke of her grandson. "He's so like his father at this age." She hugged herself with the memory. "My sweet Locrinus was such a good boy—so, so beautiful, but that will not surprise you."

Knowing Locrinus, Gwendolyn could no longer consider him beautiful because his heart was hideous. Still, she said nothing, humoring the queen, torn now between the tray and the staff. She defended the tray, knowing that Ely's wellbeing could be at stake.

"And yet," continued Innogen. "This has left me to wonder, Gwendolyn... You see, dear, I've witnessed firsthand how contentious siblings can be, even amidst true blood." She nodded. "You're quite fortunate to be an only child."

Hardly so, Gwendolyn thought. She would have preferred a brother to assume the throne. It would have gone so much easier for him. And a sister might have been divine.

Innogen lifted a brow. "Even as we speak, Kamber and Albanactus both vie for fair shares of this wretched little isle. Though fortunately for me, neither is so ambitious as my Locrinus, and my Kamber should be pleased enough to take Loegria when his brother has no further use for it." She sighed now. "Meanwhile, Alba has again set his sights upon the north..."

And now she paused, allowing Gwendolyn a moment to consider that news, but not for long. "I must imagine such rivalry cannot be helped," she said, too serenely.

Perhaps amidst spiders or sharks, Gwendolyn mused.

Queen Innogen's smile tightened. "Naturally, you wouldn't know such things."

"What has any of this to do with me?" Gwendolyn asked impatiently.

"Well, dear..." Queen Innogen looked at her askance, and then once more at the tray at Gwendolyn's back. "You must realize... if my son gets you with child... and that child should be a boy, I fear it may bode ill for you... *both*." She gave one last heavy-lidded glance at the tray, her expression purposely bored, but there was something behind her eyes that was telling.

Gwendolyn blinked now, finally comprehending.

It wasn't the gifts Innogen cared about, but perhaps poison.

Estrildis?

Given his choice, Gwendolyn knew Locrinus would never touch her, but she also knew that the entire point of their wedding was to produce an heir to her bloodline, and this was still the intention, with or without the fulfillment of Gwendolyn's prophecy[1].

However, that didn't mean Gwendolyn's child needed to live long enough to inherit. One could easily imagine his fate solely by the way they'd dealt with Urien...

And yet, Estrildis was as willful as she was bold, or foolish...

"Yes, dear. I see you've come to the same conclusion—so bright you are," Innogen suggested with false affection. "In recent days, I've had a change of heart. Really, darling, I know you must realize I empathize with your cause. Unfortunately, Estrildis is young and biddable. Sadly, you are not. But I must ask you, Gwendolyn... wouldn't it be a terrible shame for me to hold a sweet, new babe in my arms, only to love him, and then—" She grimaced, sliding a long, black-kohl painted fingernail across the pale flesh of her throat, her lips spreading into a mirthless smile. "You might imagine how this would make me feel. I fear poor Estrildis is growing impatient—"

With her sights again on Gwendolyn's tray, she made to walk around Gwendolyn, and then stumbled over the quarterstaff. Gwendolyn cursed silently. "What is this?" she asked, confused.

Diverted for the moment, she bent to lift the whittled stick, then flicked a glance at the window with sudden comprehension. "Oh, no!" she said, sounding alarmed, and when Gwendolyn moved to take it, she said, "No, no, no!" And she stepped out of Gwendolyn's reach, spinning at once for the door. "We cannot have such things lying about!"

She sent Gwendolyn a disapproving frown over her shoulder, and Gwendolyn cursed herself again for not placing the practice sword beneath the bed. Now she would have to make do without.

The Queen Mother walked away, holding the staff between two fingers, as though it disgusted her. "Fret not!" she called back as she went. "I really do hope you are not too hungry! Don't you worry, I shall return with a surprise!" And with that, she slammed the door so hard it shook the walls. But the instant she was gone, Gwendolyn turned to reconsider the tray.

It looked like it typically did—as unsavory to eat as it was to look at, but poison was not something that could easily be detected.

Just to be certain, she lifted the plate to discover nothing beneath, and knew intuitively it was not the gifts Innogen came searching for.

Unfortunately, Gwendolyn knew more than she wished to about poison. She'd been ingesting a special elixir of toxicants in minute doses since she was only a child, a measure against treason since poison too often was the traitor's weapon of choice.

However, Innogen was not the one she was concerned about—at least not over this matter. If Gwendolyn turned up dead before Locrinus had the chance to secure at least a majority of the tribes, their marriage would come to naught, and forging these alliances was the point, after all.

Also, so long as Gwendolyn lived, Innogen's son could not remarry, and the Queen Mother would remain chatelaine of this house—something she truly believed the woman preferred. So, of course, she would appear to champion Estrildis. With Loc's young lover by her side and Gwendolyn imprisoned, Innogen was the true *meistres* of this house, and she ruled it more ruthlessly than Gwendolyn's own mother could ever have thought to.

She'd claimed Estrildis was growing impatient, and Estrildis was certainly stupid enough to be impetuous. Innogen was not. No doubt she knew Gwendolyn had not had the benefit of her elixir for months and months—not since before the massacre at Chysauster. At this point, her immunity would be gone. But regardless of Innogen's reasons for the warning, Gwendolyn was smarter than both, and she didn't intend to be dispatched so easily.

"Thank you," she whispered, as she lifted the tray and walked straight to the door, opening it calmly.

With a quick smile for her guards, she hurled the tray out. It landed with a clatter, and she slammed the door after.

------

1. At Gwendolyn's birth, she was given three gifts by the Fae: a prophecy for her future, a gift of "Reflection," and a golden mane—literally, every lock of her hair will turn to gold, provided it is cut by her one true love.

THREE

Later that same afternoon, when another rap sounded on Gwendolyn's door, she clenched her teeth. Gods knew she hadn't the presence of mind to deal with Innogen again so soon—nor Estrildis, gods forbid. She certainly couldn't be held accountable for anything she might say after that stupid wench had tried to poison her—presumably.

For a moment, Gwendolyn said nothing, hoping they would think her asleep and go away; but the knock came once more, this time more insistently.

"Enter!" she said with a note of pique, wondering why either of those women ever bothered to knock. The run of the house was theirs, though perhaps they were wise enough to understand that, in a certain mood, Gwendolyn could still be dangerous, particularly whilst still in possession of her cousin's blade.

The heavy door creaked opened, and Gwendolyn was startled to find it was neither Estrildis nor Innogen. Her brows lifted at the sight of the face that emerged—a little more gaunt, eyes shadowed and sad, but oh, so beloved!

"Bryn!" Gwendolyn stood, crossing the room at

once, intending to embrace him. But his already pale face drained of color, and Gwendolyn thought she detected the slightest shake of his head. She froze midway.

"Majesty," he said tightly, and winced.

They both knew that in this palace that title was a mere formality.

And more, it was a bitter reminder of her husband's betrayal. If life had proceeded as it should have, she would still be a princess, enjoying life with her new husband, and her father's head would still be firmly attached to his shoulders, still wearing his crown.

Like hers, Bryn's hair was unkempt, his dark curls as slack as his shoulders. He appeared entirely defeated, and Gwendolyn understood that much of his ill-fortune had begun with her. After all, she was the reason he was demoted. It was her childish antics that prompted her father to strip him of a position he'd trained for all his life.

To be sure, they'd not yet overcome that unfortunate business before finding themselves embroiled in this travesty. For all Gwendolyn knew, he loathed her for it.

She wanted so fiercely to hug him.

There was so much she longed to say—but the presence of her guards forestalled her words, especially knowing that everything said or done in this room would be reported to Queen Innogen, and in turn, to Locrinus.

The only reason nobody knew about her daily dancing with her make-do sword was because they'd given her a door to close.

Only belatedly, she realized Bryn was staring, and

it occurred to her it must be her hair—as yet he had not seen her with it shorn because on the morning after her nuptials, she'd hidden the proof of Loc's violence with a scarf—the same scarf she still wore most days.

Not that Bryn would ever know it, since she only ever spied him from her window, practicing out in the yard. Anything he knew about that night's humiliation, he would know only through Ely. But that suited her well enough, because Gwendolyn was mortified for Bryn to know—in part, because she'd feared his response.

Perhaps he would say nothing to Locrinus... in fear for his sister, or even for himself. It was far too easy to say what one might do in the face of adversity, still another amid strife.

But if he was still the Bryn she knew and loved, she feared he would challenge Loc, and under the present circumstances, there would be no one who would rise to his defense—not even Gwendolyn, because there was nothing she could do for anybody, including herself.

The state of her hair should attest to this.

"Why... have you come?" she asked.

Her old friend straightened, seeming to compose himself. "Majesty," he said once more. "I've come to apprise you... we'll be entertaining visitors for the evening's feast."

Gwendolyn knit her brows. "Visitors?"

"Emissaries," he said, and she blinked.

Had her father's allies bent their knees so readily?

Gods. She was afraid to ask but did so anyway. "Which tribes?"

"Atrebates... and... Durotriges."

27

Gwendolyn's heart flitted, but she hid her excitement, only nodding, suddenly understanding what he was trying to convey with his eyes... in part, a warning... to remain on her best behavior... for his sake and for Ely's. But this was Bryn's uncle who'd come—a man Gwendolyn had considered among the closest of allies. It could be that this would be fortuitous... or it could be the end of all hope. Whatever the case, tonight, for the first time, Locrinus would certainly have need of her, and, no doubt, he intended for it to appear as though he had her support.

As though she weren't his prisoner.

With hair shorn, eating cold gruel.

She sensed now that Bryn chose his words more carefully. "Remember," he said, and one guard cleared his throat. In response, Bryn seemed to rethink his words, his blue eyes simmering with loathing... *for Gwendolyn?*

Did he hate her now?

"Remember," he said again. "When last we met my uncle?"

"I do," she said, unable to hide the slant of her eyes.

"Please... try not to repeat the offense, will you?"

Offense? Once more, Gwendolyn blinked, this time rapidly in succession. Her brows knit with confusion. *Did he mean the hunting excursion?*

As far as she could remember, it was Adwen who'd arranged that event in her honor. For once in her life, Gwendolyn had had very little to do with any misconduct. Still, she bit her tongue, sensing he was trying to say something, but what it was she couldn't tell.

"That is all," he said, and a fresh wash of tears

brimmed in Gwendolyn's eyes. She crossed her arms and clenched her fists. "I will return later to escort you," he said.

For the sake of appearances, Gwendolyn realized. "Yes, of course." She nodded.

"I am still your Shadow," he said, and Gwendolyn swallowed convulsively because there was a wealth of meaning in those five little words: *I am still your Shadow.*

Was this the *surprise* Innogen had intimated? At long last, she would be allowed to bathe, and sup in the hall like a human being, instead of a caged beast.

Please don't leave, she silently begged.

The little girl in her longed to cast herself at his feet and beseech him not to go.

There was so much she needed to say.

Now seemed her only opportunity.

"Naturally," she said, shaking her head, fighting back tears. "We... mustn't... do anything... untoward... to alarm our ambassadors." And when the guards peered into her room, she presented Bryn a glance that could have been mistaken for pique, and said, "Do tell. Have you so readily changed your allegiance?"

They both knew what she was asking, and she also knew how he would answer, perforce. There was nothing Bryn could say to reassure her, but this was her way of keeping him here, if only for a moment longer...

She and Ely were close, but never quite like her and Bryn.

Not only had Bryn served her as her Shadow for more than a decade, he had been her confidant and friend since birth. Only months ago, they'd been like siblings, carefree and easy. No words left unspoken. Now... so much was left unsaid.

"I serve the true king," he said carefully, and despite the iciness of his tone, Gwendolyn understood what he meant by the glimmer in his eyes.

Her father was the *true* king—that he could not say he served his heir, was only to be expected. "You mean the usurper," she argued, and her anger wasn't altogether feigned—not for Bryn, but for Loc's betrayal. "I warrant it will take more than parading a hostage queen before the ambassadors to convince anyone to follow an Outlander. You and I both know that without the support of *all* tribes, he will never succeed in his bid for my father's throne."

"Gwendolyn," he said. "He already has the throne. *And* the crown."

Gods. He did. This was true—but how many times must she remind herself?

Bitterly, she remembered how they'd handed the crown to Loc on the morning of their arrival—a crown of bronze with depictions of flowering myrtle. Her father's crown. "He'll need more than that," she said. "Neither a throne nor crown will make him High King."

"Agreed," said Bryn. "But that is why I have been sent to... advise you. You must contemplate the evening carefully. If you are not convincing... enough..."

His words faltered, and Gwendolyn's brows lifted. "If I am not convincing enough?"

A muscle ticked at his jaw. "The first blade is spoken for, and it will not be yours."

Fear sidled through Gwendolyn's veins. "Whose? Yours?"

He shook his head slowly, his blue eyes betraying something akin to fear, but Gwendolyn knew it was not for himself.

Ely.

"Will you deal the blow yourself?"

"If I must."

Bile rose at the back of Gwendolyn's throat, and she turned away, if only for an instant, to conceal the maelstrom of emotion she could no longer hide.

She knew Bryn would die before ever harming his sister, and yet... if he knew they intended to torture her... he would strike that blow... and another for himself.

And then... she would truly be alone.

However, Bryn was a careful man—in *all* ways. Every word he uttered was precisely considered, like his father. It was Gwendolyn who'd so oft led him astray, and she knew there was more to his warning, though she could still not glean what it was.

"Do we comprehend one another?" he said.

"Yes," she lied, and her heart thumped madly as she turned again to face him. "So... is there aught more you would say to me—another warning?"

"Nay, Majesty. That is all," he said. "Only that you are required to attend the evening's festivities, and—"

"Perform?" she finished curtly, with a defiant lift of her chin.

"Indeed," he said, blinking. "Perform."

Only this time, when he opened his eyes, he slipped her a wink, and Gwendolyn turned away, lest her surprise betray them both.

There was nothing else she could say or do to forestall him.

Her actions here and now—tonight—would have dire consequences for both him and for his sister. For Gwendolyn as well.

"You may leave now," she said, and her heart thumped madly as he closed the door.

After a moment, she heard his footfalls ebb.

CHAPTER FOUR

T ry not to repeat the offense, he'd said.

Gwendolyn scoured her memory for clues, quite certain that Bryn's warning hid a message.

Only what could it be?

As the youngest Durotrigan, scarcely older than Bryn, Adwen had been the last in line to inherit his father's lands and titles. Four years ago, after Bryn's grandfather and eldest uncle both perished in a raid, the stewardship was offered to Bryn's sire. Talwyn Durotriges remained in his hard-won position as Mester at Arms for Pretania's High King. Loyal, and true as any man could be, he'd preferred a position of service over the bestowal of lands and titles—for himself and for his son. When he'd refused, the lands and the title fell to his younger brother, Adwen.

But Adwen was a good choice for Duke. Gwendolyn had always considered him to be the most charming of his brood. And perhaps they'd gotten on too well.

That day in question, Adwen was not yet the steward of his father's lands. Like any younger son, he was puckish and full of mischief, unconcerned with matters of propriety.

Early that morning, when he'd arrived in Trevena, he came with the gift of a bow for Gwendolyn's Name Day, and then he'd convinced her to go hunting to try out the new bow—not a difficult task, since Gwendolyn was ever eager for diversions.

Only later, much to her dismay, Gwendolyn's father accused him of improprieties—most unfairly because there was never any misconduct between them, and they were never even alone—always in the company of Bryn. On her mother's counsel, they'd sent Adwen away and Gwendolyn never saw him again thereafter. She'd even missed the conferral when he was awarded his dukedom because her father sent her off to Chysauster.

What offense did Bryn mean? Aside from the tiniest ruse they'd employed to escape the morning's fast, there was nothing she had to regret.

Was it that, even now, he was worried Gwendolyn harbored some small feeling for Adwen?

But that made little sense either. The time for winning or giving favors ended when Gwendolyn took her vows at the Elder Yew.

And yet, there was something she was missing, because she knew Bryn too well, and she sensed he was trying to tell her something.

In fact, she became so consumed with thoughts of her last day spent with the youngest Durotrigan that only belatedly did she realize how late the hour grew.

Already, the sun was setting, dimming the light in her room. But, as yet, neither Ely nor Bryn had returned, and neither had Innogen with her promised "surprise."

A feeling like bees buzzed about Gwendolyn's belly.

Had they changed their minds about allowing her to attend?

Had Loc decided he didn't need her?

Had the ambassadors already sworn their fealty without thought for Gwendolyn's agreement?

If so, what would that mean for her?

AT LONG LAST, it was Estrildis who arrived with Gwendolyn's "surprise."

Garbed every bit as a queen, missing only a crown, she delivered one of her missing coffers—the most precious of all, her dowry chest. Seeing it, Gwendolyn nearly wept with joy.

Two servants carted in the chest, placing it hurriedly on the floor, then turned and fled.

"There," said Estrildis, entering the room after them, and indicating the chest with an angry flourish of her hand. Her full lips twisted as she said, "As you can see, I've brought your stupid coffer at the queen's behest!"

Gwendolyn lifted her brow. She was the Queen. Loc's mother was Queen Mother, and no longer even a consort. The title was merely a courtesy, though Gwendolyn didn't bother to correct her, when she must already know. The girl was spiteful and determined to slight Gwendolyn at every opportunity.

"If it were up to me—and someday it will be—I would give you nothing."

"Thank you so much for the chest," Gwendolyn said, unwilling to spoil the moment. It didn't matter why it was delivered, only that it was—at last.

Estrildis had no such compunction. "I hope you won't mind," the girl said indignantly. "I borrowed a few items of note."

Gwendolyn didn't bother to ask what. It wouldn't matter. Whatever Estrildis wanted, Estrildis got. By now, Gwendolyn had complained enough about her missing possessions to know that her protests would fall upon deaf ears. However, if Estrildis was "asking" there must be a reason... and Gwendolyn would not willfully antagonize her, though neither would she abet her.

"The forehead crown with the moonstones," she announced, without prompting. "I intend to wear it this eve."

Gwendolyn said nothing, determined not to risk her one chance to be out of this room, so the ambassadors might judge for themselves whether she had willingly taken part in this travesty.

"After all," continued her husband's lover, her tone growing more embittered with every word she uttered. "I am a princess, too! Shouldn't I be allowed to present myself as one?"

How conveniently she forgot; Gwendolyn was not a princess any longer.

Again, it didn't matter; she refused to be baited. It would serve no one, most especially not Gwendolyn. At the moment, Estrildis wasn't wearing the crown. But she was wearing Gwendolyn's oyster shell dress —the one with the wide sleeves and matching surcoat she'd worn the night of her Promise Ceremony, and she wondered if Estrildis knew this, though she gathered she did not.

More than anything, she hoped the little horror would attend wearing both the dress and crown—

apparel certain to be noted by anyone who'd attended Gwendolyn's Promise and wedding ceremonies. The choice would reveal much about Gwendolyn's part in this farce of a marriage.

No bride would freely allow such precious wedding attire to be used by her husband's lover and there was little doubt that everyone knew precisely who Estrildis was by now—especially considering that it was her chamber, not Gwendolyn's, that lay adjoining the King's.

When Gwendolyn still would not respond, Estrildis tried another tack, inquiring a bit more sweetly, "Perhaps you know of some reason I should not?"

A reluctant smile tugged at the corners of Gwendolyn's mouth, mostly because she was so entirely transparent. The girl was as spectacularly beautiful as she was vapid, though certainly she was clever enough to understand that people would notice such things.

However, she was not quite clever enough to go ask Loc's own mother, considering that the Queen Mother was there that day as well—at least for the wedding.

Gwendolyn could only hope that Estrildis wouldn't ask Innogen or Ely, or anyone who could warn Locrinus' mistress about what a folly it was to wear the moonstone crown. Doubtless, Locrinus himself would not have bothered to notice what Gwendolyn wore during their nuptials.

Growing noticeably annoyed, Estrildis rolled her pretty blue eyes—eyes that were as bright as her skin was tawny. "I already asked the Queen Mother," she said furiously, as though she'd read Gwendolyn's mind. "She did not remember you wearing the crown."

Gwendolyn shrugged. "There you have it then," she said, but the girl's voice lost all trace of civility. Her eyes narrowed to slits, burning with incandescent fury. "Far be it from you to be of service, you wretched creature!" Her lips twisted viciously. "Unfortunately for you, the hour grows late. I fear you'll have to make do with a *whore's* bath," she said, emphasizing the word "whore." "The Queen Mother has been otherwise occupied all day long, and certainly you're of no import to her. She gave your care to me. Alas, there's no time to bring you a tub. But don't you worry, your interval in the hall will be fleeting at any rate."

Gwendolyn's smile persisted. "Do not concern yourself, Princess. I will make do," she reassured. But Loc's lover was too much to bear. So much as she tried, Gwendolyn couldn't quite keep herself from baiting the hateful girl. "Still, I wonder," she added. "Will you be gracing us with your company this eve? Will you also be seated at the high table?"

Of course, Gwendolyn knew the answer. She would not be. So long as Locrinus was still hoping to curry favor with the ambassadors, the girl was still only a mistress, and as his mistress, she would not be suitable for the high table. They would note such an insult to their queen and it wouldn't matter whether they suspected Gwendolyn's part in Loc's coup. Centuries' worth of tradition could not so conveniently be disregarded. She was still her father's heir, and the rightful queen. Her words hit their mark. Estrildis' features twisted with rage.

"I hate you!" she hissed. "One day you'll regret

your impertinence, you stupid, ill-favored bitch!" And then she smiled thinly and said, "Next time, I'll *not* be thwarted!"

Next time? Gwendolyn blinked. Was it true, then? Did she attempt to poison Gwendolyn and had the most unlikely champion come to her rescue? *Loc's mother?*

Even so, the prospect was disheartening. If Innogen knew what Estrildis had done and did little more than put a glimmer of suspicion in Gwendolyn's head, without ever revealing the attempt upon her life, or removing the tray, then it was only a matter of time before Estrildis attempted it again and perhaps succeeded. Gwendolyn had better watch her every meal.

And now she must wonder about her "gifts"— perhaps only a cruel jest to make Gwendolyn believe she had allies when she had none. Though maybe it was also meant to distract her from the poison. Gwendolyn opened her mouth to speak, but no words came, and this time, Estrildis seemed to relish her silence. Her blue eyes glinted.

"You think I don't know your poise is an act? I smell your fear, Gwendolyn, and believe me, 'tis warranted. Only pray you'll act so well this eve, because if you disappoint my sweet darling, he'll make you pay, and I will watch with glee!"

Of this, Gwendolyn had no doubt.

"More's the pity for you. I believe he loathes you more than I do," Estrildis said, and then she laughed delightedly. Simpering, she spun to leave, with Gwendolyn's magnificent dress swishing as she moved. For the second time this day, the door slammed in her wake, and Gwendolyn had to stop herself from screaming after the girl. So much did she share her loathing.

But then, once Estrildis was gone, her mood lifted at once, if only to see her mother's precious gift—an heirloom that once belonged to her grandmother, and to her grandmother's mother before her. Her dowry chest.

Her heart lighter than it had been in weeks, she fell to her knees beside the chest, her throat bobbing with a dry swallow, for fear of what she would not find inside.

Of indeterminate age, the coffer bore many of the same markings embroidered on her mother's wedding gown—none of which she understood as yet.

As Gwendolyn did the first time she was presented the chest, she reverently fingered the artwork, loath to mar the delicate paint with even with the faintest of touches.

Sweet gods. It still smelled of lemon oil.

At long last, mustering the nerve, she sucked in a breath and lifted the lid... only to discover the interior was nearly empty. She couldn't help herself; her eyes stung with unshed tears.

Really, it wasn't so much the lack of *things*... Gwendolyn had never had much that was only hers. Indeed, for so long, she had shared her mother's gowns and jewels. But this was the first time she'd had a trousseau all her own, and those Prydein heirlooms were precious.

There was only one gown remaining. It lay on top —a piled silken fabric imported from Akkadia. A rich shade of lavender that reminded Gwendolyn of the petals of a green-winged orchid, it was one dress she'd never worn. The fabric was rare and expensive, but there must be something wrong with it if Estrildis did not want it.

Lifting the dress to inspect it, she promptly discovered why... a rip in the seam beneath the armpit. However, rip or no rip, she would have to wear it.

The only other choice she had was her Prydein gown, and she knew how much Loc detested it. Therefore, resigned to the lavender dress, she laid it aside to rummage through her remaining treasures, hopeful of finding some of her mother's Prydein gems.

At the bottom of the chest, she discovered the Minoan earrings—the dangly ones with the golden bees. She also found the silver armband.

As she'd already expected, the crown with the moonstones was gone, but the silver hairpin remained—the long one with the fish knob and sapphire eyes. And much to Gwendolyn's relief, she also found the lunate pendant, though, of course, without many of its jewels.

Here, too, was her mother's brooch, the one fashioned in the shape of a fish with an arrow through its gob. Undoubtedly, Estrildis had found little value in these items, with so much patina to mar the sheen. Compared to her shining jewels, these would seem timeworn and unworthy of even the effort to clean them, but all had once belonged to Gwendolyn's grandmother and she cherished them deeply. Clasping the brooch in her hand, she sat cross-legged on the floor, as she used to do in her bedchamber at home... examining the brooch.

It seemed a lifetime ago that she and Ely had been so carefree, giggling over absurdities.

Back then, Ely had not yet acquired the duties of

her lady's maid, and their relationship was so much less complicated. But who could ever have imagined that, in such short time, so much would change? That Gwendolyn would find herself a prisoner in her husband's home, subject to the whims of his mother and mistress?

That her father would be dead.

That her beloved Trevena would be occupied by the enemy...

And her mother...

Dead as well?

Much to her regret, she remembered their final moments together... That day on the ramparts, on the night of her wedding, Gwendolyn had been so furious with her. She'd longed so desperately for an embrace, and to have her mother tell her how much she would be missed in their home. Instead, she'd been reprimanded, admonished to smile, then lectured on the differences between a woman and a child... as though Gwendolyn did not know.

Alas, though there was truth in her final lessons, Gwendolyn resented that this should be their final memory—along with that fleeting moment by the yew, when her mother ultimately proclaimed how proud she was of her only daughter.

For so long Gwendolyn had waited to hear that, and now, even those words stabbed at her heart like a shot of yew poison, administering grief and self-loathing every time she remembered her mother's words... killing her slowly.

"Today you have brought great joy and healing to our people and our lands," she had said.

But nay, Gwendolyn hadn't. If aught, she'd been the catalyst to this end.

And Demelza?

More than her own mother, she thought of the maid as her dam. After all, it was Demelza who'd swabbed her fevered face, Demelza who'd mended her knees and her dresses.

It was also Demelza who'd wagged a finger in her face, offering unsolicited advice... always with so much love in her deep, dark eyes.

More tears filled Gwendolyn's eyes, spilling down her cheeks, only this time, unlike the last time she'd prepared for a special occasion, there was no kohl to be smeared, nor any galena to stain her face. She sighed and then reconsidered Bryn's words.

Should she take them strictly as spoken, he was only issuing a warning—"behave," do as Loc expected, or he would kill Ely, and worse, he'd make Bryn strike the blow.

"Remember when last we saw my Uncle?" he'd asked. *"Try not to repeat the offense."*

Try as she might, Gwendolyn could still not make sense of the rebuke, and when Ely arrived, unsmiling and reticent, the guards made her keep the door open, preventing Gwendolyn from speaking freely.

"Majesty," Ely said, with a bow, and her sweet blue eyes, so much like her brother's, were red-rimmed, as though she'd been weeping.

What did she know?

The question bedeviled her, but Gwendolyn asked gingerly, "Have you spoken to Bryn?"

Ely nodded, and then promptly changed the subject. "I really think you should wear your mother's gown!"

"Truly?" Gwendolyn asked, screwing up her face, more than a little surprised.

Ely nodded, moving at once to the dowry chest, proceeding to empty it of every piece of her mother's jewels—the Minoan earrings, the silver armband, the lunate pendant, and then she plucked the brooch out of Gwendolyn's hands. "Wear them all," she advised.

But... Gwendolyn blinked, confused. The silver armband would be hidden beneath the sleeve of her tunic. And if she wore her mother's wedding garb, the brooch would be too difficult to apply through the leather. Only the pendant and earrings would be visible. But when she gave Ely a questioning glance, Ely begged with her eyes, and Gwendolyn capitulated.

"You really *must* be prepared," Ely said, and then without another word, she helped Gwendolyn dress, in finality pulling a bright yellow scarf from the belt at her waist, meant to replace Gwendolyn's soiled scarf. "A gift from the Queen Mother," she explained, as she wrapped Gwendolyn's tresses, taking great care to tuck all the shorn ends beneath the cloth, before fastening it with her mother's brooch.

CHAPTER
FIVE

A feeling like dread thrummed through Gwendolyn's veins, her heart galloping faster and faster the closer they came to the hall...

Bryn had said he would return to escort her; he did not. Neither did she recognize the guards who'd came to collect her. One now preceded her down the hall. The other followed behind, both silent and stone-faced, as though they were escorting her to her execution.

Only because Ely insisted, she'd worn her mother's gown, and, along with it, every remaining bauble in her dowry chest. The result was garish, and the choice was certain to displease Locrinus, but Gwendolyn didn't care. Even now, her mother's silver bracelet strangled the tender flesh of her upper arm, but she didn't care about that either.

This would be her first opportunity to send a message to the tribes, and she still could not conceive how to accomplish this without speaking her true heart, or even whether there would be allies in attendance to hear it. If she played her hand—whatever that hand might be—and her message was ill received, those ambassadors would leave her to Loc's mercy.

But he had no mercy.

And nevertheless, if she didn't try, they could perceive her silence as compliance, and this would be the greatest folly of all.

Breathe, she commanded herself. *Breathe.*

Around every dark corner, the smell of urine drifted from the cut stones to choke away her breath, and she lifted a hand to her nostrils, even as her belly roiled.

Obviously, these people had no care for this palace. To entertain amidst such filth was unimaginable. Her mother would have wept. But this was not a home; it was a garrison. They turned another corner, coming closer to the hall, and Gwendolyn inhaled deeply, fighting a surge of nausea. Whatever she did tonight—or did not do—could change the course for all. The steady drone of voices grew louder, more obnoxious, and she straightened her spine, disturbed to hear such revelry. Although it wasn't the same infectious laughter she'd witnessed amidst her father's vassals, it was still laughter, and it grew louder and bawdier the closer she came.

When ultimately she arrived, a ponderous silence fell over the hall, prompting her husband to peer up from his goblet. He fixed her with a look of contempt —no doubt because of the gown.

Keep walking, she told herself. *Don't stop.*

She mustn't falter in her step.

Followed by her guards, Gwendolyn made her way straight toward the dais, her gaze seeking and finding Estrildis at one of the lower tables. The woman's bright blue eyes locked on Gwendolyn, her lips pursing with indignation. Gwendolyn offered a smile as she passed, pleased to see she was wearing both the oyster-shell dress and the moonstone crown. *Good.* She hoped everyone present would note her choice of dress.

It was only once upon the dais that Locrinus stood to greet her, the frown now banished from his handsome features. He was, for the benefit of all, a doting husband, extending a hand to receive his loving bride. But this was a far cry from the last time they'd supped together, with Gwendolyn so eager to greet him she'd nearly tumbled down the dais in her excitement.

She was a fool then—a silly child, with dotish dreams.

Pasting another smile on her face, she accepted the hand Locrinus gave her, and then turned once she stood by his side, bowing to their guests—mostly so the scrutiny would end. Nearly at once, the revelry recommenced and her gaze sought Adwen, but she didn't see him amidst the crowd. Letdown, she turned to Loc, hoping he couldn't read her disappointment. "I was told Durotriges sent an emissary?"

The look in his eyes was triumphant. "The Duke himself... but if you must know, Gwendolyn, we sent him the gift of a knob gobbling, so I'm certain he'll be late. Your reunion will have to wait."

Gwendolyn's belly turned. The thought of Adwen accepting such a gift, and from Loc of all people! *A knob gobbling, truly?* Adwen was always... unconventional, but had he fallen so far from grace that he would receive such gifts for his favor?

No. The Adwen she remembered would not need

to have his favors bought and paid for by others. The Adwen she knew would not bend the knee to a pretender.

And yet maybe he was not the same Adwen. Perhaps there was nothing more to Bryn's message than a simple warning, and Gwendolyn had only imagined some greater plot.

Blood and bones. The thought of Adwen turning his coat to serve a faithless serpent was heart-rending. Of all her father's dukes, she had liked him most —principally because he was a man with a mind and heart of his own, like herself. Stubborn, right-minded, ready to stand for what he believed in, they had never been more than friends, but if she'd been free to choose a man to wed, it might have been Adwen.

Disgusted, she tried to put her wayward thoughts out of her mind, and, as she had so many a feast before, she searched for Bryn's face amidst the attendees... and then Ely's, finding both conspicuously absent. *But of course.* Why should either be invited? Loc valued them less than he valued Gwendolyn, and doubtless, if he expected that either would give her some measure of comfort, he'd quickly disallow it.

The laughter in the hall resumed at full volume now, with Gwendolyn forgotten, thus she did what she'd never done before in all her life: she reached for her goblet of mead to drown her sorrows, fearing it would hold the only virtues she would need tonight.

It was no wonder Alderman Crwys drank so much. That poor soul never had one thing go his way, and despite that Gwendolyn herself had not agreed with his *politiks*, she now understood what it felt like to be like a leper amidst men.

"Smile," demanded Loc, his eyes sliding to hers, his gaze slippery as an eel, and Gwendolyn could scarcely bear it, remembering a similar rebuke from her mother. Regardless, forcing a smile, she said for his ears alone, "Why don't you go hang yourself, *my dearest love*?"

He laughed without mirth. "I presume you are being well tended?" he said. "Perhaps too well fed? You haven't lost a pennyweight." His gaze fixed upon the bulk of her arm, where the material of her gown bulged because of the hidden armband, and Gwendolyn lifted her glass to her lips, trying so desperately not to toss the contents in his face, wanting so much to reassure him that her sinew was quite well-earned. She'd had so little to eat these past few months, but her arms and legs were very well hewn after weeks of practice—indeed, more so than Loc's.

Calming herself, she took her time savoring the mead before swallowing, then put the glass down, letting her hand fall beneath the table to the hilt of Borlewen's blade.

There was no love lost between them, and Gwendolyn did not expect kindness, not even for the sake of others, but she didn't expect their discord to be so quick and cruel.

She heard the amusement in his voice. "And here I feared this evening would be a gruesome bore," he said drolly, lifting his own cup, and shifting in his seat so that he could better watch her.

To anyone else, he would appear a loving husband, flirting with his new bride, but he said beneath his smile, "Attempt to use that for aught more than your medallions of beef, *my dearest love*, and I will seize it from you once and for all, and test that blade by carving out your dull, gray eyes."

Despite herself, Gwendolyn shuddered, and in response, he smiled, leaning closer to whisper in her ear. "What was your cousin's name?" he asked cheerfully. "Wasn't it... Borlewen?"

Gwendolyn's hand froze midair, squeezing the stem of her goblet.

"Yes, that was it, Borlewen. She was a lovely little whore—offered me her cunt if only I would spare her life."

Blinking back the sting of tears, Gwendolyn put her Goblet down. "And did you?" She prayed with all her heart that he had her locked away—somewhere, she could somehow be rescued.

One word filled with disgust. "No."

For a single heartrending moment, Gwendolyn had thought perhaps she might learn he had spared her, but then her heart shattered to hear his next words.

"I did not avail myself of her, but I did cut her throat."

Bile rose into Gwendolyn's mouth. Angry tears burned her eyes. If she'd thought she'd loathed this man before, it was nothing close to the hatred and fury that welled in her breast at his disclosure. Whatever hope she'd had for Borlewen vanished, but she refused to shed more tears under Loc's scrutiny, knowing it would give him far too much pleasure— and neither would she give him an excuse to punish Bryn or Ely.

"Good girl," he cooed. "You are only here for one reason," he told her. "Play your part, Gwendolyn, and you will enjoy a hearty meal. Defy me and I will reconsider the wisdom of keeping you about."

If only to hide her quivering lips, Gwendolyn lifted her goblet again, gulping another mouthful of mead, loathing him to the core of her being, trying not to spew the sweet drink all over the table.

"My mother believes otherwise," he continued, "yet I do *not* need you. As of now, I have already secured the West and South. Only Atrebates and Durotriges have yet to bend the knee, and here..." He waved a hand to point out the feast. "Tonight, they shall."

Gwendolyn emptied the last drop in her goblet, and then hastily poured herself another, all her hopes for the evening quashed.

"After tonight," he continued, recognizing that he'd upset her. "I intend to turn my efforts to the East —with or without you, and..." He shrugged. "I must say... preferably without you."

He cast a pointed glance toward his lover, who sat pouting at a lower table, watching them with a look on her face Gwendolyn interpreted as fury and indignation. "Certainly *she* would prefer it to be without you, and I am eager to give the lady her due."

"*Her* due?" Gwendolyn said. "What of the promises you made to me?"

His lids lowered with the thinning of his smile. "What of them?" he asked. "Indeed, Gwendolyn, you bore me. So much righteous fury. Even now, bereft of allies, you still cannot see the mountains for the clouds in your head."

Gwendolyn's hopes dimmed with every word he spoke—not only because he was so cruel, but because he could be cruel with impunity.

Deliberately lifting Borlewen's dagger above the table so he would not mistake her intentions and plunge his own dagger between her shoulders, she momentarily considered stabbing him in the face, but poked at a medallion of beef instead.

"Well," she said, after a while. "I'm certain she'll make you so proud wearing all my castaway ribbons and gowns. Though I wonder," she added, with as much poise as she could muster. "Do you like that dress she's worn tonight? Does it look familiar? What of the crown?"

Locrinus frowned, glancing toward Estrildis with a look of genuine confusion, and Gwendolyn understood then that he'd never truly seen her, nor did he notice the lover he claimed to wish to give her due. He was too vain—self-amused. He didn't care about Gwendolyn, but for the first time, Gwendolyn pitied Estrildis. Whatever she wished of this man, he did not know how to give it. There was never anything Gwendolyn could have done to please him.

She added for good measure, "She's an outsider, as are you. *Her* son will never rule these lands."

"And you'll not bear me an heir," he shot back, apparently mistaking her complaint. "The blood of your precious conservators is done," he said. "All I require is for the tribes to believe I will sire a child with you. I needn't actually do it."

It didn't matter that she hadn't eaten a proper meal since she'd arrived, Gwendolyn wasn't hungry. Still, she shoved a bite of meat into her mouth, forcing herself to chew, realizing he spoke true. The tinny taste of animal blood made her tongue tingle, and when she swallowed, she gagged before it settled in her belly—like his odious news.

Only now, she wished she'd refused this invitation, and she was glad she'd worn her mother's gown. Tomorrow she might regret everything—and she might even be dead—but tonight, she hoped her presence made him as miserable as she was.

"Lest you mistake me," he said, still smiling. "I would not even covet you as a brood mare, despite that you could pass for one." He leaned closer, laying his chin into his hand, as though he were a mooning lover, but the look in his eyes could not be mistaken. "Really, has no one ever apprised you that you have a face like a horse? 'Tis no wonder you admire them so well."

Gwendolyn's jaw tautened. She tried with all her might not to spit her chewed and bloody meat into Loc's face. But for all her attempts at keeping her aplomb, his barb stung.

So the evening continued—a far cry from the last meal they'd shared when he'd tried so hard to impress her. And yet, Gwendolyn found him equally vain, and considered that this might well be the last meal they would share in proximity.

Undoubtedly, he despised her as much as she did him, and he clearly believed she was no longer necessary. From everything she had gleaned—and it was just as she'd suspected—it was his mother holding his leash, and he was like a rabid hound, lunging against his chains.

He would never punish Estrildis if she did what he only wished to do himself...

Peering down at her plate, she wondered if this atrocity would be her last meal, and she took comfort in this: a man like Locrinus would never so easily engender loyalties. If he should win the tribes, it would be hard earned, and perhaps at the cost of much blood. Like his mother, he was as treacherous as a viper, and just as lethal, and someday that would be the end of him. But if death should be her own fate, perhaps she would do well to stab him now and be done?

All of it—his cruel words, Estrildis with her stolen crown, the idle chatter of so many faithless vassals—it was enough to make Gwendolyn ill.

Lifting her glass once more, she choked back a long, unpleasant gulp... and then... quite abruptly... and quite by accident... the answer to Bryn's riddle struck her...

It wasn't that he *didn't* wish her to repeat the offense; it was that he did wish her to repeat it, and the mysterious offense he was speaking of was that silly little ruse they'd employed to steal away from the morning's fast, where after, Gwendolyn was to have gone with her mother to prepare all day long for the evening's celebration. The notion of sitting there all day, merely brushing her hair, painting her face, trying on insensible dresses had truly offended her. Instead, she'd much preferred the thought of being out in the wilds, with Bryn and Adwen. So, eager to test that bow, she'd hatched the most fatuous of plans. And really, it would seem uncouth and graceless, but then it was a child's machinations. Yet that didn't matter; it was as brilliant as it was desperate—particularly if all they needed was a simple distraction.

While Loc was making flirtatious eyes with his hateful lover, Gwendolyn stuffed more food into her mouth, and then more and more and more—as much as she dared, until she couldn't fit one bite more into her cheeks. Looking like a greedy squirrel, she considered why a distraction might be needed as she chewed, and chewed, and chewed, never once swallowing, growing more and more disgusted by her mouthful of meat and tasteless food.

Gods. This feast was nothing like her father ever served for esteemed guests, and her mother and Yestin always worked so hard to be certain the fare was anything but bland.

Here, instead of olives from An Ghréig, there was unpurged beef—as though it were slaughtered and brought directly to the table.

Instead of the imported smoked cheese Locrinus claimed he loved, there was a soft, runny *spermyse*. That alone made her long to puke.

And if there was anything less than pilchards at the lower tables, it was no wonder Estrildis' mouth remained twisted with such disgust.

When at last Gwendolyn could bear it no longer, she began with one small cough, seizing up her glass of mead for a hefty swallow. She stood then, purposely spewing the entire contents of her mouth all over her husband's finery.

Startled, Locrinus rose with a yelp, but the damage was done. His tunic was irreparably soiled, and his hair and face as well. Gwendolyn tried not to cackle with nervous laughter, but then another spray of food landed on his cheek, and the look in his eyes was, for the moment, too surprised to be angry. She couldn't help it. She did laugh, and unfortunately—or rather fortunately, as the case should be—though she was seldom sick, she had a weak constitution for the grotesque, and seeing the savaged meat caught up in his hair, she didn't have to feign her next regurgitation. It flew from her lips like a torrent, destroying the table—every plate, every glass, all tainted by puke.

In his fury, Loc cursed. Swiping himself with a look of disgust, for a full moment, he couldn't seem to speak. His face grew florid and his eyes bulged. Finally, he barked at the guards.

"Get *her* out of here!"

From that moment on, it happened quickly. Several guests rose at once to advance upon the dais. Estrildis came straight to her angry lover, mewling as she frantically swiped at his tunic, trying her best to repair him. "I cannot believe she's ruined your dress!" she cried, casting Gwendolyn a hateful glance, then continuing to tend to her sulking lover. When it was decided that his tunic could not be sorted, she encouraged him to abandon the dais.

Those same guards that had escorted Gwendolyn to sup now came to drag her, seizing her unceremoniously by the arms, their grip a little too firm. But instead of shoving her after Loc, toward Gwendolyn's chambers, they led her to another door, through the scullery, which was used for the dirty work of cleaning and storing dishes.

Here, amidst more shouts and commands, the servants scurried back and forth, filling buckets with water to clean the dais and high table. No one seemed to notice Gwendolyn, so excited did they work, and Gwendolyn didn't resist when the guards pushed her down yet another corridor.

Come whatever may, she must be at peace.

Wherever this led, she would face the consequences with her shoulders back and her head high, knowing in her heart that her time here would be short, regardless.

Tonight, Loc could hardly contain his abhorrence of her. If what he'd claimed was true, and the western tribes were already aligned with him, all he needed now were a few more tribes to have a consortium. Once he had a large enough army, he would persuade others to join forces with him.

Gods. Had he truly confessed to murdering Borlewen? Even now, she wanted to wrench herself free, go run after him, and plunge her cousin's dagger into his miserable back.

The grip on her arm was brutal. The guards shoved her this way and that way, dragging her here, then there, and for one terrible moment, Gwendolyn feared this would be the end. Perhaps they were going to drag her behind the palace and execute her —as ignoble an end as could be.

At least her father had been beheaded before an audience. They would end her life in an alley behind the scullery, perhaps leaving everyone to believe she was safely ensconced in the palace—a good little wife for the Usurper King.

Blood and bones. She had perhaps set the course for something that could never be turned back. But then, when they turned down a long, dark corridor, Gwendolyn spied a lit torch at the end of the hall, in the hands of all people... Queen Innogen.

"You?" Gwendolyn said, aghast.

The woman dangled a thick set of keys in one hand, hastily finding the one she needed, and shoving it into a rusty lock. "Really? You didn't believe you could simply leave?"

"Leave?"

"Without help," Innogen said, as she pushed opened the heavy door.

Confused, Gwendolyn blinked, finding that the door she'd opened led outside... though not just out-side... outside the gates.

With something akin to a growl of frustration, Queen Innogen shoved her into the night, where vines with thorns pricked at Gwendolyn's face, clinging to her headscarf, threatening to unveil her hair. But once she passed the tangle of bushes, there stood Adwen... and Bryn and Ely, along with six well-fitted mounts.

The guards who'd manhandled her now slipped out of their red cloaks, revealing Durotrigan livery, and Gwendolyn turned to look at the Queen Mother in shock.

Innogen shrugged. "Nothing will rally the tribes faster than a martyr," she said. "I've already surmised my son intends to kill you if you remain. Either he will, or Estrildis will, and in either case, the result will be the same."

Gwendolyn didn't know what to say, though now she understood why Ely had been so adamant that she wear all her mother's jewels and the gown.

Perforce, her dowry chest would remain in this hateful palace, and there would be no way to retrieve it, but at least she had the most precious of her pos-sessions.

No doubt, Loc would rush to his apartments to repair himself. Ultimately, he would return to his guests. But unless he cared to reprimand Gwendolyn before returning to the feast, he would not miss her for the rest of the evening.

Still shocked, she met the Queen Mother's gaze

one last time, and the woman warned, "You've little time; use it wisely. If you return to reveal my part in this ruse, I will kill you myself." And with that, she closed the portal, and Gwendolyn heard the key turn in the lock.

She peered up at Bryn, blinking away tears.

But it was Adwen who spoke. "The simplest plans are oft the most brilliant," he declared with a wink, and then pulled her toward her waiting mount, lifting her up into the saddle.

CHAPTER
SIX

The scent of green was a welcome perfume.
Gwendolyn sucked in a breath, letting it
fill her lungs.

Freedom!

Shedding the headdress, she pledged this would
be their undoing, as she would not go silently to her
end. There were no torches lit even on the battle-
ments, and Gwendolyn knew they had Innogen to
thank for that, at great risk to herself. But that did not
diminish the loathing she felt for the woman who'd
lied to her face at her wedding, then abused her for
months.

Barely a sliver of moon gave light to mark
the way.

Mounted, clutching one end of her headdress—
the end with her mother's pin—she let it fly behind
her like a golden pennant as she made swiftly for the
woods, delighting in the feel of horseflesh between
her thighs. It had been so long!

Behind them, the castle ramparts tumbled into
darkness.

"Go!" urged Adwen, and Gwendolyn held her

breath as fiercely as she held the reins, her horse's hooves consuming the ground beneath them. Tears of relief stung her eyes as she leaned forward to embrace the beast, feeling herself as one with her mount.

No shouts resounded from the courtyards.

No horns wailed.

There were no barking hounds.

For now.

Fearing that escape had come too easily, that Innogen meant for her to be caught and slain in her flight, Gwendolyn braced for an ambush that never came. The night greeted them with silence, welcoming them into its inky embrace. Eyes ahead, riding at full gallop, no one spoke. Everyone understood what was at stake. If they did not put distance between them and the Loegrian palace, they would risk facing Loc's army, reported to be more than five thousand strong.

They slid into the wooded darkness without consequence, and then, cloaked by shadows, Adwen took the lead. Behind him filed his youngest guard. Gwendolyn behind him, with Ely after her and Bryn at their back, the elder of Adwen's guards riding by his side.

Gwendolyn marveled Loc had not recognized those men who'd escorted her into the hall, but neither did it surprise her. Excluding a chosen few who served him directly, he never paid his soldiers any mind. In her heart, she knew his men followed out of fear and no more. If she could but show them another way, they would turn their hearts as easily as his own mother had betrayed him—and she had. This was coming clearer and clearer, with every advantage they gained.

No archers took aim from the trees.

No soldiers lay in wait to greet them.

No breath but their own and that of the forest's creatures reached Gwendolyn's ears...

An owl hooted in welcome.

A few conies started as they passed.

The gold-green eyes of a lynx glinted against the velvety night.

For at least half a bell, their party rode without stopping, the pace slowing only perforce once they'd entered the woods, yet still they pressed onward, until eventually they emerged into a clearing beyond sight of the palace.

"For now, it appears we've escaped them," said Adwen, leaning forward to pat a hand against his horse's withers, calming the black beast as it struggled for breath. "There's no telling how long we have."

Gwendolyn drew up beside him, her heart pounding as she waited for the others. "He is vain enough that he'll linger to repair himself," she reassured. "We've at least that much time to gain some advantage."

She knew the cretin well enough to know that his first concern would be himself, always. As little as he thought of her, he'd never suspect her childish ruse, and she knew that, even if someone else noticed Adwen's absence from the hall, no one would wish to face him in his state of pique.

She also suspected Innogen had put the notion of a knob gobbling into her son's head for a good reason —to explain his prolonged absence from the hall.

"But, no doubt, as soon as his vanity is appeased," Gwendolyn continued, "he'll return to the hall. He was quite pleased with the prospect of your bending the knee," she apprised Adwen. "Eventually, he'll note your absence and, make no mistake, he will ride against Durotriges."

Adwen's eyes were darker for the woodland shadows. "Nay. He will not," he said with certainty, and Gwendolyn allowed herself to be distracted, noting how the years had treated this man. He had grown to be quite handsome and virile—well formed, with a well-chiseled face—but with circles beneath his eyes that betrayed the burden of his leadership. Moreover, the easy smile she remembered was displaced by a frown.

"If we travel together, his men will overtake us," suggested Bryn, arriving, but he did not look at Gwendolyn. Neither did Ely. She sidled over to the other side of Bryn, fidgeting on her horse, nibbling nervously at a thumbnail, her eyes glistening with unshed tears.

"Has he hounds?" asked the younger guard.

Bryn nodded. "He does. But those poor beasts have not been fed properly since Brutus died. All but one or two will tire quickly."

"He will drive them to death," assured Gwendolyn. "Once he sets them loose, he will not stop until they are dead, or we are found."

"That pinched-nosed bastard!" said the elder guard. "Did you see his face when the Queen soiled his tunic?"

The other guard barked with laughter, and Adwen chuckled, too, finding humor in the ordeal despite the circumstances. "Good show at the banquet, Gwendolyn," he said, with a nod of approval. "I feared you'd grown too old or too soft to employ such a ruse." He gave her a familiar wink. "I'm glad you remembered."

Bryn's frown was firmly etched upon his handsome face. "We haven't time to waste," he interjected, his black hair shining against the dark night. He cast an anxious glance over his shoulder in the direction they'd come, and then at his sister, reaching over to tap her arm, drawing her fingers away from her mouth. Gwendolyn's heart ached—not only for the worry he must be feeling for his little sister, but because she feared she had forever alienated her two dearest friends. He'd risked much to help her in this escape, but he didn't have to like her to perform his duty to her. At the moment, his demeanor was cold and removed in keeping with his manner earlier this day.

"Whatever we decide, one of us must return to Durotriges to be certain we are prepared," the elder guard suggested.

To this, Adwen nodded, his gaze returning to Gwendolyn, giving her deference. "The decision must be yours, Majesty. How will you have us proceed? Do you wish us to travel together? Or should we separate?"

Intensely aware that all eyes had turned to her... except Bryn's, Gwendolyn fidgeted under so much scrutiny, fiddling with her reins.

She was *not* the one who made such decisions, and she didn't know how to respond. If they separated, wouldn't they lose whatever strength they had in numbers? And if she sent someone in the wrong direction, she would bear the burden of their fate.

Indecision paralyzed her tongue.

Adwen seemed to understand. His gaze softened.

"I could send Beryan to Durotriges with Jago and remain with you, if you'd like?"

"Nay," argued the elder guard. "You will be needed. There will be much unrest when they are told what has transpired and they'll not listen to any but you."

Unlike Trevena, Durotriges was not a walled city. Nor did Adwen keep a large army. His men had served her father, and those warriors had most likely resided in Trevena, training with the Mester at Arms. Until Loc's treachery, no one would have dared attack one of the King's villages for fear that her father would strike to defend. The last true raid on any of Cornwall's villages was the one that took Adwen's father. But no matter what Adwen claimed, Gwendolyn knew Loc would seek revenge. He would presume accurately Adwen was the one who took her, and if he did not catch her, he would send his men to Durotriges. Those people were in peril. "I agree," said Gwendolyn. "Adwen, you return to your people. They need you now more than ever."

"As you wish," he said, giving her another wink that brought a hot blush to her cheeks. "Beryan, ride with our Queen."

"What of my sister?" asked Bryn, a note of trepidation catching in his voice. "I do not wish her to be anywhere near Durotriges."

Adwen turned to face Ely. "How well do you ride, niece?"

Looking as frightened as she ever had, Ely shook her head. "Not well," she confessed, and this was true. She could not ride the way she danced.

"Very well," said Adwen. "If we are agreed, Bryn

should escort Ely to some safer location—far from Durotriges... and... far from our Queen."

He turned to give her that familiar winsome smile, and Gwendolyn had the most undeniable urge to fling herself into his arms and weep. Right now, he appeared to be her one true friend.

Awaiting Gwendolyn's agreement, the mood between the warriors grew tense now, their eyes skittering from face to face. Gwendolyn had the sudden sense they were keeping something from her, but there was no time to press. "I agree," she said.

At long last, Bryn met her gaze, with a hint of gratitude apparent in the shimmering blue of his eyes. "Thank you," he said.

No more needed to be said.

If things had been different, Gwendolyn knew that, as her Shadow, nothing would have separated them. Like his father, he would do his duty, no matter how he felt about her. But Loc did not fight fair. He fought to win, and he would send his entire army against six.

If anything should happen to Ely, Bryn would never forgive himself... nor would he forgive Gwendolyn. And neither would she forgive herself.

The distant wail of a horn blew against the night. "We've been discovered," said Beryan, and Gwendolyn gave him a nod, commanding, "With me!"

She would not be the one to bring her friends to harm.

Everyone had already risked too much to free her, and she'd not begrudge Bryn the chance to keep Ely safe.

She did not linger for goodbyes.

Spinning about as the horn wailed once more,

louder this time, rejoined by the sound of barking hounds, she gave her mount a heel.

Tonight, five had stood in her defense, placing themselves in great peril to see her escape, but if she and Beryan didn't stay ahead of the dogs, everyone's efforts would come to naught.

And this time, if Locrinus captured her, he would not spare her life. The time for uncertainty was done. She must be strong, beginning now.

SEVEN

After a while, the cry of dogs fell silent.

Still, they daren't rest—not yet. Gwendolyn had spoken true; She knew Locrinus would drive his hounds till they collapsed. And if by some odd turn of fate he should listen to sound advice and rest them a while, that didn't mean he would rest himself, nor would he rest his scouts.

Better than anyone, Gwendolyn understood how bitterly he hated to lose, especially to her. He wouldn't stop searching till he turned every stone, but not because he considered Gwendolyn a threat, because he so earnestly despised her.

Locating the river by its scent, they followed the dwindling stream vigilantly so they could slip in and out of the shallows to mask their scent, and the thing that struck Gwendolyn as they wended their way northeast was the stink of decay that wafted in the air—putrid, like Porth Pool the last time she saw it.

Against a breezeless night, even the mist failed to stir, suspending itself midair in writhing serpentine veils that, over time, coiled about so thickly that it threatened to strangle the very air—so dense in fact that Gwendolyn could hardly see her mount's ears.

With each snap of a twig, and every owl's hoot, the animal's flesh quivered between her thighs, responding as she responded to every new sound—twitchy and not solely because of the midge flies. When finally the breeze lifted, sweeping aside the fog, a crook of moon glinted against the inky waters, its sickle-shape revealing the swarms.

Continually, she heard Beryan slapping at his head and bare arms and was grateful for the protection offered by her mother's tunic and leathers. He, too, wore leather, but with the summer heat, his jerkin was sleeveless and hers was not.

Later, as the mantle of night lifted, and the hounds remained silent, Gwendolyn dared to hope... until the grey morning light arrived to reveal a forest consumed...

Blood and bones.

In such a short time, the Rot had spread so far north. After less than three months locked away, she could scarcely believe how much this land had declined. In what should have been the peak of summer, everything was dull and brown. Whatever green she spied was peaky and pale, and the boughs of trees, save for the hardy evergreens, were nearly bare, their diseased, yellowing leaves clinging for life. Too many now blanketed the forest floor, causing their horses' hooves to sink to the knees in decomposing bracken. As though it meant to defend them, embracing them, tendrils of mist curled jealously about the wizened trunks of wasting oaks.

Presently, they encountered an ancient wych elm, with its lichen-covered branches stretching far across the stream. Halfway across, one large branch succumbed to decay, and now lay damming the river.

Here and there along a muddy bank lay a small carcass—a bird, a rabbit, even a boar.

"This is dreadful," Gwendolyn said. "How far has this spread?"

"Much too far," said Beryan, with a heavy sigh. "At least now you know why we had no choice but to barter for your freedom."

"Barter?" Gwendolyn straightened in her saddle, a frisson of fear rushing down her spine. But even as she asked, she knew—all this time she'd been wondering how in the goddess's name they'd convinced Innogen to aid them. "*What* did you give her?"

The elder man's voice grew heavy with regret. "Durotriges," he said, without equivocation, and Gwendolyn shut her eyes, remembering Adwen's words... spoken so heavily with such certainty... *Nay. He will not,* he'd said.

And now she understood why he was so sure Loc would not declare war.

He wouldn't need to because Adwen had already promised Durotriges in return for Gwendolyn's freedom, yet Adwen did not know Loc the way she did. He would destroy Durotriges merely because they'd abetted her. Their only chance was Innogen, and Gwendolyn knew his mother well enough to know how her mind worked. She didn't care about Durotriges or its people. This was a strategic move on her part, certain as she was that Locrinus still held the advantage.

Well, he was bound to be angry, but perhaps with some persuasion, she could make clear to her son that

Gwendolyn was not a threat to his rule—at least not for now.

With the fall of Trevena, he already controlled much of the southernmost regions—all the Dumnoni territories, and Atrebates and Durotriges. And now, because he'd retained control of Westwalas, it would make his advance into Catuvellauni territory all the easier, allowing for his armies to approach both from the north and south.

Gwendolyn had wondered why only Atrebates and Durotriges were present this evening; now she understood. When he was ready, Plowonida would be Loc's for the taking, and purely by allowing Gwendolyn to go free, Innogen had delivered her son the means by which to accomplish his dream without ever involving the Dobunni or the Druids.

Worst case, if Loc could not be appeased, and he reneged upon Innogen's bargain with Durotriges, he would still hold those lands. Durotriges could never defend against his growing army, and Gwendolyn was quite certain that Innogen had sacrificed the entire village for her contrivance.

No doubt, her primary aim had been to remove Gwendolyn from Loc's hands. She perhaps understood that Gwendolyn's death would give birth to a martyr, and a martyr in this time of unrest was far more dangerous than a flesh and blood queen—one whose part in this ruse was still untold.

And perhaps she even feared that, with Gwendolyn's blood on her son's hands, he might turn the hearts of those who were still undecided. Better to release Gwendolyn and leave her to answer to her kinsmen. After all, even if she could win back her people, she would still have to find those loyal to her father, and fear would make that a perilous task.

Additionally, with her father's armies all scattered, whatever offer of protection she would make would be empty and few would be so trusting of a would-be queen who'd already presumably aligned herself with a kingslayer. It didn't matter that Gwendolyn was innocent, she must now prove she'd had nothing to do with Loc's coup. And even if she did this, they were still bound to mistrust her "Prophecy" now, when their once celebrated princess and valiant king were so swiftly and soundly defeated. Indeed, why should anyone fight for a house abandoned by the gods?

And the final blow was this... with the land dying, it was only a matter of time before the people's outrage turned to Gwendolyn.

Innogen.

Even if she lost, she would win.

It was only now, in this very moment, as Gwendolyn pieced together the story that she realized she had perhaps lost her greatest opportunity to cut off the viper's head. Without his mother, Loc was only another greedy, vicious man; however, with Innogen by his side, he was far more dangerous. She was so much more cunning than Gwendolyn ever supposed.

Considering this, she rode quietly, filled with dismay, praying that Ely and Bryn had escaped, and only to be sure, she planted the golden scarf tangled about her fingers, letting it slip to the ground, peering over her shoulder to watch it settle—a bright yellow stain on the forest floor.

Bryn had said those hounds would tire. Hopefully, that would be the case. But if they made it this far into the woods, bright as her scarf was, no one would miss it.

Gwendolyn knew how to defend herself as well as any man, and considering that, it was far better to lure the hounds in their direction, knowing she and Beryan had a better chance against Loc than Bryn alone with Ely. Their paths had diverged only marginally, but if she could, she would keep Loc and his men from following her dearest friends, and somehow buy more time for Adwen to safeguard his village.

CHAPTER EIGHT

Gwendolyn felt awful that Beryan was the unlucky one chosen to accompany her, particularly knowing those dogs would eventually come searching for her.

He was a quiet man, a little guarded, though Gwendolyn could tell by his actions and his demeanor that he was dutiful and constant.

And yes, of course, she would confess about the scarf, but not until there was no chance of him turning back for it. For himself alone, she knew he'd not bother, but for her sake, for his queen, he would feel obliged.

She didn't intend to argue with anyone about the value of her life. So far as she was concerned, her life was worth no more than Bryn's or Ely's—and assuredly not the entirety of Durotriges. Even if Beryan were willing to risk his village for her, she could not allow it.

If she fell in battle, she suspected Adwen might even be the one chosen to lead, and he, more than most—perhaps even more than Gwendolyn—had the best chance to unite the tribes. He was a man, for one, but there was a good reason she hadn't seen him since her fifteenth Name Day. During these short years since he'd come into his title and lands, he'd been a force for good, working faithfully for peace in her father's name. With the greatest respect, Durotriges might not compare with Trevena, but even without the walled city, Adwen drew followers from many of the nearby tribes, giving them refuge. His village had grown immensely since the old duke's death, and so had his tributes. Conversely, who did Gwendolyn have?

The answer rang like a death knell in her head.

Perhaps she had some small chance to convince her mother's people to ally with Cornwall, but probably not. So much had fallen with Trevena.

No longer would she have control over their mines.

Neither did she hold the port, nor govern the trade.

She didn't even have control over the city.

And now it struck her that *all* their elders had likely been executed along with her father—Yestin, Morgelyn. Crwys, all who'd remained true to the old king.

In her *konsel*, there would be fewer men like Beryan, whose knowledge came from age and experience. Their future would depend upon a new generation, with untried warriors and legates, all meant to be guided by a fledgling queen... and this gave her the greatest pause.

Gwendolyn had spent many years studying under the Mester Alderman. She'd studied all the war maps. She knew every leader of every tribe, but she had never done more than attend her father's *konsels* and sit and listen. He'd never given her a voice, and to be sure, much of the time she'd sat there, thinking of ways to be excused. *Gods.* She had wrongly believed she would have more time, and even when her father was so sick... she had still believed she could fix him, that he would live many years more. After all, how could a legend like her father perish so ignobly as to waste to his bones? Little did she realize... it could be worse.

In the distance, too close for comfort, the hounds bayed again, and Gwendolyn cast a nervous glance at Beryan. In the daylight, she could see his many scars —one thick white line on the back of his upper arm, another small one parting his right brow, and another that followed the outside of his forearm, as though a blade skimmed the length of his arm.

"Did you fight beside my father?" she asked, sidling up beside the elder warrior. If they were meant to die here together, she would at least like to know more about the man who would give his life to defend her.

He gave her a lift of his chin. "More than once," he said, and then he grinned. "I was there the day he dispatched Gogmagog."

"Were you?" Gwendolyn asked, with a modicum of surprise. Not that Beryan wasn't old enough—he was at least as old as her father—but she had never met someone who'd witnessed the end of Gogmagog firsthand. "Did he truly pluck up a tree, as I was told?"

The elder warrior peered back at her. "Gogmagog?" He shrugged "Neh. Not so much a tree," he said. "But your father did lift him up with three broken ribs and tossed him headlong into the River Dart."

Gwendolyn smiled wistfully, wishing she could

have seen it for herself. Men still told that tale wherever she went, and she still enjoyed it every time she heard it. And yet, the man her father had become before his death was barely a shadow of that much sung hero.

Ravaged by illness, her father had been too frail even to stand unassisted for long. The last time Gwendolyn saw him was at her wedding, and that was the best he'd looked in months. Gwendolyn had only dared to hope that her marriage to Locrinus was the beginning of his healing journey. After all, the land was the king, and the king was the land. This was the sole reason she'd agreed to wed Locrinus in the first place, and she foolishly believed her marriage would strengthen their alliance. If the people were contented, it made sense that the land would heal, and her father's health would return with the land. But she had been wrong. *Oh, so wrong.*

"I was proud to fight with him," Beryan said. "As I'll be proud to fight beside his daughter."

Gwendolyn bit at her lower lip, worrying, because the chance was greater than he realized. And regardless, they would put forth a good fight. If she must perish in these rotting woodlands, her name and legacy forgotten in a battle that would be remembered by no one, they would at least take as many of Loc's minions with them as possible, and hopefully Loc himself.

She lost herself in thought, loathing what she saw in these woods...

Years ago, when the Rot first began, she remembered how many of the tribes sent their aldermen to the capitol. Together, led by the Awenydds, Gwyddons and Druids, the tribal *konsels* had all put aside their animosities for the sake of the isle, because, despite that they were all so different, they had one thing in common: a fierce love for this land. Somehow, some way, this is what Gwendolyn must appeal to again... and perhaps dreaming of vengeance wasn't the answer. Where had such fury gotten her so far? For all these long months, she'd been so intent upon revenge. It was only now, with her freedom, that she dared consider all that was lost... and more, all that must be done to salvage what was not.

"Have you a wife?" Gwendolyn asked, curious.

"Aye," he said, but then he corrected himself. "Rather, I did, Majesty. Only my daughter now. Her name is Taryn."

"How old is she?"

"Full grown," he said with a warm smile. "Yet do not ask me how many years. I don't even know my own years. All I know is that she was born before the Great Southern Storm."

Gwendolyn remembered that storm only vaguely. It flooded much of the southern coastlands, razing forests, and sending many of the southerners fleeing into northern territories, looking for higher ground and shelter. It passed through Trevena with scarcely a whimper, but what she remembered most at the tender age of four was the influx of people who'd arrived, cold and shivering, with only their cloaks on their backs.

That was also the year her father built the public *piscina*.

And then, two years later, a second wall to surround the city's expansion. Some of those newcomers were Atrebates by birth. Still her father had turned none away.

"All are Pretania's children," he'd said, envisioning a day when all the tribes would live as one, when peace would reign in a kingdom without borders...

It was a beautiful dream, but, alas, it seemed more impossible now than ever.

Gwendolyn's jaw worked as she considered all the terrible choices made.

In retrospect, she could see every mistake...

If she had it all to do over again, she would have done at least one thing differently: She would have run Alderman Aelwin through. Consequences be damned—her father's temper be damned!

The last time she saw that traitor they were carting him off to a prison cell, and more than likely Locrinus had set him free to strut about her city as though he himself were Mester—and perhaps he now was, but that very notion infuriated her, that his betrayal could be so easily rewarded. If she'd never traveled to Chysauster with his infernal prunes, she might never have suspected his treachery, but if she'd not gone, her uncle and family might still be alive. That faithless bastard murdered one of his own peers, intending to lift himself into a higher position, and quite likely he would have murdered the Mester himself, if her misconceived journey to Chysauster hadn't happened. But though his perfidy was revealed to her through this series of unfortunate events, she was hard-pressed to say any of it was worth it. After all, where was Aelwin after plotting with Locrinus? She hoped as dead as her father but doubted this had been his fate.

As for Brutus, they should have ousted him from these lands the day he'd arrived on their shores seeking asylum. Barring that, her father should never have allied with an outlander, and they shouldn't have trusted him so easily. Neither should they have given him so much—no lands, no titles, no marriage alliances. Everything Brutus became, he became because her father allowed it. And, ultimately, it did not matter that Brutus was betrayed, too, because he'd brought with him a culture of lies, betrayal and murder. Worse, he'd sired Locrinus, and for that alone, he should have been crucified, as the Assyrians would do.

She sighed then, considering this—reconsidering Beryan.

This sweet, true-hearted man had placed so much faith in her—a vanquished, angry young maiden whose fortune now depended on the kindness of strangers.

Gwendolyn wasn't so ignorant that she didn't comprehend she was only a beggar now, dependent upon the mercy of others—like the Atrebates who'd come knocking at their gates after that storm. It really didn't matter what blood ran through her veins. Left to her own devices, she would be no more than a mud lark pecking at scraps.

This was a humbling thought—an impression of herself she had never once considered, having lived so finely, with servants to care for her every need. Now, with her father's death, her beloved Cornwall was a broken dream... soon to be a memory.

And so would she if Locrinus found her.

LATER, when the barking grew louder, Beryan commanded Gwendolyn to ride ahead. "You lead, I shall follow," he said, and she obeyed, giving her mount a heel to lift the pace.

"Should we keep to the *bourne*?" she asked.

"Hmmm. I'm thinking we should slip back into the woods," he replied, but no sooner had advised this when an arrow flew by Gwendolyn's ear.

"Down!" Beryan shouted. "Down, Majesty!"

He moved behind her to shield her back and Gwendolyn bent low over the horse's withers, grasping desperately at its mane to lie as flat as she dared. But even as she did so, another missile flew by. *And then another.*

And another.

At her back, she heard Beryan yelp in pain. "Ride!" he demanded. "Don't stop!"

Fear sent thunder bolts through Gwendolyn's heart. But she still couldn't see where the arrows were coming from. But if one struck Beryan in the back, they must have come from behind. Peering over her shoulder, she found the old warrior keeping pace, tugging an arrow from his shoulder. Giving the mare another heel, she prayed the horses wouldn't protest after such a long night. Already, it was past time to rest.

Another barrage of missiles flew by, and once more, Beryan yelped, though he somehow kept his saddle.

Gwendolyn's mind raced with every recourse. If they veered into the woods, their pace would slow. If they ran alongside the river, they would remain viable targets.

If only these were Brigantes, she could stop and try to barter with them, but she knew they were not.

A rumble of hooves shook the land, approaching

faster, closer, closer—so close she could feel the thunder of their hooves leap up into her heart.

"Agh!" Beryan grunted, and this time, she didn't have to look back to know he'd fallen.

This time, she heard his body tumble from his horse, and the animal surged forward out of fear, saddle empty, keeping pace beside her.

Another arrow struck Gwendolyn's horse in the rear, and she felt the beast's hooves leave the ground, preparing to buck her. Smelling blood, it grew frenzied and confused.

One more bolt in the backside, and it did rear.

Gwendolyn heard the scream of pain and knew she hadn't seconds to lose.

But all was not lost. She wasn't merely a good horsewoman. She was an excellent horsewoman. Wasn't this what she told everyone?

Her heart twisting with as much grief as fear, she seized Beryan's reins, then stood in her own saddle, struggling for balance. Despite having lost its rider, Beryan's horse was steadier than hers. She leapt into his empty saddle, even as another missile struck her animal's flank.

Her horse went down in the stinking river and didn't again rise. Gwendolyn's heart wrenched to hear its scream of pain. But she didn't stop.

Settling herself atop Beryan's mount, she snapped the reins, giving it a knee and veering sharply into the adjacent woods, hoping to lose her pursuers amidst the trees and low-lying limbs. If this animal was worth half its weight, it would know how to read her cues, and Gwendolyn rode best under extraordinary circumstances.

Behind her, she could hear her pursuers gaining ground. She urged her mount to ride faster.

Her hand slid back across the animal's flank to assess the situation behind her and came away with a greasy coat of blood.

Gods. Oh, Gods.

Beryan's horse was bleeding, too.

The animal's sides heaved, exhausted.

There was nowhere to go.

Once more, she scanned the woods, seeing no escape, and her heart squeezed painfully. No one could anticipate the fear that rose in the throes of battle. This was her first taste of it; it was sharp and tinny.

Her heart tripped violently as the horse tripped, losing its footing in the soft bracken, stumbling to its knees, spilling Gwendolyn rudely onto a bed of rotted leaves.

The horse groaned, and tears brimmed in Gwendolyn's eyes, hearing the stamp of hooves behind her and knowing they were done for at last.

The shouts grew louder, and now she could hear the hounds snarling as well. One barked excitedly, having caught her scent, and Gwendolyn scrambled to her knees and then to her feet and ran, not caring that every low-lying limb slapped her full in the face.

I am done! she thought. *This is how it ends!*

She would die fighting, or by Loc's hand. Worse, if he returned to the palace, his mother would put a dagger through her heart as easily as she had betrayed her son. Knowing this, Gwendolyn summoned the last of her reserves and ran faster than she thought she could.

She ran for her life.

Ran for Pretania.

Ran for her father.

Ran for her people.

It was difficult to gauge her footing amidst uneven terrain, concealed by so much detritus. Gwendolyn tripped, and then tripped again, unable to stifle a yelp as behind her, she heard another squeal of protest from Beryan's horse.

Holding back a sob, she bounded to her feet and slid quickly behind a fat oak, trembling from head to toes, standing with her back against the rough bark, hands flat against the wood, praying to any god who could hear her—old and new!

Please, please, please...

"This way!" she heard one man shout, and then she heard the rush of a thousand feet as they came in her direction.

Warriors.

Horses.

Hounds.

Done.

I am done.

Closer.

Closer.

Closer.

"Over here!" said one man, his dog yapping wildly.

Intuitively, Gwendolyn's hand flew to Borlewen's dagger, unsheathing it, making herself ready. She didn't know how many she could take down before she died, but she would take as many as she could. A thousand years passed in a heartbeat. A hundred fears roared through a single shiver.

Gwendolyn's heart hammered fiercely, and still

she could hear even the tiniest of sounds... the leaves rustling as the dogs nosed for her scent... the jeers of men as they pursued the dogs.

"Here! Here!" She heard one man bellow. "Over here!" And then every sound became one sound... like the roar of thunder.

Biting her lip to keep from crying out, she tried to make herself as small as possible, willing them to turn in another direction—and then suddenly, inexplicably, she felt the ground shift beneath her feet, and for one terrible, heart-stopping moment, she feared she had swooned. *Gods.* They would come upon her prostate in these leaves and skewer her through—but nay, it was as though the tree she was hiding behind grew limbs...

Round and around and around the boughs went, encircling Gwendolyn, trapping her. Round and round and round.

She grew disoriented and tried to wrench herself free, but found she was trapped. Dizzy and frightened, she opened her mouth to scream as another limb encircled her head, restraining her, and no sound emerged from her lips.

Fear gripped her heart, then squeezed.

Gwendolyn gasped for breath, but couldn't breathe...

And then suddenly, she could.

Breathe.

How?

Within moments, Loc's soldiers had infiltrated the area, searching high and low behind trees, uprooting bracken. Yet somehow, while Gwendolyn could see them, they couldn't see her—all save for one snarling hound. Teeth bared, it pounced after her, then back, looking both frightened and fierce at once. Ears folded back, it returned to sniff at her feet, but even to Gwendolyn, her feet no longer appeared to be feet.

How could this be?

Málik?

Absurdly, she *felt* him. It was as though his arms were enfolding her. She sensed the unmistakable warmth of his cheek against her own, the sweetness of mint at his breath, and her heart pounced into her throat. Only belatedly, she heard his voice in her ear.

Shhh, he said. *Be still. I am with you.*

Was it really him?

Was she mad?

His whisper was like the sound of wind rustling through the boughs of trees... unintelligible... and yet... she understood.

Be calm.

Two arms enfolded her, but it felt as though she were caged by a thousand unyielding vines, pressing her mercilessly against the rough bark, giving her scarcely room to breathe, much less scream.

You left me, she thought, bitterly. *You left me when I needed you most.* Yet even as hot tears pricked at her eyes, a thumb caressed her cheek, impossible as it seemed.

"Damn the bloody get! I saw her!" shouted one of Loc's soldiers. His hound continued to sniff at Gwendolyn's legs. "She was here!"

"Shut up, you blind bastard! If you saw her, she'd still be there. You let the bitch get away."

"We had her!"

"Aye, well, you don't now, do you? And let's see what the King says about that. I warrant he'll pluck out your blind eyes if you claim that lie to his face. No woman vanishes like a puff o' dirty smoke, not even one cursed by the Fae."

The man with the hound sounded more uncertain now. "But... you saw her too." He scratched at his head. "You told me you did. She ran this way. We both saw her," he mewled.

"I did not see her," denied the other hotly. "I came this way because *you* said you saw the bitch and your dogs, too. But clearly she's not here, you daft fool!"

Gwendolyn hadn't any notion how this was possible.

How could they not see her when she was standing in plain sight?

A moment later the entire vicinity was a crush of Loc's soldiers, all searching frantically—looking behind trees, turning up leaves, leaving no stone or stump unturned.

"Bloody hell," complained another, wading through a sea of leaves. "'Tis deep enough to conceal an army!"

"She can't have gone far," complained the man who'd scolded the man with the dogs. "Her horse is here." He pointed in the direction whence Gwendolyn had come, but the tree held her too firmly so she couldn't move.

"Did you see what she did? Leaping from horse to horse?" asked one of the passing soldiers, then whistled loudly. "I've ne'er seen a woman ride that way before!"

"Nor any man," agreed another.

At Gwendolyn's feet, the dog continued to sniff, and began to whine and Gwendolyn held her breath.

"She must be here somewhere. Evan, take two men and search that way."

Then suddenly, everyone froze as a new rider came trotting through the woods, stopping only briefly to glower at the whining dog. One brow arched as he observed the hound.

Loc.

Murderer.

Deceiver.

Monster.

She fought to stifle a sob. It stuck in her throat, a thousand curses welling up behind it.

Dressed in a white tunic and a bright golden cloak without her spew, he looked as though he'd never broken a sweat. If Gwendolyn had been free to do so, she would have stabbed him through the heart.

Dismounting, he came over to inspect the tree where the hound barked, *touching* Gwendolyn—his hands testing, grasping, probing. Despite that, somehow, he couldn't see... nor feel her. *How could it be?*

"What in the name of the gods is wrong with that witless hound?" he asked. "Have you starved the animals so long they've gone daft? Where are the rest?"

"The dogs?" The one with the dog lifted his chin. "We lost four, Majesty."

Loc turned to peer back at Beryan's fallen mount. He sighed. "I see you lost the girl as well..."

The girl. Not the Queen. Clearly, he would not have his warriors consider her that way. The men all peered anxiously at one another while the dog at Gwendolyn's feet continued to whine and sniff, then bark. "We're... not... certain, Majesty," said the man standing beside his dog.

Loc's brows collided, his amber eyes sharp as knives. "What do you mean you're uncertain?" He peered up from the dog to address the man speaking. "Her companion lies in that river. Her horse, too. I'm told you followed her afoot into these woods. Now you claim you don't know where she is?"

At his feet, the dog growled, teething Gwendolyn's leathers and swiftly but coolly, Loc unsheathed his sword, then skewered the animal through. "Worthless beast!" he complained, then turned away from Gwendolyn, perhaps to consider her fallen horse.

"Is the horse's leg broken?" he asked, and Gwendolyn fought the burn of tears—for the poor wretched beast lying at her feet, for Beryan's mount and her own. For Beryan most of all.

"Aye, Majesty."

"Go on, then. Put it down," he commanded, re-sheathing his blade. "She won't be needing it. She's outlived her usefulness to me." He chortled then, and even as he did so, Gwendolyn understood his meaning. Just as she'd suspected all along, he never intended to return her to the palace. He'd meant to see her dead. *Today. Now.* Like the hound at her feet.

In her fist, her cousin's dagger seared into her palm. She wanted so much to wield it, to thrust it into Loc's throat, see his blood spew. Never in her life had she been more aware of the feel of metal against her flesh and she raged against the restraints holding her back.

She could end this here and now—if only *he* would release her.

Let me go! she thought in vain. *Let me go! Let me go! Let me go!*

The words would not form on her tongue. Whatever binding constrained her arms, also held her tongue. She was a ghost to these men, without form or voice, and yet, she was so painfully close—close enough to plunge Borlewen's blade into the tender flesh of Loc's belly.

I will kill you, she tried to say. *I will cut out your tongue! I will shave your head in kind for the treatment you gave me! I will nail you on a cross of wood before Trevena's gates, with small wooden picks to force your eyes wide, so you can see all you have lost, and then I will call upon the Druids to summon crows to pluck out your eyes!*

"You!" said Loc, unmoved—though of course, he couldn't hear her. He pointed to a pair of men who stood idle together. "Search northeast. As for the rest of you," he said, gesturing to the rest of his troops. "Scatter and move along. Turn every stone you find. If you locate her, leave her to me. I mean to put an end to these Cornish vermin once and for all."

And with that, he turned to remount his horse, leaving Gwendolyn to stare after him, her eyes burning with fury and shivering as much with rage as with fear.

BEFORE DEPARTING, Loc's soldiers climbed into the trees, searching the vicinity as though their lives depended upon it, because they did. And then, at last, as twilight returned to kiss the forest with a soft, rosy glow, the cage of vines surrounding Gwendolyn receded.

In a matter of seconds—the same way he'd produced his Faerie flame—all returned to its usual form and Gwendolyn was no longer a tree, Málik no longer embracing her.

With a yelp of surprise, still holding Borlewen's blade, Gwendolyn tumbled free of his arms, tripping over the now cold carcass of the poor hound.

"What was that?" she exclaimed, scrambling to her feet.

Dear gods. It was him. It was truly him! And he looked so utterly magnificent in a tunic the color of night. His silver hair took on a pink hue against the dusky light, and his *icebourne* eyes were as bright as the flame now hovering beside him. In the half-light, his skin was translucent. His ears were still unmistakably pointy, his teeth uncommonly sharp. And even so, the sight of him made Gwendolyn's heart trip painfully. To her, he was the most beautiful, most wonderful, most welcome sight in all the world.

"*That*," he said with his usual mordancy, "was a narrow escape." And then he smiled, but the humor didn't quite reach his eyes. "You can thank me now," he said.

"Thank you!" Gwendolyn's brows lifted. "You should have let me kill him!" she railed. "Why did you not release me?" She lifted Borlewen's blade to show him, but he shrugged. "Bastard!" she spat, and she wasn't sure if she meant Loc or Málik—perhaps both! Gwendolyn had never felt more ambivalent. On the one hand, she longed to rush into his arms, bury her face against his sinewy chest and weep. On the other, she wanted to see him flat on his belly, with his much too-handsome face pressed into the rotting bracken, her boot planted atop his back, and a blade kissing his nape. It would serve him right after abandoning her for so long—leaving her to wonder for months and months if he would ever return. Indeed, he'd been gone so long that she'd forbidden herself to think of him, lest her heart shatter to pieces, beyond repair. And still... here he was, and her throat constricted at the sight of him, even as her hand tightened on Borlewen's blade.

Calm. Smug. Superior.

He looked so stunning, and it was all Gwendolyn could do not to fly at him, pummel his chest. *Forsooth!* As grateful as she was for his timely intervention, she was also entirely furious with him—not to mention relieved.

Shaking her head to hide the sting of tears, she slid Borlewen's dagger back into its sheath, giving him a baleful glare.

Above him, his Faerie light shimmied about his head, the edges feathering with the cool evening breeze, scattering tendrils of white and blue light.

"What I meant was," she said, a bit more calmly, gesturing at the tree—a tree, which, by the by, looked precisely like any other tree. "What was *that*?"

He turned to inspect the tree in question, lifting his brows. "I believe you would call that an oak," he replied, and Gwendolyn bristled.

"I know what it is, Málik!"

His lazy smile was infuriating. "If you already knew, then why ask?"

"Blood and bones! You know what I mean!" she returned. "What did you do to me?"

"That," he said. "I will explain in due time. For now, we mustn't tarry. Come along, Princess," he said, reaching for her hand.

Gods. He was right. Loc's men hadn't been gone long. The hounds could still be heard in the distance. Moreover, Gwendolyn was suddenly and unusually famished—more so than she'd been in living memory, and the sooner they found shelter, the sooner she could fill her belly. "You have much explaining to do!" she said, taking his hand, tears of relief flooding her eyes.

But her relief soon turned to fury, only belatedly realizing that he'd called her princess—a thing she'd not been in months, a thing she sorely lamented, a thing Estrildis persistently taunted her with, and the one thing Málik had once called her both snidely and endearingly.

"In case you've not heard," she said. "I am no longer a princess."

She hoped he would take her meaning, and all it

conveyed! He did not stay and fight for her, and now she was wed to another, though her heart would forever belong to him.

"I know," he said darkly.

He knew?

He knew!

His answer settled very poorly because Gwendolyn wanted him to feel as sick over it as she did. It galled her so much that he'd taken her father's sword, and then walked straight out of that vault, and out of her life, without so much as a backward glance...

TEN

"What else do you know?" she asked petulantly. "Did you also know they murdered my father and mother?" Not to mention, stole her city, killed her people, then cut her hair.

Perhaps disapproving of her tone, his Faerie flame whizzed between them, dancing frenetically, leaving a sparkling blue tail in its wake.

"I did," he said far too calmly for Gwendolyn's liking.

"Well, if you knew," she said. "Why did you not come?" Tears spilled into the back of her throat, making her question sound too much like a whine—she loathed the way it sounded.

"Gwendolyn..."

She also hated that note of pity she heard in his voice.

What was she supposed to do now? She'd begged with all her heart for him to return before her wedding—he did not. Neither had he cared to stay and see her wed. Though perhaps if he had, she mightn't have gone through with that bloody farce.

And then she would have fought by her father's side, with Málik at hers, and Trevena may have had a better chance.

Yet even as she considered this scenario, she knew it wouldn't have made a difference. She had considered her marriage to Loc a sworn duty, and in the end, her father had been too weak to lead.

As for herself—no matter what she might wish to believe, she was too inexperienced to have known what to do. And Málik was only one male, not an army.

Poor Beryan! He'd given his life to defend her. Now she had no means of repaying him. The poor man was as dead as her father, and Gwendolyn never even had the chance to bury either.

And worse, she had perhaps hurried Beryan to his grave by leaving that scarf to draw Loc away from Bryn and Ely. Now, guilt gnawed like termites at her guts.

Alas, they had no horses, and she was stuck with Málik, who seemed to have nothing to say to her though he should beg her forgiveness—for what, Gwendolyn didn't know, though it made her feel better to blame him when she had no one else to blame.

Except herself.

Her emotions were in upheaval, as though his arrival had set them free. For the moment, she didn't have to be strong, nor did she have to be a queen. She was simply Gwendolyn, and Málik was the one person who knew her best. Grief formed itself like a ball in her throat as she remembered his plea... *Come away with me*, he'd said.

Forswear the crown...

Come to a place where no adversity may seek you.

Gwendolyn had laughed—she'd laughed!—and now she sensed he regretted not only his part in that kiss but the heartfelt plea as well.

Suddenly recalling the way he'd released her from his enchantment, casting her away so fiercely that she'd tumbled to her knees, it made her feel as though he couldn't wait to be free of her.

Was he angry she did not choose him over duty?

He didn't sound angry—and that was, perhaps, the point. He didn't sound the least bit emotional, unlike her, and Gwendolyn didn't want him to be indifferent.

She wanted him as he was before he went away.

More than anything, she longed for him to take her into his arms and hold her and kiss her, tell her how desperately he'd missed her, and yet... how could she expect such things of him? She was the one who'd refused him.

Unbidden, a memory assailed her... that night during the New Moon... only days before her wedding, when he'd cuddled with her on the clifftop... wet from the rain, teeth chattering... the taste of his lips like summer rain...

Don't think of that, she scolded herself.

Don't!

Think.

Of that.

Because if she did, she would entirely cease to breathe—give up. Here. Lie down. In the muck. Curl up and die.

More tears brimmed as she trudged onward, the ground beneath her boots so soggy and damp she left puddles beneath her feet. And yet, mercifully, as unrelenting as the hounds had been, only silence pursued them and with every step she made, she felt the burden of her regret grow heavier and heavier, even as muck crept into her boots, pushing silt between wrinkled toes.

It was a good thing it was summer, because in winter, she would lose her toes as swiftly as she had lost her heart to this damnable *Fae*. And truly, she had. That much was clear. Though the most upsetting thing of all was that, even as her heart longed for words that were never forthcoming, all Gwendolyn really needed to know was that he was as pleased to see her as she was to see him.

Instead, he offered dry wit and pity.

He knew, he knew, he knew...

And this is how her brain worked and worked and worked as she marched into the wee hours until exhaustion claimed her. Without forewarning, Gwendolyn found a tree and slid down beside it... only to rest. Somehow, she'd been able to ignore the gnawing in her belly—a pang unlike any she'd ever experienced. She was spent, and she hadn't even the energy to keep her eyes open. Outrage alone had given her the strength to go on—that far more than fear. But now she was well and truly exhausted.

Loc would pay, she thought.

Someday.

Her fingers itched to return to the hilt of Borlewen's blade, but she'd missed her opportunity and now she needed rest. Blinking against the inexorable weariness, she knew only vaguely that Málik came and sat down beside her. He drew her into his arms, guiding her down to cradle her head in his lap... as he did so long ago.

But, nay, that only felt like a long time ago. In reality, mere months.

So much had transpired since then, and Gwendolyn was no longer the same. Málik was no longer the same. Nothing would ever be the same.

And even so... in that moment, as he folded Gwendolyn into his arms, she felt as though the world itself sighed, and she dared to curl up and forget...

Forget she was running for her life.

Forget, too, that her *husband* was a murderer and thief.

Forget that the land was suffering. Her people, too...

Forget that Málik seemed too distant.

Right now, she didn't care where he had gone, only that he had returned. He sat combing his long fingers through her curls, teasing her scalp with sharp nails, until her lids grew heavy and closed. Tomorrow would be soon enough to demand answers.

Tonight... she must... sleep.

GWENDOLYN AWOKE to the scent of cony turning over a flame.

Warm and cozy beneath Málik's cloak, last night's inexorable heaviness weighted her limbs, and she couldn't move. Eventually lifting one lid, she found Málik sitting opposite her with no coat at all, his bottom resting atop a rotten log, one elbow lifted over his knee, only staring into the flames.

This was how she remembered him best... all those nights they'd spent in Chysauster, huddled together beside a cozy fire whilst her family cele-brated... how her heart ached for this past.

But her uncle and cousins were gone and no amount of regret could bring them back.

Nor could it soften the awful truth that Gwen-dolyn had unwittingly been the catalyst to their end. It was she who'd led those men to their village, simply because she'd had a stupid yen to investigate Bryok's death—a matter that, in truth, should have been left to her father's *konsel*. She'd been a stupid little halfwit, merely playing at being a sleuth.

Spoilt, Málik had once said, and looking back on it now, Gwendolyn realized he'd spoken true. She'd called him arrogant, when in truth, the arrogance was hers, thinking she was good enough to best a mester at arms. She had fought him at every turn, even defying her father when he'd told her to train with Málik daily. And, after all was said and done, whatever she'd learned was all due to him.

For a moment, she lay there, belly grumbling, saying nothing, daring to enjoy the moment, because too soon, everything would change.

Resting beside him, catching a glint from the flame, lay his beautiful bastard sword. Still snug in its harness, neglected for the moment, but she knew from experience that he was ever ready to wield it. Never in her life had she met a man with keener senses than his... but then, he was not a man, was he?

Her gaze returned to the muscles in his thighs, so easily discernible when he lurched forward to test the make-do spit.

"Good morning," he said, catching her awake.

Gwendolyn's cheeks burned, but she did not turn away.

She had endured too much to be embarrassed by this brief moment of pleasure, unseemly though it might be. She didn't feel wedded, and she was a virgin still, her body untried, and her mind filling with wonder over the differences between their bodies—even more perceptible now because of the desire she no longer felt compelled to deny.

As vexed as she was with him for having left her so long at Loc's mercy, she was equally relieved to have him so close. Particularly since she knew it wasn't his fault. He'd only done what she'd asked. Gwendolyn was the one who'd sent him away.

Rubbing her eyes, she stretched, the smell of breakfast rousing her completely. "Morning," she said sleepily. "Did you hunt?"

"Hunt?" he asked, with some acerbity. "Alas, for this poor beast, he had the ill fortune to encounter me." There was a note of regret in his tone, and for all Gwendolyn knew, he'd ensorcelled the poor creature. More and more, she was coming to understand how little she knew of Málik's *rás*—his people, his breed. There was so much about him she didn't understand, and she mustn't forget he wasn't Bryn. Indeed, he might kiss like a man, flirt like a man, but he was not a man. He was a child of the gods, a creature not of this world.

And if ever she needed a reminder of this, she needn't look too hard—only peer into the maelstrom of his eyes or note the whetted fangs.

Fae, *Sidhe*, Danann, whatever his pleasure, Málik was nothing like her, and still she seemed so intent upon forgetting this. From the very first, she had needled him relentlessly, and notably so when she'd believed he'd stolen her best friend.

Now she had neither Bryn nor Málik—or rather, she had him here in form, but his demeanor was colder than he'd ever been. Colder yet because they had once been so close.

"I've some hob cake as well," Málik said. "Though we'll save that for later. At the moment, you need something more." A lock of his pale hair fell into his face, and he pushed it away. "I took a chance to roast the cony, knowing Loc's men would be slow to rise."

"How would you know such a thing?"

He grinned. "Let us say... I made certain to give them a reason for it."

"Oh?" Gwendolyn returned. "Did you somehow find them and poison them?"

In her darkest of hearts, she hoped the answer would be yes. As terrible as that would seem to wish for a man's death, she'd like to see Loc choke till the little veins burst in his eyes.

Málik's answering chuckle was dark. "Something of that sort," he confessed. "Though not precisely. *He* wasn't there, else my answer would be different."

There was no need to explain who *he* was. Gwendolyn knew. That was the way she thought of *him* herself—a nameless, heartless, soulless fiend.

Málik blew out a weary sigh. "As it was, I encountered only a few men whose worst crime as yet is to be born under a dark star. Though it might seem judicious to slay them and be done without offering a chance for defense, that would be a crime against my people's laws."

"Your people?" Gwendolyn frowned. She had never considered that they, too, might have laws of their own. She had rather thought of them as she did the gods, or ghosts, or fables—whimsical, supernatural, romantic... but not subject to... laws.

He looked at her now with brows lifted, and the gesture wrested a blush from Gwendolyn. "We are not really so different," he apprised.

"I must disagree. I have not yet met a man or woman who could turn people into trees," she said, and sat, wincing as she reached up to pluck a leaf from her hair. *Gods.* It was one thing for Málik to run his fingers through this tangle by night, yet another for him to see it by day.

"That is not precisely what happened," he said, but then he did not explain, and Gwendolyn watched as he poked at the cony with a finger, testing its doneness.

"What then?" she pressed. Still he answered with silence.

Gwendolyn sighed. Knowing him as she did— that he would tell her only when he was good and ready—she shrugged off his cloak, setting it aside. "Thank you for this," she said, gesturing to the cloak. "You needn't have gone without for me."

"Keep it," he said, turning away. "As you must know, I do not feel the cold as you do."

She had already surmised as much. "Still another way we are different," she pointed out.

But then she wondered: Was it only one winter past that he'd arrived in Trevena wearing summer clothes during winter? Indeed, it was.

So much had transpired since then—most of it disastrous. But she would never forget the sight he'd presented, cantering in through those gates, his hair free and billowing with his cloak.

Wistfully, Gwendolyn's thoughts returned to that

moment on the ramparts, standing beside Demelza and Ely. "Who is he?" she'd asked.

"No one for you to be concerned over," came Demelza's curt response.

But Ely was quick to disclose all she knew. "He's an Elf!" she'd said in a sing-song tone, pleased with the gossip. "My father says he has come to enthrall our King, and we'd best take care."

"Bah!" said Demelza. "If you leave them be, and stay out of their way, they'll leave you in peace." But that wasn't precisely true, because Gwendolyn had done nothing to warrant their visitation at her crib side. She was only a babe then, and neither her mother nor Demelza had summoned those creatures. They'd come of their own accord, with their gift of a prophecy, and a stupid blessing that felt more like a curse.

She could not say with any good faith that she knew what everyone saw when they looked at her, but the most obvious consequence of her "gift" was that people treated her differently depending on how they viewed her countenance.

"Salt," Ely had then said, undeterred by Demelza's rebuke. "Salt or a necklace of marigolds will ward them away." And yet it wasn't long thereafter that Ely had changed her mind about him. Instead of wearing marigolds, she had followed him about with a daisy in her hair, like a love-sick pup. And truly, Ely's affection for him had perhaps been the first blow to their friendship—the first, not the last. Because he *was* enthralling, Gwendolyn soon discovered. In truth, he may not have beguiled her father, but he certainly had her. There was something about the swirling depths of his silvery eyes that always made Gwendolyn forget herself... as she did now.

Catching herself staring, she continued to repair herself while he removed a bit of cony from the skewer, offering the first piece to Gwendolyn. She grasped it, her mouth watering even before she had the chance to taste it. But then, once she did, she was famished for more. "Delicious!" she confessed, pleased to see that he was tearing more bites and placing them on a strip of cloth.

They shared a look, and Gwendolyn licked her fingers, not meaning to behave like a starved animal, but she couldn't help herself. The instant he handed over the napkin, she shoved everything into her gob, the taste and scent so unimaginably satisfying.

For all these months, she had existed on only gruel. At supper the evening past, she'd hardly eaten a bite, so disgusted was she by Loc. And later, she'd been too excited, and then nervous to worry about food. This morning, however, she was so ravenous she could eat an entire stag.

And that was yet another thing she was grateful for this morn—that Málik knew how to cook, because Gwendolyn never learned how. The most she'd ever attempted was to drop two eggs in a pot of boiling water after watching her aunt do the same. But she never even had the chance to discover if her efforts proved edible, because that was the day those men had tracked them to Ia's farm. Interrupted from the task, she and Málik had battled for their lives, then departed without ever seeing to their bellies. For all Gwendolyn knew, those eggs were still sitting in that same pot, though she hoped not because that would mean Ia and her parents never returned. That possibility dulled her appetite, though not enough to keep her from eating every bite offered. When it was gone, she blinked in surprise, only belatedly realizing that Málik never ate. "Aren't you hungry?"

"Not at the moment," he said, and Gwendolyn considered the fact that she'd never actually seen him eat. Not truly. Not even during their time in Chysauster, although he did join them to sup. Very distinctly, she recalled he drank from her cup, only to tease her, but never once did he take a bite from their shared trencher. "Don't tell me you only eat berries?" she joked.

His eyes narrowed to slits of gray smoke. "Do these appear to be the denticulation of one inclined to berries?" He bared one tooth, the look in his eyes wholly feral—quite at odds with his actions as he sat serenely, declining the feast he'd made.

He added, "You'd be wise to note there are few occasions when the goddess' creatures are made without regard to need, Gwendolyn. If you see claws... or fangs..." His silver eyes glinted, his pupils dilating as a hunter's would when focusing on prey. "You should run."

Gwendolyn tilted him a questioning glance, jesting. "Should I now?"

He shrugged. "That would depend..."

"On what?"

He smiled lazily. "Do you wish to find yourself my morning feast?"

Gwendolyn blinked, uncertain of his meaning, sensing there was something forbidden and carnal in the jest. "Are we talking about food?" she dared to ask.

"Perhaps," he said, his grin spreading slowly, revealing two gleaming rows of sharp white teeth... with the canines sharper than the rest.

Why had she never wondered about this before?

It made sense, though. Why was any creature born with fangs if not meant to use them? Simply because his *rás* was said to exist in harmony with nature did not mean they did not have their place in its hierarchy—as hunters. Wolves were nature's beasts, but they would gladly sup on a man's flesh and bones. More than ever, Málik was a mystery to her, and clearly disinclined to alter this truth. However, there was something she needed to know, and now seemed as good a time as any to ask. "Where did you take my father's sword?"

"Home... where it belongs."

Gwendolyn lifted both brows. "Home?"

"*My* home," he said. "*Claímh Solais* was ours before it was yours."

As quickly as the tension between them had eased, it stretched taut once more. "And yet it would not burn for you as it did for my father. So I must argue it no longer belongs to your people. It belongs to mine, and you stole it!"

"To the contrary," Málik said. "It was given to me for safekeeping, in case you don't recall."

"Oh, I do," Gwendolyn said, her fury mounting. "But that sword was granted to you by a sickly man, who did not know what travesty was soon to come."

"You must not give your father so little credit, Gwendolyn. He understood he was dying and did not believe his heir was up to the challenge of defending that sword. You cannot possibly imagine its worth."

His words cut deeply. Gwendolyn pointed to her breast. "*I* cannot imagine its worth?"

Men died to defend that sword—men known to her since she was a child. The aldermen had guarded it with their lives. In the end, her father had sequestered that sword, leaving untold riches free to be stolen—gold, copper, tin. None of it had merited the place in her father's vault.

Moreover, how could he imply she would not know her father? Or that she might underestimate his cunning? She better than most knew her father's worth, but Málik did not understand how much he'd wasted, nor how much Gwendolyn had worried for him, searching for remedies, worrying incessantly about Porth Pool, even so far as to consider summoning those Druids. Gods, she'd married a rotten gobshite solely for his sake!

"You didn't even know it was there," he argued. "Did you?"

It was true. She did not know the sword was in her father's vault. And this was a great burden to carry—to know her father had not even trusted her well enough to tell her.

Gwendolyn bounded to her feet, vexed again, though this time she had a good reason. And it wasn't only about the sword.

She had a sense that Málik knew more about everything than he was willing to admit, and if he'd known what was about to happen to her father, why hadn't he spoken up to warn her—or at the least, stay to defend the true conservator of this land?

After all, wasn't that what he'd claimed he'd been sent for—to defend Trevena?

"I'm ready to leave," she said, slapping a hand across her tunic to rid it of cony grease. Far from looking like a queen, she feared she looked and smelled like a homeless beggar. And perhaps she was, though if she doubted it, Málik's next question emphasized the truth.

"Where would you have us go?"

Where, indeed?

Anywhere far from here—far from Locrinus, and for the moment, far from Málik, as well!

"North," she snapped, and with that, she bent to lift his cloak, tossing it back to him, wanting nothing from him that wasn't owed—and verily, he owed her nothing. Even his oath of fealty as her Shadow did not come without an expiration date.

Furious again, she turned and marched away.

CHAPTER
ELEVEN

Tired and hungry, her shoes damp and her heart feeling trampled as well, Gwendolyn refused to complain, nor did she wish for Málik to discern how much he'd hurt her feelings—how much he wounded her every time he opened his mouth.

Why was he so compelled to speak so forthright, with no thought for softening his words? Much as she wished to know the truth from him, and even respected it, he showed no thought for her feelings in his disclosures. It was as though he meant for her to loath him.

And yet, no matter that she desperately wanted to, she could not.

For now, it was better not to speak to him—not even to ask about the cake he said he had. By now, whatever vitality the morning's victuals had provided was well and duly squandered, and still she trudged through these changing woodlands, lips pressed firmly together and teeth grinding with remembered fury.

Nearly spent, she followed as he led her through

lands that were thicker with brush, and she wanted to ask where they were going, but Málik had never been less forthcoming.

Like hers, his lips were sealed tighter than a clam at high tide.

All the while, they traveled, not more than a few feet apart, she felt the distance grow between them, widening like a chasm. Along with a tumult of emotions, a multitude of questions marched through her head, all vying for a turn on her tongue. There were so many things she wished to know, not merely about her parents, about Málik as well.

Where had he been all these months? Why had he returned? Why now, when he didn't bother to do so all those miserable weeks she'd prayed so desperately?

Whatever the case, he still hadn't even told her *what* he'd done to her yesterday.

It was an astonishing feat. The entire time he'd held her in his arms by that tree she'd felt unchanged, as though she were still flesh and blood, but Locrinus and his men had looked straight through her.

Moreover, it was late morning when Loc's men first gave chase, and twilight when Málik released her from his enchantment. Meanwhile, it seemed only minutes had passed, but she'd lost an entire day, emerging from his—whatever it was—famished and prepared to devour anything that crossed her path.

Unfortunately, at this moment, her strength was quickly diminishing, and her state of mind as well. The only thing she knew for certain was how sorely she missed her horse.

"Where are we going?" she asked when she could bear it no longer.

"You said north."

"I did, but you seem to have a particular destination in mind," she suggested.

Because he did. She did not miss his sure steps, nor his attention to the path. But Gwendolyn didn't recognize these parts. And truly, though she didn't wish to complain, she felt as though Málik was punishing her somehow—perhaps to illustrate how spoiled she was.

But she wasn't. Despite those long hours of practice in her room, she wasn't so hale as he was. And no matter, she kept walking, refusing to concede, reassuring herself that whatever manner of toil she must survive during these days at large it would only strengthen her body and soul.

Ahead of her, Málik stubbornly gave her his back, his mood growing darker with every step they took, and Gwendolyn had to restrain herself from leaping at his back and pummeling him soundly. Somehow, he brought out the worst in her, even now.

Yet she would not give him the satisfaction of her anger, and therefore, they journeyed most of the day in silence, encountering not a soul along the way, until the woods grew dark and still.

Eventually, they crossed into what appeared to be the beginnings of the northern pine woods—a vast expanse of woodlands that some claimed ambled all the way to the North Sea.

Here there were fewer oaks and elms and more of those great northern pines—trees that grew to enormous heights, in defiance of soil and weather.

It was said those pines were as defiant as the northern people, and Gwendolyn could easily believe it. Despite that, the land here was drier and the soil less rich, the trees were still hardy, growing tall enough to blot the sun.

This brought to mind her mother's people, said to live amidst this shifting landscape, where the tribes were as changeable as the land. No matter that the southern folk referred to them as a confederacy, those northern tribes were actually many tribes—seven, whose kings were known to her father as thanes. But those thanes ruled only the largest of the northern provinces, and for every known thane, there were seven more whose names were as yet unknown.

This was the reason her grandfather always claimed the Prydein would forever remain unconquered, subservient to no one. The most anyone could ever hope for was to form an alliance with one of the larger tribes, and then pray that, by virtue of the respect this tribe engendered, it would facilitate relations with the others. But despite her father's marriage to Gwendolyn's mother, though it changed some aspects of their dealings with the northern tribes, it never made them closer. They were still not allies. They were not even friendly. And though she had kinfolk amidst the largest of the Prydein tribes, they were as much a mystery to her as was Málik.

The more she thought about it, the more she wondered if going north was the right thing to do, or even if her mother's people would bother to aid her.

After all, why should they? For her mother's sake? A woman who'd not once returned to her birthland after her espousal?

Neither had her grandparents ever inquired about their long-lost daughter or granddaughter. More than nineteen years Gwendolyn had been in this world, and through all those years, she never once recalled an inquiry from her grandparents.

She frowned now. For all she knew, she was well and truly alone—entirely so now that Bryn and Ely had abandoned her. All she had left was Málik, who could no longer abide her. Whatever transpired during the time they'd spent apart, he no longer felt the same about her.

She felt it in her bones.

"I've not heard those dogs in quite some time," Gwendolyn said, spent with the silence, wearied of the discord and growing tired of endlessly marching.

"With a bit of luck, my flame will lead them astray."

Naturally, Málik didn't bother to turn to see if she was keeping up. He merely assumed she could. "You sent it away?"

Gwendolyn remembered how it behaved in her uncle's *fogous*, like Yestin's loyal hound. Clearly, those wisps had a will of their own.

Her belly grumbled again and Málik must have heard it, because he turned to hand her a wafer. Gwendolyn grasped it at once. "Thank you!" she said, eagerly tearing a bite, then swallowing, shocked to find it settled so quickly.

In fact, she was prepared to take another, but stopped midway to her mouth to inspect the curious wafer. It appeared to have so little substance, so light and airy it melted against her tongue, but the moment she swallowed it, she couldn't imagine putting another bite into her mouth. Her hunger wasn't simply appeased; she felt as though she'd eaten an entire brick of clay!

What was more, she'd eaten it so swiftly, but she

imagined it tasted like a pudding in cowcumbers, made with the most flavorful of baby cowcumbers, in a buttery broth of pork... stewed with sultanas and cloves. This was her favorite dish as a child.

After another moment, she was no longer so tired and her eyes felt as though she could see more keenly. What was more, her legs felt as though they were light as feathers, and more—as if she could march another hundred leagues. "What is this?"

"Hob cake, I told you," he said. "Don't eat too much. A nibble will do."

Gwendolyn peered down at the cake in her hand. "Hob cake?" she whispered with wonder and then bristled when she heard Málik's answering chuckle.

TWELVE

I t was like a *drogue*.

Not for the first time, Gwendolyn stole another glance into the pouch wherein she'd stashed the rest of the hob cake.

In fact, there was nothing caky about the wafer Málik gave her, and she had no doubt now; her eyesight *was* keener, her hearing more acute, and her scalp felt more and more tingly by the moment. She suspected his hob cake was responsible, though she daren't ask about it, because, despite Málik's warning, she'd been sneaking "nibbles" off the wafer all day long... only to be sure of the taste. Her investigation grew utterly confusing. One nibble tasted like pottage stew, another like mushroom pasties, yet another like crispels basted in honey. Her last bite had tasted like those pilchards she'd eaten at her uncle's home in Chysauster—all favored meals, though not one bite the same, and the only thing Gwendolyn grew certain about was that the onset of whistling in her ears was equally annoying as the tingling in her scalp.

After a while, the whistling grew so loud she

feared Málik could hear it as well, though he said nothing, and neither did he bother to speak to her, so lost was he in his own brooding silence.

Fine.

She didn't really need to talk to him, anyway. Talking was overvalued. It wasn't as though she'd been alone for months and months, only praying for companionship... eager for news.

Nay. She needn't talk to the bloody elf, and if he was vexed with her, she should be twice as vexed with him, because Gwendolyn had the greater cause for enmity.

What cause had *he* to be angry, anyway?

Regardless, his scowling face remained centered on the vicinage, his eyes quick to investigate every sound. Gwendolyn felt alone in these woods.

Alas, even though she would never dare admit it, she rested easier in his company, concerning herself less with Loc and his men, and more with this peculiar confection Málik had provided.

Light until she ate it, it assuaged all hunger, but although it sat heavily in her belly, it did not make her feel as though she needed to nap, as so often was the case when she ate too much. She was well and truly satisfied, but without the heaviness that accompanied a large meal. *Curious.*

When finally Málik deigned to address her, it was close to twilight, and then it was only to insist they should rest for the evening. But Gwendolyn was too animated to sleep. In fact, when she should have been exhausted after a full day's exertion, she felt as though she'd been sucking on willow bark all day long. "There's no need," she insisted. "If you're concerned about me, do not be."

Somehow, she'd managed not to complain at her worst and now that she was feeling more energetic, she really wanted to continue. There had been no sign of Loc since yestereve, but his men were not traveling afoot as they were. So, as far as she was concerned, if they didn't need the respite, they shouldn't take the risk.

He turned to fix her with a pointed glance, lifting a brow. "I'm certain you can persevere, *banríon*. But no matter that the effort of yesterday's glamour was mine, you'll eventually reap the effects and the rewards."

Banríon?

Gwendolyn frowned, unfamiliar with the word, though he'd said it much the same way he used to call her princess, and that needled her, because, really, he'd so often called her that, not as a matter of deference, but to emphasize the lavishness that was her life.

But that simply wasn't true. Her father and mother had never heaped riches into her lap. She had earned everything she'd ever owned. The state of their vault should have attested to this, and that none of the yield from their mines could be found within the city's stores said quite a lot. Because it was used in payment to their people, for goods sold in the market, or in payment to men like Brutus for weapons and defense.

Only her mother had ever had a closet to be envied, and even so, Queen Eseld had shared all she had with Gwendolyn, sometimes gifting her gowns to others, including Ely.

The only thing her mother ever kept entirely for herself were the jewels she'd brought from her home in Prydein, and it was clear she'd valued those things above all.

Meanwhile, the only thing her father was ever lavish about was the city's amenities—all for the sake of the people. Their palace and buildings were constructed with the people in mind. But if the king had been less generous, perhaps Trevena's coffers would have been full enough to mount a better defense, and Locrinus would not be sitting on half the isle's store of tin, copper and gold.

"I need not be coddled," she apprised. "There is no reason we should stop now. If Loc merely searches in another direction, we will easily be found. I insist we go on."

He lifted a brow. "You insist?"

Gwendolyn lifted her chin. "Yes. I must."

"And still here we will stay," he said, his tone brooking no argument.

Officious as ever, but he did not remember his place! Even if he were still Gwendolyn's Shadow, she would be the one giving orders, not the other way around. Yet he gave up that title the day he abandoned her, and if he thought he could return now as her most trusted advisor and confidant—just like that!—and that Gwendolyn would do all he said without question, he must think again!

His steely gaze settled on the pouch at her waist —a silent rebuke?

Did he know?

Yes, he did.

His gaze lifted to her face, his eyes studying her. "You feel invulnerable, don't you?"

Unable to lie when he looked at her so directly, Gwendolyn nodded.

"Perhaps even drunk?"

Gwendolyn crossed her arms, tilting her head. "I wouldn't say... drunk... not precisely."

"It's the hob cake," he told her. "And once it wears off, you'll close your eyes without warning. If you push yourself too far, you'll not wake for days. Here, we stay," he said once more, and with a flourish, produced another of his Faerie flames, tossing it into the air—decision made whether or not Gwendolyn liked it.

He was right, of course—he was always right, maddening as that was. Still, she didn't have to like it, nor did she have to obey. And nevertheless, when Gwendolyn opened her mouth to protest, he said the only thing that could have moved her.

"*I* need to rest, Gwendolyn."

"*You?*"

No matter what they had endured, Málik was never worse for the effort, and even when she herself looked like a rumpled mess—as no doubt she did now—his appearance was unspoiled and his mood annoyingly well disposed. As her Shadow, he'd never once employed the use of her antechamber. The entire time they'd remained in Chysauster, she'd never even learned where he'd made his bed, nor whether he'd slept at all. And later, down in the *fogous*, he'd held her all night long, but she couldn't remember him sleeping a wink. It was only on the cliff side, on the way home, on the night he'd kissed her, that he'd dared to rest awhile, sharing her blanket. But even then, he was gone by first light, risen to tend the horses before Gwendolyn ever opened her eyes.

"I don't believe you," she said, certain he was exaggerating for her sake.

Gwendolyn didn't need to be cosseted. She was tired of everyone brushing her aside, locking her away, ignoring her requests as though she were still only a child, instead of the rightful queen of these isles.

"Have you known me to lie?" he asked, and Gwendolyn responded with arms akimbo, lifting her chin.

"In fact," she said. "You told me you'd never leave me, and yet you abandoned me!" The complaint burst from her lips before she could think to stop it, but now, at least he should understand the reason for her ill temper.

Her feelings were hurt, and she wanted him to know it—especially since she sensed in her deepest of hearts that his presence in Trevena during the Feast of Blades could well have changed the course of fate. He'd failed her when she needed him most.

"Believe what you will," he returned. "I cannot lie." His lip curled at one corner—like a snarl—giving her a glimpse of one sharp fang. "'Tis a weakness of my people," he lamented, and then added, "Take care what you ask if you don't wish to know the answer." His Faerie flame whizzed by, growing frantic with his mood. "Trust me, Gwendolyn. If you heed me, you will thank me later." His chin lifted as he added, "Having said that, I did not abandon you. Never once did I tell you I'd be every moment by your side. But I am here now, and if I've returned, you cannot claim to be abandoned."

That was true. He was here. But he was not the same. She wanted him back the way he was—not this cold replica of the Fae she grew to love.

Still, blaming him for what happened in Trevena might seem unfair... unless he somehow knew what would transpire, and somehow, Gwendolyn feared he might. Considering the Faeries' gift of prophecy for her, it really made her wonder.

His *icebourne* eyes glinted hard as he shrugged off of his cloak. "I'll be back," he said. "Please stay." And then, daring Gwendolyn to refuse by the dark look on his face, he handed her his cloak.

Arms crossed, Gwendolyn didn't at once accept it, defying him for reasons she didn't altogether comprehend. She was truly grateful to have him again by her side, so why couldn't she stop being angry?

"No fire," he added. "It's too risky."

For the longest moment, they locked gazes, and Gwendolyn wished so desperately to tell him no, she didn't want his cloak. She wanted to go where he went, and despite this, there was a warning in his manner that dissuaded her, and she seized the cloak, even as it vexed her.

"Yes, of course!" she said, and she wondered inanely if the offer of the cloak was a purposeful decision made so he could keep his distance from her—Gods forbid they should share it. "Where are you going?"

"I'll be back," he said again, without further explanation, and then he marched into the woods, leaving Gwendolyn to stare after him, vanishing so swiftly that she was forced to blink, mistrusting her vision. It must be the hob cake, she decided. Playing tricks on her mind.

THIRTEEN

One bell. Two bells. Three bells.

If there were bells to ring, that's how many Gwendolyn believed must have passed all the while she paced. Without thinking, she lifted Málik's cloak to her face, inhaling deeply of his scent—a musky woodland spice unique only to him. But then, catching herself in the act, she tossed the cloak away, beside an old ash tree.

What was wrong with her?

Why did his presence in her life always turn to matters of the heart when there were more important matters to consider?

Where had he gone? Having spent more than enough time alone with him to know his habits, Gwendolyn didn't believe he'd slipped away for privacy, especially for so long.

Down in those *fogous,* it was always Gwendolyn rushing off to tend to her needs. Again, today, all day, it was her, and Málik had stood waiting for her with no sign that he'd ever wandered away.

Indeed, for all that he was a living, breathing creature, he sometimes appeared to be altogether devoid of needs—no sleep, no food, no love, no affection. In all the time she'd known him there had been so few occasions when he'd appeared to covet anything at all, and... well... let us merely say it was difficult to understand his motives.

Clearly, that kiss had meant less to him than it had to her.

For months, whilst she'd lamented Loc's repudiation of her, the memory of Málik's kiss had sustained her, even fearing he might never return. In her heart, she'd contented herself with the notion that somewhere out there, someone cared for her.

At least that's what she'd told herself, when she'd decided for Loc instead of him—that even if she never saw him again, she would carry his memory in her heart, cherishing his kiss above all.

Only now that he had returned, it seemed to Gwendolyn that he couldn't care less about her, and yet she was still his burden, and his demeanor made that all too clear.

Well, at least he'd cared enough to leave her with the damnable cloak and his Faerie light. The flame hovered close by, as though watching her, pulsing with a gentle blue light.

"So here we are," she said aloud, speaking more to herself than to the orb. So far as Gwendolyn could recall, Málik only ever spoke to it once, and in that case, she'd suspected his actual words were meant more for Gwendolyn than for his flame. So often, it simply did what he wished of it. And sometimes, there were more than one. They came and went, vanishing with the morning light, and returning whensoever they pleased. Gwendolyn didn't know where the orbs made off to—perhaps out there luring some poor muggin to his doom. Like the *piskies* in Porth Pool, there was something other-worldly about them.

This one... like a wolf stalking its prey, it circled her, and Gwendolyn watched it suspiciously. "Are you his spy?" she wondered aloud.

The orb's blue light brightened to white, and she said, "You are, aren't you? That's why you're here? So you can tittle-tattle?" She eyed the flame with a lifted brow.

In answer, it bounced around, off the trunks of trees, crashing through leaves, burning brighter, then dimming and despite herself, it wrested a reluctant smile from her lips. But she was quite certain now that it was responding to her questions.

"Do you understand me?"

It brightened, but still she frowned. "I don't understand you," she lamented.

The orb dimmed.

"I don't suppose you have a name?" she asked, feeling silly for asking.

It flickered, looking... bewildered?

"Name," she said, pointing to herself. "I am Gwendolyn."

She tapped her breast, but the orb didn't respond, and Gwendolyn slid a glance about the campsite, hoping against hope that Málik wouldn't return now to find her hopelessly gabbing with a ball of blue flame, as though she were so desperate for a friend.

But she was, now wasn't she?

The orb followed when she gave a turn to inspect the camp, and she said, "Mayhap I should call you *Sterenglas*?"

It meant blue star, and it suited the wisp well. It

reminded her so much of a wee star borne to earth. "Do you know where he's gone, *Steren*?"

Excitedly, the flame zipped over to Málik's cloak, perching there, then blinking slowly like a cat blinking its yellow eyes.

Gwendolyn frowned. "That's only his cloak," she said, but the orb was undeterred, shimmying itself into its folds, snuggling—of a sort. Gwendolyn peered at the silly little sphere, half considering taking it up and tossing it into the woods to see where it might go.

"Well, I don't care where he's gone," she told the orb. Spy or not, she didn't intend to sit idly waiting for him to return. There must be something she could do.

Unfortunately, they had no blankets, and Gwendolyn had no belongings, except for what little she carried on her person—a handful of Prydein jewels and her cousin's dagger.

And, really, much as she valued her mother's belongings, they would eventually be of more use in the purchase of a mount and supplies. It would pain her immensely to surrender them, but she couldn't justify keeping them only for the sake of keeping them. Although she might keep the armband, if only to prove her identity to her grandfather.

Since Málik didn't wish for her to kindle a fire, there was really nothing more to be done, except sit and wait... and wait... and wait... and wait—something Gwendolyn should have become accustomed to by now, but there was nothing in her demeanor inclined toward indolence.

Princess she might have been, but she'd never actually considered herself a lady, and never in her life had she been content to sit about sewing or doing such things as her mother's ladies clearly enjoyed—Ely could attest to that. So could Bryn.

Even so, here she was... again.

Waiting.

Still.

As though she hadn't already waited months and months.

Unsettled by the persistent tingling in her scalp, her gaze returned to the Faerie flame still snuggled by the ash tree—directly below a small, sturdy limb growing sideways from the trunk. One corner of Málik's cloak caught upon the limb... but that gave her an idea.

"I'm going to whittle," she told the orb.

It blinked at her, then scurried away as she approached and Gwendolyn unsheathed Borlewen's knife to cut herself a length of wood, then sat with her back against the tree.

Without being asked, the Faerie flame sidled close again, lifting itself to a position over her head and there it remained, providing ample light to whittle by.

Slowly, methodically, while Gwendolyn sat conversing with an animated blue flame, she carved out the tip of an arrow, fashioned the way her father once taught her.

"Ash is not the best wood," she explained. "But it will do."

Her father's preference was yew because it outlasted all other woods. But also because the yew's poison did not die when the tree died. This was why her father's army so oft used a tincture made from the yew sap on their arrows. If the poison pierced the skin, it was quickly absorbed, and if the arrow didn't do the job on its own, the poison would ensure they'd not live to see the morn.

There were bones in the woods near Trevena... some claimed to be the bones of hapless travelers, but some were clearly wounded soldiers who'd crawled into the cool shelter of the woods to die. Gwendolyn imagined them with their brows burning with fever, their knees to their bellies, and mouths agape with silent screams. No one ever dared touch those bones; because it was bad luck to do so. Taking morbid pleasure in the thought of Locrinus dying that way, Gwendolyn imagined herself with a bow, taking aim... *He* wouldn't be grinning so easily if he had a yew arrow through the heart, would he?

Inspecting the newly carved tip, she ran her fingers across the length of wood, feeling for knobs. "The trick," she said, glancing up at the Faerie flame. "Is to find a piece as straight as possible." Eventually, she would shave the bark and bend it over the heat of a flame, to straighten it, then fire-harden the point. Even though her fletching skills were far from the best, she could still do it well enough to serve a purpose.

This mightn't be magic, but the discipline took years to develop, and before his death, her father was still trying to work at his. So often in the quiet moments, she would find him there in his chambers, whittling at wood...

She laid back, shoving the memory away, knowing she shouldn't dwell on a past she couldn't change.

Peering into the woods, she wondered when Málik would return, and then, eyeing the Faerie flame, she remembered the wafer in her pouch—hob cake, Málik had called it, but that told her little more than how it was made, not what it was. At home, the cake they'd served to break the fast was also hob cake —made in a flat pan—though it certainly didn't have the same qualities.

Craving it even now, Gwendolyn refrained from stealing another bite, wondering idly why the gods turned against the Tuatha'ans. Had they also betrayed their conservatorship? Was this why Málik had returned now? To right some wrong committed by his people?

To make sure that Gwendolyn didn't make the same mistakes?

He certainly hadn't come to return her father's sword, she thought bitterly. And judging by his unsociable behavior, he hadn't returned for her...

She glanced again into the woods and wondered why he wouldn't tell her where he was going. Why couldn't she go with him?

So many questions marched through her head, with so many riddles to be solved.

There was so much to do in order to see her father's legacy restored... and despite that she spoke so boldly in anger, Gwendolyn didn't know where to begin.

Right now, the only thing keeping her from falling into a squashy little puddle was... the one person who couldn't seem to abide her.

At last, when he returned, he did so without an explanation and Gwendolyn didn't bother asking where he'd gone. If he didn't wish to tell her, so be it.

Flicking her the briefest of glances, he divested himself of his shoulder harness, laying down his sword. Then, without a word, he slid down the tree opposite her, and closed his eyes—if not to rest, then perhaps so he wouldn't have to look at her.

His Faerie flame moved closer to him, and Gwendolyn whispered beneath her breath, "Traitor." It made a sputtering sound like a hissing kitten, then ignored her now as well.

Beneath its light, Málik's face took on a bluish hue. He reached back to pluck a black ribbon from his hair and drew his locks over one shoulder like a fount of pale silk.

Gwendolyn watched him, and, for the first time, it occurred to her how much longer his hair was than hers—something else he'd not yet bothered to mention, and mayhap that rankled her as well? On the one hand, she didn't want him to notice her hair.

On the other... she longed... so much... to have him see her—well and truly see her—to understand how much she'd endured.... to draw her into his arms and say, "Don't fret, Gwendolyn. All will be well." But he did not. Annoyed that he could so easily dismiss her, afraid she couldn't sleep with so much hob cake in her belly, she lifted the arrow she'd begun to carve, and once more whittled furiously, first shaving away the worst of the notches, then peeling away the bark.

"Gwendolyn," he said, after a while, his tone too much like a complaint. "Please rest," he said. "We've a grueling day on the morrow."

No one knew this more than Gwendolyn did, and if she could sleep she would, but she *couldn't*. Her senses were still reeling, and her heart beat too fast.

Blood and bones! Somehow, they must be done with these strained relations, and if she did not make the effort, he might never.

"I'm not sleepy," she said.

"I wonder why."

There was no need to voice the reason because she sensed he knew. Only now was the perfect opportunity to find out what it was she'd been nibbling on all day long.

"What is hob cake?" she demanded.

"My people call it ambrosia."

She stopped whittling. "What's it made of?"

His answer betrayed a twist of a smile. "A pinch of hope, a wodge of dreams, a sprinkle of dread... and the shimmer beneath a *piskie's* wings." He smiled then, and his fang glinted blue beneath his Faerie light.

Gwendolyn resisted the urge to roll her eyes. Determined to be as annoying as he was, she persisted with more questions. "What is a wodge?"

"More than a wedge, less than a podge."

Disappointed in so many less than forthright answers, Gwendolyn hurled her ash stick and said, "Very well! I see. You don't wish to talk to me. Never mind!"

"Gwendolyn... if you are so concerned we'll run out of the hob cake, do not be. There's plenty more. And yet, I must warn you... if you eat too much, you may turn into an *Elf*."

Gwendolyn blinked. "Is that true?"

"No."

He was needling her, she realized, and despite that it felt more familiar, it nettled her anyway—in part for his use of a word that was never spoken with good intention, although Gwendolyn was sometimes guilty of using it herself. Did he know she'd sometimes referred to him that way in anger? *Gods*. She hoped not. Determined to find some way to bridge the chasm between them, she persisted, "Where did you go?

"That is none of your concern."

"Oh," she said, tears now stinging her eyes, wishing for some way to make him understand all she wanted was the return of his friendship.

She missed him so desperately, and never more than she did right now when he was seated only an arm's length away. More than anything in the entire world, she wanted to crawl over to him on her dirty knees and nestle in beside him... lay her head atop his chest and... rest.

"Gwendolyn," he said low, his voice hoarse with exhaustion. "I would really like to say I am sorry..."

"You would?" Her throat burned with raw emotion—and hope.

"I would, but cannot," he said darkly, dashing all her hopes. "I cannot change my actions," he said. "Nor do I wish to. I know what you want, and I cannot give it."

"How can *you* possibly know what I want?" Gwendolyn shot back.

He sat abruptly. "Do you wish to know the answer? I mean, truly, Gwendolyn?"

"Of course!" she returned.

He lifted a brow. "I must warn you, you'll not like the answer," he said, and a shiver rushed down her spine, remembering that, once before, in her uncle's *fogous*, he'd said something very similar. Yet Gwendolyn sorely regretted that she did not press him that day. If she had, perhaps everything thereafter would have transpired so differently. "Tell me," she begged.

"Very well... you wished to know what happened

back at the tree. I will endeavor to explain. All living creatures have what you mortals call a soul."

Gwendolyn's face twisted with confusion.

Did he now mean to give her a lesson in the mystical?

"You believe it exists within you," he said, glancing up at his Faerie flame. "But it exists without you as well. Neither is it unique to sanguine creatures."

He patted the tree at his back. "Take this tree, for example," he said. "Its roots run deep and long, all connected. What one knows, all will know."

Gwendolyn furrowed her brow.

"Do you understand what I am telling you?"

"I... think so," Gwendolyn lied, glancing nervously at his Faerie flame as though it could give her another clue. It sat blinking as she did.

Málik gave her another moment to consider, then glanced away and back. "Let me ask you this way... did you realize it was me before I spoke to you?"

"In the tree?"

"Yes... though neither of us were actually in the tree," he explained. "It was only an illusion—a *glamour*." He must have sensed her confusion because he lifted both brows. "Let me put it another way: *How* did *you* know it was me?"

"Because..."

Gwendolyn tried to remember when exactly that she'd realized it was him, but, truly, she'd understood it from the first—even before Loc's hound came sniffing... certainly before Málik had whispered into her ear.

"In order to include you in my *glamour*, my *anam* absorbs yours. For this interim, we are one," he explained. "Like the trees. All that transpired before... I may perceive... as clearly as though it happened to me. Do you understand?" he asked again.

Gwendolyn blinked. "So... now you know... everything?" She didn't know if it was wonder or mortification that made her voice sound so small.

"Everything you know I may know," he said, with a nod, and for a long, uncomfortable moment, silence fell over the woodlands.

"I cannot lie," he said. "I went searching for Loc tonight."

In the shadows, his hand slid to his dagger. "I regret no choice I've ever made, save one. But here and now I will make you a promise, Gwendolyn..." A pinprick of blue flared in his eyes, like twin flames. "I spared him that day in your Dragon's Lair. I spared him again whilst I held you in my arms by the tree. I'll not make that mistake again."

Gwendolyn blinked. All the while she'd been sitting here, cursing him, he'd been out there searching for Loc... intending to kill him?

Those weren't the actions of a man who did not care for her, and some part of her thrilled over the revelation, even as it confused her. But then... quickly on the heels of this revelation came another, and this one shook her to her bones.

Málik knew everything.

Gods, oh gods, oh gods.

He'd been privy to her heart, and still he'd called her spoilt!

He knew what she felt for him—*knew it*, and still could not say the same.

He knew that too oft when she looked at him, she

was staring with deepest longing at his mouth...
Willing him to kiss her.

Remembering his taste.

Wishing for his love.

He understood how desperately she'd prayed for his return, how heartbroken she was when he did not come. He'd tasted her tears as though they were his own and knew how humiliated she was when Loc repudiated her before the marriage bed—how enraged she'd grown over the ensuing months, weltering in fury until it stole her breath and even her will.

Even now, he must have sensed her crippling doubts. Every fervent wish. Every fear. He knew every time she'd thought of him, and how long she'd dwelt upon his kiss. And he knew all this because of his enchantment—Fae magic that gave him admission to her most private thoughts. And so much as she wished to regret it, she couldn't, because if he had not, she'd have taken her final breath against that oak, with Loc's hound drooling on her toes.

I cannot change my actions, he'd said—*nor do I wish to.*

Had he to do it all over, he would do it again.

That admission stole any words she might have uttered. She laid down and turned away from him, snuggling under his cloak, grateful to have it so she could hide her ruby-red face.

Sleep came with difficulty.

CHAPTER
FOURTEEN

I f yesterday the hob cake gave her too much energy, this morning Gwendolyn felt precisely the opposite. Already, she was bone-weary, and she had only just opened her eyes.

For so long she'd lain awake, trying in vain to sleep, alternating between feelings of hurt, fury, resentment and chagrin, fearing every indiscretion she ever committed must be etched irrevocably into Málik's brain. *Bloody, rotten elf.*

Nay, that wasn't a nice thing to say, and still she hoped he could read her mind, and just in case he could, she mentally called him every terrible epithet she'd ever heard slip from her father's mouth—and then a few more.

Bleary-eyed, she rose at first light, and with no need to repair the camp, she returned Málik's cloak, dumping it unceremoniously over his resting form.

He didn't stir, but she knew he wasn't sleeping.

It didn't matter.

She didn't need him, she told herself.

She didn't need anyone!

And yet even as she thought it, she knew it wasn't true. She needed help more than ever.

Pride battled with reason, and reason won. Without her father to back her, without her beloved city, without the king's army... who was she? Indeed, for all her bold talk, she was powerless to do aught more than rage against the Fates.

Fortunately, she didn't have to beg him to come. By the time she had walked less than thirty feet, he was already by her side, though he said nothing, and neither did Gwendolyn. Still, his eyes flashed with a quality she'd never noted before—pity?

It brought a fierce new sting to her eyes.

I know what you want, he'd said. *I cannot give it.*

And he knew what she wanted... because he'd plundered her thoughts like a thief. Even now, her cheeks burned uncomfortably over his confession, and even as a seedling of something like hope fluttered to life within her belly over the knowledge he'd gone seeking retribution, she imagined crushing it beneath her feet before it could gain a foothold.

There was strength in fury, and she could not afford to be weak.

No matter how heartfelt he'd meant it, saying he would kill a man on her behalf only meant he cared for her welfare, but caring for her welfare was not the same as love.

He'd once told her he was both summoned and sent. Gwendolyn understood now that it was her father, not her mother, who'd summoned him to Trevena—not to train the king's warriors, as was first presumed. He'd come, not for the honest employment, but to retrieve a treasure that sat undisclosed in her father's vault—*Claímh Solais.*

And that was another thing that infuriated her. No one *ever* bothered to give her a chance to see if that sword would burn for her. The instant her father gave it to him, Málik took it away—far from her. And far more than the fact that he'd left her in the first place, she resented that most of all—that neither her father nor Málik had ever believed her worthy of that sword. Like Cornwall's crown and throne, it should have passed to Gwendolyn, but *he* took it without regret.

But that was the reason Cornwall's crown had fallen to an outlander—a man, because a woman could not rise to the task.

But she could! And she would!

As for Málik, he'd made her promises he'd not kept—not only as her Shadow, but as her friend. The vow he took to serve her was not an oath to be made lightly. His duties as a Shadow could not be forsworn. Therefore, he was bound to her still.

Woman, or nay, she would and must hold him to his pledge, and yet, even now, reaching into her pouch to retrieve the last bite of her wafer, she tried to summon the nerve to send him away.

After all, why should she trust him? His return to her was only because of some mysterious sense of duty he'd not yet disclosed, and Gwendolyn knew that, too, because he'd said so, and so he said, he could not lie. But she must not release him, not now. Whatever his reason for returning, she could not do this on her own, and she would not cut off her nose to spite her face.

Alas, for all the broken promises, the one that upset her most... was the one he'd made to her when they were alone under the stars, when he'd said he would never leave her. Now, every time she thought of that moment... the way he'd held her... the way he'd touched her... the fact that she'd dared to trust him... the way she'd...

Gods! You do not love him, she told herself.

But that lie weighed heavier than the burden on her back—her duty to her people, the responsibility she bore to Pretania. It was enough to keep her mood perpetually sour.

All day long, she studiously avoided Málik's gaze, embarrassed by all the dreams she'd unwillingly shared.

At some point, she fell behind and let him take the lead. She followed simply because... as he'd pointed out, there was nowhere else to go. She was a queen without a country or crown!

By midday, her belly was growling fiercely, and her feet grew heavy. Still, she persevered.

With the last of her wafer consumed, the final bite was nearly her undoing, because it tasted too much like Málik's lips, and she refused to ask him for more.

Pressing at her lips in remembrance, she stared at his back, admiring the cut of his shoulders and hips. He carried his sword on his back so effortlessly, as though it were nothing but a dagger. Lean as he was, his presence filled these woods, larger than life. He was as at ease on his two legs as he was on a horse, and somehow, after two grueling days of travel, he was hardly worse for the effort. Meanwhile, Gwendolyn was fagged.

There were many views about the Fae. Some believed they were akin to gods. Others claimed they never existed at all, and were simply tall tales, meant to frighten wee children into behaving. Still others believed they existed but were long gone, and their *rás* mustn't be any different from mortal men. After all, they were so soundly defeated by Gwendolyn's own kinsmen—men with no godly gifts or graces. How inconceivable was it to believe there could be kings who could replace entire limbs with new ones made of silver? Or that ships could sail upon storm clouds?

This was what the Mester had taught Gwendolyn in her lessons.

Her Prophecy was a story told to rekindle the wonder in her people. Her father had been of this mind, too, though he'd rarely spoken his thoughts aloud, because, to do so, was to disparage her mother, and her tale about Gwendolyn's crib-side visitation.

Only Demelza claimed it was all true, even if she wouldn't say too much about the encounter at her mother's behest. She'd enlightened Gwendolyn re-gardless, with bedtime stories intended to counter the Mester's dismissals, which to Gwendolyn had seemed far more plausible. Even so, some small part of her had entertained the tales as truth—because, of course, one *must* believe in some measure of fancy to believe one could be blessed by Fae. Still, Gwendolyn had entertained doubts, and ultimately, all her sense of wonder was lost long before her hair turned out to be nothing more than hair under Loc's snicking blade. She'd watched those curls fall into her lap with so much trepidation and dismay, and yet a little voice deep down had whispered, "I knew it! I knew it!" Even as Locrinus had called her a liar.

Indeed, until he'd hurled Borlewen's blade into the bed behind her back, she had preferred to believe it all a beautiful lie rather than to consider that Loc might be the wrong man.

What a fool she had been.

Though when first she'd met him, so resplendent in his finery, his smile so bright and his appearance so golden, she'd wanted so much to believe in him... and yet, even blinded by this golden beauty and all her wellspring of hope, she'd kept close the things that would make her people vulnerable—the workings of their Dragon Lair, Porth Pool... her father's illness and his connection to the land. Only now that she understood there had been a reason for her distrust, she also understood that she herself was not totally blameless.

Alas, she knew her father's heart as she knew her own, and if Gwendolyn could be honest with herself, none of their actions had ever truly put first the spirit of this world.

Even before her father's illness, her capitulation to the alliance was simply for the advancement of his interests—and hers as well, truth be told. It was never a truly selfless pursuit.

Gwendolyn had viewed her betrothal to Urien as the means to an end—the unification of these lands under one king... and eventually, one queen.

The entire time she'd kept her eyes upon Porth Pool, worrying, fretting, her one-true concern had not really been for the land itself, but for her father's health.

Indeed, everything she ever did was for her father, and for Trevena and Cornwall.

But perhaps the land was dying, not so much because of her father's illness or his death, but because her people had too long forgotten to seek wonder in this world?

This was what she must now reconcile: What was true, and what was not. What was still possible and what was lost.

Intuitively, she understood Málik held the key to her answers, and no matter what she felt about him —no matter what he felt about her, she must rise above it all and seek the truth.

"There's a village ahead," Málik apprised, when she feared she would sink to her bottom and never again rise.

"At last!" Gwendolyn exclaimed, but then she blinked as she took in her surroundings. Regardless that she had never actually ventured this far north, she recognized the rising landmark from the map in her father's war room. Before her stood six stones, painted with blood and carved with daggers...

The Druids' Crossroads.

FIFTEEN

The village Málik spoke of was the one Gwendolyn feared.

Even at this early afternoon hour, with the sun shining so brightly, there was a pall to the glade, giving Gwendolyn a frisson of fear.

Unlike the Llanrhos Druids, who worked with Pretania's tribes, serving as arbiters, this order did not welcome tribunals, nor visitors. And despite that they, too, were arbiters simply by virtue of their ancient order, their judgment was offered without mercy, and no man—no woman—was foolish enough to disturb these men.

"Málik?" she said, halting abruptly, but to her horror, he kept walking. "Málik!" she cried out. "This is no place for me! Neither for you, truth be told!" She rushed up beside him, daring to seize him by the hand, tugging frantically. "Please! No! Let us go!"

To her surprise, his fingers wove themselves through hers, and he squeezed reassuringly. "Trust me," he said, gently. "This is one place Loc's men will not seek you."

"Doubtless!" Gwendolyn agreed. "Really, you

143

must realize they'll not welcome my kind, not even a queen."

He lifted a brow. "Your kind?"

"A woman," she hissed with horror. "I'm a woman, Málik!"

"Indeed, you are," he said, with a wink, as though they hadn't quarreled so bitterly only yestereve, and then gone for much of the day without speaking. Gwendolyn was relieved to see the end of their enmity, but this was neither the time nor the place for jests.

And she really, really didn't wish to be here!

"They *will* welcome you," he insisted, dragging her along.

Gwendolyn had no choice but to follow. "Blood and bones!" she said, relenting. "I really hope you know what you are doing."

"I do," he said. And despite that, she worried.

This was the order that once made their judgment about a man's innocence by shoving a dagger into his belly, slicing him to his entrails, then concluding their opinion by the way he stumbled and fell, and thereafter, by the way his entrails revealed themselves.

"The last man I know who came crawling to this village ended up eating a stew made from his own innards!"

Málik had the ill graces to laugh.

"It is true!" Gwendolyn insisted.

"And you know this because he returned to recount this gruesome tale, even without his innards?"

Gwendolyn frowned, tilting her head as she considered this, and then she shrugged, wondering, in truth, how that story came to be told, if the man no longer had his innards. No matter, there were too many stories like this one for it to be dismissed.

"Perhaps he traveled with a companion?" Gwendolyn suggested.

"And this companion also ate the stew?" he asked, turning to offer her a toothsome grin, and a wink— more like himself than he had been in too long.

Nervously, Gwendolyn peered about, shuddering with revulsion as she noted the knotted meshwork hanging from the trees, many of which cradled the sun-bleached remnants of what she surmised must be hapless trespassers. If Málik were not so firmly holding her hand, she would have run.

"Doubtless you've met a few Druids whose temperaments lacked in good graces and humor, but they are not what people suppose."

"And now you intend to teach me about Druids?" Gwendolyn asked, acerbically. "I know the Druids!" They were custodians of truth, and all that was sacred, arbiters of the law. As bards, they were entrusted with the memory of all tribes. This was why they were so oft sent to witness their ceremonies.

"What you know is the Llanrhos Order," Málik suggested, squeezing her hand. "The Lifer Pol Druids are ovates and healers. Some are prophets. They are, in fact, the most ancient order. And, yes, 'tis true, they do not welcome guests, and much of what you see here..." He gestured about at the nets. "Is meant to keep trespassers at bay. But there is a good explanation, and soon you'll understand."

As far as Gwendolyn could see, there was no clear path to any flourishing village—only an odd tomb, surrounded by blood-stained stones.

The entire glade was eerie and misty, and she

could well imagine it was swarming with ghouls and knockers—mischievous little goblins she'd sometimes heard called coblynau, or leprechauns, or klokers or brownies. "What is this place? A tomb?"

"Nay," he said, explaining that it was a hothouse, constructed over a pool, not unlike Porth. But this one was used for ceremonies.

"What manner of ceremonies?" Gwendolyn asked dubiously.

He didn't answer, but Gwendolyn relaxed a bit after he took her inside for a peek, and she found nothing more than a mist-filled chamber, with a little pool. There, he pulled a bell before returning to wait by the entrance.

"What about the blood on these stones?" Gwendolyn persisted.

"Bulls most likely, sacrificed for protection."

"Art certain not human?" Gwendolyn had also heard they sacrificed men in osier cages, burned them alive, but for what reason she didn't know.

As a child, she had been terrified of Druids, until she was assured, quite vehemently, that the Llanrhos Order did not employ such savagery. And yet, all she knew right now was that a *lot* of bulls had lost their lives to paint these stones.

"If they sacrifice me, I will return to haunt you," she promised.

Málik chuckled. "If they do, I will apologize."

"How reassuring," Gwendolyn allowed. However, she'd like to see him apologize for something. He wasn't the type. At least Gwendolyn knew when to apologize.

Mercifully, they didn't remain long before men emerged from the mist, their robes pristine white, their beards long, and bound with ribbons. Their hair was likely washed in lime water to give it that stiff texture so many of them seemed to prefer. Some had perhaps used it a bit too much because they had only sparse hair atop, but plenty in their beards. Their faces and bodies were painted in the same fashion as the Prydein.

"Málik?" she squeaked.

Some wore strange ear sheaths that were fashioned to look like Málik's pointy ears, but unlike the Llanrhos Druids, they wore no piercings on their bodies.

Málik squeezed her hand again, and said again, "Trust me, Gwendolyn."

God help her, she did. She truly did. Why then did she suddenly have another swarm of bees buzzing about her belly?

The Druids surrounded them, speaking in a strange tongue.

Peering up at Málik, seeing him so at ease, Gwendolyn pasted a smile on her face.

SIXTEEN

The Druid village was concealed by the surrounding woodlands, their dwellings hidden high atop the trees, where men would never think to look.

There was an initial climb up a rope ladder, which was drawn up as soon as they reached the landing, then a series of ramps winding throughout the twisting boughs of trees—a network so vast and so complex that Gwendolyn walked along, mouth agape.

As they ascended higher into the village, she stayed close to Málik, grateful when every so oft, he would squeeze her hand, because for all their welcome reception, the air itself was... odd... unearthly. Sometimes Gwendolyn saw nothing at all in the mist, save for a billowing fog. Sometimes, she saw half-clad men seated along nearby bridges. Cross-legged, hands on their knees, they bared the artwork on their bellies, all wearing expressions as naked as their forms. Gwendolyn had a sense they were praying, though she couldn't tell.

"Fly-agaric," Málik explained, bending to whisper into her ear. "Flesh of the Gods."

Gwendolyn peered up in confusion.

"Balgan-buachair," he tried again, and when she still shook her head, he said, "Pookies."

"Ohhhh," she said, remembering that sometimes the Druids used mushrooms and herbs to provide their visions. In fact, the Llanrhos Order never once visited Trevena without paying a lengthy visit to the Yew, under which no normal man could remain for longer than half a bell without finding himself surrounded by *piskies* and a terrible headache to follow that persisted for days. However, mushrooms would explain the expressions of these men she encountered, and Gwendolyn suddenly understood why visitations might be frowned upon. Gods knew these men were not in any condition to defend themselves.

One by one, their escorts fell away, perhaps returning to their various tasks, until only one remained, and this one led them all the way to the top of the largest of all the tree dwellings, wherein they discovered an elderly Druid, dressed in white, like his peers, though he sat atop a small dais, grinning widely as they entered.

Returning the old man's smile, Málik released Gwendolyn's hand, bounding forward to fall upon one knee, then finding and lifting the veiny old hand, kissing the back of it deferentially.

"Prionsabail!" greeted the Druid. "You are a sight for sore, old eyes."

"Máistir Emrys," said Málik, and the Druid's face broke into a wider grin.

Quicker than a spider clambering across his net, he caught both of Málik's hands in his own, patting them with great affection. Gwendolyn didn't believe he moved like a man of advanced years.

"I'm so pleased to see you have returned," he said, and then the old grey eyes drifted beyond his shoulder to Gwendolyn. "With a guest, so it seems..."

Málik turned to extend a hand, beckoning Gwendolyn forward. "I am certain she is no mystery to you, but allow me to introduce Gwendolyn of Cornwall, heir to these isles."

"Welcome!" said the elder man exuberantly, and the smile he gave her was genuine, but it still raised the tiny hairs on the back of Gwendolyn's neck. "I am so pleased you've found your way."

Gwendolyn knit her brows. She hadn't, really. She'd naturally followed where Málik led, but she nodded jerkily, wondering now if that had been a mistake.

Returning his gaze to Málik, speaking in a tongue Gwendolyn did not understand, they conversed for a moment, until Málik gave him a single nod. Suddenly, both again turned to address her—and why did she suddenly feel like the prey in a spider's trap?

"I confess we expected you, *Banríon*. To celebrate, we've prepared... a special fare."

He inclined his head toward Gwendolyn, and Gwendolyn tilted Málik a questioning glance, remembering that he, too, had called her this name once.

"Queen," he explained. "In the tongue of my kindred."

Queen. Gwendolyn blinked. Clearly, these Druids still held some manner of communion with the Tuatha'ans? But how was that possible when they were banished behind the Veil?

The elder Druid released Málik's hand, reaching now for Gwendolyn's, then patting it in turn. "Welcome!" he said again, giving her a jovial wink. "Welcome, welcome!"

And then another voice hailed from across the room... a woman's voice, and Málik's gaze shot up. "Welcome," she said silkily, and a growl erupted from Málik's throat, the sound so feral that Gwendolyn started.

SEVENTEEN

She was extraordinary.

Perhaps the loveliest creature Gwendolyn had ever beheld—until she smiled, revealing teeth that were sharper than Málik's.

Danann.

She was Danann.

On her back, she carried another bastard sword, as Málik did, and as it was with him, the weapon settled there, like a natural limb, only waiting to be used, and otherwise forgotten.

Her gaze settled upon Málik, and Gwendolyn couldn't help but note the look they shared—one she intuitively understood, despite that she didn't know their story.

Undaunted by Málik's scowl, the Faerie's eyes glinted with unbridled delight despite his displeasure. And then, suddenly, he bounded to his feet, rushing to her side, pulling her away, into an adjacent room. But he didn't have to force her. It was as though she glided backward at his touch, as gracefully as a flame bowed by a breeze.

"Lovers!" declared the elderly Druid and his gaze returned to Gwendolyn.

Gwendolyn swallowed.

She had already surmised as much, but her heart ached to hear it even so. So, then, was *she* the reason Málik could not offer Gwendolyn his heart?

There was nothing about their interaction that was the least unfamiliar. Gwendolyn could still see them through the arched doorway, their faces intimately close, their bodies so attuned to one another, and she couldn't help but gawk, peering back and forth between the Druid and the couple in question. To her it appeared they spoke entirely with their minds, their animated gestures the only clues to what was being said. He was not happy. She did not care.

All this time, the Faerie's smile never wavered, and neither did she peer back into the hall at Gwendolyn, so certain was she of her worth. Gwendolyn should take a lesson from her.

"I never had the good fortune to meet your father," said the elder Druid, catching Gwendolyn's attention with a wave of his hand. "But I admired him greatly. He did not deserve such an ignoble end."

Unbidden, tears pricked at Gwendolyn's eyes. "Thank you," she said, swallowing her grief, but whether that grief was for her father, or over the couple she couldn't help but steal glances at, she wasn't entirely certain. And yet, what the druid said was true. Her father did not deserve to find his head on a pike. Sickly as he'd been, he should have lived out the rest of his days until he was called to rest. And then he should have quit this world with dignity, with a king's farewell, horns sounding, and drummers strumming. At the very least, he should have had a proper tomb, with a hero's interment, his grave filled with all the things he would need in the Afterlife.

This was the way of her people. While the pyre was preferred for common folk, on the off-chance that duty called him again, and the gods should wish to restore a king to his throne, he should rest with his armor and his sword.

Instead, his head sat withering in the sun, with crows pecking at his eyes, and his body... well, no one knew where that was, or at least no one had said. Knowing Loc, Gwendolyn suspected he'd ordered her father interred in some common grave, with no one to speak his rites.

The thought turned her belly and tore at her heart.

Wrenching her gaze away from Málik once and for all, she asked herself why she should care about love when there was still vengeance to be had.

The elder Druid studied her another moment, before saying, "If you'll pardon me for saying so, *Banríon Dragan*, I see you still wear your child's cloak. But it does not suit you."

Blinking, Gwendolyn opened her mouth to tell him that nay, this was Málik's cloak she wore, but then she remembered that she'd given him back the cloak, and she was wearing none.

The elder man's eyes twinkled with mirth as he watched her, and Gwendolyn understood suddenly that the cloak he spoke of was metaphorical.

"You cannot rage against the Moirai," he said. "Instead, you must seek the thread and staff, the spindle and the scroll, the shears and Book of Fate. They are now yours to wield."

Like Málik sometimes did, he spoke in riddles.

The Morai were the Fates, and their sister, Aether, was the Goddess of Gwendolyn's people. Her name was the essence of life. But Gwendolyn did not know of threads, or staffs, or spindles or scrolls. Even so, the Druid's advice was soundly given without the least antipathy, and Gwendolyn took it in good faith. He was such a strange old fellow.

The robes of his order were bright white, brighter than any white she had ever seen before, made all the brighter by the light that entered this dwelling—a strange blue-green hue that owed its color to the trees and swirling mist. He, too, wore the ear sheaths, delicately carved, and fitted closely to his ears, as though he meant to pass them off as his own.

Clearly, he wasn't through with his lessons. "Grief is a boon not meant for queens or kings," he continued. "Neither is love nor hate. These are emotions that will cloud your reason. Rather, your greatest love must be this land, and your joy begot by its stewardship."

Gwendolyn considered the elder man's words as best she could, her gaze returning against her will to the couple in the adjacent room.

She had been little more than a bundle of emotions for so long—fury, grief, sorrow, doubt, and even fear. She knew these things had all clouded her judgment, but she did not agree that a king or a queen must live a loveless life. Her mother and father had had such a great love, and Gwendolyn once hoped for the same.

The Druid was still watching her, Gwendolyn realized, but she had no chance to ask what thoughts gave his lips such a knowing curl, because Málik returned with the woman at his heels.

The Faerie slid forward to embrace Gwendolyn, every motion as graceful as her form. "Gwendolyn," she purred, her voice warm, like a swim in a Porth Pool. "You are indeed as lovely as I've been told."

Surprised by the compliment, Gwendolyn said, "Thank you."

But, really, she'd never felt less lovely than she did at the moment, and this was saying quite a lot, considering that betimes in her life she'd felt rather hideous based on the actions of others. But there was absolutely nothing about this woman's demeanor that gave her pause. She clearly meant it, and Gwendolyn found she liked her, even if she was a rival for Málik's affections.

"I am Esmerelda," the Faerie said, pressing a cheek against Gwendolyn's face, her skin as warm as Málik's. "You may call me Esme."

"Hello, Esme," Gwendolyn said.

"Come now," the Faerie demanded, taking Gwendolyn by the hand and drawing her away. "Let us visit whilst the men converse. You know how they can be —self-important and full of blether. You and I have far more important matters to attend."

Disinclined to be separated from Málik, Gwendolyn peered back at him desperately, but when he gave her a nod, she went. Reluctantly.

"I must confess he is not so pleased to see me," Esme allowed, completely without regret, her voice like the music of a lyre.

She cast a glance backward, into the room as they departed, and Gwendolyn followed her gaze to find

Emrys and Málik speaking now, their expressions sober.

Gwendolyn didn't know what to say. He was clearly not pleased. But she was ill-equipped to assuage the Faerie's ruffled feelings when Gwendolyn's own heart was still wounded and weeping from his confessions.

Instead, she thought it best to change the subject. "I never expected these Druids would be so... amicable." Feeling silly now, particularly after Málik's recent disclosures, she added. "I was led to believe they would tear out my woman's heart if I ever dared to seek their counsel."

"Ah, well, you are not merely any woman, Gwendolyn. You are *the* Dragon Queen," Esme said. "But you must not be fooled by the Druid's demeanor. Emrys will slay a man sooner than he will harm a spider. They are fierce in their love of nature, and, truly, even above my *faekind*, they have curried favor with the goddess." She waved a hand about. "This place... they know its worth and will guard its secrets with their lives... and, if needs be, the lives of others. That is the true reason you mortals are not welcome here. It has little to do with your womanhood."

A warm breeze pushed about a mist that was light and yet somehow still impenetrable, so that even as one passed through it, even knowing what was left behind, or what lay ahead, all sense of what was gone was lost, and a glance backward revealed nothing but swirling mist. Looking ahead gave one a sense of keen anticipation, though for what was unclear.

"But enough of that," Esme said with a hand to the small of Gwendolyn's back. She led Gwendolyn down several twisting paths until they came to a cluster of small dwellings. "I come bearing gifts, *Ban-ríon na bhfear.*"

"Queen?" Gwendolyn said, and Esme offered a nod of approval, adding, "Queen of men. You learn quickly," she said, approvingly. "Your husband may yet rue the day he ever met you." And she smiled as she said this, the smile transforming her face until it was a thing of terror.

CHAPTER
EIGHTEEN

The "gifts" Esme came bearing were many, but the most magnificent of all was neither the clothing, nor the accoutrements. It was a bath. Warm, scented, it reminded Gwendolyn of a miniature version of their *piscina*, although she was gobsmacked that any such structure could exist so high in the trees—at least she believed they were still in the trees. She couldn't be certain. She had a sense of great height, but the swirling mists prevented her from seeing anything beyond their immediate environs. It was the strangest experience Gwendolyn had ever had.

"There is a hot house below," Esme said. "But that bath is not used for washing. It is ceremonial. This one is simple but serviceable."

"Where are we?" Gwendolyn dared to ask.

The Faerie answered in a singsong tone. "Oh, neither here, nor there," she said.

Not helpful. And yet, wherever they were, the room was far larger than Gwendolyn had expected upon their approach, and once inside, Esme went straight for a stone tub, dipping in a finger to test the water.

After considering it a moment, she tilted her head, and a burst of steam erupted from the pool. Gwendolyn blinked with awe.

Esme said, "As you must have gleaned, Gwendolyn, this place defies your earthly laws. It was constructed by my kinfolk when we were still masters of this realm. It became our final refuge, and though it remains concealed behind the Veil, it exists betwixt worlds, neither in this, nor the next. Somehow, these Lifer Pol Druids found it, and made it their own."

She spun about then, her movements so elegant they put even Ely's dancing to shame. And then, again, she closed the distance between them, although Gwendolyn never even saw her feet move. Once she reached Gwendolyn, she at once began to disrobe her without invitation.

"The bath will be lovely," she promised. And when she laughed thereafter, the sound was like poplar leaves tinkling against a warm summer breeze. "Perhaps long overdue?" she suggested, without intending the slightest insult, Gwendolyn sensed. Still, she lifted a finger to her nose, pushing it up as she smiled. "When was the last time?"

Embarrassed, Gwendolyn said, "Not since..."

"Your wedding day?" Esme surmised. Then she slapped her forehead and shook her head. "The cruelty of men will never cease to amaze me. And yet, so I understand, your care was left to his mistress and his mother. Is that true?"

"Yes," Gwendolyn said, still embittered, and Esme huffed another sound of disgust. "Mark me, they might both live to regret their choices."

"Estrildis has a son," Gwendolyn confided, wondering why she felt compelled to speak so candidly.

Oddly, it felt as though they'd met before.... somewhere, but, in truth, Málik was the first Fae she'd ever met—or at least the first that Gwendolyn remembered. She couldn't recall those Faeries at her cradle.

Esme drew up Gwendolyn's arms. "I know," she said, and tugged the tunic up and over Gwendolyn's head. "You may need this later," she suggested, making a face of disgust. "In the meantime, we shall have it repaired. Until you have need of it, I have another garment better suited to the task you will face. A queen must not go about looking like a dirty little waif!" she said brightly and gave Gwendolyn a wink.

"Thank you," Gwendolyn said, as her tunic was discarded.

Esme at once rolled down her leathers, tugging them off as well, then discarding those, too, atop the Prydein gown—both utterly filthy. She blushed hotly, unaccustomed to any such solicitations, and when Esme paused at her mons, tilting her head, then peering up at Gwendolyn with a question in her eyes, Gwendolyn's face heated, though she didn't know why.

Gwendolyn had never stood under such intense scrutiny before, but she had always considered her hips a bit too wide, her breasts too small, and her mons... Golden like her hair, Esme's gaze narrowed there, her brows slanting with surprise.

Did Faeries have no mons? she wondered.

The look Esme gave her made her think they must not, but perhaps there was another reason for her twisted little smile. Gwendolyn daren't ask about it. She was far too embarrassed, and particularly in contrast to Esme's striking beauty.

As Esme suggested, she felt like a dirty little waif

in comparison—and it was only then that she dared to look, really look, at her arms, her legs, her feet, taking in the disgusting layer of filth that had embedded itself into her flesh. She must look as though she'd been wallowing in a pigsty!

Unlike her mother, whose hair and gowns were impossible to don without aid, Gwendolyn had rarely allowed herself to be assisted by Demelza. And even once she'd had her own maid, Ely knew her too well to try. Gwendolyn was not the sort who enjoyed being dressed or adorned, still she allowed it with Esme, perhaps even enjoyed the ministrations.

Then again, she had wallowed in her own sweat and filth for many months now, and it felt... divine to have someone care for her just once.

They lingered in silence for a while, and then Esme returned to the subject of Estrildis, her tone far more sober. "I must ask you, Gwendolyn. Given the chance, what would you do with that child?"

The child?

Oh! Not *her* child. She'd meant Loc's child and heir.

But then it was difficult to concentrate on a good answer because Esme reached out to bounce one of Gwendolyn's breasts in her hand, testing it as though it were the most natural thing to do, and Gwendolyn gasped with surprise. "I-I don't know!" she confessed. "I've never considered it." In fact, aside from what it would mean to her own child to have a scheming stepbrother so like his father, she had tried not to think of Habren much at all—mostly because to consider Estrildis as a mother confused Gwendolyn. It made Estrildis seem... a normal woman, but she was not.

Neither was she kind, and Gwendolyn had a difficult time imagining her treating any child with any great affection.

Habren was less than two, Gwendolyn believed, which meant Loc had taken up with his mistress quite some time before their Promise Ceremony, wherein he, too, had promised himself to Gwendolyn. How could she have been so naïve?

And Brutus... he'd stood by and watched his son forswear himself, knowing Estrildis awaited him at home, his grandson as well.

As for Innogen... she'd certainly embraced Gwendolyn on her wedding day, kissing her cheeks so easily, when all along, she'd had another "daughter" at home, one who'd already born her a grandson.

But it was not Habren's fault that his father was a liar, a thief and a murderer and his mother was a bitter, greedy wretch—nor that his grandmother was a scheming witch.

It was not his fault, and yet, his presence imperiled Gwendolyn.

His mother might be many distasteful things, but she was no common whore. She was a well-born daughter to a well-respected king, or so Innogen had been quick to reveal. In time, with Gwendolyn stripped of her crown and her power, the tribes could come to accept Estrildis as their queen... and, in turn, her son as the natural heir.

Still, Gwendolyn could not imagine herself murdering a babe, not even to save her throne.

"Well," prompted the Faerie. "You should... consider it. A woman's heart is her true fate. So much as we might like to believe elsewise, even with a prophesy, one's destiny is not entirely predetermined.

There are many possibilities, not just one. What we believe with our hearts may come to pass merely because we make it so. Do you understand what I am saying, Gwendolyn?"

"Yes... I believe so," Gwendolyn said, but like Emrys, and ofttimes Málik, Esme, too, spoke in confusing riddles, flitting from one topic to the next. It was difficult to follow their conversation, even as she found difficulty processing these environs. "You are saying the gods might favor a man, but 'tis a man's... or a woman's... turn of mind that will decide her fate?"

"Precisely," said Esme, with a smile in her voice as she encouraged Gwendolyn into the bath.

Gwendolyn needn't any coercion. She slid into the tub, considering Esme's words, and much to her surprise, she found the tub so much deeper than should have been possible.

Shocked, she peered outside the tub's rim, and Esme laughed. "You will find the unexpected here," she said. "I told you, this place defies the world as you know it. But there is no place in this realm or the next, where you will be closer to the truth of creation."

Gwendolyn peered up at the Faerie with a sense of marvel, but then, overcome by the deliciousness of the bath, she laid back to wallow. The water felt utterly delicious—impossibly warm, as though it were newly filled with buckets of water straight from a simmering cauldron.

Esme continued. "I must also caution you not to listen to wizened old men. When you think like a child, your imagination is free. Everything is possible. The trick is to know when to use your child's eye, and when to see with your woman's heart."

Gwendolyn wanted to respond with something

wise, but all thoughts fled from her mind. Sinking deeper into the water, she dared to relax, contented enough to listen to Esme chatter, and the things Gwendolyn learned were nothing short of remarkable, each new thing more fantastical than the one revealed before.

For one, Gwendolyn learned that this order of Druids only aged when they ventured beyond the Veil. Here, they were frozen in time. It was only when they descended into the woodlands or ventured down for one of their ceremonies in service to men that their aging recommenced. Emrys was the eldest of the entire lot, and Esme placed his age around seven-hundred and two.

She also learned that this order of Druids were envoys, slipping easily between realms. To preserve their affinity for this ability, they remained highly attuned to the natural world. The Danann referred to them as Children of the Greenwood, despite that their combined ages would span the annals of time. They were by no means young, and still the wonder in their eyes, despite the elder druid's proclamation, was akin to that of a child's.

Conversely, Gwendolyn felt she was born an old soul. Throughout the years, she'd come to doubt all she'd ever been taught as a child—all the bedtime stories Demelza used to tell.

Eventually, as she grew into her womanhood, she'd become skeptical of everything, until, after a while, she'd even struggled to believe in her own prophecy.

But why shouldn't she doubt the prophecy?

There had never been one tangible thing to grasp at—not even her own reflection in the mirror. What she saw was ultimately the same to her, always, and even when she'd suspected others saw something different, she could never quite glean what that was.

Really and truly, even suspecting that her own mother saw only the accursed child—that her heart prevented her from seeing any beauty in Gwendolyn at all—*what* she actually saw was a mystery to Gwendolyn. And now, it would always be so.

There was nothing Gwendolyn could do to change that truth, and no matter that she'd always longed to be closer to her mother, Queen Eseld died virtually a stranger. Some part of Gwendolyn mourned this, as no doubt she mourned her father, yet so much as she had wept during those first few weeks after learning of their fates, she was now benumbed by the loss.

Strangely, it was only whilst she was in Málik's presence... the two of them alone... that she felt safe enough to be her truest self... vulnerable betimes, angry betimes... mostly herself.

And yet, she really didn't wish to explore any of the questions that arose with this revelation—especially in the presence of this woman he was embroiled with.

Esme was oddly endearing, and whilst her features and form were as elegant as any lady's Gwendolyn had ever met, she radiated a sense of strength that Gwendolyn admired.

Her hair was fairer than Gwendolyn's, not so silvery as Málik's. And while her teeth were sharper, and her ears more pointed, her skin was a paler shade than his as well, and slightly iridescent... like pearls. Her eyes were neither blue, nor gray, nor green, but every shade in between, perhaps depending on her mood.

Her beauty was as delicate as a helleborine orchid, though Gwendolyn had every sense that, no matter how fiercely the wind blew, Esme's spine would neither bend nor break.

Gwendolyn peered up at her now, studying her delicately chiseled face. She appeared so serene as she sat on the edge of Gwendolyn's tub, her face so utterly pleasant—so long as her mouth remained closed. Alas, when she smiled, it put Gwendolyn in mind of a porbeagle, with its sharp, jagged teeth. Not even Málik's smile was so full of menace.

However, it unnerved Gwendolyn that, as it was with Málik, Esme knew too much about her.

"Esme... would you tell me about the *anam*—how does that enchantment work?"

Esme blinked. "Enchantment?" She sounded confused, but only for an instant. "Ah! The *anam* is not an enchantment, Gwendolyn. But you are perhaps wondering what Málik has gleaned of your thoughts after the *glamour*?"

Gwendolyn nodded.

"Well, you must consider it this way: Every trial we endure leaves a scar," she explained. "But that is not the same as reading your thoughts. While his intuition is seldom wrong, he may only interpret your scars. Does that make sense?"

Gwendolyn nodded.

"But he is afflicted with the disease of so many."

"Disease?"

Esme's bark of laughter startled her. "He's a man," she said, followed by a slow grin. "And since when have you known a man to interpret a woman's heart so unerringly?"

Gwendolyn laughed now, too, and Esme moved behind her to lift what remained of her curls. "Let me wash it," she proposed. But she didn't wait for Gwendolyn to assent; her fingers sank into Gwendolyn's tangles, working them loose, massaging her scalp. In response, Gwendolyn sank lower into the tub, daring to enjoy it.

Demelza's hands had never been so delightful. She was always so impatient, scrubbing too vigorously, dunking her head like one would a willful child's.

Esme's hands were gentle, unhurried... almost worshipful. It left Gwendolyn ill-prepared for the emotions it engendered because this was the first time in all her life, except for Málik's one kiss, that any hands besides her own had touched her so tenderly.

And not at all the way a mother would—but then again, Gwendolyn couldn't say she knew a mother's touch. She didn't. Queen Eseld had so rarely touched her, and never once was she the one to bathe Gwendolyn or dress her.

But even Ely's touch was different—that of a sibling's—and though Gwendolyn knew intuitively that this woman was her rival for Málik's affection, she brought out in Gwendolyn a sense of devotion... almost as though she might be enthralled. Even her voice was seductive.

"If you must know," she said at Gwendolyn's ear, giving Gwendolyn gooseflesh. "The glamour he performed was not so complicated as you might believe. We are *all* the same in this world, living and dead.

The *Aether* absorbs our emotions; this is the *ysbryd y byd*. *The spirit of the age.* It weeps as men weep, over time, seeping into everything it touches."

Gwendolyn had never considered it so thoroughly.

Certes, she was raised to consider the *ysbryd y byd* in all things. After all, this was the reason she had connected her father's illness to the decline of the land. But a thought abruptly occurred to her...

"So, this is the cause for the Rot?"

"It is."

"And do you believe it will continue to spread?"

"Perhaps," said the Faerie. "But there are lands where the *ysbryd y byd* is not affected by Pretania's trials. In truth, while all lands are subject to this Rot, as you have called it... not all lands will Rot merely because *you* have failed to oust a usurper."

You, she'd said, leaving all responsibility with Gwendolyn. "So then... if I fail, Pretania falls?"

"Perhaps," said Esme again. "But not certes. The answer is not so simple as you wish it to be, *Banríon na bhfear*. But if Locrinus prevails, the future is, indeed, bleak."

'Here now," she said. "I think we are done." She came about and took Gwendolyn by the hand, pulling her gently up from the tub. "Quite improved!" she exclaimed. "You clean well, Dragon Queen."

And then, having said as much, Esme graced her with another full, tooth-baring grin.

Gwendolyn couldn't resist. She grinned back, noting the sincerity in Esme's eyes, and no longer quite so alarmed by the fangs.

It was like that with Málik as well. At first, when she'd looked upon his face, she'd thought him the most beautiful creature, until he'd opened his mouth. But Málik never so generously bared his teeth. He only ever gave her glimpses of those fangs, and despite that it gave Gwendolyn a shiver the first time she saw them, it was... somehow... utterly alluring.

"I brought you a gown in the style of my people," Esme announced. She moved swiftly over to lift a length of folded cloth.

The tunic she presented was not unlike the one Málik wore. Black as a moonless night, fashioned like Esme's as well, except that Esme's was a shade like buckskin. The one she handed Gwendolyn shone more like polished obsidian. But it was not made of any material Gwendolyn had ever seen. It was... the airiest of... metals? And still finely woven like a good silken cloth, slightly iridescent.

"Black mithril," revealed Esme. "Woven by Arachne, a student of Athena's, the very finest of weavers. But her tale is not such a joyful one. She hung herself. This is the last thing she ever wove."

Gwendolyn was horrified. "She hung herself?"

"Indeed," said Esme. "Alas, if only that were the last of her torment. Athena turned her into a spider, but now, at least, she still weaves."

"That is..."

"Monstrous, yes, I know, but at least it should please her to know that her finest of works will be worn by the Queen of Pretania."

Gwendolyn shook her head. "I may be queen, but queen of nothing," she said bitterly.

Esme tilted her a look of admonishment. "You must realize self-pity is unbecoming."

However, the instant the words were spoken, her smile returned, and she commenced to dressing

Gwendolyn again, pulling the black tunic over her head and settling it down over Gwendolyn's form. However, unlike the first time Gwendolyn tried on her mother's stiff Prydein gown, this one seemed only for a moment too large, then of its accord, it melded itself against her form, settling itself over Gwendolyn's breasts as though it were made only for her. The leathers did the same, even though were not made of the same cloth, but a type of buckskin so soft that it felt like *boge*. Remarkably, once Gwendolyn was dressed, she still felt as though she were nude—much how that hob cake settled in her belly, there but not there. After a moment, the bodice fitted snugly to her form and somehow hardened like steel, while the rest of the tunic adjusted in all the right places, giving her ample room to move about... to wield a sword if she must.

To fight.

Gwendolyn wiggled her arms with the realization.

Forsooth. She had never in her life worn something so... mutable.

She tried moving every which way, and no matter what she did, the material stretched to accommodate, leaving her free to move how she pleased. She couldn't help herself. Grinning, she spun about in wonder.

Esme laughed and said, "I've also brought you a sword, though it is not the one you might hope for. Would you like to see it?"

Gwendolyn nodded at once.

NINETEEN

E sme led her out of the bathhouse, and then down one of the many suspension bridges, turning this way and that, onto another, and then yet another, taking her up and down so many corridors that Gwendolyn would surely have been lost without her guidance.

Inconceivably, this was a sprawling village. Mist curled about the area, creeping along the pathways, stealing into every dwelling. Gwendolyn didn't remember climbing so high on their ascent, but she had the sense now that she was high, high amidst the clouds. And yet, no matter how she tried, she couldn't spy the ground even when they traversed the bridges.

Eventually, they arrived at yet another chamber. This one boasted only a simple bed, on a wooden dais, piled high with furs. And though it wasn't at all like the luxurious bower she'd once occupied in Trevena, it was still nicer than any room in Loc's palace, and quite sumptuous for this strange woodland palace.

The chamber walls were made of a substance Gwendolyn didn't recognize, shimmering in shades of green. Although it wasn't actually transparent, it was gossamer like spider silk, and still it somehow sustained her weight when she leaned into it.

Like the mist itself, it was there, but not there, nothing corporeal.

But though Gwendolyn couldn't see any of the trees from her room, and her room had no windows, she had every sense of being surrounded by boughs, lush with leaves, with light spilling into the chamber and a gentle breeze lifting the smallest wisp of her curls. It was magical.

Esme moved straight to the bed, where a sword lay nestled amidst the soft, white furs. She lifted it up, turning to display it atop her hands.

"Pure Adamantine," she said. "Undiluted by any alloy from the realms of men. Forged in the fires of Mount Slemish. This was the same sword once gifted to Helen of Troy... or Helen of Argos, as she was known before the war. Lovely though she was, she was not to be trusted."

"Helen?" Gwendolyn whispered, thinking it mustn't be a coincidence that Helen was Trojan and so was Loc.

"The sword itself may not be destroyed, but a single drop of Adamantine will strengthen all alloys, even those of this realm, and..." She tilted Gwendolyn a look. "As you may have guessed, this is the source of your Loegrian Steel." She sighed wistfully. "However, *this* weapon is sacred. Not quite as precious as the Sword of Light, but I hope you'll be pleased with it, regardless. It is designed as you would like it... in the style of Málik's sword."

Had Málik told her how much Gwendolyn liked his sword? That she'd wanted one designed like it? It would stand to reason he must have because somehow Esme knew it.

"Use it wisely. Use it well." Gently, she laid it upon Gwendolyn's upturned hands and Gwendolyn gasped with surprise over the feel of it—so light, she could scarcely believe it was metal.

All along the flat of the blade, there were runic inscriptions inlaid, glittering impossibly, like minuscule diamonds. But this sword was lighter than the one Málik used. That one, lovely as it was, was heavier and less shiny.

Esme brushed a finger along the glyphs, and they glowed, as though infused with fire. "Kingslayer," she whispered. "Appropriate, don't you think?"

CHAPTER TWENTY

Twice in the space of a single day Gwendolyn had been called lovely—and, indeed, she felt *more* than lovely. Dressed in Esme's black mithril and leathers, with a sturdy pair of matching boots, she felt... *invincible*.

For too long in her life so much of her self-worth had been tied to her face, but she would no longer allow herself to be judged based on this thing she had no power over.

Her face might well be lovely to some, hideous to others, but Gwendolyn could no longer take joy in such provisional flattery, hoping to be judged as a woman of merit, simply because of the way one viewed her countenance.

And yet, she understood a queen should not go about looking like a "dirty little waif." Nor would her unruly appearance engender confidence, so she dared to wear this gift of Esme's with joy, and dared to walk tall and proud, reassured that she was a good person, a great horsewoman, and a more than adequate warrior. No matter what Loc thought of her, no matter what anyone thought of her, she had worth. Even so, the breath caught in her breast when Málik turned to meet her gaze as she entered the Druid's feast hall. A hush fell over the room and his *icebourne* eyes swirled with emotions Gwendolyn couldn't read—surprise, but not precisely.

Wonderment, perhaps?

At once, he rose to greet her, and once he did, the Druids all resumed their discourse, whispering feverishly amidst themselves, as though there were some great mystery they must decipher.

Esme excused herself as Málik approached, kissing Gwendolyn ever so gently on the cheek, and then gliding away as gracefully as she had appeared.

Gwendolyn felt... oddly bereft without the Faerie's presence at her side, missing her at once, though she scarcely knew her. She wondered if her feelings for all Fae would be so strong—and if so, perhaps she was truly ensorcelled. And yet, never did her heart beat so furiously as it did this minute, at Málik's approach.

"It suits you," he said silkily, taking her hand, gesturing to her tunic, and when her heart pounced against the cage of her ribs, she knew irrefutably that what she felt for him was not the same thing she felt for anyone else...

This was... *different.*

"Thank you," Gwendolyn said, swallowing despite herself, flicking a glance at Esme, and wondering if Esme resented this attention to her rival. But it didn't appear so. Esme was, as Gwendolyn wished to be—composed and assured.

"Locrinus will not know you when he sees you," Málik suggested, placing his hand on the small of Gwendolyn's back and compelling her toward the table. The shock of his touch sent a bolt of lightning up her spine. "Especially since he may not see you." He chuckled darkly, murmuring into her ear. "Black mithril has the most delightful effect of concealing its wearer by night."

"Oh?" said Gwendolyn, turning to blink into his eyes, her heart tripping as she did. "Esme did not tell me that..." She smiled nervously. "But she told me a few other interesting tales today, some about you."

His mood darkened at once. "Yes, I'm certain," he allowed. And there was a note of displeasure to his voice, though Gwendolyn didn't believe he cared one whit for what was said, only for who said it. There was that about Málik that dismissed anything except for what he himself deemed of import.

Once arrived at the table, Málik settled her between himself and the elder Druid she'd met earlier this day—or at least she thought it was the same day. This place... it had the most disconcerting effect of giving one a sense of timelessness and only a vague sense of place. Truly, she did not know where they were—lost in the *Aether* for all she knew.

"As I said, *Banríon*... we have prepared a feast in your honor," announced the elder Druid as Gwendolyn took her seat beside him—not in a chair, on the floor, with legs crossed. Fortunately, Gwendolyn's tunic gave when it should, allowing her to sit without embarrassing herself.

Also, much to her surprise, this table was round, instead of long, and the only other face she recognized was Esme's.

Málik's 'lover' sat on the other side of the table, her gaze now and again returning to Gwendolyn or Málik, but elsewise she sat conversing genially with men Gwendolyn had once believed to be mean and churlish on their best days, murderous on their worst.

Nothing was as once she'd conceived.

Emrys handed Gwendolyn a fluffy pastry meant to be eaten along with the main course, which was yet to arrive, he explained.

"You must forgive me in advance," he told her, then chortled. "I cannot be held accountable for the fare. We do not oft have guests, and the first time for you may be rude."

Rude? Did he mean meager?

Gwendolyn frowned, not entirely certain of his meaning.

She set down her bit of pastry and smiled reassuringly. Much to the contrary, it wouldn't matter how mean his fare. She would be eternally grateful for the Druid's hospitality, and, at this point, any supper would be delectable. The pastry alone looked scrumptious, and she was already salivating merely over the scent. Gods only knew, after eating little more than cold gruel for so many months, she would be delighted by anything warm, regardless of the taste.

The scent of the cony Málik made her still simmered in her memory, like manna from heaven. Quite easily, she could forgive even a bad cook, and nothing could be as bad as what they'd served her in the Loegrian palace. Really and truly, it was enough that they'd welcomed her so warmly, and that they had offered her a seat at their table—like any well-respected man.

"Art comfortable?" Málik asked.

Gwendolyn nodded and then leaned to whisper in

his ear. "Quite, but I've never had the pleasure of sitting at a table without chairs."

"You'll be glad enough to be seated on your arse," he said with a wink.

"Hmm," she said, wondering at his answer. It was strange, to be sure, yet no stranger than the unveiling of the main course. A giant kettle had been placed in the center of the table, and when the lid came off, a great puff of smoke arose from the pot.

Emrys rose quickly, lifting a ladle, and then began scooping portions into each of the bowls, then passing them around, beginning with Gwendolyn's.

But... it was... only broth.

Confused, Gwendolyn peered down at the few small bits of mushrooms and grass in the bowl, then turned to peer at Málik. He grinned, revealing his elusive fangs. It was the first time in so long time he'd bared so many teeth.

"Thank you," Gwendolyn said to Emrys, nodding, smiling, reaching again for her pastry, thinking that she'd best eat every bite because that broth would not sustain her.

"Eat hearty," said Málik, tearing a piece of his own pastry, then shoving it into his gob. Surprised to see him eat, she did the same, concealing a grimace when it tasted like burnt parchment—not that she'd ever consumed burnt parchment. But that was precisely how she imagined it would taste.

T ime slowed.

Voices melted together.

Smoke rose to spin away everything in Gwendolyn's presence.

She had been fairly certain she was eating a bland, distasteful stew, but now, it appeared, she was no longer at the table. She was somewhere... else... on her mare... the one lost to her in Chysauster... Gods, how much she'd missed the sweet beast.

This was Trevena, on a market day. Everyone scrambling to prepare their booths. So many familiar faces—the baker and the cordwainer.

Gwendolyn waved as she rode by, cantering toward King's Bridge. Usually, this was where the merchants congregated, just inside the inner gates, hawking wares to anyone who ventured past. "Early spears!" called one merchant.

"Nettle tops!" cried another. "Nettle tops!"

It was a day like any other day. The sun shining. The air was full of sweet pollen. Children rushing about. Laughing. Giggling. Lifting kites into a clear, blue sky.

One particular kite caught Gwendolyn's attention... it was emblazoned with the Loegrian serpent, yet in gold, not red. *How strange. How strange.*

Gwendolyn reached down to pat her mare, so grateful for her return.

When was she lost? Why did it seem she'd been gone so long?

And now, though she couldn't recall why she was riding toward the city gates, she gave her mare a gentle heel, and made for King's Bridge, passing a few small carts, then several men with packs on their backs, and finally a petite young woman with a little girl. "Myttin da," said the girl, but there was no smile in the child's dull brown eyes.

The mother's face was bloodless, her lips grey.

"We've come to sell morels," said the child without emotion, pointing to her mother's basket.

"Oh!" said Gwendolyn brightly. "I love morels." She reached into the pouch at her belt to produce a silver coin, ready to toss it at the girl, but when she peered back at the pair, they were transformed, giving her a fright. The mother's face was pale, with circles beneath her eyes, her eyes themselves black as coals, her pupils lost amidst the blackness. And then, when she pulled back the lid of her basket, it was filled with maggots wriggling over the King's decapitated head.

Gwendolyn gasped, swaying backward, and for an instant feared she might tumble from her horse as her gaze returned to the girl to find the child smiling with a mouth lacking teeth. Her flesh, too, was pale as death, and when she blinked, her blue eyes turned black.

Gwendolyn might have screamed, but then, quite suddenly, she was peering into a smallish room, no longer seated upon her horse, staring at the form of a weeping girl...

Ely?

Was it Ely?

The girl's feet and hands were bound behind her back, and she was sobbing disconsolately, peering up suddenly, her pink lips quivering, as Gwendolyn walked into her room. "Oh, Ely!" Gwendolyn said, rushing to her side. "Please tell me! What is wrong?"

For a moment, Ely didn't speak. Her lovely blue eyes were red-rimmed, her face encrusted with filth and mud. "Gwendolyn?" she sobbed. "Is it you?"

"It is!" Gwendolyn said. "I am here!" Flinging herself atop the bed, she groped about for some means to set Ely free, but the ropes binding her hands had no beginning or end; they couldn't be loosened.

"Have you found Bryn?" Ely asked. "Please, tell me he is not lost?"

"I don't know what you're talking about, Ely. I've not seen Bryn—not since you left me."

Ely shook her head, fat tears streaming down her cheeks. "Oh, no! Gwendolyn! We did not leave you— can't you see? *You* left us. Bryn went in search of you and never returned."

But, nay, that wasn't true, Gwendolyn wanted to say.

She would have welcomed both in her company. Bryn wanted nothing to do with Gwendolyn. He was still so furious about it all, and it was his idea to separate, not hers. Gwendolyn had only agreed because his eyes had begged her. "I did not leave you," she insisted. "Blood and bones, Ely! I cannot find the means to free you! Who did this to you?"

"You did," said Ely. "You did."

"I would not!" Gwendolyn said, and then, frustrated with her inability to untie Ely's bindings, she looked about the room, for the first time studying their environs. She didn't recognize the place.

"Where are we?"

Ely buried her face in her crude blankets, weeping again, inconsolably.

"Oh, gods Ely!" Gwendolyn soothed. "Speak to me. Please. Where are we?"

Her eyes as black as the little girl's from the market, Ely turned again and said, "I am where you sent me!" And suddenly, the walls rose about them—dirt walls. The ceiling vanished, leaving them under a thousand winking stars. Ely's weeping persisted, but now there were more bodies on the bed, and the bed itself vanished, folding into itself, leaving Gwendolyn with the horrid impression they were lying in a mass grave.

When Ely's weeping ceased abruptly, Gwendolyn feared she might be dead because the scent of death clogged her nostrils, making her gag and cough.

The bodies mounted, the mound growing higher and higher, and, instinctively, Gwendolyn fought to make her way out, grasping, groping, searching. Even as she ascended, more bodies rolled into the grave, knocking her backward, impeding her progress—more and more and more. Desperately, she clawed her way through rotting flesh and bones, leaving her with flesh beneath her nails, moving further and further from Ely. Her dear friend's sobs were muffled by dirty rags and blankets and decomposing flesh.

Gods, oh gods! If she didn't get out of here, she would die as well. But she couldn't leave Ely. If she did, she could never face herself in the morning.

Somehow, she must find some way to save her.

More bodies rolled into the grave, and Gwendolyn's heart beat painfully as she turned back, diving again, deeper, deeper, searching for warm flesh amid putrid corpses, guided only by Ely's sobs, which grew louder and louder, until finally—at last! Gwendolyn reached down and found a familiar soft hand—Ely's hand... it was so soft, without blisters...

Ely was so genteel, so lovely—everything Gwendolyn could never be.

Standing over her, her mother sighed with disgust, shaking her head and pinching her nose. "What for the love of the Goddess have you been doing, Gwendolyn? Blood and bloody bones, child, what will I do with you?"

Gwendolyn's voice sounded faraway and small. "We were only playing, Mother," she said, lowering her head with shame.

"With Bryn, no doubt? You don't see Ely engaging in such vulgarity, do you? Will you never outgrow this shameful behavior? How will you be a respected queen if you'll never behave like one?"

Gwendolyn shrugged.

"Where is Bryn?"

Gwendolyn shrugged again.

"Go, find him," her mother demanded angrily. Then suddenly, her expression darkened, and she seized Gwendolyn by the arm, shaking fiercely. "Go, find him," she said again. "Find him!"

GWENDOLYN BLINKED, opening her eyes to discover Esme seated on the edge of her bed, with a cool, damp cloth pressed to Gwendolyn's forehead, smoothing it over her brow.

Was it only a dream?

Esme's smile was genuine, though her brows knit with concern. "You gave us a terrible fright, *Banríon na bhfear.*"

Gwendolyn tried to rise, but Esme shoved her back down, her eyes twinkling with good humor. "All is well, do not worry. We simply failed to consider the hob cake you consumed. There are properties within each that are much the same, and perhaps you ingested too much?"

She tilted her head in question, and Gwendolyn's cheeks heated, remembering Málik's warning about the hob cake. At once, she reached back to inspect her ears, and then breathed a sigh of relief when she found them unchanged.

Very amusing. Damnable creature!

"Where is he?" Gwendolyn asked, lifting an arm to inspect the loose gray robe she was now wearing. So big, it consumed her entirely, and—Gwendolyn pinched the sleeve, lifting it to her nostrils, sniffing. It was rancid, with too much sweat. Someone had undressed her, then dressed her again in a *tupik*.

"I am sorry. It was not something we anticipated," said Esme. "At home, we do not sleep with such trappings. But Málik insisted we not leave you unclothed, and that is all I could find." She turned up her palm, making a disgusted face. "At any rate, he is waiting outside the door—precisely where he's been since I banned him from your room. He was quite beside himself when you swooned."

Gwendolyn's brows knit. "I swooned?"

Esme nodded. "Straight into your soup, dear.

Málik swept you up and brought you here. And here you've remained for nigh on three days."

"Three days!" Gwendolyn sat up again, startled by the news.

Yegods! Málik had warned her. And now his warning had come true. Nay, she did not turn into a Faerie, but she'd closed her eyes and slept for days, despite that they could ill-afford for her to lie abed. "Where are my clothes?" Gwendolyn asked urgently, moving Esme out of the way. Then, hearing whispers outside her room, she rose and made her way to the door.

Those dreams... odd as they were, she knew they were omens. Some had perhaps already come to pass, and some she must prevent.

Deep in her heart, she understood that Ely and Bryn needed her, even as Trevena needed her, and nothing or no one could keep her from rushing to their aid.

She tore aside the curtain to reveal Málik and another Druid she'd not yet met but remembered from the supper. Gwendolyn didn't wait for an introduction. "We must leave," she said. "Now!"

CHAPTER
TWENTY-TWO

The entire order of Lifer Pol Druids couldn't have prevented Gwendolyn from leaving. Fortunately, no one tried.

This time, when she and Málik set out, they would not go alone. Esme insisted upon traveling with them. So did the young Druid Gwendolyn met outside her chamber, named Lir. Fortunately, neither would she need to spend her mother's jewels to procure their supplies. The Druids provided everything needed, including horses and a healer.

As little time as she'd spent here, most of it abed, Gwendolyn would be heartily sorry to leave this place unexplored. Even with Esme's ready explanations, she would depart with more questions than answers, and yet, now that she had a better understanding of the Order's purpose, she felt certain she could return. The tales she'd heard of these men were false, and though she understood the telling of them had a purpose—to keep people away—they did not do the Order justice.

She wondered why her father never sought them because it was certain he must have searched. The map in his war room gave evidence to that, though perhaps the seeking itself was not enough. Gwendolyn was beginning to suspect that perhaps her father's legacy was not aligned with the Druid's purpose, just as she understood why Málik had brought her here: So she could rediscover something lost.

These Druids were more than simply scholars or ambassadors. They guarded the only remaining portal on this side of the Veil. If anyone sought them without that knowledge, it was perhaps for the sacred herbs they grew, and the visions the herbs imparted—more potent for the locus, because here is where visions were born, here in this magical, ageless place, where the impossible and the possible melded together.

The feast they'd provided upon her arrival wasn't meant for sustenance. They'd served her a potent brew intended to arouse visions, and, indeed, it had, although, much to Gwendolyn's trepidation, it wasn't possible to ascertain which of these dreams were merely glimpses into the future, which were still changeable, and which had already passed.

This morning, she heartily feared that everything she'd witnessed was already done, and that she would arrive too late to save the two people she'd known longest in this life.

Pretania could wait just a while longer.

So could her mother's people.

There was nothing she could do to save her father, nor her mother, but Ely's cry for help was one she could and would heed. After losing so much, if she lost Ely and Bryn, too, she might never survive it. She must believe there was still a chance, though one thing was certain: If she did nothing, if she sat about feeling sorry for herself, only wondering whether she could live up to this task she was born to, it would certainly be too late. No matter that the Druids' Crossroads remained frozen in time, the world beyond the Veil was not, and Loc would not stop until he saw this entire isle vanquished and prostrate before him.

Gwendolyn must be the one to stop him.

One quest at a time.

First, she must locate Ely and Bryn.

Preparing for their departure, she retrieved and donned her wonderful new tunic and a borrowed cloak, securing the coat with her mother's brooch. The rest of her belongings—all but the silver armband—she entrusted to Emrys, along with her mother's Prydein gown.

She didn't care anymore about the shortness of her hair, or her face, but thanks to Esme, she would look the part of a warrior queen.

Once dressed, she joined her company in the glade, where Emrys stood with his staff in hand, overlooking the preparations. His wizened brow smoothed when he spied Gwendolyn.

"Your satchels have been filled, anticipating your needs. If there is aught you do not have, I will argue that you will not need it." He gave her a wink, opening his mouth at the same time as though the gestures were physically linked.

Gwendolyn smiled. "Thank you... for everything," she said. "I must apologize for the abrupt departure, but I hope you will receive me again."

"You needn't ask," said the elder druid, reaching out to clasp Gwendolyn's shoulder more firmly than an old man should have had the strength to allow. "I understand," he said, with a knowing glimmer in his eyes. "'Tis oft this way with the sight. Go with the Goddess," he said. "Return to sup with us another day. You'll be welcome any time."

Gwendolyn lifted a brow. "Something more than pookies?" she suggested, and Emrys barked with laughter.

By now, Esme and Lir had already retrieved the horses, making certain they were geared and settled —beautiful mares with long silver manes, large black eyes, and broad chests. These, too, were Esme's contributions, brought, she'd said, from the Fae realms.

Their trappings were simple—nothing like the showy horse Loc had given Gwendolyn as a bridal gift. There was no gold in the saddles, no gilded horns, no armor with golden scales. They were fitted only with simple, well-oiled leather, soft and supple, so the saddle and fittings melded as closely as possible with the curves of each horse, and each to its rider.

"Where to?" Málik asked, bringing Gwendolyn the reins.

"East," Gwendolyn said. "That is all I know right now."

I am where you sent me, Ely had said in her dream. Bryn had been quite adamant that they should not return to Durotriges, and knowing what Gwendolyn knew now, she understood why, though perhaps danger awaited them in the east as well?

If Gwendolyn could, she would intercept them before they presented themselves to the Iceni. Unfortunately, as it was, they'd already lost a good three days here in the Druid village, and even before then, they were two days removed from their parting in the glade.

They had at least a *sennight's* worth of travel to catch Ely and Bryn, but the Iceni village lay deep in the southeast—a good sixty leagues or more. Esme reassured Gwendolyn that, given time, their Fae horses could catch them. Considering this, Gwendolyn led her mare to the fore.

Sometimes in life, one must know when to defer to others, but this was not one of those times. If she would be queen, she must lead, and no longer could she afford to defer even to Málik.

Gwendolyn had trained the entirety of her life for this moment, and right now, all those things she'd worried about so incessantly only yesterday seemed of so little import. If she would spend the rest of her days as a widowed queen, then she would gladly accept this fate, if only she could return peace to this land, and her people.

There was only one thing she knew with certainty this morn: Locrinus must be defeated. She didn't know how, or when, but that was her charge. And regardless, to accomplish this, she would need good men and women to ride by her side—Bryn, for one.

Her gaze slid to Málik, who now stood checking the cinch of his mount, adjusting the larger saddle and fittings.

She was glad he was with her, and in the aftermath of his *glamour*, they were bonded in a way they were not before. Gwendolyn couldn't say that she could read his mind, nor could she glean anything from his thoughts, but instead of abandoning her when he'd discovered her insecurities, and all her frailties, he'd remained by her side, regardless of his affiliation with Esme—whatever that entailed. He was not her Shadow. Bryn was her Shadow. Málik was something more but defining this was impossible. Life was no longer so simple. Matters were complicated and grown infinitely more so after this visit to the Druid village.

Her gaze shifted to Esme, taking in her regal bearing and manner of dress. She wore no crown, but she didn't need one to proclaim her supremacy. It was quietly stated, ingrained in her very being, every movement and gesture. Esme was not a woman accustomed to taking commands from any man, and Gwendolyn wasn't certain she was prepared to take orders even from a queen, no matter how helpful she seemed, or how obliging she might be. She was a bit like pine liquor—heady and warm in small doses, exhilarating going down one's throat, but set the bottle too close to a flame, and it would explode, kindling a blaze nearly impossible to put out.

Dressed in a tunic similar to Gwendolyn's, hers was now a deep forest green, bearing something like scales that reminded Gwendolyn of a serpent's skin—slightly iridescent to match her skin. Málik had said Gwendolyn's mithril would conceal her by night, but Esme's attire would seem to blend itself against the environs, changing colors as quickly as did her eyes.

For his part, Málik wore his usual black tunic and leathers—as simple and supple as the leather of their saddle trappings, giving Gwendolyn a shocking eyeful every time she dared to look his way. It was... unbearably revealing. And... there were things she noticed this morning that she daren't before—such as the way his leathers molded themselves to his sinew, rolling across the landscape of his body like a sheet of liquid night.

As for the Druid, he'd shed his white robes for this journey; he now wore undyed leathers in the fashion of a Shadow. He'd also eschewed the ear sheaths at Esme's request, and Gwendolyn noted an underlying current of *something* between those two.

Unrequited mayhap, the young Druid admired Esme, though if Esme shared his regard, she had a strange way of showing it—with a tongue as biting as Gwendolyn had ever heard. Yet, as unpredictable as their fellowship was—for all of them, not simply Esme and the Druid—Gwendolyn sensed a fidelity to her cause. In short, she didn't know if any of them would be in accord with one another—not even Gwendolyn and Málik—but she knew they would be steadfast and loyal. For good or ill, the quest to save Pretania must begin.

Once she was ready to ride, Gwendolyn hoisted herself into the saddle, pleased to discover that, just as she'd anticipated, her new tunic didn't impede her movements. Reveling in the feel of strong horseflesh between her thighs, she gave the signal to move out.

"Welcome back, *Banríon,*" said Málik with a slow, dazzling grin. "How I've missed the fire in your eyes."

"Have you?" Gwendolyn asked with a lifted brow.

"Indeed I have," he said, winking as he tossed her an apple.

TWENTY-THREE

By midmorning, they'd ridden beyond the point when they should have stopped to rest. Still, Esme insisted they continue, pushing the horses beyond the normal endurance.

Fleet of foot and nimble, their horses galloped on silent hooves, hardly winded no matter how swiftly they flew. Like Esme herself, it was as though they glided over the woodland terrain, veering more swiftly, more sharply, more intuitively than any horse Gwendolyn had ever had the pleasure of riding.

Pleased with the mare's performance, Gwendolyn leaned forward to tangle her fingers through the long, soft mane, then slowed, riding for a moment, simply listening to the horse's even breath against the snapping of twigs beneath her hooves.

"They'll never be winded," Esme insisted, reaching over to pat her own mare's neck. "These are superior to mortal breeds."

Gwendolyn's gaze snapped up in surprise. "She's not mortal?"

Esme tilted her head one way, then the other, vacillating. "Well," she said. "Let us say that even gods are not truly immortal, Gwendolyn. Age will not defeat us, but a good spear will do it."

Gwendolyn understood Málik was... older... but immortality was not a concept she understood—particularly now, when so many people she knew and loved had already gone from her life. Still, she thought of him as invincible, and the very thought that something could happen to him left her unsettled.

"Only ask Nuada," suggested Esme. "Though I promise you he's as dead as dead can be."

"Nuada of the silver hand?" Gwendolyn surmised. The king who grew himself a new limb so he could be made king again, but then was murdered by Balor of the Evil Eye. "I've heard that tale," she confessed. "My mother's maid used to recount these stories to me when I was young."

The Faerie's eyes twinkled. "Perhaps at bedtime to frighten you into remaining abed?"

Gwendolyn laughed softly. "Not precisely. You see, I had a Mester who was far too cynical to believe in my Prophecy. I suppose she told them because she felt it was important I should hear them."

"Considering the prophecy?"

Gwendolyn nodded.

"I see... and did she tell you any other such tales?" She flitted her hand between them. "Perhaps the story of your crib-side visitation?"

Startled by the question, Gwendolyn slid the Faerie a curious glance. Her visitation wasn't a secret. Anyone who knew Gwendolyn knew of it, but she had never actually discussed it with anyone, much less a true-blood Fae—not even Málik, truth be told.

"Yet I wonder," continued Esme, without waiting

for Gwendolyn's answer. "Perhaps she felt it vital you believe her story?"

"Story?"

Esme's brows lifted. "Indeed. Wasn't she the one who came upon the Fae in your nursery? She and your mother?"

Gwendolyn blinked, then nodded.

Once again, none of this was undisclosed, but Esme was the first ever to speak of it so boldly—that she was also Fae, gave Gwendolyn a vague feeling of... not quite unease... nor was it quite foreboding, but there was something about the look in Esme's eyes that made her wonder... And yet, in truth, it should be far stranger that no one ever spoke of it, because in part, this was what had led Gwendolyn to doubt her prophecy. Stories told in whispers were too often gossip or lies.

"You know... Balor was my grandsire," the Faerie disclosed.

Gwendolyn's brow furrowed. *Her Grandfather?* Time, as she was coming to understand, was a malleable experience; even so, Balor's death would seem to have been so long ago. "When did he die?"

The Faerie's eyes glinted sharply, then turned a bright shade of blue. "Quite some time ago," she said, though she didn't elaborate, and then her gaze slid to Málik, riding ahead, conversing with Lir.

The two were quite the pair—Málik with his silver hair and lithesome form, Lir with his hair black as midnight, and shoulders wide enough to rival the breadth of his horse.

What Gwendolyn truly wished to know was how old Málik was—or rather, that was not the thing she *most* wished to know, but it was something she'd asked him repeatedly, and for which she'd not yet received a proper answer. "How old is Málik?" she dared, and the Faerie lifted a brow, turning to tilt Gwendolyn a curious glance, her eyes still sparkling, though now a mix of green and blue, like the Dragon's Bay in spring.

"Ask me anything," Esme said, after a moment. "I've no secrets, you'll learn. But that is *not* my story to tell. If you would know it, Gwendolyn, ask him." She hitched her chin ahead at Málik's back, and her lips turned ever so slightly at one corner. "However, I will share one thing I know you are eager to learn..."

Gwendolyn's heart jumped, knowing intuitively what it was Esme meant to share. The question had hovered on her tongue from the moment Emrys had proclaimed them lovers.

"He is *not* my intended, despite that our fathers would like to see it so. You may put your thoughts at ease over that."

So they were *not* betrothed. A powerful sense of relief rushed through Gwendolyn, despite that she was compelled to deny it. She shook her head, but when she did so, so did Esme.

"No," said the Faerie, lifting a finger to her lips. "You cannot deny it, Banríon." She leaned closer, somehow bridging the distance between them as she whispered. "I smell desire."

Again, Gwendolyn opened her mouth to repudiate the claim, but it was true, and when she closed it again, Esme laughed, returning her attention to the pair ahead. "If you ask me, you two would be better served to be done with it—clear your heads for the task ahead. Nothing is quite so distracting as lust," she declared. "Alas, do not fret, Gwendolyn, I'll not speak of it again, and *his* obstinance will surely rival yours."

In all her years, Gwendolyn had met no one like Esme. She was a study in contradictions. Sometimes chatty and warm, other times as stubbornly aloof as Málik.

Sometimes she was painfully amusing, other times achingly mortifying.

Sometimes coy and clever, other times sweet and soft.

Sometimes she made Gwendolyn blush hotly, pouncing on her weaknesses with the prowess of a wolf scenting blood.

Other times she made Gwendolyn feel as if there was no one more important than she was, catering to her every need.

From one moment to the next, there was no telling what version of Esme you might face, and despite that, the more she came to know the Faerie, the more Gwendolyn trusted her.

At least she was honest, even in her recalcitrance. And yet, as closed-mouthed as she was about Málik, she had no such reservations over talking about anything or anyone else.

Quite literally.

Gwendolyn learned every dark secret about every Faerie in existence, save Málik. Esme had no qualms even recounting her own sins—which were a multitude, judging by the small sampling of stories she'd already shared.

She'd once lain with a brother, and also claimed to be the one who blinded Balor in one eye, hurling a dagger into it for an insult to her mother. "So, your mother was Balor's daughter?" Gwendolyn asked, trying to follow.

"Ethniu," Esme revealed.

"And she was Lugh's mother, as well?"

Esme smiled. "He is my Half-brother."

It took little to determine that the brother she'd lain with must be Lugh, particularly by the twinkle in her eyes, though Gwendolyn didn't actually want to know for certain.

"Cían was his sire," she told Gwendolyn. "Mine is... someone else." And that someone else, Gwendolyn surmised, must be the man who'd see her wed to Málik. With a little patience, she might actually discover everything she wished to know—precisely who was Málik?

About nearly everything else, Esme was a font of information, and Gwendolyn also learned a bit about the Lifer Pol Order. For one, she did not realize Lir was Emrys' brother, as well as the youngest of the Order, though, in truth, he was not so young. His earthly days numbered six-hundred-ninety-nine, despite that he looked scarcely older than Gwendolyn.

The Lifer Pol Druids had now occupied the Fae village for nearly six-hundred-and-seventy-seven years, placing Lir's age at about twenty-two when he crossed the Veil. But, unlike his brother, he'd not emerged from the village during the interim of their occupation, and this was why he still appeared so young, and conversely, his brother appeared to be twice his age or more. Simply by appearance, they could pass for grandfather and grandson, although in reality there were only three full years between them.

As for what lay between Esme and Málik, that was

impossible to ascertain. Though whatever it was, it shouldn't concern Gwendolyn. Already, Málik had apprised her that his heart was not hers to have, so she shouldn't need to be told twice. And now that Gwendolyn had met Esme, she would be the last person to part them—even if she could, and she could not.

However, now was not the time to pore over matters of the heart. She had a job to do, and her thoughts must not be turned from it.

Those two might not actually be betrothed, but they still behaved like an old, wedded couple, bickering every time they spoke—or really, it was more Málik's discontent. For whatever reason, he did not relish Esme's presence among them, and regardless, he had no control over what the Faerie did or didn't do. Esme was unaffected by his moods, answering his churlish tone with only dulcet words. Nothing appeared to ruffle her, although she seemed to be less than enthralled by Lir. Those two were like oil and water—both different and unwilling to conform.

Gwendolyn also discovered a curiosity.

Once, when Lir caught her staring at Esme's ears, he explained that the pointier the ears were, the older the Fae. Thus, Esme was older than Málik, though by how much Lir couldn't say.

Clearly, *faekind* did not live by the same mores as mortals, although betimes neither did men. Urien was older than Gwendolyn by far. Only now she wondered if everything would have transpired so differently if Urien had lived...

As a wee one, she had so oft imagined herself married to a man more like her father—someone who would cherish his wife and his family. Her mother was her father's consort in all ways, ruling by his side, and betimes even lifted above his heir. Yet, this was never something Gwendolyn begrudged, because she had always known she was meant to leave Trevena, and, until the day her father was called to his eternal rest, her mother should have had the people's respect. Therefore, regardless of what Gwendolyn had felt about her mother, she'd respected Queen Eseld without fail. And she had so oft prayed that she, too, would wed a man whose love for her defied a nation.

Indeed, for a while, Gwendolyn had sorely lamented her impending marriage to Urien, only because he was so much older than she—he, who'd lived half his life before her birth. But even then, she had aspired to be a worthy helpmate, and she had vowed to please him. It was only after the choice of Locrinus was placed before her she'd dared to hope for more...

What a mistake that was.

She wondered about Kamber and Albanactus— were these two equally horrid as Loc? She decided they must be, and Loc had better watch his back, because even if Gwendolyn failed in her retribution, there was no love or respect in that family. If they could go along with killing one brother, regardless that he was only half their blood, they could betray another.

"You've been quiet," suggested Málik, as he sidled up beside her. "A silver for your thoughts?"

Gwendolyn arched a brow. "So much?" she said, offering him a smile, reaching down to pat her mount's neck, nervous in his presence though she couldn't say why.

"Silver seems a pittance for all I'd give for peace," he said.

So would she, in truth. "I didn't realize we were quarreling," she allowed, flicking a glance at the two riders trotting ahead, both so thoroughly engrossed in their own discourse they hadn't spared a thought elsewhere for at least a full bell.

Apparently, Esme found it irksome that the Lifer Pol Druids all wore those ear sheaths. She considered it an insult, and utterly pretentious, though Lir attempted, in vain, to explain it was only meant with the greatest of admiration and respect. "You are mortals," Esme said. "Do you wear them hoping the gods may forget and bestow you with immortality?"

Lir replied, "Have they not already?"

Esme flipped a hand dismissively.

"Somehow, we've endured these seven hundred years and more," Lir persisted.

"Seven hundred and TWO," Esme countered, and Gwendolyn could sense the roll of her eyes in the bored tone of her voice. "You mortals do count your years as you do coppers!"

Pursing her lips, Gwendolyn tried not to laugh.

"That," Málik said, pointing at the pair ahead. "Is a quarrel. Still, I would like to see us cry peace."

"I'd like that, too," Gwendolyn confessed. It had been far too long since she had counted Málik among her close friends, and now she needed friends more than ever.

Up ahead, their companions continued their row.

"You merely exist," Esme berated the young Druid. "Sitting about all day with your knobs in hands, rotting your brains with pookies, dreaming the lives of others—that is not living."

Lir said nothing in response, but he straightened his spine, riding as stiffly as a length of wood.

On and on they continued, and Gwendolyn had an inkling that Esme thoroughly enjoyed the needling... as she seemed to enjoy needling everyone, including Gwendolyn.

After a time, listening to her poke at the Druid, Gwendolyn began to think of Esme much as she did *piskies*—indescribably beautiful on the outside, perhaps equally so on the inside. But if you rubbed one the wrong way...

And sometimes when she smiled exactly so, it brought to mind Demelza's description of the Faeries by Gwendolyn's cradle... with their bright eyes and sharp, savage grins.

TWENTY-FOUR

That evening, they settled near to where the River Dee curved north and west. Another furlong, thereabouts, and they would have returned to the location where Beryan fell.

Gwendolyn recognized the old wych elm and couldn't help but consider Beryan's daughter. Would she worry about her missing father as much as Gwendolyn worried about her mother and Demelza? Likely so, and it was the not knowing that was so terribly hard. At least if she knew that her mother was dead, she would rest easier knowing that she wasn't suffering, and stop worrying and hoping. But if she was dead, there would be no redemption for either of them, and particularly for Gwendolyn. After all that she'd witnessed and endured, she now understood that everything Bryn had said was true: Everything her mother ever did she'd done in Gwendolyn's best interest.

More than anything, Gwendolyn wished she could see her again, and explain that, not only did she forgive her, but she finally understood and loved her fiercely for her care and protection.

Poring over those dark thoughts, Gwendolyn found a good, dry spot for their pallets. Meanwhile, Esme tended the horses, and Málik went searching for their supper, and Gwendolyn followed Esme down to the river, intending to help with the horses, determined to do her part.

She didn't wish to be like Loc, sitting atop his golden throne, merely watching his warriors spar from his dais, staying clear of the blood.

Gods knew, even his coup was designed to keep the blood from his hands, with him long gone from the city as the deed was done, with Gwendolyn culpable simply for having wed him.

She was still furious over that. *Utterly and irreversibly.*

With a look that Gwendolyn read as amusement, Esme watched as Gwendolyn checked her mare for galls caused by the gear.

"You won't find anything," she declared. "These are Enbarr's daughters."

And, of course, she spoke true. Gwendolyn found nothing. The animal's flesh was pristine.

"Her name is Aisling," Esme revealed. "It means dream."

She tapped the horse directly beside her on the flank and said, "This one is Sheahan. It means Peaceful One; for good or ill, it is why I lent her to that silly druid. How annoyingly unflappable he is. One would think him made of stone." So then, she *was* needling him on purpose.

Pointing to the others, each in turn, Esme called out their names. "Daithi—Swift, and Lorcan." The last one was hers, and she grinned. "In my tongue that means 'little fierce one.'"

205

"Like her master, I presume?"

"Perhaps," said Esme coyly, her smile turning crooked.

"And they are all mares?" Gwendolyn said. But it wasn't a question because that was the first thing she'd noticed. Her father had been of the mind that, in battle, mares were better than stallions or even geldings. For one, stallions too oft suffered from blood frenzy, and in the throes of battle would unseat their riders. But it wasn't altogether a matter of blood frenzy.

Once during practice, Gwendolyn watched a very determined stallion attempt to mount a mare in heat with both riders still attached.

And truly, despite that geldings were cheaper than mares, they were not much better behaved. Therefore, while many warriors seemed inclined to match their egos with their mounts, choosing great, imposing stallions, her father always insisted on good, sturdy mares for his troops, and from an early age, he'd taught Gwendolyn the importance of their training and care.

He'd put her on a horse when she was two and had her cleaning stalls by the time she was four—for many reasons, though primarily because it was her father's heartfelt belief that a horse's loyalty was given first to the person who tended and fed them. As it was with warriors, loyalty was essential. Therefore, it didn't matter what one's royal standing, a shovel of shite now and again was the price to be paid for the certainty of a mount's fealty.

"Indeed," said Esme. "As randy as the sire may be, he'll never produce stallions." Her expression shifted to one of disgust. "You see, Enbarr was a gift to Lugh from Manannán, and, of course, that old windbag would leave nothing to chance. For my part, I was surprised to learn he could breed at all."

Gwendolyn lifted both brows. "Do you mean the sea god?"

Esme waved a hand dismissively. "You say god, I say imbecile. He's a selfish old wanker, though I suppose he loved his foster son enough to gift him three of his most prized possessions: Enbarr, plus a boat and his sword." She peered back toward their camp. "That is the sword Málik now wields—the Answerer."

One more nugget of information.

"You said 'loved', so was Manannán slain, or has Málik found himself disfavored?"

"Nah. The old goat lives, but you mistook me, Gwendolyn. Málik is not *his* son. I was speaking of Lugh." She bent to lift a palmful of water, splashing it gently on her mare, then rubbing away a bit of mud.

Gwendolyn filed these things away to mull over later. "So he gave his boat, his horse and his sword to Lugh?"

"He did, but the only reason that mucky traitor offered anything was to ensure he'd have visitors. You see, he, too, was exiled after our banishment. Forbidden to enter our Fae realms. But it served the bastard right since he's the one whose tricky tongue saw us banished beneath those hills." She rolled her eyes. "Of course, the boat he gave Lugh was self-navigating, and the horse can traverse both land and sea, so you tell me whether he had an ulterior motive. But then, when Lugh never visited, he claimed all these gifts were lent, and insisted Lugh return them."

"But he didn't?" Gwendolyn surmised.

Gods or nay, Esme made them sound as petty as men. But Gwendolyn knew a few aldermen who'd behaved that way, doing nothing for anyone unless it served them first.

"Why should we?" Esme said. "Enbarr is quite the stallion. So long as he lives, he'll continue to fill our stables and his progeny may not be so blessed, but they are remarkable, even so. Wouldn't you agree?"

"I would," said Gwendolyn, her thoughts returning to Málik's sword. "So is Málik's sword Faerie forged?"

Esme peered up the hill. "Merely blessed, though it's quite handy. I'm sure you'll agree." She sucked at her teeth, then lapped at her lips. "With that blade to one's throat," she revealed. "No man can tell a lie." She smiled then, adding, "Nor woman."

"Really?" Gwendolyn said, and she could think of a few people she'd like to use it on, including Málik, despite that he claimed he could not lie. As far as she saw it, a lie of omission was still a lie. "So how did he acquire that sword if it was gifted to Lugh?"

Esme lifted a brow, her lips turning crooked. "That, too, will be a question for Málik." She inclined her head in his direction. "Why don't you go ask him?"

And just like that, their discourse was done.

Gwendolyn frowned. Esme seemed intent upon sending her off to Málik for questions. But as curious as she was—immensely so—she was not curious enough to go pulling at Málik's coattails. Particularly when she knew he would be disinclined to answer— and so soon after their truce, she didn't wish to be annoyed with him. Thus, that question, along with a multitude of others, could wait for some other day.

Bored perhaps, because she didn't get the response from Gwendolyn she was seeking, Esme abandoned Sheahan to drink, turning her attention to Daithi.

Meanwhile, Gwendolyn returned Aisling to her post near their campsite, leaving her to graze along with Lorcan. And, knowing intuitively that Esme would prefer to handle her own mount, she went in search of Lir to help him forage.

"She's maddening," the Druid complained. "I know not how you bear her!"

"Esme?"

The "young" Druid nodded, his lips pursing with what Gwendolyn presumed was irritation.

"She has her moments," Gwendolyn allowed. "What are we searching for?"

"Cobnuts," Lir said, and Gwendolyn immediately set about to helping him locate a few.

At home, their cook often served cobnuts with a hen and bacon stew, but Gwendolyn liked them best crushed and baked with honey bread and summer fruit, topped with fresh cream.

Ely's favorite way to eat them was roasted, with nothing on them at all, and tonight, they would have no choice but to roast them or eat them raw.

Unbidden, the memory of Ely in the dream accosted her, bound and weeping, and Gwendolyn had the most overwhelming desire to take Aisling and rush to her defense.

CHAPTER
TWENTY-FIVE

L ater that evening, once their bellies were satisfied, everyone huddled about a dwindling campfire to discuss the morrow's plans.

Málik's Faerie flame bounced about the campsite, like a curious kitten, exploring and Gwendolyn supposed it was no strange thing to Lir, because the Druid scarcely noticed, merely swatting it away without thinking when it came too close to his face.

As for Málik, Gwendolyn noted that, regardless of how annoyed he appeared to be with Esme, he chose a seat close to her, both resting atop a fallen log. Gwendolyn told herself it was only because the ground was so wet, but a niggle of jealousy pricked her. Shrugging it off—because she must—she told them about her dreams. "What do you believe it means?" she asked.

"Some dreams are merely dreams," Málik suggested. It was the first he'd spoken since returning from the hunt.

"That I do not believe," said Lir, with his usual flair for discourse. "If you are attuned to them, even the most inconsiderable dreams will have much to say." He lifted a cobnut, attempting to crack it between his teeth and failing. "I like these better roasted," he complained.

"Indeed? And perhaps you brought a pan to roast with?" suggested Esme, a little too sweetly. "Or mayhap you might like to hold them over the flame with your sweet little mortal fingers?"

The Druid gave her a narrow-eyed glance, and Gwendolyn suppressed a smile. "I believe that, too, Lir," she said. "My Demelza used to caution me to remember the lessons of my dreams."

"What is a Demelza?" inquired Esme.

"A woman after my heart," said Lir. "Who is she?"

"My mother's maid." Gwendolyn said. "But I must presume she is dead."

A fresh wave of grief rushed over her, remembering Demelza's loyal service. Even more than her own mother, Demelza had been the one to care for her, and despite that she had long outgrown her tutelage by the time she left to be wed, Demelza would be sorely missed—as one missed a favored aunt or uncle. Alas. There were so many good people whose blood stained Loc's hands.

"Ah," said Lir, casting her a glance beneath his dark lashes. "Bad business, all that," he said. "I am sorry, Majesty." It was the first time he'd used her formal title in the common tongue. She was getting used to hearing *Banríon,* though none of them spoke that word with the diffidence Gwendolyn was accustomed to seeing when people had addressed her father. Still, it didn't bother her. She thanked the Druid, then, plucking up a cobnut, cracked it, and pulled out the meat, pitching the broken shells toward Málik, wondering over the peculiarities of his mood. He did not say so, but despite his call for a truce, she sensed he disapproved of this digression to search for Bryn and Ely.

Though perhaps that was not all. His mood had been six-degrees of sour since encountering Esme in the Druid village, and now she must wonder why. Was it because he disliked Esme? Or did he like her too much, and perhaps he didn't wish for Gwendolyn to know it? Or mayhap her presence here reminded him of duties left unfulfilled?

Or... Esme had rebuffed him, and Málik was still angry over it?

Whatever the case, he wasn't too pleased with Gwendolyn for having done the same, no matter how innocently she had done so.

And regardless—so it seemed, he'd had no right to ask her to run away with him, and she ought to tell Esme about it, except she couldn't stomach any more discord. As much as she wished to confront Málik with these accusations, Gwendolyn knew it would not be the best course of action. She needed him.

Once again, he had consumed none of his supper, despite being the one to provide it. For her part, Gwendolyn knew she ought to eat more in anticipation of tomorrow's travels, but her belly felt as though it were full of stinging nettles. Whether this was because of Málik's mood, the lingering disease of her dreams, or simply the fact that they had stopped so close to where they'd encountered Loc and his men, wasn't discernible. All she knew right now was that her stomach had grown sour, and every time she thought about Beryan's body out there, somewhere, rotting in the river, disrespected... she couldn't rest easy.

"I fear I've sent my friends into danger," Gwendolyn fretted, and once again, it was Málik who responded.

"The Iceni might have no love for Cornwall, but I do not believe they'll mistreat anyone who comes to them in peace. If Ely and Bryn have gone to them, they'll be welcomed in good faith."

Gwendolyn furrowed her brow. "How can you be so sure?"

"For what it's worth, I believe he speaks true," agreed Esme. "Regardless. I warrant as yet your friends will not have had time to arrive so far southeast. It will be another two days travel for them if the way is easy, and another *sennight* if not. Did you say whether they rode with suitable mounts?"

Gwendolyn shrugged. "Certainly not Enbarr's mares," she said. "And I do not believe they could retrieve their own horses from Loc's stables before our departure. Their removal would have been noted. Still, I must presume Queen Innogen would have given us suitable mounts, or else what would be the point of freeing us?"

Lir shrugged. "Perhaps she intended for you to be caught?"

Gwendolyn shook her head. "I did consider that, but I don't believe it. She warned me specifically against returning—said she would kill me herself if I did."

Lir persisted. "Perhaps she knows her son too well, and surmised he would kill you sooner than he would return you?"

Gwendolyn cast a glance at Málik, knowing that

he, too, had overheard Loc's avowal—that he intended to do precisely so. Still, Gwendolyn persisted, "I do not believe she would take that chance. The *politikal* climate is too unstable. If I were to die by Loc's hands... well, he would surely make me a martyr and Queen Innogen is shrewd. She would have left nothing to chance. I do believe she will have provided horses that are hale enough for travel, and likely not from Loc's personal stables. I've heard he is not kind to animals."

"'Tis difficult to imagine *King* Locrinus being kind to any creature," suggested Esme, and Málik grunted his displeasure over the mention of Loc's name with his title though he said nothing more. Naturally, Gwendolyn shared his disgust, but she was certain Esme intended no insult. She was coming to know the Faerie well enough to know that she was an equal opportunity antagonist, yet none of it was meant to engender ill will.

"Whatever the case, Esme is right. Even so, they must travel through Plowonida, or near it," said Lir, as he lifted another cobnut. He tried to smash it between his teeth, but it would not break, so he cast it away with a look of disgust. "The area is much embattled," he finished. "What chance they were waylaid?"

Málik lifted a cobnut to sniff it. Gwendolyn watched him curiously. "Quite probable," he said. "No matter what Loc believes, the Catuvellauni will not so easily relinquish what they have built. Anyone passing through the area will be vulnerable." He popped the cobnut into his mouth, cracked it easily, then eyed Lir with a lifted brow. However, once he put it into his mouth, he made a face and hacked it back out. Gwendolyn would have laughed if she hadn't remembered his warning...

You'd be wise to note there are few occasions when the goddess' creatures are made without regard to need, Gwendolyn. If you see claws... or fangs... you should run.

Gwendolyn peered from Málik to Esme, then back again, loathing that he was still so much a stranger to her—even after everything they'd endured. In some ways, she was beginning to know Esme better than him! There was so much she still didn't know about Málik. Betimes she felt as though she knew less about him now than ever, and he was never less inclined to share his truth.

And yet, despite Esme's assurances, his relationship with Esme aggrieved her most. Gwendolyn must have conveyed it through a glance, because when she met Málik's eyes, his pupils dilated until they were large enough to swallow the silvery-blue.

Gwendolyn averted her gaze, and he rose from his seat before the fire, and said. "We should rest. Tomorrow's journey will be long."

And then he swiftly departed, wandering again into the woods. By the time he returned during the wee hours, everyone was already abed and asleep... except for Gwendolyn.

She laid there, listening to his footfalls about the campsite, and knew it was him, because she knew his cadence... knew his scent.

She heard him approach her pallet, then halt beside her, but she daren't turn. Lying on her belly, cuddled beneath her borrowed blanket, she peered beneath her lids at the bracken in front of her, and then, after a moment, she sensed he put down an object, and turned away.

After that, it took Gwendolyn a long, long time to rest easy, and even then, she was too acutely aware of his warm Fae body lying so close.

CHAPTER
TWENTY-SIX

It was the arrow Gwendolyn had been carving before their arrival at the Druid village... except... now it was complete... with all the proper fletching.

She blinked at the sight of it.

During her argument with Málik, she'd cast it away, and when she awoke the following morning, his disclosure was still the only thing on her mind. She'd completely forgotten about this.

Did he return last night to search for it?

Nay, because he would have needed time to work on the shaft and create the fletching. Somehow, he must have gone after it that morning before Gwendolyn awoke, or else he'd retrieved it the night of their argument after she fell asleep.

Had he kept it all this time, working to perfect it?

Lifting the arrow to inspect it, Gwendolyn found it perfectly straight now, with no evidence of having been cured over a flame. The tip was fashioned as her father would have done. Intrinsically perfect, except... she didn't have a quiver, nor a bow—not any longer.

Later she would, she vowed, as she folded her

blanket, placing the shaft in the middle before the final roll to keep it secure behind her saddle.

This wasn't precisely a gift—not when she was the one who'd thought to create it. But it felt like one, because Málik had thought well enough to retrieve it, and then, evidently, took some time to create the fletching—no easy task. It was thoughtful of him, Gwendolyn thought, even if it was useless for the time being. Later, she would thank him for it, and perhaps this was his way of making amends? For herself, she desperately wished to find some way to restore their friendship—if not back to where it was before wedding Locrinus, then as close as they could come.

It was entirely possible he was still put out with her for refusing his offer to go away with him, but so it seemed, they were both wronged, because, considering Esme, he never should have asked her. And yet, regardless of their recent discord, he was still the one Gwendolyn trusted most—even more than Bryn, he was also the one she felt inclined to lean upon. In fact, she thought back to her parting with Bryn in the glade. Regardless that she'd understood his reasons for leaving, and it saddened her he'd wished to go, if that had been Málik, she would have been lost. That he was here with her now—whatever the circumstances—gave her hope.

THEY HADN'T GONE FAR down the riverbank when suddenly Málik stole Gwendolyn's reins, leading her into the adjacent woods, straight back to that oak where he'd discovered her. But Gwendolyn's breath caught at what she found there. Directly beside the oak lay a newly dug grave, and atop the grave lay Beryan's shield and sword.

Málik.

He had done this.

When?

Last night?

Swallowing the lump that rose to choke away her breath, she slid down from her mount, and then fell upon her knees by the old warrior's grave, tears swimming in her eyes. She couldn't look at Málik for fear that he would see the naked emotions she couldn't hide.

He must have dragged Beryan out of the river, then buried him...

For her?

Certainly not for Beryan, because he didn't know this man.

Poor, sweet Beryan.

Placing her hand atop the freshly turned soil, she finally cast a backward glance, grateful beyond words. Despite that, for the longest moment, words continued to fail her... neither did she trust her eyes to remain dry, so she averted her gaze again, reaching out to brush her fingers across the flat of Beryan's sword.

This gesture, like the arrow, was quietly done, with no pomp or ceremony. Simply knowing how she'd felt, Málik applied himself to the task, and even now, remained mounted and silent, allowing Gwendolyn time to grieve. She knew without it being told that he didn't even expect her thanks, though she would give it, regardless.

Gods.

He was confusing beyond words.

She sensed he cared for her immensely, but his words never expressed this. And neither was this the same as a tender glance, or a warm embrace... certainly not the same as a kiss... Still, it betrayed some deeper affection... sentiments that words alone could not express.

With a heartfelt sigh, she buried her fingers into the cool, damp soil, closing her eyes, whispering a fervent prayer for this man whose life was lost in defense of her.

No one spoke. No one rushed her. But she knew they could not linger, and when Gwendolyn was finished with her devotions, she turned and said, "Thank you, Málik. This is a kindness I did not expect." He hitched his chin at her, and she added, "I am only surprised they did not take his sword." The shield was clearly ruined—broken in two, so she understood why they'd left that behind. Alas, though, he never even wielded it, so quickly did Loc and his men fall upon them. It was all they could do to ride.

"It was beneath him," Málik explained. "They would not have seen it without moving the body, and clearly, they were in too much of a hurry to bother."

There was no sign of either of their horses, Gwendolyn noted, and no corpse for the dog, but she knew they had been here. Somehow, Málik must have also disposed of them, but she daren't ask how. If he could call upon the forest to embrace her as he had, he could certainly call upon the earth to inter them—or perhaps he'd cast a glamour to conceal them from her eyes, so she wouldn't have to see them. A courtesy she hadn't the means to repay—not yet.

But she would...

Once she could.

"Poor, sweet man," she lamented, wishing there was some way to atone for his death. "I should take the sword," she announced. "If I find his daughter, I will give it to her."

"And the shield?"

"Leave it to mark his grave," Gwendolyn suggested, and Málik did not wait to be commanded. He slid from his mount, came forward to sweep the sword up, then carried it back to his mount, placing it into the empty sheath attached to his saddle.

But, of course, that sheath would be empty. Unless he was sleeping, his own sword never left the harness on his back. He never let it out of his sight.

"When did you do this?" she wondered aloud, peering at him, watching as he secured Beryan's sword, before moving to adjust the cinches on his saddle to account for the new weight.

"Last night," he said matter-of-factly, and, without another word, he swung himself back into his saddle, not bothering to await her leave to go. He clicked his reins and trotted away.

"So that's where he went," said Lir.

Esme said nothing at all, but she cast Gwendolyn a curious glance, before peering after Málik.

TWENTY-SEVEN

All day long, Gwendolyn was acutely aware of the arrow wrapped in her blanket, but no less so of the one who'd returned it to her. In all her life she'd received so few gifts, and this was the first time she'd been given something so unexpected by someone not of her blood, or a close relation. And for no reason at all. Simply because.

As fortunate as she had been, even her dresses and jewels were mostly borrowed from her mother, but this was nothing she would dare complain about after witnessing the penury of others.

Her father had not believed in hoarding riches whilst his vassals went hungry. His standard of sacrifice for others was a bedrock of their customs, and even her father's dukes had lived meagerly compared to Gwendolyn.

Her uncle Cunedda had so easily shared all he had with his neighbors. En finale, he'd given even his life for Gwendolyn, never having been asked.

And her sweet, beautiful cousins, as well. The sisterly joy they'd shared with so much laughter was their greatest treasure, and their belongings amounted to nothing more than a shared comb and several dresses—most of them gifted by Gwendolyn.

Remembering that little girl from the market[1] whose eyes had shone so brightly when Gwendolyn tossed her a coin for her morels—her joy was minuscule compared to the earnest gratitude she'd spied in the mother's eyes. It was the look of a woman who'd been handed a year's worth of meals for her hungry children.

Charity was the way of her people, and her father was a fine example, but he did not pinch coppers for the city or its people. Gwendolyn, too, had been taught this principle of self-discipline, and anything she'd owned were things she'd needed and used—a horse, a dress, a sword, a comb, a pair of good slippers, and a good pair of boots and leathers for hunting and sparring.

Indeed, this was what had upset her so much about her mother—Queen Eseld's obsession with the *dawnsio*, her dresses and her station. And perhaps that was only fitting she should be that way. Along with the Druids, the *dawnsio*, Awenydds and Gwyddons all served important roles for the kingdom—as priests, historians, philosophers, and scientists. They continued an ancient tradition, teaching epochs of history through a choreographed dance. But it was only now that Gwendolyn understood something about her mother that wasn't clear to her before— that her need to belong was as great as Gwendolyn's need to be known. And it was only after seeing what true rapacity and affectation looked like—through Estrildis—that she'd understood the difference.

Not even Queen Innogen had been so pretentious or grasping, although her greed was certainly farther reaching. Unlike Estrildis, who appeared to want *things*, Queen Innogen wanted something far less tangible. She wanted power. In all Gwendolyn's time at the palace, not once had Loc's mother ever concerned herself with Gwendolyn's stolen belongings. Estrildis had claimed them all and Queen Innogen seemed pleased enough to allow her son's mistress the distraction.

As for Brutus, he was never so fastidious as his son.

Gwendolyn remembered his state of dress when he'd arrived for her Promise Ceremony—boorish and foul-smelling, although she'd excused him for his travels.

Conversely, his son had left her waiting for hours and hours while he'd pandered to himself, but, at the time, Gwendolyn had considered it a gesture of his care. It was only after seeing where he'd lived all his life that she suspected how much he'd resented his father's frugality, and she sensed he must have secretly coveted Gwendolyn's home and life—luxurious in comparison.

Indeed, it wasn't until arriving in Loegria that Gwendolyn had witnessed true privation—the very squalor his people endured.

But now her thoughts returned to the bow Adwen had given her...

How odd that two of the three most random gifts she'd ever received were so connected—a bow and an arrow. Perhaps she should have aspired to archery?

Certainly she could fight as well as any man, but her archery was nowhere near her swordplay and her swordplay was nowhere near her equestrian skills. Still, she was quite good with a sword—good enough that she'd often bested Bryn. Good enough that her father decided her teacher needed a teacher—and thus entered Málik. At least, Gwendolyn had believed that was the reason.

She remembered the first time she'd ever defeated Bryn. He'd commemorated the feat by giving her a cornflower. Gwendolyn placed it on her windowsill, and every morning, the sun would shine past the blossom, casting its bristly shadow against her bedroom wall. Thereafter, she'd woken for weeks, feeling anew the glow of Bryn's gift—until her mother discovered that flower on the windowsill, and plucked it off, admonishing the maids to better clean her filthy room.

Gwendolyn had wanted so much to explain that it was a gift from Bryn, a reward for her accomplishments. But she knew in her heart that Queen Eseld would have mistaken it for something else. In retrospect, Gwendolyn understood that her mother was trying to protect her and doubtless, she'd feared Gwendolyn would lose her heart to the Mester's son.

That would never have happened, because even as a wee child, Gwendolyn had understood her duty. And so, she'd believed, she knew better than to allow her heart to wander to such places. Bryn was only ever her friend, and nothing more. But she'd been naïve, because she'd long suspected that he'd harbored some small affection for her, despite that he would never disrespect her by saying so. He knew she could not forget her duties, nor allow herself to be thwarted by misadventures of the heart. But perhaps she had been blind to his feelings and perhaps she had expected too much of him—to accept the futility of one's heart's desire. Gwendolyn must confess... it hurt.

A glance in Málik's direction found him watching her again, though he averted his gaze when she looked his way.

Alas, so mindfully guarding her heart against Bryn, and despite having kept her wits about her so many years, Gwendolyn somehow lost her heart to a damnable fae. And, as certainly as it was for Bryn, Málik's heart was already promised to another.

Esme.

Even though, clearly, she didn't feel the same for him.

Gwendolyn had consoled herself that she'd not encouraged Bryn's affections, but neither had Málik encouraged hers. From the start, he'd worn that same mask of insouciance Esme now wore, and if Gwendolyn could be honest with herself, it was she who'd first coveted Málik. She'd thought him utterly magnificent, and she'd loathed the fact that he'd judged her—loathed it so much that she'd set about to prove herself to him, at first, needling him every chance she got.

All those months whilst he'd practiced in the Mester's Pavilion with Bryn... Gwendolyn had spied on them from the ramparts... jealous, though not of Málik for stealing Bryn's attention, as she'd once told herself. She was envious of Bryn... for the friendship those two so easily engendered.

And meanwhile, Málik seemed to have had nothing but contempt for Gwendolyn. It had sorely vexed her. She'd marched by in a pique nearly every day, dragging Bryn away when she dared.

But, if anyone was to blame, it should be her father for pushing them together because, until he'd made him her Shadow, Gwendolyn had kept him at bay with the flimsiest of excuses. It was only thereafter that she'd succumbed, and though she'd raged over that turn of events, she'd also secretly rejoiced in it as well—that she would have a perfect excuse to face him every day.

As for that stupid investigation after the death of Alderman Bryok—the need to find and speak with his wife, Ia, to satisfy her own curiosity about unanswered questions—Gwendolyn sighed. She would like to believe she'd had some great intuition where that was concerned, and perhaps she had, but the true reason she'd dragged Málik away from Trevena was to have him alone, to herself... away from all her mother's spies....

Away from Ely as well.

And yet, for all that, even knowing where it would lead and how she would feel, Gwendolyn had no regrets. For a while, she and Málik had enjoyed one another's company, and she had selfishly wanted to create a few memories, needing something of her own to keep for all time... something not contrived by her mother or mandated by duty.

Conversely, she had not liked Locrinus from the very first day she'd spent in his company—self-aggrandizing, mean-tempered, brute—and her loathing for him had somehow opened the door for... something else. Something she daren't confess even now.

Málik peered over his shoulder, wheeling his horse about, his wintry eyes impaling Gwendolyn and her heart leapt into her throat as he paused, waiting for her to catch up, his eyes fixed upon her. He was looking straight at her, though Esme and Lir also rode ahead of Gwendolyn, both still bandying words. When they passed Málik by, Esme gave him a finger—a crude gesture in a manner she'd witnessed with Locrinus' guards. It embodied the phallus, with the fingers beside the middle finger marking the testicles. Esme laughed when he rolled his eyes and shook his head at her.

"What was that about?" Gwendolyn asked.

"Esme being Esme. She needs no reason," he said.

Gwendolyn did not know whether to laugh or weep because, whatever else it might be, the gesture was immensely intimate. She wished she could ask him directly what he felt for Esme, but she couldn't. The words rose as far as her throat and then stuck there.

"At this pace, we'll be in Catuvellauni territory by morning," he said, once again sidling up beside her. "There's no surety of what we may encounter there. I warrant the Catuvellauni are licking their wounds after their recent losses, but they might have gone south, or they could well have retreated into these northern woods. I would advise we should stop early to regroup... and perhaps spar?"

"You and I?"

He tilted her a questioning glance. "Unless you are afraid you've forgotten how to fight?"

Gwendolyn laughed. "Hardly," she said, and didn't bother revealing how hard she'd practiced with her whittled stick. He didn't need to know that. She arched a brow. "Must we practice for my sake?" she asked. "Or yours?"

"For his sake," he said, pointing to Lir. "He might well be a skilled healer, but what good will that do us if he is dead?"

Gwendolyn laughed again. "True," she said, flicking a glance at the sword at Málik's back, remembering all that Esme had told her about it. Only now she understood why he'd chosen that sword over the Sword of Light. It was arguably more precious.

"A little more practice will do us all good," he suggested. "Even Esme, no matter that she would never admit to it. Once we are faced with battle, it will be too late."

It had been months since Gwendolyn had practiced with an actual sword, and longer since she'd practiced with Málik. "I'd like that," she said, and meant it.

And then he went and spoiled everything by saying the worst thing he could have said to her. "I warrant your *husband* will stop at little to find you. I do hope you realize it's only a matter of time before we face him, Gwendolyn. We are not prepared—none of us."

She might have agreed, but her tone was icy. "Please, do not refer to him that way." It was perhaps a testament to how much she loathed Locrinus that she was far more upset with Málik's reference of him as her husband than she was over the prospect of facing Loc and all his armies in battle.

"I would say I warned you against that wedding, but I realize that would be unkind."

She lifted a brow. "And yet you just have."

"Have I?" he said, offhand, his silver eyes glinting with a measure of good humor, although Gwendolyn was hardly amused.

"Must you always be so churlish? Is this why Esme rebuffed you?"

Both his brows lifted now. "Did she tell you that?"

229

"Nay. She didn't have to," Gwendolyn said, sensing she must have hit close to the mark because his expression changed, and he cast Esme a narrow-eyed glance.

"She's really quite beautiful," Gwendolyn allowed, and meant it, though it wasn't said with the most charitable spirit.

"That she is," he said.

Gwendolyn straightened her spine. "You would be blessed to have her by your side."

"Would I?"

Gods. She knew what she was doing, but she couldn't stop herself, even knowing that such manipulations, subtle or elsewise, would never work with Málik. He was far too clever, and yet all she really wanted was to hear him deny his affection for Esme.

"She is, indeed, quite lovely," he agreed.

Her traitorous eyes burned to hear the sincerity in his words, but she fought her tears, refusing to dishonor herself any more than she had already.

"And yet," he said, vacillating. "Do not allow her ostensive good nature to fool you, Gwendolyn. She's as dangerous as a viper, and just as swift in her vengeance."

Gwendolyn turned to look at him to find that all traces of his smile had vanished. "Is she?"

He nodded before hitching his chin at the riders ahead. "Mark my words. Lir will learn his place in good time... unless he somehow weasels his way into her good graces—and perhaps he will. She has a soft spot for the young ones."

Gwendolyn steeled herself for his answer. "Art jealous?"

"Me?" He laughed quickly, the sound bitter, his

lips settling once more into some semblance of a smile. "What do you believe, Gwendolyn?"

"I think you are insufferable," she said. And he was. "But I should thank you for the gift of my arrow before I am compelled not to because of your delightful wit."

"You are welcome," he said, smiling, but not with his mouth. She could see the twinkle in his eyes.

"And for Beryan," she added, peering down at the longsword strapped to his saddle. "Thank you mostly for that. He was a good man."

Málik's gaze sought and found hers, held it, his eyes softening to a pale shade of winter. "I did not know him," he said. "And yet... anyone who fought to defend you merits my gratitude and service."

"Thank... you," Gwendolyn said awkwardly, but her fingers tightened on her reins as firmly as did her resolve. She was pleased by their truce, but she could not afford to allow herself to soften any more.

Your greatest love must be this land, Emrys had said. *Your joy begot by its stewardship*. He was right. She must not allow herself to be distracted by Málik anymore than she was.

---

1. In book one, Gwendolyn met a young child walking with her mother. They were on the way to the market to sell morels. Gwendolyn gave her a gold coin.

TWENTY-EIGHT

With less than three bells of sunlight remaining, they halted to water the horses. Weary and peckish, Gwendolyn dismounted and slumped to her knees next to a dwindling *bourne*.

She still had some hob cake in her pouch, but knowing they meant to stop early, she was saving her appetite for supper, and the hob cake and salted meats for tomorrow's travels. Only now, enervated and tetchy, she was rethinking the wisdom of that decision.

Not trusting the stale *bourne* water for consumption, she splashed a bit on her face, unsettled to find the temperature was warmer than her heated flesh.

Unfortunately, despite that the black mithril was perfectly fitted for her body, it also absorbed the sun's rays, trapping too much heat beneath the armor, making her sweat profusely and robbing her of energy so much that she considered taking a small bite of her hob cake. She'd had none since her three-day nap and was wary of it now.

Turning to find Lir marching her way, she decided that he, too, was worse for the wear, his face mottled, his dark hair dripping with sweat.

Gwendolyn felt terrible for him, certain that his role as a healer and seven hundred years in seclusion had ill-prepared him for the discomfort of travel in the heat of Pretania's summers.

However, on the bright side, he must be quite well accustomed to an empty belly, judging by that pookie broth they'd fed her at supper.

Peering down into the water at her own reflection, she grimaced at her disheveled appearance. It wasn't so much that she cared for her own sake. Though perhaps she'd been too hasty to dismiss her appearance if she intended to win any favors. None of those tribes would care to follow a weakling child, and though she wasn't a child any longer, that wasn't apparent simply at a glance. Even though her curls had grown so much since Locrinus butchered them, her hair was still too short and uneven. Even with her recent bath, it was unruly, making her look like a dirty little boy.

Red-faced and clearly spent, Lir walked past her through the shallow stream with his horse in tow, only to kneel on the opposite bank, facing Gwendolyn, leaving Sheahan to drink by his side. Over the course of the day, Esme had worn him out.

There, he too quietly refreshed himself, every now and again, his gaze seeking Esme—perhaps because he liked her, or perhaps because he didn't. Both possibilities were entirely conceivable.

Whatever the case, the horse Esme had chosen for him suited him well. Judging by his enduring patience under Esme's relentless goading, he was as peace-loving a man as was ever begot. Even now, saddle worn and red-faced, he didn't complain.

As for Esme... Málik's warning still rang in her ears—in part because Gwendolyn couldn't get a feel for the Faerie's true intentions. Sometimes it seemed she could be Gwendolyn's dearest of friends, and sometimes... well, Gwendolyn wasn't so certain.

There was something about the glimmer in Esme's eyes that made Gwendolyn wonder—sometimes appearing to be simple delight, other times... something more.

Only time would tell.

Meanwhile, Gwendolyn's belly grumbled and Esme must have heard it as well because she, too, complained as she knelt beside Gwendolyn. "He's going to kill us," she said.

Gwendolyn needn't ask who; she knew.

Málik's mood was as mercurial as Esme's. He had driven them ruthlessly all day long, stopping only when the horses needed respite—which was scarcely ever. "I've a bit of hob cake left," Gwendolyn offered. "'Tis yours if you'd like it?"

Esme scoffed, twisting her face. "Hob cake?" she said, shaking her head adamantly. "Gods, nay! I've had enough ambrosia to last a thousand lifetimes. Really, Gwendolyn!" she said, lifting a brow. "That is what we were forced to make-do with during our confinement. If I never suffer another bite, I should be quite content." And then her eyes narrowed, and she tilted her head. "I wonder though... you do know those tales are all true?"

"What tales?" Gwendolyn asked, confused.

Esme grinned then, proudly displaying her por-beagle teeth. "Well," she said, with a feral gleam in her eyes, flicking a quick glance at Lir, saying loudly enough for him to overhear. "Some of us *do* eat babies."

Gwendolyn's brows collided. "Babies?" She hadn't the first notion where that came from—perhaps another argument between Esme and Lir. But despite that Gwendolyn had heard those stories, they were always so disingenuously told, and she'd never truly believed them.

"The younger the better!" Esme declared, before splashing her face, and then she said, "Fret not, Dragon Queen. I prefer my meals to run on all fours."

She tittered then, and rose, drifting away, leaving Gwendolyn with the disturbing vision of a horde of *Fae*, all with sharp fangs, mauling wee babes. Horrified by the thought, she peered at Lir, and the Druid lifted a shoulder, shrugging at her unspoken question. But if he believed Esme, he didn't appear the least bit concerned. What was the purpose of that? Gwendolyn wondered. Did Esme not wish for Gwendolyn to rest easy in her company? Or was it she didn't want Gwendolyn to trust Málik? "Argh," she said, considering that she'd once kissed Málik with that mouth.

She'd looked straight into his too familiar eyes, imagining him no worse than men who dined so greedily on roasted pig... yet perhaps he was worse?

Glancing over her shoulder, she found him brushing his mare's hindquarters, but his attention was now fixed upon Esme, watching her as she returned from the stream. When she neared, he hissed something beneath his breath, and Esme returned the exchange, marching by to see to her mount as it grazed. There really was something between those two... something Gwendolyn couldn't precisely resolve... something beyond the obvious.

Gwendolyn sensed Málik would never betray her... but then again... trust was not something she could afford to give so freely—and this was a lesson hard learned.

Even with Málik, she'd be wise to keep her wits about her—especially with Málik.

HEARTILY RELIEVED to find that Málik appeared to have forgotten their date to spar, Gwendolyn abandoned Lir to his foraging and went to retrieve her blanket from the rear of her mount.

Much as she needed practice, she was thoroughly exhausted, with too much on her mind, and it didn't matter what Málik returned with for victuals. She would be content enough to nibble on hob cake and pass out.

She found a good spot close to the campfire, still far enough away that she could rest out of the path of trampling feet, and then bent to roll out her pallet.

After departing yestermorn without breaking their fast, and last night's meager repast, then a full day of travel with little sustenance, she was bone-tired and preparing for bed before sundown.

The pinewoods were thinning now, interspersed with sprawling elms and oaks. By early tomorrow morning, they would cross into Catuvellauni territory, and this filled her with dread.

For one, no matter how fierce Esme and Málik might be, they were still only two Fae, accompanied by a Druid healer. And regardless that Gwendolyn felt certain she could fend for herself, the Catuvellauni were much like the Iceni, fiercely territorial and jealous, and if they caught her under these circumstances, her name would curry no favor. They might not return her to Loc, but they could well finish what he'd started.

At the beginning of her father's reign, Dumnonii lands had consisted only of Cornwall proper. Eventually, they'd stretched from Land's End to the Wrikon in Cornovia, including Durotriges.

Before assuming the throne, her father had won himself a reputation as a brutal commander, and many had considered him over-reaching. His marriage to a Prydein daughter, though it gentled the northern tribes, engendered little confidence.

Until her father arrogated Durotriges and Cornovia, no tribe had ever even considered uniting banners. That he did not force them did not actually matter to the Catuvellauni, who considered this aggressive expansion a threat to the Brothers' Pact—if not in fact, then certainly in spirit.

There were a number of laws drawn by the sons of Míl after the defeat of the Tuatha Dé Danann, but this was the First Law: No tribe of Pretania could occupy lands not their own, without a sanctioned alliance. It would be one thing to append a tribe, but not since the Brothers' Pact had any chieftain defied that law. If Locrinus succeeded, he would be the first to disregard the Pact in more than a thousand years.

This was why Plowonida remained abandoned. No tribe would stand by and allow another king with his armies to march in and take lands belonging to another.

However, as a matter of course, after the annexation of Durotriges and Cornovia, the Catuvellauni and Iceni both began similar campaigns to annex Cantium and Trinovantes, citing their own right of blood to rule.

That was when the trouble began, compelling her father to ally with Brutus in hopes that a more united front in the west would quiet the discord in the east. For a while, that worked.

Eventually, both the Catuvellauni and Iceni sent ambassadors and *dawnsio* students to Trevena, but only on the condition that their tribes be recognized as sovereign states of equal bearing with Trevena and their sovereigns as kings—which, of course, her father was quick to agree to, because there was already such fierce infighting betwixt those eastern tribes and he did not care to inherit their strife. But then, Cantium, which was traditionally allied with the Catuvellauni, gave a younger daughter to be wed to the Iceni king, uniting both tribes by marriage. In retaliation, the Catuvellauni chieftain turned about and kidnapped the Iceni king's bride, igniting a years-long feud, which culminated with the recent attack on Plowonida.

Málik was right: After this recent loss, the Catuvellauni would be on high alert, guarding their borders, fully prepared to defend them. But there was little love lost between Caradoc, the Catuvellauni chieftain, and Cornwall. His compassion over her father's death would go only so far, and if they'd caught

Bryn and Ely en route to the Iceni, they might take this as a sign of Gwendolyn's favor for the enemy.

It would not bode well.

Gwendolyn pored over this as she rolled out her pallet, hoping that somehow Ely and Bryn would evade the Catuvellauni.

Their capitol might be difficult to avoid because of its central location, but as far as Gwendolyn knew, Plowonida still sat unoccupied, and she dearly hoped that Caradoc had drawn his men south, closer to the Dobunni border, near the Cod's Wold, where the Iceni would be more reluctant to seek them.

Whatever the case, she had so much work ahead of her if she meant to unite any of these tribes, and her greatest chance lay in her hope that the three Cornish tribes might still be turned if they could simply oust Locrinus from their territories.

And perhaps with some luck, Atrebates as well.

Locrinus might not yet be strong enough to hold both Loegria and Trevena, much less take and hold Plowonida, but he was getting close.

According to his own words, he'd won allegiances from eight of Pretania's twenty-one tribes, which left her with terrible odds, considering that seven of those remaining were Prydein, and the other six included the Brigantes, who never took sides. But also the Iceni and Catuvellauni, who both hated one another as much as they mistrusted Cornwall.

However, Prydein accounted for a third of this isle. If she could but convince her grandfather, Baugh, to ally with her, and if she could then convince the Iceni... those tribes alone would make up for the eight Locrinus had already won.

Even before Locrinus, the Iceni had come close to

Cornwall's might, particularly now, allied with Cantium and Trinovantes. Add to that their association with the Parisi to the north, and they were now the third largest confederacy on these isles.

Somehow, she must convince the Iceni king to ally with her. However, just because they had once halfheartedly joined her father's alliance, did not mean they would do so again. Nor would they so hastily embrace her father's heir, especially whilst she was still wed to Locrinus. Even so, the Iceni must be her primary goal right now. Negotiations like these were a delicate matter; fortunately, she had witnessed enough failure from her father's aldermen to know that there was a critical order of progress to be undertaken, else all negotiations would fail.

For instance, if she went first to the Caradoc, she feared the Iceni would take offense, and if she went first to the Iceni, the reverse would be true. But if she went to the Iceni, Cantium and Trinovantes would follow, and perhaps Parisi as well. The more allies she amassed, the better it would all go. Eventually, Caradoc and his warriors would have to choose a side. Gwendolyn hoped it would be hers, though she had better work quickly if Albanactus had already turned his sights to the north, because if Prydein fell to Albanactus, or allied with Locrinus, all hope would be lost.

At this point, it would be impossible to wrest the four tribes of Westwalas from Loc's control. It would have been far better if her father had never given him those lands, but that was water long gone under the bridge, and there was nothing anyone could do about that.

Completely fagged, Gwendolyn closed her eyes

for a moment, inhaling a breath. There was too much to be done, and she didn't know where to begin. Needing to see to her mount, she lifted a knee, not entirely certain she could follow it with the other.

"On your toes," she heard Málik command, and Gwendolyn rolled her eyes, exasperated that he would choose this very moment to engage her. She was about to turn and tell him nay, but his demand was followed by the hiss of metal leaving his scabbard.

She peered up in time to see the raised sword. He didn't offer a moment to consider, bringing it down unerringly, straight into the spot where Gwendolyn had been kneeling.

Moving intuitively, Gwendolyn hurled herself out of the sword's path, rolling over a sharp branch, and crying out in pain. Quickly, she bounded to her feet, rushing for her sword.

Stupid, stupid!

She was unprepared.

She should have known Málik would test her.

It was too uncomfortable riding with her sword in the scabbard at her waist, so she'd opted to leave it in the saddle sheath. Of course, Málik wore his behind his back, and he'd withdrawn it so easily, wielding it deftly. Irritated beyond measure, Gwendolyn seized her sword, then rapped Aisling on the rear, sending the mare out of harm's way as she turned to face Málik with her sword drawn.

Esme and Lir drifted over to watch—Esme with a delighted gleam in her now smokey eyes.

"I am not ready," Gwendolyn complained, keeping her eyes on Málik's sword.

"You'll never be entirely prepared."

"But I am weak from lack of sustenance," she argued.

"And whose fault is that? Do you think Caradoc will give you the courtesy of a warning?"

Gwendolyn frowned. Damn him. He was right, of course.

Moreover, he had warned her, giving her ample time to prepare.

She fought the urge to strike first in anger, knowing that, in her present position, it would send her into a spin. For the moment, he was too far out of her reach, and too nimble. With this new sword, both their swords were now of equal length and Gwendolyn no longer had the advantage of reach.

"Make use of the grip for leverage," he reminded her, and then, without giving her time to adjust, he rushed her. Gritting her teeth, Gwendolyn withheld her swing, sensing her feet were still positioned all wrong.

Blood and bones.

It had been too long.

She knew intuitively when to strike and when not to, but Málik was faster than any opponent she'd ever sparred with, and the weight of her new sword was unfamiliar.

He said nothing, only smiled, and it was hardly reassuring—particularly after Esme's gruesome revelation about supping on babes.

"Why did you not tell me you ate children?" she hurled at him, hoping to unnerve him, wielding her words as ruthlessly as she knew she must her sword. "If I'd known, I'd never—"

Lacking the confidence to advance properly, her energy too much spent taunting him, she stupidly stepped sideways, trying to find better footing. He grinned, seizing the advantage, stalking her. "Never what?" he asked, his question as vicious as the sharp edge of his sword.

Gwendolyn's cheeks burned.

Never have kissed him, forsooth!

Never have loved him!

But she didn't want to say.

"I warned you the goddess arms her creatures, accordingly, did I not?"

"Oh, indeed, you did." Gwendolyn parried, trying to regain her aplomb as he circled her, slowly closing the distance between them. "Yet I did not figure you for a child eater."

His smile drew back over his teeth before he answered. "I do *not* eat children," he said definitively. "And neither does Esme, though I'm certain she delights in having you believe it."

The soft titter of laughter confirmed this announcement, and Gwendolyn felt herself grow flustered. "You know me well enough," he said, still circling her.

"So it appears I know you not at all."

His eyes glinted. "Trust your instincts," he said, and Gwendolyn took this time to reposition her hands as he added, "Keep your eyes on *my* sword. Raise the pommel, pull back as you thrust. Control your emotions, Gwendolyn."

The glimmer in his eyes was too unnerving. Gwendolyn knew he was trying to help her, but, for a paralyzing moment, as she stared at him, all her fears came rushing to the surface, crippling her thoughts as inexorably as they did her limbs. Her heart beat faster and faster, noting the predatory gleam in his eyes—and that too wicked smile.

Remembering the first night they'd spent in these woods after his return, something about the look in his eyes thoroughly unsettled her. *I cannot change my actions,* he'd said. *Nor do I wish to. I know what you want, I cannot give it.*

Why was he here? she asked herself again. Why had he returned, if not to stand by her side? Why must she long so desperately for something that could never be?

She swung, crying out in frustration when the effort displaced her and she spun about without intending to—like a fledgling swordswoman. Málik gave no quarter. He caught her easily, turning her about and putting the sharp edge of his blade against her throat.

"You put too much hip into your cut," he admonished, holding his cold steel to her throat, embracing her from behind so she could feel every flex of his sinew. "You are *dead*," he whispered, and Gwendolyn frowned.

"I told you I was unprepared."

His warm breath tickled the back of her ear. "And I ask you again, do you believe Loc's men will allow you the courtesy to prepare?"

His blade remained dangerously close to the flesh of her throat—close enough that she could feel the cool kiss of steel. If she moved but a fraction of an inch, the sharp edge would draw blood.

Knowing he spoke true, Gwendolyn carefully shook her head, and meanwhile her hand reached up to draw away his hilt, giving herself room to breathe and finally pulling the blade's edge free of her neck.

Only then his lips moved closer until she could feel them brushing against her lobe. "Now tell me... what is it you'd never do again?"

Kiss him, she had been about to say.

She would never again kiss him.

Or love him.

Both answers danced on the tip of her tongue, with the overwhelming desire to be spoken, and without truly intending to she opened her mouth to speak. It was only the prick of Málik's blade that stopped her.

That sword. Remembering Esme's disclosure— that no lies could be told with the sword at her throat, she prayed he'd not ask her again, because if he did, she might not hold back the words.

Even now, they longed to be spoken...

"It is true, Gwendolyn," Málik whispered. "I am a predator. So is Esme, but if she has taunted you with such an ill-favored truth, it is only so you'll remember: nothing is as it seems."

Gwendolyn could smell him so near, his scent too intoxicating.

Never mind the sting of his blade, he pressed those hot lips against her flushed, sweat-dampened cheek, lingering an instant too long before dipping his head and parting his lips to nip one cold, sharp fang against the tender part of her throat. And then she couldn't focus, her thoughts blurring, even as his blade continued to kiss her so coldly. She longed to turn around... fling herself into his arms.

And then he spoke again, lifting the fog in her brain.

"Esme lies, though she did not lie about this, Gwendolyn... I, too, smell desire," he said, and her cheeks flushed. Blinking away all remaining confusion, she reared back, planting the heel of her boot over his knee. And then she wrested herself free, sliding away to glare at him.

Vexed, but not with Málik—feeling vulnerable, and not simply because he'd caught her unawares, and nearly forced her to confess her heart's desires—she spun about, marching away.

His dark chuckle pursued her.

CHAPTER TWENTY-NINE

Málik quite bemused her.

She was undone by his teasing—if he didn't want her, why did he seem so intent upon trifling with her? Or, perhaps it wasn't flirtation, and it was all in her imagination, and she was doomed to mistake his every gesture, wishing it meant something more than it did.

That night, again, she had trouble sleeping. Was it any wonder?

She lay brooding over the day's unpleasantness. Although for all the rudeness of Málik's lesson, his words struck true to their mark—so much so that when she'd crawled atop her pallet, she went dragging her new sword. She kept it close thereafter, with the hilt cradled in her palm, ready to wield if she must.

War was not convenient. A surprise attack could happen at any moment. She had learned this in her training, and yet, it was one thing to know it and another to experience it.

Her people had too long been at peace, spoiled by the knowledge that, together with the Kingdom of

247

Loegria, they were unmatched amidst the island's tribes.

In the peak of their alliance, not even the Prydein had been a match for them, although, in truth, no one knew what strength lay in a united confederacy. Those northern tribes were only weaker because they were such a multitude of clans loosely governed by the Seven.

No doubt Locrinus meant to engage them, but *how* was the question... would he woo them as allies, or face them as foes?

And if he pursued an alliance, would her grandfather agree to it? There was no surety that the Prydein king would show loyalty to a granddaughter he'd never met.

Random thoughts hammered through her weary brain, all of them demanding answers, none of them producing any.

Peace was not Loc's ultimate ambition, but he would say or do anything to move his game pieces across the board that was Pretania. He would ally himself with Prydein, lie to the Druids, promise the moon... but he would be satisfied with nothing less than annihilation.

She knew him well enough to know that by now.

And she was fairly certain she understood why he'd returned to Loegria, even after that city was taken, despite his contempt for his father's achievements. He could endure nothing that reminded him of Gwendolyn's worth. That's why, even before he'd revealed his true self, he was already boasting about future conquests, setting his sights on the taking of Plowonida, instead of contenting himself knowing that someday he would rule both Loegria and

Trevena, with a doting queen by his side—Gwendolyn before she'd understood what a villain he was.

And now, he would rape her beloved city, and leave it to ruin, and he would take his ill-earned rewards to his precious Troia Nova to start anew, with nothing to remind him of the people and places he'd destroyed to achieve his dreams.

Gwendolyn didn't know yet what to do to stop him, but she knew it must be done.

Now, if Bryn and Ely revealed Loc's intentions to the Iceni, would they take Plowonida for themselves? Defy the Brothers' Pact? Had Gwendolyn done the Catuvellauni a disservice?

Gods. It was not so easy to lead and now she understood why her father was so often prickly about her studies and her training, even before he'd grown so ill.

Tomorrow, she would begin afresh by practicing with her sword, even in the saddle, become accustomed to its weight and feel, until it felt like an extension of her person.

The enemy would not care whether she was distracted, or whether she ate, or didn't eat, nor whether she felt weak, or sick, or tired. Every decision she made henceforth must be wiser, more thoughtful, designed, not solely for the moment, or for the future, but with all things in mind.

In like fashion, Trevena had prepared for every circumstance, save one. Her grandfather had built that city on a stone isle, attached to the mainland by the narrowest of bridges. It was protected on all sides by natural defenses, and still he had erected two inner-city walls, just in case men escaped their archers. Towers were also appointed at intervals, not merely overlooking the harbor and bridge—the two most vulnerable locations—but the cliff side, as well, in case they were attacked by men who could scale those cliffs. There were a multitude of precautions in place, and this, despite that her people had been so long at peace... but those defenses had meant nothing in the end. They were infiltrated; the city overtaken by Loc's treachery. They'd found a peaceful way in through those gates and vanquished Trevena from within.

She needed to be prepared. She needed to practice every chance she got, even during their travels. And she must remain prepared, and if she was not, she would fail—not only Ely and Bryn, but Trevena as well.

And yet, right now, at this moment, she loathed *he* was right yet again—loathed even more that she had so swiftly turned her thoughts from the bite of his sword to the bite of his teeth.

Gods. As much as she would like to believe her heart had hardened against him... and much as she wished to honor his ties to Esme... she was too easily undone despite her best intentions.

Tomorrow, she swore she would keep her wits about her. And in the meantime, she would be good for little if she didn't get some rest...

Blinking against the dark night, she suddenly realized there was no sign of Málik's Faerie flame. It was gone.

The only visible light came from slivers of moonlight where it sluiced through the canopy of trees. Once again, she had been too distracted to notice, and Málik and Esme were gone.

Were they out there... *together? Embracing? Kissing?*

Gwendolyn daren't confess how much that notion aggrieved her.

Without intending to, she rose to search the camp, blade in hand. Lir was still sound asleep under his woolen blanket. The fire hadn't been kindled in hours. Burnt to embers, it faded against the chill of the night. But, suddenly, she heard a snap, and the distant murmur of voices, and instinctively, Gwendolyn slid behind an oak to listen...

The voices came closer and her brow furrowed. It didn't sound like Málik and Esme... nor was it the sound of lovers coupling... or even arguing.

She turned to peer at the horses and found them prancing nervously.

Gwendolyn moved swiftly to where Lir slept, shaking him awake, grateful at least that her tilt with Málik had left her sleeping so lightly. She pressed her free hand over his mouth to keep him from speaking. His sleepy gaze met hers, focusing on her face, and Gwendolyn lifted a finger to her lips, then tugged him up, urging him to his feet, and shoving him behind her.

If she was so unready, Lir wouldn't last long.

As best as she could, she would defend him until she could not, and hopefully, Málik and Esme would cease their cavorting and return to help defend them. "Shhh," she said, but then she blinked, spying Málik's silver hair glinting beneath his Faerie fire.

Esme came quick at his heels—no sword drawn, despite that they were followed by men on horseback. Confused, but no longer alarmed, Gwendolyn exhaled a breath she'd not realized she'd held as the thicket parted to reveal visitors—three strangers, traveling with four horses, one saddle empty, one dragging a litter. Málik was the first to step into the glade, followed by Esme, and then came the lead rider behind them. But it wasn't until Gwendolyn moved closer that she realized it was a young woman in the saddle—her red hair thickly plaited.

"I come seeking my father," she announced. "In return, I have brought you a son of Trevena."

"Father?" Gwendolyn asked, confused.

The woman lifted her chin, her dark eyes glinting against a shaft of moonlight.

Esme turned to Málik, and Málik fixed his gaze upon Gwendolyn.

"My name is Taryn," announced the stranger. "In my litter I've Bryn Durotriges."

It was only then that Gwendolyn's gaze found Jago's, recognizing him from her rescue party. And then, slowly, her gaze fell upon the litter strapped to his mount.

THIRTY

T hey settled near the fire, rekindling it to keep
Bryn warm.

As they spoke, Lir tended his wounds—
the most critical being a blood-and-filth-encrusted
gash below his ribs. His body was feverish, yet his
lungs were strong—evidenced by the wail he emitted
when Lir dug into the wound to extract a bit of detritus. The blow had missed vital organs, but there was
bruising at the temple where the backside of a war
hammer had pummeled his head. This was perhaps
the injury Lir felt certain was keeping him insensate.

Taryn explained that, as yet he'd not opened his
eyes, and Gwendolyn sat dutifully on one side of
Bryn's litter, clutching his cold hand, fearing he might
not make it through the night.

Seated by the fire, next to a man called Ives, Jago
tugged up a weed, rendering it in two, his fury and
grief both notable in the tic of his jaw. "They attacked
as we were evacuating the women and children," he
said.

Loc. So quickly he'd moved upon Durotriges.

He must have gone straight from the search for

253

Gwendolyn to take his fury out on the people he deemed responsible for her escape. That, else he had dispatched a part of his army straight to the village while he pursued his search for her. Either way, Gwendolyn wondered if Queen Innogen cared that he'd undermined her efforts. After all, why attack a village that was already promised?

"Of course they would," interjected Taryn, casting an angry glance at Jago. "We should have begun the process long before Adwen surrendered our village!"

Jago did not meet her gaze. He said quietly, "We did not know we would be presented such an opportunity." But Taryn's face remained a mask of fury.

"Opportunity?" she countered furiously, and it was clear to Gwendolyn that she must have tempered her outrage to save it for this moment.

"To free the Queen," Jago explained.

Taryn's gaze moved warily to Gwendolyn, but that didn't prevent her from speaking her mind. "Yet you attended the feast for that very purpose. What did you believe would come of it?" Jago said nothing, merely shook his head, and Taryn continued. "It would have been far wiser to call for an evacuation *before* you left, not *after* you returned, when it was already too late."

In the answering silence, tensions mounted.

"And regardless, Jago, what I am most furious over is that you sent my aging father to defend our queen—the eldest of our warriors. You should have gone in his stead!"

"We believed—because she gave us her word— no harm would befall our village, and as for your father, he's the one who volunteered. Would you have me disrespect the man by questioning his compe-

tence? Your father wielded a sword before I learned
not to piss down my own legs."

"But that is the point," argued Taryn.

"Now is not the time for quarrels," interjected
Esme, who, till now, had remained silent, only
listening.

They'd happened upon the small party in the
woods as Esme and Málik were scouting the area,
concerned about Catuvellauni. The three had arrived
bloodied, battered, and glum. Clearly, Taryn blamed
Jago for this travesty, but it was not his fault.

"I must take full responsibility," Gwendolyn interjected. "I sent Jago with Adwen to secure your village, believing myself capable of fighting beside your
father."

There was more to it, of course, but she didn't
wish to say that she'd also sent Bryn away to keep Ely
safe, knowing that Loc and his men would pursue her
with Beryan. She swallowed her guilt, remembering
the scarf she'd dropped to lure their pursuers away
from the others.

Gods knew she'd embarked upon a suicide mission, and she felt as though Beryan had known this as
well, that he'd wittingly made this decision. Like
Jago, she would never have disrespected the man by
questioning his competence. She had understood
even then that, no matter how well the rescue party
could fight together, they could not have defeated
Loc's party. Beryan must have known this, too, and it
was Gwendolyn's decision to support him.

Whatever she believed, Taryn did not argue. She
said nothing, but averted her gaze, peering again at
the litter and the figure lying so still upon it, his face
bloodless, even against the warm glow of the fire-

light. "I thought he had ridden to the Iceni," Gwendolyn said.

"He did," said Jago. "On the way, he was captured."

Gwendolyn's brow furrowed. "So, how did he end in Durotriges?"

It was Taryn who spoke now. "He arrived with two Catuvellauni warriors. So I'm told... they did not trust him, and they came to speak with Adwen. Regrettably for them, they arrived as the battle engaged. Bryn rushed in to save me from a beheading but fell to the same axe."

A sting of tears pricked at Gwendolyn's eyes. That was so like Bryn—ever ready to fight for what was right.

"Without his intervention, I'd not be here to tell this tale."

A sudden rush of fear squeezed Gwendolyn's heart. "What of his sister?"

Jago shook his head. "The lady did not return with him, Majesty. But there was no time to speak of it before he fell, so we do not know what became of her. We only know what we know because Wihtred told us before he succumbed to his wounds."

"Wihtred?"

"Caradoc's son. He fell, too."

Gods. The Catuvellauni chieftain's son. This, too, boded ill.

Taryn added, "Bryn was unrestrained when he arrived with them, and he seemed to come of his own free will, fully armed, so I must believe they are merely detaining her."

Poor Ely. How much more was she bound to suffer?

"What of Adwen?" Gwendolyn dared to ask.

"Dead, Majesty." Jago turned his head, the apple in his throat bobbing. "He, too, fell in battle. I... I made certain... before leaving him." He shook his head. "He... was gone."

Gwendolyn swallowed. "Dead," she whispered. But that did not seem possible.

She blinked away the sting of tears, scarcely able to understand how far they had fallen from grace. Adwen had been so young... she had liked him so very much. His death simply wasn't fair, and it was so inconceivable that she must now bear the responsibility of yet another death, one more person she cared for so deeply. "What of Durotriges?"

"Taken," affirmed Jago.

"By the time Bryn fell, it became apparent how the battle would go," explained Taryn. "We dragged him away." She peered at the litter. "I could not have left him after he saved my life, and I did not believe his wound would be fatal."

"That remains to be seen," Lir said. The Druid was still working furiously to cleanse his wounds. Gwendolyn swallowed again with some difficulty.

Durotriges, *fallen*. Ely, *taken*, Adwen, *dead*.

Bryn's uncle had risked so much to free her, and now he, too, was gone. So virile and handsome, cut down in his prime. But Gwendolyn could not bear it if Bryn died, as well. Though he was not raised with Adwen, he would still be grief-stricken when he learned of Adwen's fate.

"Locrinus must have gone straight from his search for you to Durotriges," surmised Málik. He'd been listening intently, allowing Gwendolyn to steer the conversation.

"I believe so," said the man called Ives—a tall,

brawny fellow with a snarled golden beard and strong violet eyes. With two fingers, he tugged at his tangled beard.

"How many attacked?"

"Perhaps fifty, but we took twenty at least."

"So, perhaps thirty remain?"

Ives shrugged, then nodded. "Perhaps," he said. "But if he has not yet sent for reinforcements, I am sure he will. If what you say is true, and he intends to take Plowonida, he'll no doubt use Durotriges to launch his attack."

All together, they were seven now—eight if Bryn survived the night. The odds were overwhelmingly against them. Locrinus had more than five thousand men at his beck and call, and it was certain that the number would grow.

For now, Durotriges was lost, but Ives had counted more than fifty men who'd gone to defend the women and children. They were now awaiting instructions from Adwen—instructions that would never come.

"We needn't decide anything tonight," said Málik to Gwendolyn. "Rest and let us speak again in the morn." His gaze slid to the litter, then returned to meet her eyes. "Tonight, your *Shadow* needs you," he said, and despite that he'd said it without animus, his tone was sour.

Gwendolyn gave him a nod as he rose from the circle they'd formed, disbanding the group merely by that action. The others immediately followed, leaving Gwendolyn alone with Lir and Bryn. "I believe he'll wake soon," Lir said. "See his eyes."

Gwendolyn moved so that the firelight could better illume Bryn's face to find his eyes beneath his closed lids were dashing back and forth, back and forth.

"If that blow had addled his brain, he would not be dreaming so vividly."

Lir rose then, excusing himself to seek his bed, instructing Gwendolyn to summon him at once if she noted any change.

Retrieving her blanket, Gwendolyn settled in beside Bryn, with her cheek close to his face so she could feel his breath. She placed her arm over him as well, careful not to disturb his freshly applied bandages, nuzzling closer, taking comfort in his familiar scent.

She had known him so long—since they were sprouts, with Ely toddling about after them, her sweet blue eyes as luminous as her shining hair.

How much they had endured since then...

How lost she would be without her friends.

As of now, she had no one left to call family—no one at all. Not her mother nor Demelza, not her father, nor her uncle, and none of her cousins.

Gwendolyn still hadn't a clue about Lady Ruan and her husband, but she considered them both now, wondering if either had survived. If they had, how sad they would be to learn of Bryn's death... if he died. How cruel life could be, and how swiftly death arrived.

Her throat grew thick as she remembered her cousin's final moments. There hadn't been time to say goodbye, and already Lowenna, Briallen and Jenefer had fallen by the time her uncle sent Gwendolyn into the fogous. So much blood... even now, she couldn't bear to remember.

During her childhood, she'd been close to her

cousins, though far more so with Borlewen as the eldest of her uncle's brood. They'd loved all the same things—knucklebones and ninepenny *marl*, *hevva* cake and blueberries, Beltane and quarterstaff contests. Her cousin had been quite skilled with a blade, displaying feats of deftness that even Málik had admired. However, the one way she and Borlewen were not alike was in Borlewen's plainspokenness. Gwendolyn only aspired to such boldness, and she had so much admired Borlewen, not merely because she always spoke her true heart, but because she always did whatever she wished to do. She had spoken of pleasure as though it were a woman's right, embracing consequences as though they were blessings.

All three of her cousins had been quite unafraid to speak their minds, and all had come by it honestly through their father—a man who neither lamented the passing of his years, nor his lack of sons to continue his legacy. It had not mattered that his wife remained barren until her death. He'd loved her no less, taking such joy in her company as he did her body, not caring if his daughters witnessed those torrid displays of affection.

It was no wonder that all three spoke so freely of cocks and bald-pated Druids.

Gwendolyn swallowed hard. That was the last thing she remembered them speaking about the evening before the raid. And then... the following morning...

I did not avail myself of her, but I did cut her throat.

Even now, the vitriol of Loc's words cut like a poisoned blade, the malice of his admission spreading like venom, hardening her heart.

I. Will. Kill. You. She vowed.

It was only once she turned her thoughts to Málik that her heart softened, and when at last she dozed, she slept with thoughts of him holding her close... down in her uncle's *fogous*... in the dark, with only his Faerie light as their witness...

Gwendolyn knew she was dreaming when she felt his husky breath on her face. He drew her up from his lap to kiss her so sweetly and fully on the lips, tangling his hands through her hair, grasping her neck. "Gwendolyn," he whispered gruffly. "I can smell you."

How utterly embarrassing—that he could scent her desire, like the sweet perfume of pollen in the air. The thought filled her belly with a warmth that slid between her thighs. It made her clamp her legs together and wiggle in her sleep, and she moaned desperately, turning her face up to seek his kiss... *so achingly sweet.*

As necessary as water.

As delicious as fresh peaches from Qin.

He pressed his mouth against her trembling lips, and then he, too, moaned hoarsely, the sound so utterly tormented as she parted her lips to accept the gift of his tongue.

Gods. She had so long dreamt of this moment—so starved for his embrace. For all those months locked away in Loc's prison chamber, she had prayed for Málik's return... and now he was here, and she could not and would not turn him away...

But this was only a dream...

At least here she should take unrepentant joy in the unnatural warmth of his body... rejoice in his hunger as his tongue swept into her mouth, exploring... suckling, and kissing in turn.

"Gwendolyn," he said, again, with the most desperate of yearning, and her heart kicked an irregular beat, as she opened her eyes to an achingly familiar face... but it was not Málik's.

"Bryn!" she exclaimed, bounding up from the pallet, her hand going straight to her traitorous breast, the nipple even now pebbled in anticipation of Málik's touch.

Her cheeks suffused with warmth, but she daren't say anything to disarm his weak smile. "You're awake!" she said, and then, uncertain what more to add, she shouted for Lir.

CHAPTER THIRTY-ONE

The head injury had knocked him insensate, but it was the festering wound that had kept Bryn out cold. With his wound now cleaned, his fever subsided, he was now seated, wrapped loosely in Gwendolyn's woolen blanket, shivering in response to a lingering fever, but conversing even so.

It was just as they'd feared. Ely was being held by the Catuvellauni. They intended to keep her until the envoy's safe return. Bryn had ridden unfettered, knowing that if he attempted to escape, or if they found his account to be untrue, Ely would pay the price.

And, simply to be certain, his escort had been the chieftain's own son. Only now, if they returned without him, there was no telling how the Catuvellauni would respond.

Gwendolyn didn't know what to do.

This hadn't been her plan. It was, in fact, the worst turn of events, because she needed the Iceni king's support, and she would not receive it if she had Caradoc riding by her side.

Moreover, even if that wouldn't deter him, the Catuvellauni were not known to be allies of anyone. They had long contested her father's annexation of Durotriges, and much like the Iceni king, Caradoc had aspirations of his own for annexing the surrounding tribes, and it was perhaps to his continued indignation that so many continued to call him a chieftain, not a king.

There was no easy way to proceed.

Gwendolyn could not rise against Loc's men at Durotriges with only eight warriors. And, no doubt, by now, Caradoc would have received word of the attack, although Gwendolyn could not return Bryn in his state.

Neither could she go herself. Even without so much discord, prophecy or nay, few outside of Cornwall would jump at the opportunity to follow a woman—particularly one they still had so many questions about, wondering whether she'd taken part in Loc's coup against her father.

Considering all this, Gwendolyn sat, flicking her thumb against the black pearl of Borlewen's blade, considering her best recourse.

With Adwen gone, there would be others who shared Taryn's outrage over Adwen's dealings with Innogen. Regardless, Gwendolyn's quest for allies must begin somewhere, and the Catuvellauni appeared to be her only option.

Her best bet would be to send word to those who'd fled the Durotriges village and call them to her side. They were still her father's banner men, and they owed Gwendolyn their service. But she would not risk them unnecessarily. Diminished though they might be after the Iceni raid on Plowonida, the Catuvellauni still had far greater numbers than she had at her disposal. It would not be wise to face Caradoc until she had more. Therefore, it was decided that they should not remain in such a vulnerable location, where Caradoc could easily locate them whilst awaiting reinforcements. After dispatching Ives to retrieve the Durotrigan refugees, they would then retreat north to an abandoned hill fort Lir spoke of—one that belonged to a Brigantes chieftain who'd come seeking healers after a skirmish between his tribe and another. Too far gone by the time he'd found the Druid village, he'd died in their care, but now his misfortune was Gwendolyn's boon.

According to Lir, the village was only a short ways north. Abandoned now, like Plowonida, it would remain so in deference to the Brothers' Pact; but borrowing a village was not quite the same as appropriating it, and the gods would surely not object.

Gwendolyn had only one thing to do before leaving.

She marched over to Málik's horse to retrieve the sword he'd kept in his saddle sheath, returning it to Taryn. There was no need to explain what it was. She recognized her father's sword at once and took it from Gwendolyn with fat tears streaming down her cheeks.

"Thank you," she said. "I'll use it to honor my father's final wishes—to serve the queen he believed would lead us from ruin to prosperity."

Gwendolyn smiled gratefully. "From your lips to the gods' ears," she said, and she vowed she would do her best not to let these people down.

. . .

By MIDDAY, they were already en route.

Mercifully, Bryn could now sit upright. He rode beside Gwendolyn on his own horse, with her wool blanket draped over his shoulder, wrapped about his middle, then trapped beneath his leg. He said nothing about the kiss. Neither did Gwendolyn.

Already, even before that kiss, there had been enough tension between them, and now, she could scarcely look him in the eye because she had truly believed that kiss was Málik's, and she had kissed him back with equal fervor—until she'd realized it was Bryn.

At least she now knew that one kiss was *not* the same as another.

The problem was, so did Bryn.

Even as weak as he'd been, he must have seen her face when she'd realized who he was, because his brows had slanted so sadly, and his blue eyes dimmed.

They were still dull, even as he sat shivering, barely able to hold his reins, much less his sword. Still, Gwendolyn remained by his side, studiously avoiding all thoughts of that kiss—and Málik as well. Instead, she considered these lands between the Confederacy and the South...

Like the Prydein, the Brigantes were not merely one tribe, and their territory bled east into Parisi lands. The Brigantes themselves were not a warmongering people, but they certainly owed their prosperity to the Prydein, who in times past had willfully raided the south lands, trading their plunder with the Brigantes on the return journey home.

After her parents were wedded, the raids ceased,

but peace brought its own web of challenges, and without the Caledonii raiders to supply their villages, Brigantes tribes rose and fell, villages came and went. There were many hill forts along these parts, some still flourishing, though many more in ruins. This one was perhaps defeated by bloodshed, but Gwendolyn wondered if the Brigantes now regretted their associations with the northern tribes, because, in truth, it was impossible to trust any man whose welfare benefitted from the misfortunes of others.

Not unlike Locrinus, who'd stolen his brother's title.

Gwendolyn wondered now if King Brutus had ever suspected the cause of his elder son's death, or if he'd trusted his viper of a wife.

Poor Urien would have been a better man. After all, it was Urien her father had first met, and Urien he'd so readily embraced, singing his praises, so much so that he'd been willing to betroth his only daughter when Gwendolyn was still only a babe.

Indeed, she had known she was to wed Urien from the moment she could understand what it meant to be wed, and the importance of their union had been driven into her heart and mind every day of her life. That she later found herself affianced to the younger brother was only because of Innogen's clever sleight of hand. To deny Locrinus after so readily accepting the elder son would be to forswear their alliance, and to make an enemy of Brutus. Yet, the instant Gwendolyn's betrothal to Loc was agreed upon, her fate was sealed.

Not for the first time, Gwendolyn considered Loc's mother. Locrinus must die, but so, too, should

Innogen. And nevertheless, Gwendolyn suspected Innogen would be difficult to vanquish—like striking at smoke.

THIRTY-TWO

Forty-three men and twelve women returned with Ives, all armed and prepared to fight.

One came bearing the King Corineus' crimson mantle, recovered from Trevena's courtyard after his beheading. The King's bloodstains remained, even after having been washed.

Gwendolyn recognized the young man who delivered it to her as one of Lady Ruan's household guards, but, unhappily, he came bearing a gruesome tale along with her father's cloak.

They'd forced King Corineus to kneel in the courtyard, dressed in full regalia, wanting everyone present to witness how the mighty were felled.

Then, after the deed was done, both dead kings' headless bodies were dragged through the city streets by their ankles. Her father's cloak, having nothing to restrain it, caught about a merchant's stall at the beginning of its journey. The young man saw it and seized it, then fled the city. So, he claimed, Bryn's parents were neither seen nor heard from again. It was supposed that both, having held such prominent positions and seats at the high tables, were likely slain in the great hall, where Brutus met his end.

Gwendolyn's throat grew thick with emotion as she listened to the young man's tale, and she accepted his offering, thanking him for the thoughtful gift. But it was all she could do not to weep inconsolably as she brought the mantle to her nostrils to inhale the last traces of her father's lingering scent...

No longer had he smelt of horse, or sweat, or even sunshine, so ill had he been... but it still smelled strongly of the cloves he'd used in his coffers to ward away moths.

She would wear it proudly, bloodstains and all.

Someday soon, Loc would pay for what he'd done, she vowed. Gwendolyn would not rest until he and all who served him were vanquished—including his mother and mistress.

She would build her army from this meager beginning. They were few compared to Loc's vast infantry, or even those her father had once led, but she would be eternally grateful for every soul who rallied to her cause.

Unfortunately, once they were joined by the refugees, the Brigantes village was no longer serviceable, even for so few as sixty-three. So as soon as Bryn felt himself well enough to travel, they once again took to their saddles, wending their way south... toward Plowonida.

While he was still in the company of the Catuvellauni, Bryn had counted more than twice their numbers among them, and if Caradoc meant to fight, Gwendolyn's fledgling forces would doubtless lose. However, a new thought wended its way through her brain, and she reconsidered her options.

No one knew Trevena better than she did, and why should they continue to travel from hill fort to hill fort? If Trevena's gates were all closed and the towers were all manned, there could be no safe passage onto the Stone Isle, neither by land nor by sea.

Unless...

There was a narrow passage where the *piscina* siphoned from the bay, a bit of brilliance that came to her father through a Phoenician merchant. But unless one knew how it worked... unless they'd had the chance to study the blueprints—which Gwendolyn had—they would assume the pool was filled by the same springs that were so plentiful in the area.

But it was not.

Gwendolyn was not some silly, tattered waif, even if she looked like one. She was her father's heir, and she had a gods-given right to hold Trevena. And perhaps she could do it if only she could convince the Catuvellauni chieftain to ally with her. Considering what argument she would use, she commanded Bryn to give her a full account of their affairs.

"Caradoc will not relish the loss of his son, but thanks be to the gods, Wihtred was not his heir. I was told his eldest son also fell against the Iceni. But he has one more."

Gwendolyn nodded. "What was the elder's name?"

"Lund, I believe."

Up ahead, Málik rode by himself, neither with Esme nor with Lir. Although he avoided Gwendolyn's gaze, she felt their bond much the same as she once had, and knew he was as aware of her as she was of him.

"Lund," Gwendolyn repeated, wondering if she'd

ever met him. Caradoc had not visited Trevena often, but he had daughters he'd enrolled in the *dawnsio*.

"As I said... thankfully, he still has one son remaining," Bryn disclosed. "Kelan." Both his brows lifted. "He took a liking to Ely at first sight, and I believe she may have to him as well. It was she who suggested I go to Adwen and leave her in good faith."

Gwendolyn lifted her brows, surprised. "Ely did that?"

She was pleased to know that some of her own daring had rubbed off on her friend, but mayhap this wasn't quite the time for it. It could work to her detriment if negotiations didn't go well.

Bryn nodded.

Aisling ambled easily alongside Bryn's mount, ignoring the occasional forays his stallion's curious nose made into her soft, white mane. If it weren't for Aisling's unflappable temper, there would be no way Gwendolyn could travel beside him unless she demanded someone switch Bryn's horse. As it was, Aisling was as equable as her Faerie masters, only now and again shrugging her head as though to rid herself of a nuisance fly. But it wasn't a fly harassing the poor mare, it was Bryn's lusty stallion. But this gave Gwendolyn a notion of how to proceed.

Lust was a powerful motivator, and so long as Ely shared the son's interest, it could prove to their advantage.

Once more, she peered over at Málik, daring to allow her gaze to linger.

Even knowing that Bryn was watching, she couldn't help herself. Málik's proximity was intoxicating, stirring her blood and clouding her thoughts, even when she tried to stay focused.

With some effort, she averted her gaze. "What of the remaining son? Is he like his father?"

Bryn lifted a brow. "Kelan?" He shrugged. "If you mean, 'Does he have an eye for the ladies?' the answer is definitively, aye. If you mean, is he as bearish as his Caradoc, then no? He's more sensible."

"Good," Gwendolyn said, considering. If negations faltered with the quick-tempered father, perhaps she would take them to his son.

However, surliness wasn't the worst of traits. Bryn's father was quite crotchety betimes—sober and peppery, but loyal to a fault. Even when he'd had the chance to inherit lands of his own, to pass them on to his son, he'd chosen a life of service for himself and for Bryn. One could not fault a man who would do such a thing, and Gwendolyn mourned his loss.

Some of her father's aldermen were also quite ill-natured, and she'd had to learn to deal with them according to their vanities. Only a few had not succumbed to her flattery, and Gwendolyn often thought this was because they, like her mother, had found her countenance... unbecoming.

Alas, it was one thing to yield to a pretty maid, yet another to be cajoled by a plain-featured miss.

At this point in her life, Gwendolyn understood intuitively what it felt like to be treated under both circumstances. But if the prophecy wasn't true, there was certainly immense disparity in her treatment, simply based on her appearance.

Remembering the sway her mother held over all men, not simply her father, she sorely hoped the Catuvellauni king might consider her lovely—not because she wished for him to favor her, but because she'd have a far easier time if he did.

Unfortunately, that was not something she could control, and it wouldn't help matters much that she would arrive looking like a rag doll whose hair had been snipped by a three-year-old child. Really and truly, she no longer cared about her appearance, but she knew others would.

Gwendolyn must conquer each small battle one at a time, first things first, and she no longer intended to leave things unsaid. Tomorrow was simply not promised.

"Bryn," she began, hoping to lessen the unease between them. "I don't know if you can forgive me for what I've done." It was because of her he'd first lost his position as her Shadow. "But if you will endeavor to do so, I will spend the rest of my days making right the things that I've made wrong."

He was silent a long moment, peering down at the reins in his hands—his face still too pale, though his strength had much returned. He answered after a moment. "No," he said. "It is I who must ask forgiveness, Gwendolyn. I was, in truth, angered by my demotion... I blamed you unfairly for my parents' deaths, yet I was more enraged by myself."

Gwendolyn blinked in surprise. "Why should you have been? No one could have known what was to come, Bryn. Only Locrinus and his brothers could have known, and not even poor Brutus caught wind of their plans. How could you, so removed from their lives?"

"True," he said. "That is true. But the same should go for you," he argued.

And then he added, "But it was more than that, I must confess. When you returned from Chysauster, I saw you were so changed. I sensed the reason.... beyond the loss of your kin." He glanced at Málik. "I must confess, it wrecked my heart."

Gwendolyn's own heart ached over his full-hearted admission. She knew how difficult it was for him to say so much. He had never been entirely forth-coming, and she had too often pressed him to no avail. "I am sorry for that, Bryn. Truly. You must know I'd never wish to cause you grief."

"I know," he said.

But it wasn't enough simply to know. Gwendolyn wanted him to understand that it was not her true choice—if only things had been different, if she were simply a girl, and he a boy... but they were not. Their roles in this life were cast in stone upon their births—at least regarding whom they must wed, or not. Still, it wasn't fair because, as her Shadow, Bryn had been forced to relinquish any chance for a family, devoting himself entirely to her. From the moment he took his vows, he was fated to watch as she loved another.

But at least now he wouldn't have to. One of them should be happy, and perhaps that would be one of the first things Gwendolyn would change when she could. Perhaps a Shadow needn't commit himself so fully if he wasn't serving alone? Like the aldermen with the Treasury, perhaps they could serve in shifts? But this would mean there would be a lack of inti-macy and trust, and that could be a problem, in truth. Simply consider Locrinus with his guards—none of them ever the same guard, none of them loyal beyond the gold in their pockets.

Still, there must be some way to accomplish this so that a Shadow mustn't be fated to live a loveless life... She wanted Bryn to have choices—to choose his own life, and perhaps a wife. If she could ease his heart, she would do so, though she couldn't offer him her heart.

That was already taken, much to Gwendolyn's dismay.

She sighed, casting a glance ahead, her eyes daring to note the contours of Málik's back... the sword that couldn't hide the lean, but well-muscled cut of his shoulders.

All too easily, he had set her aside, and it hurt. "You must know... if I were truly master of my own heart," she told Bryn, "I'd never give it to *him*."

Gwendolyn didn't have to explain who. He knew.

Bryn, too, peered over at Málik.

About a half a bell ago, Esme had ridden up beside him and he and his Faerie counterpart now rode side by side, although while Esme seemed intent upon giving him a taste of her thoughts, he continued in silence, ignoring her, every once in a while peering back to meet Gwendolyn's gaze. But that was all. He'd had so little to say to her since Bryn's return, and Gwendolyn wondered if he was jealous—wondered, too, if he'd awoken during the night to find her kissing Bryn...

The very thought of that brought a new sting to her cheeks.

Bryn nodded. "I can well imagine you wouldn't offer him your heart. He's—"

"*You* liked him well enough," Gwendolyn interjected quickly, before he could speak against Málik, not really understanding why she should care what he said or thought about him—it would all be true. Málik was not an easy one to love... even so, Gwendolyn did.

"I did like him," Bryn offered. "I *do* like him," he

amended quickly. "But he's a difficult one to know." Gwendolyn rolled her eyes. That was putting it mildly.

"What is with those two, anyway?"

Gwendolyn peered again at Bryn. "Esme?" He nodded and Gwendolyn sighed, lifting her shoulder. "How should I know?"

Esme had certainly had plenty enough to say when they were in the Druid village and some on the ride out, but little enough since. Indeed, it was much as though she were two people, and she had not seen the *other* Esme in quite some time.

"She seems..."

"Fierce," Gwendolyn finished, knowing what he would say only by the look on his face. She knew him only too well. "She is. Quite. And still she is a conundrum because she is thoughtful and patient, as well." She sighed again. "It is she who dressed and armed me," Gwendolyn revealed.

Bryn gave her another close look, once again examining her vestments. His eyes skipped past her breasts and Gwendolyn smiled knowingly, sensing his unease. "No one ever accused me of having womanly curves, but this armor molds itself to my form."

She wiggled a bit, as though to loosen it, but no matter how she moved, the garment adjusted itself to accommodate. It was as though she wore a second skin, and the only thing loose was her wild, unkempt hair.

"It's quite... interesting," he said.

"Black mithril," Gwendolyn apprised him. "Woven, not forged."

"How is that possible?"

Gwendolyn shrugged. "Fae magic?"

"Whatever the case, I've seen nothing like it."

Except, of course, for the one Esme wore. Like Gwendolyn's, Esme's was fitted to her person, except Gwendolyn's armor was black, and hers was a shade of green that reminded Gwendolyn of the patina on her mother's Prydein jewels—at least today. The first time she'd noticed the garment on her, it had been a shade of buckskin, and the next, a deep forest green.

Like the hob cake, the colors of her garment shifted according to her environs—subtly though enough that if one was watching for it, it was easy to note.

"She's refreshingly candid," Gwendolyn said, not quite realizing that her attention had returned to the Faeries conversing ahead—nor what that gesture might imply to anyone watching.

"He's well and truly stolen your heart, has he not?"

Gwendolyn didn't bother to deny it. "More's the pity."

"Have you told him?"

Gwendolyn eyed her good friend with chagrin, then lied to him for the first time in all their days. "No. Why should I? As you can see, those two are—"

"*Not* enamored," Bryn contended. "That is not what I see. And, really, you should tell him, Gwendolyn. I know I am not the man you will love... you need not coddle me like a babe. Nor need I forgive you for following your heart... and neither for what has happened to our parents. You grieve as I grieve, and if I ever gave you the impression I blamed you for any of it, 'tis I who must apologize."

Gwendolyn was grateful for his absolution. It was true, she could not help whom she loved, and if she could, it really wouldn't be Málik. Loving him was problematic.

"Indeed, if you must know," he continued. "I forgave you long ago for my demotion, as well as for loving Málik. *Gods*. How could I not when you honored your promise to Loc, even though I knew you loathed him? I merely could not find it in my heart to forgive myself for leaving you to rot in that chamber, with no aid forthcoming. And I knew what they were doing to you, still I did so little for too long."

"Oh, please! What could you have done?" Gwendolyn argued. And then she answered for him. "Naught, Bryn. There is naught you could have done."

"But that is where you are wrong, Gwendolyn. *I* am the one who summoned Adwen. I am the one who suggested to Innogen she might barter with him for your release."

"You?"

He nodded. "I knew she was wise enough to understand that her son meant to kill you, and that your death would make you a martyr, crippling his reign before it began. I went to her with this, and she understood, even agreed. With her permission, I arranged it all under the guise of my loyal service to Loc. But I came to know a few good men who did not condone his treachery. He has many among his ranks who, while they'd not be willing to oppose him, would lay down their arms if only given half a reason to do so—an opponent they can believe in."

Her spine straightened of its own accord. "But... not me?" Gwendolyn surmised by his tone.

Bryn sighed, the sound like a whoosh of wind. The circles beneath his eyes appeared to deepen with the slant of his eyes.

"Because I am a woman?"

He shook his head, pursing his lips.

"Because I am too young?" she pressed.

He shook his head again. "I don't believe so. They see you as weak..."

Weak. It was the very thing Gwendolyn feared—that too many would see her as her father's daughter, but not her father's heir.

"These men do not wish you ill, Gwendolyn. Still, there are many who do not believe you have what it takes to defeat Locrinus. He is ruthless and will stop at nothing to win. He was raised by that bloody witch to believe himself the only suitable candidate for Pretania's throne, and the only reason he did not murder his sire himself is because his mother beat him to it."

Gwendolyn's eyes widened in shock. "Innogen killed Brutus?"

Bryn tilted her a look. "Did you not know? Even before the *drogue* was fully in effect, she plunged a dagger between his shoulders."

Gwendolyn's hand moved to Borlewen's blade, her palm cradling the hilt. "Gods," she said. "What a viper!"

"Aye, well, you only know the half of it," Bryn said. "She called me to her bed more than once. I'm certain you did not know that either?"

Gwendolyn blinked quickly in succession. "Her bed?"

He nodded.

"And you went?"

Now it was Bryn's turn to flush. "You may think me crass, but I'm not sorry I did," he said. "How do you think I proposed the trade for Durotriges?"

"Gods," Gwendolyn said, again. In a thousand

years, she could never have imagined Bryn selling his body for favors.

"Apparently, she likes black-haired boys," he said with contempt. "Yet believe me when I tell you that, with Ely in her antechamber, it was impossible for me to pleasure her the way she required, and... well..." His cheeks reddened. "I should apologize to you for where my tongue has been."

"Your—" Gwendolyn began, and then hushed abruptly, not really wanting to know more. Once again, she'd been kissed by lips she didn't want to imagine where they'd been before. "Gods," she said again because words failed her.

She really needn't know such things, and, as for the other revelation—the fact that no one had faith in her ability to lead... Gwendolyn didn't like his answer, but she understood.

Bryn flicked a discomforted glance at her hair, much grown now, but still definitively ruined. It was becoming unmanageable, falling into her eyes now and again, blinding her. For obvious reasons, she no longer had Innogen's scarf to bind it.

In truth, Gwendolyn had never looked much like a proper lady. Now, with her new armor, she didn't precisely look like a dirty little waif any longer, but she still didn't look like a lady—a woman perhaps, but not a lady, nor a queen.

Conversely, Ely had a way about her that was exquisitely feminine. It was no wonder the Catuvellauni's son had immediately taken a liking to her, and Gwendolyn hoped the man was equally deserving of Ely's admiration. "Ely will be alright," she reassured. "I intend to prove all the naysayers wrong, Bryn. I'm meant to lead Pretania. I know it. I feel it in my bones," she lied again, knowing intuitively that if she didn't at least sound like she believed it, no one else would either.

Come what may, Gwendolyn must face the Catuvellauni king with the surety of a queen, not the timorousness of a child.

"I know you will," Bryn said with conviction, and his answer surprised her.

"You do?"

He smiled then. "You are the Dragon Queen, are you not? Little did Locrinus realize that, when he joined your two houses, he would seal his own doom. The dragon banners are united, Gwendolyn. This is all the prophecy demanded—not that your union provide you with wedded bliss."

THIRTY-THREE

B ryn was right.

The notion struck Gwendolyn with such force that it moved her heart—not with love, but perhaps with some inkling of the passion she would need to persuade the Catuvellauni chieftain.

Those Fae never once mandated that she must rule by her husband's side, nor that their children be the hope of this isle, only that their *draig* banners be united to stem the Red Tide. Thus, it would not matter whether they stood united in their sovereignty.

Now Gwendolyn must find some way to wrest control from Locrinus, and, for the first time, it no longer seemed entirely hopeless.

Considering that, she drove their numbers south, settling after two days' travel in Dobunni territory. A little further south lay Atrebates, and betwixt the two provinces stood the Temple of the Dead—a holy place Gwendolyn had long hoped to visit. But not today. She'd not disrespect that sepulcher by bringing bloodshed to its door.

Stopping short of the Temple, they made camp

directly in the Cod's Wold—primitive lands said to still be as wild as its people, only disguised as gentle, rolling hills.

Here, foolish fire was said to maunder aplenty, tempting wanderers into bogs where hobbs and boggarts were still reported to abide, along with great packs of monstrous hounds boasting fangs and claws like bears. These had once been Faerie lands before they were driven north, and below—the very heart of Pretania. Forces, not entirely dark, still lingered here, and despite that travelers were not always so fortunate, the Dobunni themselves remained mostly untroubled by otherworldly mischief—perhaps in part because of their Temple, their tribute to the Ancients.

The Druids were also invested there. So, too, were the Gwyddons and Awenydds—the former with their laboratories, and the latter with their academy of *philosophia*.

No tribe—even if they had a mind to and were not frightened of the creatures remaining in the area— would ever dare to disturb the peace in this province.

The closest anyone ever came to annexing Dobunni lands was in Cunedda's marriage to Lowenna, but that counted for little then, and less now that he and Lowenna were both dead.

Gwendolyn always marveled over the irony that this one small territory in Pretania, which cared so little about kingdoms and borders and legacies, had somehow remained freer than most, annexed by no one. Even her father's own ambitions had left the lands untouched, and their Cornish borders had ended with Durotriges, recommencing again farther north to the Wrikon in Cornovia.

Simply by its wildness alone—its blue-green

thickets so gnarled as to become impassable, its endless rolling hills, its moorlands painted in shades of pink, lavender and rose, and the boglands, where the unwary might be taken by the ankles and dragged down into the darkest depths of the unknown—this land proclaimed itself Noman's-land.

It was the perfect location to make a stand.

Even realizing their campfires would be visible for leagues, Gwendolyn planted her dragon pennant on the highest hill—retrieved by her Durotriges banner men. It was a bold move, but destiny did not favor the meek.

She was Pretania's rightful queen, and she must no longer hide from her destiny.

Within a stone's throw of the Temple of the Dead, she would mount her campaign, unafraid to face Druid, or Fae, hobbs or boggarts—let them all come!

From a seedling, a mighty trunk would grow, and this was where she would plant the seed of her sovereignship.

THOSE WHO CAME from Durotriges came with the tents and supplies.

Gwendolyn ordered the tents to be erected in the vale, with banners raised, be they dragon or other. If she would be queen of all, she must not oppress them.

Thereafter, she dispatched a scout to Durotriges, and another to surveille Trevena, and yet another to summon the Catuvellauni king, who no longer had a city to preside over.

She must not be seen as a beggar crawling to his

door. Based on all that Bryn had told her, she sensed she knew him well enough—lionhearted, but fair.

He might not come simply because she'd called him, but she knew that if she went begging, he would never respect her.

After all that Bryn had said, she felt reassured that Ely would come to no harm—not if she had truly caught the eye of the King's eldest remaining son.

It was true. She had no army as yet. No vast supply of weapons. She did not command the north, nor the east, nor the west.

She did not even have Cornwall returned to her as yet.

But even though they were only sixty-three strong, they had the Druids' blessing, and Lir to attest to this. They also had Esme and Málik, and even if Málik could pass for human—which he could not— there was no way anyone could mistake Esme. All that proclaimed Málik Fae was multiplied tenfold in Esme, and their ancient counsel must count for something.

Only one thing continued to trouble her. Though she was dressed like a queen, and she was beginning to feel like a queen, Gwendolyn couldn't forget the look Bryn had given her when they'd spoken of her legacy, and some men's opinions of her.

She must leave them all with no doubt.

Something must change—beginning with her appearance.

At twilight on the seventh night after their arrival, she called together a new *konsel*—Bryn, Málik, Lir, Esme and Taryn—and when she had them all together on the hill, outside her tent, she unsheathed her dagger, handing it to Bryn. But though he accepted it, he looked at her, confused.

Undaunted, Gwendolyn marched over and sat on a boulder, and for a moment merely sat, surveying the heathered moorlands from her make-do throne... only to be certain.

A sense of peace perfused her heart.

There was such beauty all around her... in the golden hue that fell over the gently rolling hills... in the familiar faces now peering at her so expectantly... in the multi-colored tents erected down in the vale... so much diversity. She need not be a beauty to rule these lands as the gods ordained. She only needed to be fair, and just.

She took a deep breath and peered directly at Bryn. "Cut it," she demanded.

Blinking with confusion, Bryn peered down at the blade in his hand—the very tool Locrinus had used to ruin Gwendolyn's tresses—and then he arched a brow at her, as though he thought her mad.

"Cut my hair," Gwendolyn commanded once more. "Do it now."

Bryn stepped backward as though he'd been struck by her words. He shook his head vehemently. "Nay!" he said. "Forgive me, I will not do it!"

"But you must," Gwendolyn said, more gently. "For one, this hair..." She tugged at her curls with disgust. "Will impede me during battle. And since I can no longer plait it, will you have me blinded by my tresses and doomed by a stupid curl?"

Still, he shook his head, refusing.

"Bryn," she said, more gently still, understanding why he would refuse. He still saw her as the girl he would love, and she could see the hope that lingered in his eyes... and this too must be carved away. Gwendolyn was not meant to be his love, nor anyone else's. He must not continue to see her as she was—naïve, mischievous, far too capricious. He must do this now, and it must be done with Borlewen's blade—to come full circle after Loc's violation. This would make her whole again—to cut her tresses by her own choice, not Loc's, or anyone else's. "You must," she begged.

Suddenly, Esme swept over to steal Borlewen's blade. "She speaks true," the Faerie said. But then she turned and handed the blade to Málik, with a knowing turn of her lips, and for the longest moment, Málik stood staring.

He peered up at Gwendolyn now, his silvery eyes meeting her stormy grey, his gaze locking with hers, as though he would look into her heart...

"Art certain, Gwendolyn?"

He said her name with such tenderness, the lack of title not intended as an insult. At the moment, she was among her closest friends, and these were the people she must convince. She was ready to rule. She must arise from this boulder a woman changed...

She must slay the child and rise a queen.

Holding Málik's gaze, she nodded affirmatively, planting her hands on her thighs to keep them stilled, because in truth, it would pain her immensely to lose the only thing that had ever mattered to her—her golden hair... the measure of her worth...

"I am ready," she said, and Málik stepped forward, wielding Borlewen's blade so the setting sun glinted off the shimmering steel.

THIRTY-FOUR

Málik stared at the blade, his hand trembling though he didn't know why. He stood before Gwendolyn, ready to do his worst, and she peered up at him, and said, "Please. I've never been more certain of anything in all my life."

But *he* was still uncertain.

"When I face the Catuvellauni king," she reasoned. "I will not have him look at me as so many have—like a child, a slip of a girl, a shade of his own son. I would have him see at me as his equal."

"He may never look at you that way," Málik said, but not unkindly. "It is a failing of men to admire their own likeness."

"Nevertheless," Gwendolyn told him. "It must be done..." She flicked a quick glance at Bryn. "If my closest friend, my Shadow, will not do me the honor, I beg you then, as my... friend... as my—"

Unwilling to hear what else she would call him, he stepped forward quickly, his smoke-filled eyes glinting as sharply as Borlewen's blade. But before the snip, they shared one final glance.

. . .

AT THAT MOMENT, it was just the two of them... Gwendolyn and Málik. All others faded away. Including Bryn and Esme.

Gwendolyn dared to speak with her eyes.

My love, she thought. "'Tis only fitting you should do it," she whispered, and though she didn't confess why, she knew... he knew. She could tell by the look in his eyes.

He knew.

It didn't matter if he couldn't love her in return. She loved him truly. And regardless of what came next, she would have no regrets.

From the day of Gwendolyn's birth, she was told that her hair was her crowning glory. It was the means by which her true love would someday prove his love for her. The snipping of her hair would heal her. It would remove any doubt anyone had that she was only waiting for a man to save her. And even if Málik loved her, he was already promised to another. Neither was he a king nor a prince, only a lowly huntsman. She could not rule with a commoner by her side, not even be he Fae. Therefore, when he snicked her hair, he would not do so for confirmation of his right to wed Cornwall's queen... he would do it... because she'd asked it of him. No more.

At long last, he nodded, and for a moment, he seemed uncharacteristically shy, unhurried, even hesitant to touch her. Gwendolyn dug her fingers into her thighs, preparing herself as the last ray of sunlight dipped under the distant trees, turning the entire hillside a rosy gold.

The breeze shifted, then seemed to hold...

They shared one final look, and Gwendolyn

sensed the question in his gaze. "Do it," she whispered. "You must."

He nodded, then reached out to tangle his fingers into her hair, and Gwendolyn's head fell back with a gasp at the feel of his hands in her curls.

Blood and bones.

She felt his touch even in the tips of her breast as he tugged on a curl... pulling it straight... preparing to snip... but first, ever so slowly... caressing between his long fingers... admiring it.

Unshed tears burned her eyes, and she closed them against the indignity of it—not because he was about to cut her hair, but because she couldn't bear the feel of his hands or the look in his eyes as he cut it.

"Open your eyes," he commanded softly. "I would have you look at me whilst I do it, Gwendolyn. I must be certain you'll not regret this, nor loathe me for complying."

Then, uncaring of the audience, he added, "I've always thought your hair so beautiful. I would cut out *his* heart only for this... and now you will ask me to do the same."

Traitorous tears gathered in Gwendolyn's eyes, caught by her thick lashes. But she prayed they would not fall, lest he mistake them.

He thought her hair beautiful?

Never once had he said so.

Nor did she remember him ever speaking to her with such tenderness.

There was a sadness in his eyes that she wanted so badly to allay... but not here... not now.

She lifted her gaze to his, careful not to blink.

Gods. He, too, had unshed tears glistening in his

ice-blue eyes, glittering like diamonds—fierce as the blade in his hand.

"You must," she persisted, and with a final nod, he swept the blade forward to snick.

One lock fell... and then... solidified upon her knee... one unmistakable coil of pure gold.

In the distant woodlands, a murder of crows erupted from trees, screaming into the heavens.

"Gods! It's true," whispered Taryn, her voice filled with awe. "It's all true!" she said as she knelt.

THIRTY-FIVE

Drawn by Taryn's shout, an audience gathered as Málik sliced more hair, and more gold tumbled into Gwendolyn's lap. A collective gasp rose as he cut more, and more and more gold fell.

Again.

And again.

And again.

Málik kept snipping, and snipping—if only to prove that his eyes did not deceive him.

But no.

A thousand years of emotion caught in the lump at his throat, like dry cake left unswallowed.

Gold.

The hair on her lap was...

Gold.

And he knew.

He knew by the look in her eyes. By her face laid bare. By the way her silent tears slid over the apple in her cheek, and those achingly familiar lips, quivering, but emitting no sound.

All at once he was transported to a field by the

lake at the Dragon's Mouth, with sunflowers blooming under a warming sun.

More than anything, he longed to close the distance between them, take her into his arms and kiss her, find some way to make her remember who she was, but there were forces beyond his bearing that would stop at nothing to keep them parted.

Accepting their love, embracing her now, mating with her, would not only put her prophecy at risk, but her life as well, and he could not bear it if he lost her again.

He turned to peer at Esme and saw the truth writ upon her face.

How long had she known?

What role in this had she played?

Suddenly, so much made sense.

What of his father? Did he know, too?

Did everyone but him?

Was this again why, no matter how much he'd longed to be free of Gwendolyn's influence, he'd returned here again and again?

By Balor's unholy breath, soon enough, he would be forced to serve her unto his father in order for her to fulfill her destiny—her Prophecy. But if he did so, with him by her side, as her lover, it would seal her fate... yet again.

Outraged, unable to finish the task, Málik handed the blade to Esme, his eyes darkening to the color of storm clouds, urging her to seize it from him—before he could be tempted to gut Esme with the infamous blade as well.

They locked gazes, Esme reveling in the moment, and he understood she had wanted this truth to come to light—that she could not tell him herself only meant that she was bound by promises.

Bound to whom? To the Moytura Konsel? To her father? To the Sisters?

After a moment, she took the blade, her smile all-too-knowing, uncowed by Málik's fury, but knowing the task must be completed and she was the only one who could do it in such a fashion to soften Gwendolyn's appearance. He trusted her to do that for his dragon queen—the lover his father stole from him, withholding her fate and her name.

And every time he came close to finding her again, she was slain again—martyred for his father's amusement.

But not this time.

It could not happen again.

NOTHING COULD HAVE PREPARED Gwendolyn for the pain of Málik's rejection.

She watched him walk away, and those tender vines that once defended her heart grew thorns as sharp and deadly as her cousin's blade.

If Gwendolyn had believed Loc's betrayal to be the worst of what she would endure, this was far more devastating.

But then she took heart.

As Esme chopped her hair, cutting it close, carving symbols into the golden down, she grew more and more certain of her purpose, and her heart...

Reaching down into her lap, she lifted a golden curl, studying it closely.

It *was*, indeed, gold. The Prophecy was true. Therefore, no matter what Málik's reaction, no matter how dark that look on his face, this gold betrayed him.

Esme gave her a wink, gathering up all the golden curls as everyone watched, mouths agape. With night lowering, she worked quickly, pressing them all into a single ball of gold, the heat of her palms melding it all together, then pulling, tugging, weaving, forming it into something else... a shining band... a crown... a new crown.

Her fingers worked deftly to create points and spikes... then intricate filigree, branches of flowering myrtle, a dragon effigy, stars, runic symbols...

When at last she was finished, she placed the golden crown atop Gwendolyn's head, as one by one, points of light appeared on the landscape—some only campfires, others like Faerie flames, with their bluish hues lifting the shadows and painting the vale blue-green.

"The King must die," bellowed Esme. "Long live the Queen!"

THIRTY-SIX

After three days, Málik was still nowhere to be found, but Gwendolyn understood he had matters of the heart to resolve, as did she.

For her, it didn't matter that they couldn't be wed, nor that they couldn't or wouldn't be lovers. It was enough to know his true heart—and now, regardless of what he claimed to feel, she knew he loved her, and that must be enough.

Your greatest love must be this land, your joy begot by its stewardship, Emrys had said. It was sage advice, and Gwendolyn intended to heed it.

Moreover, she now understood how much her faith had wavered, and whatever else it said of her relationship with Málik, the crown on her head, made from the gold of her own tresses was indisputable proof that her Prophecy was real, and knowing this, she would stop at nothing to fulfill it. Everything she had endured would be worth it in the end.

For the return of her faith, she would be grateful. Now she must follow her heart, and trust that it would not lead her astray.

Plucking the golden crown off her head to examine it, she studied the impossible design work. Esme had fashioned it for her all-too easily—her hands working magic. She wondered now that this must have been the way Málik fashioned her shaft, bending by the heat he produced. It was entirely remarkable. The points of light in the stars of her crown glistened as though with starlight. Even now, the memory of her working the gold left Gwendolyn spellbound.

Wherever Málik had gone, Esme did not follow, and Gwendolyn took heart in this, though she still didn't understand what happened, and how Esme had known that her hair would turn gold under Málik's hand—yet she *had* known. The look in her eyes as she'd handed Málik the blade was unmistakable. It was the look of a woman with untold secrets—secrets Málik shared though neither had bothered to reveal them to Gwendolyn.

She considered that—considered finding Esme and demanding answers, but that would be pointless. Both Málik and Esme would share only what they pleased in their own good time, and not one minute sooner. Gwendolyn might be queen, with their full support, but she was not *their* queen.

The tent flap parted to reveal Bryn. Behind him, the morning sun burned bright, leaving his face cast in shadows, creating a perfect silhouette of his body. She couldn't read his expression, but that didn't matter. His demeanor was much altered now—more like the Shadow who'd once served her so loyally, only with a new respect. No more did he question Gwendolyn's dictates. "There's a rider approaching," he said. "Bearing our standard. I believe it's Ives."

Gwendolyn nodded. "Thank you," she said,

standing, returning the crown to her head. "Gather my *konsel*. Bring Ives to my tent."

He turned to go, then hesitated, turning about, with his hand still on the tent flap, holding it back. "Málik has returned as well," he added. "Should I ask him to attend?"

"Where is he?"

"With Esme."

So he went first to her?

Gwendolyn sighed, peering down at the ground to hide her disappointment, though she really must cease to allow such things to unsettle her. "Yes, please, ask him if he would be so kind as to join us," Gwendolyn said—*ask*, because no one could command him, and Gwendolyn knew it. He was as untamable as the Cod's Wold.

"LOCRINUS HAS EMPTIED TREVENA'S GARRISON," revealed Ives. "The army marches west to Durotriges."

Durotriges was directly east, but Gwendolyn wasn't concerned their camp would be discovered. She knew many of his men would resist entering the Cod's Wold.

Neither would they relish risking the Druids' wrath by intruding upon these lands around the Temple of the Dead, especially when they didn't have to.

Once they regrouped in Durotriges, they would take their armies south to Atrebates. And meanwhile, his armies garrisoned in Westwalas would have an easy enough time, passing through Cornovii lands they had wrested from her father.

Although he'd once told her he'd meant to cross

through Dobunni lands to achieve his aim in Plowonida, and despite that many of his men were Trojan by birth, many were, in fact, superstitious Pretanians, and those men would insist upon staying out of the Cod's Wold.

Regardless, it was only a matter of time before they descended upon Plowonida, and the Catuvellauni would have no defense against them. Their only chance—Gwendolyn's best chance—was to convince the Catuvellauni to follow her, and then to usher them into the safety of the Cod's Wold. As she had the Durotrigans, Esme would reassure them. No harm would come to them so long as she and Málik remained in their company.

Gwendolyn tapped a finger at her chin, catching herself; it was her father's habit. Instead, she moved her finger across both lips, pressing them as she considered. "How many did you count?"

Ives shrugged. "Fifty. More or less. They rode too close to count numbers."

From her perch on the rock where Esme had cut her hair, she surveyed their camp—all the tents and banners, soon to be joined by another clan if she had her way.

It was Bryn who spoke now. "That will be everyone."

"And you know this, why?" inquired Esme.

"Because I listen better than I speak," he told the Faerie. "Locrinus oft said his brothers did not need to stay on that god-forsaken rock, because Corineus' good planning secured his conquest."

"So, then... if they have abandoned the city," prompted Taryn, "it means Trevena lies vulnerable?"

"Not at all," replied Bryn. "You must trust me when I say the city remains impenetrable."

"Not entirely," Gwendolyn interjected, her seedling of a plan growing stronger. For the first time in weeks, a hint of a smile lifted one corner of her lips.

If, in truth, Loc's armies were marching toward Plowonida, they would not remain in Durotriges overlong. They would remain only long enough to join the main army and then march on. But even if they marched straight through, with their numbers, so many likely afoot, it would take them two sen-nights, or more, before they could descend upon their destination.

At best, if every one of them were mounted with good coursers—which Gwendolyn doubted—they could make the journey in seven or eight days.

Considering their proximity, Gwendolyn could easily cover the distance in two days, or, at most, three, with Enbarr's mares.

As yet, Málik had not yet deigned to address her, but it was time to stop talking. "Gather our mounts," she commanded Ives, and then she turned to Esme. "Fetch Lir. We leave at once." Circumstances had changed. There was no time to waste.

"Where you go, I go," announced Bryn, excited by her energy.

"I will have it no other way, my friend," Gwendolyn reassured, offering him a wink and a smile. "And no matter, you're the only one here who can lead us."

He laughed.

"Do you remember the way?"

"You know I do."

"Good," Gwendolyn said, and then she turned her

attention to Taryn. "Please, keep the peace here. Reassure your kinsmen. We will return."

With her father's sword strapped to her belt, Taryn knelt before Gwendolyn, her fealty given without question. "As you say, Majesty. I will prepare them for your return."

"Thank you," Gwendolyn said, and she turned to enter her tent to retrieve her sword and prepare herself to face Caradoc.

THIRTY-SEVEN

Gwendolyn chose her entourage carefully: Lir, for his affiliation to the Lifer Pol Order, Esme and Málik, Ives, Jago and Bryn. Altogether, they numbered but seven, yet Gwendolyn knew intuitively that facing Caradoc with any more would prove of little advantage.

Diminished as they were, the Catuvellauni still outnumbered her paltry few, and Caradoc was a proud man, who'd stood fiercely against the Iceni, even against three times his company.

Indeed, this is when the Mester Alderman's lessons would serve Gwendolyn best—all those long hours of study under his tutelage. She had some inkling of what to say to convince Caradoc to fight for lands and people not his own, and en finale, to fight alongside longtime foes. In the end, she must stir the hearts of *all* Pretania's remaining tribes to stand against Locrinus—a task that, at the moment, seemed as impossible as the crown she wore on her head. And yet, here it was—a circlet of gold, made from her own golden tresses, molded by the hands of a true-blood Fae.

She defied anyone to look at her now and think her unsuitable or weak, no matter how few warriors rode by her side. With her Fae-given armor, and her father's bloodstained mantle draped over her shining black mithril, her short, glyph-marked hair, and the adamantine sword she now wielded more instinctively, she felt like a warrior queen, and older than her years.

Moreover, to prepare her for the event, instead of kohl and pretty maquillage for her face, Esme also painted her with the woad of her mother's people—a visual reminder that, at some point, Gwendolyn fully intended to call upon her blood ties in the north.

At the moment, she might be a disfavored queen, with an army of too few, but she would not stop until she faced Locrinus with twice his number, and more.

One by one she intended to gather Pretania's tribes, beginning with the Catuvellauni. And once she had Caradoc convinced to follow, she would take back Trevena. She only needed a few good men to help her retake her city and then hold it.

Thereafter, she would take a handful of men and ride north to barter with her mother's kinfolk. And, if she swayed the Prydein to her favor, she would ride south to persuade the Brigantes. And then the Parisi.

Finally, once she had enough warriors behind her to face the Iceni, she would endeavor to recruit them as well. And with the Iceni would come Trinovantes and Cantium.

And then, she would mount her final campaign...

Against Locrinus himself.

But first she must win Caradoc.

Gwendolyn had only met the man once, many

moons ago, when he'd first brought the youngest of his daughters to the city to enroll her in the *dawnsio*.

The elder, Enid, was already a master dancer and the youngest, Bronwen, was meant to follow in her sister's shoes. Gwendolyn had a use for those two as well, but first she must convince their father that she would be a worthy queen to follow.

After speaking with Bryn, she suspected she understood how to move Caradoc's heart. He was a hard man, a loyal man, but he was also a family man. He had five daughters he loved, but only one remaining son. His city was now destroyed, his armies vanquished, but Gwendolyn knew he still reserved hope for his people, even though they hid like animals, hungry and weakened.

He was also a fair and trusting man, else he'd never have sent the elder of his two remaining sons to verify Bryn's story, and Gwendolyn surmised he was eager for alliances.

No doubt this was part of the reason he'd sent his son to speak with Adwen—much to the son's woe. But Gwendolyn also knew he would be motivated to discover if her warning was true—if Loc's armies intended to march on his beloved city, a city he must still hope to recover. He simply hadn't the means to retake it and keep it—not without more men, not in the state it was now in, nor without walls or proper defenses.

However, that he had not abandoned the region entirely told her he had not given up. Clearly, he loved his Plowonida as much as Gwendolyn loved Trevena.

If he would help her retake and keep hers, she would return the favor, and return to defend his. But, if he should refuse, she had a good sense of what to offer in order to win his favor.

All the while she formed her plan, Bryn led the way... through chalk downlands, clay fields, and finally over gravel ridges and pasturelands riddled with brackish ditches.

As Bryn confirmed, Plowonida's hill fort stood no longer.

Once settled near the wide, flowing, dark river for which it was named, the city had been moated on the south by the great river and by fens on the north. But this alone had not protected Caradoc nor his people against the Iceni. Only a pitiful length of the ragstone wall remained, and Gwendolyn and her party rode past the blackened remnants of wattle and daub homes into fenny lands. Apparently, after the Iceni burned their village, the Catuvellauni retreated into nearby marshlands that, during this time of the year, were almost too flooded to traverse, except by foot. Only those mounted on Enbarr's light-footed mares remained in their saddles. Everyone else dismounted to lead their horses afoot, boots sinking to the cuff into stinking mud.

These were not lands that should be occupied permanently, Gwendolyn noted, and she intended to argue that they should not be occupied at all—especially when she could offer them a walled city for protection.

Unfortunately, the boggier the path got, the more treacherous their journey became. At one point, as heavy as he was, Ives sank into the mire up to his thighs, and he had to be dragged out by one of Enbarr's mares, with a length of rope Jago produced from his satchel.

At long last, as night fell on the second day of their travels, they emerged into a small glade, surrounded by peat bogs, and there they were met by Caradoc's men—thirteen well-armed soldiers to Gwendolyn's seven—six, considering that Lir couldn't fight his way out of a sack.

Carrying torches that flickered against the velvety night, they emerged from the black woodlands, led by Caradoc himself.

Gwendolyn's belly turned with nerves.

This would be the first time in her life she had bartered in place of her father, but she would not allow herself to be cowed, not when she must earn Caradoc's respect.

He stood before her—a strapping man, far younger than her sire, but still old enough to have fathered many children, some who were older than Gwendolyn. His hair was still black, and his eyes shone with a ferocity unmatched by any of the warriors he'd led from the woods.

Almost at once, his eyes found Bryn's, narrowing. "You've some nerve returning here, young Durotriges —else you are stupid, or mayhap both?"

His voice was deep like a bear's, and his body was thick as well.

Bryn slid down from his saddle, stepping forward, undaunted by the chieftain's ire. Leaving his horse beside Gwendolyn, he walked taller than she'd ever witnessed, making his way forward to face the wrathful chieftain. He said, "If you know what transpired in Durotriges, then you know your son fought valiantly by my side to save women and children. He died with his sword in hand."

Caradoc's eyes glinted, hard as steel, his jaw clenching.

Bryn continued. "I came to know Wihtred as my friend, and I'd not dishonor his friendship by cowering before his sire." He removed a bronze ring from the pouch at his belt and then stepped forward to hand it to Caradoc. "I was given this by one of my kindred who dragged me from the field. I am told she took it from Wihtred's finger. I believe it is yours."

The elder man's eyes shone fiercely against the flame of his torch, but his thoughts were indistinguishable as the mist-filled night. He said nothing, but nodded, reaching out to accept the ring, bringing it near to his torch to examine it.

"It's Wihtred's," he said, and the apple at his throat bobbed. Suddenly, his gaze shifted to Gwendolyn, and she knew... even as changed as she was, he recognized her. "What brings you to these parts, Dragon Queen?" he growled. "Has your husband cast you away so soon?"

Behind her, Málik snarled, surging forward to flank her to the right, but Gwendolyn silenced him with a hand, intending to speak for herself.

Caradoc's words might be cruel, but Gwendolyn understood something about this man that was confirmed by the look in his eyes, and the shoulders he refused to bend—woman or not, he would not respect her if she allowed anyone else to fight her battles.

Even if she must brandish her sword and challenge him here and now.

However, she did not dismount as yet, and his gaze remained fixed upon her, his dark eyes perhaps trying to read her.

"I hear tell, he's got himself a lovely new wife... a new princess... with a son, to boot," he continued, taunting her, and the intimation was not lost to Gwendolyn—a son who would inherit these lands long before her own.

Once again, Málik growled, the sound as feral as any beast Gwendolyn had ever heard, but Caradoc did not avert his eyes from her, and fortunately, she did not have to gesture to Málik again. His hands remained firmly upon his reins, although she knew from experience that he could retrieve that sword at his back before any man present could even attempt to wield his weapon.

Still, Caradoc had twice their numbers, and Gwendolyn herself had only once seen battle up close —during the raid in Chysauster. Málik said nothing, though he didn't have to. Caradoc noted the protective gesture, lifting a thick brow, his fists clenching then unclenching at his sides. His eyes snapped to Málik, then back to Gwendolyn.

Very calmly, Gwendolyn unsheathed the bastard sword from her scabbard and pointed the shining length at Caradoc. "If you know all this, Old Man, you must also realize I've no love for that fiend. I will thank you for keeping his name from your lips regarding me or mine."

Determined to show no fear, she cantered slowly forward, still brandishing the bastard sword, extending it so the blade caught his torchlight.

The sword outstretched revealed the runic inscriptions along the flat of the blade.

His torch bearers fell back as his swordsmen moved to the fore, preparing to engage if their chieftain gave them the word, but a flicker of interest entered Caradoc's eyes.

Their gazes remained locked for a moment before his dark eyes shifted again to Málik... then to Esme and then to Lir, taking their measures, each in turn. His dark eyes glinted as he moved his hand to his longsword, but still did not unsheathe it.

"Do you know what that says?" he asked, hitching his chin at the sword Gwendolyn held, noting the words of power. But before Gwendolyn could speak, Esme cantered forward, her body swaying with every step of her mare's as she came to a halt on Gwendolyn's left.

"More to the point, do you know what it says?" asked the Faerie and Caradoc's gaze swiveled to meet Esme's gaze as her lips parted to reveal her porbeagle teeth. "Kingslayer," she said in a singsong tone. "In the tongue of my people." She let him consider that an instant before adding, "The question is, which king does it call to slay?"

Gwendolyn lifted a brow. She had known Esme would not hold her tongue for long, and now she was flanked by two Fae, and Caradoc's gaze peered behind her to consider Lir, who sat quietly still, garbed in his unmistakable Druid robes. After a moment, his gaze returned to Gwendolyn. "What do you want of me, Dragon Queen?"

Gwendolyn chose her next words as carefully as she had her escort, knowing that if she spoke wrongly, the hiss of metal would follow. "I come with a proposition," she said. "Even now, Locrinus gathers his troops. At most, he is no more than a *sennight* away from descending upon your lands and seizing them for his own. And mark me, Caradoc, he will seize them. He does not come unprepared, and if you believe the Iceni were fierce, I have seen his men do battle, and they'll not retreat, no matter how many fall. He has more than enough to spare. If you ride to face him, by the time he is done, you'll have no men remaining, and Plowonida will be lost."

Caradoc shrugged. "I am more than willing to die for my lands."

"Naturally," said Gwendolyn. "As I would for mine. Yet if you would bide your time, allow him to take it... for now... and come fight beside me to reclaim Trevena, once we have turned the red tide, I will return here again by your side, and fight for your city."

The elder man's face twisted with outrage. "You would have me abandon *my* lands to fight for *yours*?"

"A temporary measure," Gwendolyn argued. "Locrinus will be embattled from the moment he takes Plowonida. The Iceni will not care who the enemy is . They will rise quickly against an Outlander, even as they would if you were to restore your claim."

And yet, neither would the Iceni take those lands for their own. This law was known. And, if not, the Iceni would have already occupied Plowonida by now, thwarting him for all time.

His expression softened, if only a little, so Gwendolyn continued.

"After we have retaken your city, we'll restore it, and I will help you fortify it. I will provide copper and gold from my wheals, and under my protection, we will call it Lundinion in honor of your eldest son, even as I will call you my friend."

Caradoc scoffed. "And how do you expect to do all that with seven warriors? I warrant, even with two

Fae and one Druid, that will not be enough to defeat Locrinus and his armies. I hear tell he's amassed thousands."

Gwendolyn lifted her chin. "Let him raise ten thousand," she said. "Like you, I would face him alone, but I will not have to." She sat straighter in her saddle, grinning down at the would-be king, but there was little mirth in the effort. "Will you allow a slip of a girl to be more fearless than you?" she taunted.

The elder man laughed then, turning briefly to address his men. He shook his head as he returned his attention to Gwendolyn. "What you speak is folly!" he said. "You'll never win against so many."

"You might not, I will," Gwendolyn argued with certainty. She touched her crown to make her point, and the stars gleamed at her touch, flashing brighter than Caradoc's torches.

Caradoc's eyes widened. His eyes flicked to Bryn, then to Málik, once again returning to Gwendolyn. "How?"

She sat straighter in her saddle, daring a smile. "The 'how' of it is not something I mean to reveal without an oath of fealty from you. Simply know I've the means to take back my city. Yet I do not simply wish to have it restored to me," Gwendolyn explained. "I'll not hide behind my gates cowering while that red-cloaked viper sweeps through our lands, stealing what is not his."

Caradoc nodded, this time with approval, Gwendolyn perceived. "You are, indeed, your father's daughter," he said. Even so, he did not capitulate, not yet, and Gwendolyn gave him another moment to consider before she continued.

"I can take the city, but I cannot hold it and still achieve the task I am given, so I must ask you to hold Trevena in my name. This would allow your people a chance to heal, eat, sleep, all without fear of reprisal from the Iceni. You will be safe behind my gates until you strengthen your numbers, and mine as well. And, in the meantime, I would ride north to engage Baugh."

Her grandfather. Most southerners knew him by name, because his name itself was legend, his image larger than life, and his good fortunes and advantages regarded to be gods ordained. Caradoc's attention was well and duly piqued now. "And you think he will come?"

"Aye. He will," assured Gwendolyn with such certainty that she almost believed it.

Caradoc's hand abandoned his sword now, alighting upon his hips, standing arms akimbo. "And you'll leave me with my own warriors to keep your precious city?"

Gwendolyn nodded affirmative.

"What makes you so certain I would return it? If what they say is true, and Trevena is so impregnable, I might wish to keep it for myself." He chortled now, tossing up his hands, and turned to address his crew, as a titter of nervous laughter left his torch-bearing companions.

Meanwhile, Gwendolyn's six remained sober and silent.

Beside her, Málik pulled gently at his reins, and she knew from that gesture he was only waiting for a reason to draw his sword.

Gwendolyn softened her voice. "Because, my friend, you are no fool, nor a coward to be handed your victories." Only to be sure he understood she was not afraid, she gave Aisling a heel, moving forward again, leaving the immediate safety of her guards.

She approached the Catuvellauni chieftain, looking down on him, and then added, "Because you love your city as much as I love mine. Because Trevena will never be *your* victory—not when it comes with an oath of fealty you must forswear in order to keep it."

He was considering it, she sensed, so she appealed to his vanity, "Someday, Lundinion will be *your* glory—and yours alone. I will help you achieve that victory, and with it, return your good name." This last promise appealed to him most, Gwendolyn sensed. He inhaled sharply, stepping back, puffing out his chest. Then he turned, peering at his men, nodding to each in turn.

All returned their king's nod, and Caradoc stepped back to whisper to the one man who stood behind him. Finally, he turned to face Gwendolyn again, but for the longest interim, did not speak.

Anticipation filled the glade. Only the pitch torches roared against the silence. Gwendolyn pressed her knees against her mount so that Aisling pranced nervously. "What say you?"

"I will agree on one condition," said the elder man.

"Speak it."

"We must seal our alliance with a promise of matrimony—my son and heir to Elowyn of Durotriges, and with their wedding should come *all* Durotrigan lands."

His gaze now flicked to Bryn, who stood before him, challenging him to protest.

Gwendolyn, too, looked down at Bryn, preparing to refuse Caradoc, but Bryn said, "If it is my queen's pleasure, I will agree," he said. "As her sworn Shadow, they were never mine to hold."

"Art certain, Bryn?" Gwendolyn persisted.

"Quite," he said, his blue eyes shining.

"It is settled, then," Gwendolyn said, returning her attention to Caradoc. "If Elowyn agrees, I'll not only bless it, I will award a dowry fit for a royal daughter. Though you must show her to me now. Allow me to speak to her. I'll not do to my friend what was done to me, barter her life to one she cannot love."

Caradoc turned then, waving at a distant figure standing in the shadows, deeper in the woods. Dressed fully in black and hooded, Gwendolyn did not realize they had an audience until the figure emerged, drawing back her hood as she came through, her smile all-too familiar.

Ely.

"I agree," Ely said, turning to glance over her shoulder at the man who'd stood behind Caradoc. He, too, came forward, sliding his arm about her waist and drawing her close, as though to protect her.

Smiling, Gwendolyn re-sheathed her sword and said. "We are agreed, then."

And she directed her next words to the young man behind Ely, whose image was the same as his father's, only younger. "I suppose you have a torc to declare the lady?"

To that, Ely drew back her cloak to reveal a bronze

necklace already placed snugly about her throat, its finish as brilliant as her answering smile.

Heedless of how it might appear, Gwendolyn slid down from Aisling, nearly tumbling to her knees. Hot tears burned her eyes as she rushed to embrace Ely. They collided, arms enfolding one another, cheeks wet with tears. "I missed you," she said, with feeling.

"I missed you too," returned Ely.

THIRTY-EIGHT

The gambit worked.

Gwendolyn now had the entire Catuvel-launi army and people at her back, marching into Dobunni territory.

Scarcely better off than the Durotrigan refugees, they seemed hopeful, chattering amidst themselves, some jesting, some laughing as well.

Somehow, Caradoc had sequestered more than three hundred souls out in the fens, with a quarter of those numbers being well-trained warriors, and a third of those mounted.

The younger children rode in wagons led by ponies and donkeys while the elder brood walked alongside their mothers—girls and boys alike, quick to lend a hand when the wagons stalled in the mire.

They'd also brought half a dozen head of cattle, a trip of goats, and an immense flock of sheep along with several dogs.

Inconceivable though it might be, they'd somehow kept and fed so many beasts.

The journey was slow, taking twice the number of days that it took to arrive, but eventually, they rode out of the wetlands, and wended their way into higher country, staying off the roads in case the Loegrian army ventured too far south.

Gwendolyn suspected they would be en route by now.

Locrinus had too long coveted Plowonida to be diverted from his ambition. She remembered how excitedly he'd spoken of it during their Promissory feast, how his amber eyes had lit over the prospect of founding a city in his honor. But there would be no Troia Nova if Gwendolyn had anything to do with it. His dream would be the first thing she would take from him, and thereafter, everything he cherished, including his mistress and child.

Esme had once asked her what she might do with Habren, and Gwendolyn still didn't know the answer to that question. But if the child lived, she knew he would remain a threat to her reign, illegitimate or nay. But could she take the life of a child?

Must she?

Life was so cruel.

Hadn't she learned as much already?

Contemplating this, and more, she reached for Borlewen's dagger at her waist, fingering the dragon hilt.

Gwendolyn didn't have a cruel streak, but she couldn't deny her desire for vengeance, and so far, Loc had taken every one of her family members. Turnabout would be fair play, and despite that something must be done with the child, she needn't decide today.

Today, she only needed to move her people to safety.

Gwendolyn felt a tremendous responsibility now

that she had embarked upon this quest, and there were too many who would suffer if she failed.

But she would not fail.

To be sure they kept every advantage, she was determined no one should spy them. Locrinus was not well-favored in these parts, but there were still some who would be too afraid of his wrath not to run and tell. Or some who might covet the gold he'd put into their palms. For Gwendolyn's plan to work, it was crucial that he not learn how far she'd come, nor that she'd pulled together both Durotrigan and Catuvellauni refugees—not that their numbers would concern him as yet. But it was better that he heard nothing, and if they were lucky, he would think her dead.

No doubt he had underestimated her.

Gwendolyn knew these lands, and she had a bond with these tribes that no Outlander could presume.

She had not yet counted her warriors, but she surmised that, between Durotriges and the Catuvellauni, there would be a few more than two hundred to command once they rose to battle. More than enough to take and hold Trevena if all went according to her plan.

Reconsidering Bryn now, she cast him a glance.

He was riding beside Ely's intended, perhaps taking this opportunity to apprise his sister's new husband about how *not* to deal with his sister.

Gwendolyn knew he would be gentle, but firm, and his commination would be well considered. Ely was clearly overjoyed, and he'd never intentionally ruin his sister's pleasure after these harrowing few months—no more than he would risk this new alliance by angering the chieftain's only remaining son.

Since she'd not explained her plans to him beforehand, his response in the fens surprised her. More than anything, she admired his dedication, and she vowed that she would never again question him or take him for granted. Come what may, he would be her Shadow, and she would not keep him from his duty.

As for Málik...

He rode behind her, alone and brooding.

Ever since leaving the Catuvellauni camp, he'd not ventured far from Gwendolyn's side, and though his actions, if not his words, comforted her, something had surely changed between them... something she couldn't point a finger to.

His look when he'd spied the golden lock on her lap was like nothing she had ever witnessed from him —far from the fury and disgust she'd spied on Loc's countenance. His was more... shock and dismay.

For her part, if she was surprised by the fulfillment of the Prophecy itself, she was certainly not surprised about the conclusion. She had known for some time where her heart lay—never with Locrinus, and neither with Bryn.

And that brought her to Esme...

Esme no doubt played a part in empowering Gwendolyn, and for that she would be ever grateful; despite that, there was something about the Faerie that made little sense.

Just as Málik kept secrets, so, too, did she.

And sometimes she looked at Gwendolyn in a way that gave Gwendolyn pause... certainly with pride, but also something darker... something troublesome.

At least for the moment, she was more jovial than Málik.

Between Esme and Lir, they were entertaining Caradoc. Clearly, he was enjoying the attention, and overall, Gwendolyn found she trusted the man. She didn't believe he would have bartered for his son's marriage if he intended to betray them. Nor was his request for Durotrigan lands any small matter. With those lands, he would inherit some of Cornwall's richest mines. And if Ely's exuberance over the union was any sign, she was clearly thrilled about the prospect of their marriage.

Indeed, she hadn't stopped chattering about it for one moment since their reunion. "Gwendolyn!" she exclaimed now, waving a hand before Gwendolyn's face, as though to call her attention. "You are too lost in thought! *He's* been staring now for hours!"

"Kelan?"

"No," Ely said, scrunching her nose, peering behind them, and Gwendolyn knew without looking who it was she was speaking of.

Málik.

Now that Ely was away from the stresses of the Loegrian court, she had returned to her usual self—a relief on the one hand, agonizing on the other because Gwendolyn needn't be reminded of the discord between herself and Málik. She was acutely aware of it without Ely's reminders.

It was growing dark again, but as yet *he* hadn't bothered with his Faerie flame in the company of so many—why?

Gwendolyn didn't know, but it wasn't as though these people didn't know what he was simply by looking at him. Gwendolyn found she missed his odd little sphere, even as she missed his biting tongue... and his crooked smile.

321

He rode silently at her back, moody and distant.

But Gwendolyn would not beg him to engage her. He would when he was ready, and in the meantime, she had more important things to consider.

"I don't understand what ails the two of you, but I am too delighted to be distressed. Really, Gwendolyn, I grieve the losses we have endured, but I find myself ever so grateful for the new bond I've gained."

"Are you truly?" Gwendolyn asked.

Ely nodded.

"I take it you do love him?"

"Madly!" Ely confessed. "Yet not from the first. He was a brute!"

"What changed?"

"I cannot say for his part," Elowyn said, shrugging. "But I was quite sad," she confessed. "One day he made me laugh."

Laughter was the greatest of balms, Gwendolyn thought. Unfortunately, she had laughed little herself since Chysauster.

Not since Málik.

Beside her, Ely cast a wary glance at the pair now riding at the fore of their cavalcade. "I do hope Bryn will not frighten him away," she worried aloud.

"They appear to be fast friends."

"Don't they?" Ely agreed and sighed happily, then changed the topic. "You know, Gwendolyn? I've been meaning to say..." Her gaze lifted to Gwendolyn's head. "It took me a while to become accustomed to it, because your hair was always your most glorious feature. But now I see your beautiful eyes and cheeks."

"You flatter me undeservedly, Ely."

"Oh, nay, dear friend! Nay! I've never seen you more lovely, nor your eyes more aglow. There is something about you that shines as brightly as the stars."

Hearing the sincerity in Elowyn's tone, Gwendolyn smiled, sweeping her palm across the soft fuzz on her head, stopping to finger one of the many runic inscriptions—symbols like those in her Prydein gown. As yet, she didn't know what any of them meant, but there was something bold about the style, even if it wasn't conventionally beautiful.

"And yet... I really must ask," Ely dared. "Who cut your hair?"

Gwendolyn sighed, knowing intuitively what she wished to know, and, truly, it wasn't as though she meant to keep it from her.

For these past two days, Ely had ridden mostly by her side, only sometimes in the company of Bryn and Kelan. None of the entourage she traveled with now would dare engage in idle talk, but the moment they arrived at camp, Ely would doubtless hear the news from others. It was not a secret Gwendolyn could hope to keep, and yet... there was nothing to say— leastways not precisely what Ely wished to hear. "Esme did," she lied.

But it wasn't precisely a lie. Málik might have been the first to put a blade to her locks, but Esme was the one who'd finished it and made it presentable.

"Oh," said Ely, sounding disappointed, and thereafter, they rode in silence—because Ely knew her too well. By the tone of Gwendolyn's voice, she must have determined there was more to this tale. Indeed, Málik had cut her hair, and it turned to gold. But then he'd walked away. Though he probably hadn't done so for the same reasons Locrinus had, Gwendolyn's feelings were far too muddled to put into words. Nor had she yet made sense of it all.

This wasn't the way she'd ever imagined her Prophecy would reveal itself... not quite. Rather, she had dreamt of this incredible, magical moment, wherein the entire world would hold its breath at the snip of his scissors, and only she and her beloved existed. He would trim her hair, see that it was gold, then take her into his arms, kiss her desperately, and afterward, they would live happily ever after, with their loved ones all healthy and happy to share in their good fortune. But that's not the way it happened.

Not for the first time, she turned to seek Málik... and found him watching her still, his smoke-filled eyes dark and foreboding.

What is it you're not telling me? she asked him silently.

CHAPTER THIRTY-NINE

Gwendolyn knew every inch of her beloved city—every nook, every bolt, every crack in the mortar.

As her father's only child and heir, she was among a select few who'd been able to roam the city at will. She took full advantage of that privilege, and because of that, knowing what she knew, delivering Trevena might prove to be an easier task than anyone supposed...

If she herself didn't die during the process.

Most of their numbers had remained in the Cod's Wold, with Taryn and Esme in command. Lir also stayed, despite that they could have used his healing talents. It was a decision Gwendolyn made knowing the Druid was not made for war. However, if all went according to plan, there should be no injuries amidst their crew.

For her own part, she couldn't say the same.

Planning according to the chart of tides, they waited to launch the attack with the spring tide, when the ebb and flow was higher and lower than usual. That would give them more beach to cross at its lowest point, and then, once the tide turned, it would surge higher and faster, aiding Gwendolyn with the second part of her plan—a detail she would share with no one... not even Bryn or Málik. *Not yet.* Málik would be the first to try to stop her, and she would not be thwarted.

On the evening of the strike, they gathered on the beach north of Trevena, just beyond the keeve, where the cliffs hid their camp from view. Here, Gwendolyn explained the most pertinent details.

Under her father's rule, both the inner- and outer-city gates had remained open—for a few reasons. As a man of the people, her father had typically heard audiences until the eighth bell, even when he was gravely ill. Therefore, he'd left the gates open so villagers could freely come and go. Yet, as generous as that was, it was the least of her father's concerns. Unfortunately, the closing of the outer city gates also presented a number of administrative problems—the first being that, whilst the gates could be easily secured by the severing of ropes, once closed, they could not so easily be re-opened. As heavy as the armored wood was, it took a string of ponies to lift the portcullis, and then an entire team of engineers to repair the mechanisms to secure it in place. In the event of fire, if those outer gates were shut, there would be no safe passage in or out of the city, and Trevena's occupants would burn along with the city —unless they should cast themselves over the wall into the bay, and it was a long perilous drop onto the rocks below. If the fire didn't kill them, the fall definitely would. And this was the primary reason those gates were left open, save during times of war—an eventuality Gwendolyn never saw till now.

And yet, Locrinus would not be overly concerned with an attack. The city's very reputation would lull him into a false sense of security, and he needn't be told it was impossible to approach the city without notice. It was easy to see. The entire locality was viewable from the ramparts, and the only tree standing for a good league was the Elder Yew. Any company approaching the city would be spied for miles. Long before anyone reached King's Bridge, the portcullis could be lowered with the simple swing of an axe.

Moreover, it was impossible to move any great numbers across King's Bridge. During market days, villagers and merchants could only cross single file. Their carts were barely accommodated, requiring great effort and care during the crossing. One too many had gone over the cliff side, smashing on the rocks below. With the towers manned, their archers could easily pick off trespassers.

There was also a small, but heavily guarded postern gate. But behind it lay a steep path down to the harbor. But much like King's Bridge, that way was not easily traversed. It wasn't simply steep, it was narrow. Only one person at a time could maneuver the steps, and one shove, one slip, one hurried misstep, and the rocks below were as unkind to flesh and bones as they were to wooden ships out in the bay. This was why all cargo was searched below, and conveyed into the city upon a lift, reserving the stairs for men.

However, unbeknownst to all but to a few in the royal household, there was one more postern gate. Not only was this hidden portal intended to be an escape for the king and his family, it was also meant to be used for the repair of the *piscina*. As a matter of prudence, no stairs were ever constructed there, and the descent was as precarious as the ascent.

From the outside, it was indiscernible. From the inside, it was hidden from view, and because it lay adjacent to her father's treasury, that area had been guarded too. This was the area Gwendolyn had found herself investigating alone.

Before Málik absconded with her inheritance, the aldermen themselves had taken well-regulated shifts, but even they had little to say to deny the King's heir. So long as she stayed clear of the vaults, no one could speak against it, and Gwendolyn had often used this spot to hide from her mother.

Drawing out a map of the palace and the surrounding environs, she pointed out all the key markers, carefully explaining the workings of the gates, along with all the reasons they couldn't be closed, and the procedures her father set forth to prepare in case of war—something Locrinus wouldn't bother to question or change, considering that he still didn't deem Gwendolyn a threat.

Moreover, whoever he'd left in charge of Trevena wouldn't likely concern himself with daily audiences —not at this point—so Gwendolyn felt certain that, with the withdrawal of the Loegrian troops, they would close the inner-city gates, if only because they were easy to reopen, and Gwendolyn's spies had once again verified that the garrison was nearly empty.

However, the steward would have been advised to leave the outer gates open, and he would be forced to do it, not simply because of the risk of fire, but also because merchants were as necessary to Trevena's welfare as breath was to man.

As efficient as the city was, its greatest failing was its inability to support itself from within. Constructed directly on a stone isle, with no chance of cultivating gardens within, they could manage nothing more elaborate than the raised herb plots they'd constructed for the cooks. All things consumed therein must be imported, and yet, particularly during these early days of his occupation, Gwendolyn was willing to gamble that Locrinus would not allow ships into the harbor without knowing who and what came aboard.

Instead, as her father had, he would favor local merchants, not because he cared for their wellbeing, but because he could search them each as they arrived, allowing entrance into the city as required.

"It is confirmed. The port is closed," Gwendolyn said.

She tapped a stick at the southernmost tower in her drawing. Altogether, there were five, four constructed near the barbican; but it was those towers nearest to the inner-city gates that would provide the city its heaviest defense.

"This one will be manned, but without foot traffic on those back steps, they'll prefer to concentrate their defenses on the towers facing the barbican, particularly considering that Locrinus will have taken the best of his archers."

However, even if he'd left a few archers, they would not compare to her father's. Loegrian defenses were entirely based on hand-to-hand weapons, and the alloy they'd touted from the moment they'd landed on Pretania's shores. But they would be prudent enough not to allow missiles into the barbican, and all new arrivals would be searched before crossing the bridge—a bridge easily defended by two good archers and an axe.

"There will be a search here," Gwendolyn said, pointing to an X she'd marked on the map she'd drawn in the sand. "They'll be looking for weapons primarily."

Kelan stood with arms akimbo. "What if our men are refused entrance? What if the weapons are seized? I'd not have my sisters, or my bride come to harm."

It warmed Gwendolyn's heart to hear him include Ely in such concerns. "I have no family remaining," she told him. "Ely is as close to any. I can assure you I'd not send my dearest of friends inside with only two guards were I not confident. Neither would Bryn."

"My sister will know what to do," assured Bryn, and then he winked, the gesture meant for Kelan. "Considering how she ensorcelled you, my friend, I'd worry more for Loc's guards."

Even against the glow of twilight, Gwendolyn detected Kelan's blush. With the palm of his hand, his father shoved him from behind, teasing him without words.

"At any rate," Bryn continued. "We've provided only short swords. The iron is old, and no longer military-grade. No one will question two modestly armed guards charged to defend a troop of dancers. Indeed, I would argue that were those dancers not assigned some manner of protection, it would raise more brows."

"That is true," Gwendolyn said. "The *dawnsio* has always been afforded protection during their travels. We've also dressed the guards accordingly." By some stroke of good fortune, Caradoc's daughters had considered their *dawnsio* regalia as crucial as any life-saving supplies. They'd kept all their gowns, veils, slippers, and the guards' uniforms. A cartload of scantily dressed women, accompanied by musicians, would appeal far more than those guards would raise concerns. Indeed, as far as Gwendolyn was concerned, the troop's arrival would be, in some part, a measure of assurance that the people were prepared to accept Loc's rule, perhaps even eager to return to life as normal. But if by some act of perfidy, the troop was forced to pass without the guards, the guards themselves were not essential to Gwendolyn's plan—not directly. Only those dancers needed be in the barbican. Likewise, if their weapons were confiscated, it simply wouldn't matter. By the time they would have been forced to draw weapons, the city would already be under siege. In the meantime, Bryn was right. Ely did know what to do, and each of those dancers were armed with ceremonial daggers. It was inconceivable that anyone would violate the *dawnsio* for any reason, considering the institutions close affiliation with the *Awenydds* and *Gwyddons*, but if anyone dared, they would lose both eyes before becoming eunuchs, and Gwendolyn had sparred enough with those ladies to know that even Ely could deliver some damage. Caradoc's daughters were hardly wilting flowers, but Ely had come a long way since the Feast of Blades. She was no longer a hapless child.

Regardless, Gwendolyn only meant to ensure all eyes remained on the most obvious point of entry. If there ended up being some little squabble, it wouldn't hurt their cause, and she felt certain not even Loegrian soldiers would risk the wrath of the tribes by harming a troop of students.

"Once the bridge is crossed," she continued. "They should be allowed to remain in the barbican overnight. That is why my father constructed it—to provide for the merchants so they wouldn't have to cross that bridge morning and night."

"What if they are not allowed to enter?" worried Caradoc.

"They will be," assured Bryn. "What better way to mollify a pack of idle old men than to provide a good show?"

"Unless they grow drunk and stupid." Caradoc crossed his arms. "Perhaps it's the last thing they intend to allow?"

"That's what our guards are for," Gwendolyn reassured. "Little doubt their presence will draw some attention, but that, too, will serve our purpose. Those guards on the towers will keep all eyes peeled on the armed guards in their barbican."

"You mean to say, whenever their greedy eyes are not on our women?" argued Kelan, scowling with arms now crossed.

"You could take their places?" Málik suggested, and this drew a bit of nervous laughter.

For the first time in days, when Gwendolyn met Málik's gaze, he gave her a reluctant smile. It sent her pulses skittering, and her heart tripped an awkward beat.

Throughout this entire explanation, he'd stood silent, with arms crossed as well, and Gwendolyn sensed he knew there was more to her plan. But he said nothing, and his smile quickly reversed into a frown.

"Whatever happens, they won't be alone for long," Gwendolyn allowed, tearing her gaze away.

"Once Bryn gives the signal, Ely will engage the musicians."

"Sunset?" Caradoc affirmed, and Gwendolyn nodded.

"While we still have light, but not till the final moments. We'll waste no time returning to the beach because the tide will turn quickly."

"I do not swim," interjected Kelan. This time, his worry was for himself.

"Can't or won't?" inquired Málik.

Kelan's brow lifted. "Can't," he confessed.

"Then don't get in the water," Málik suggested. Still, he persisted.

"What about the climb to the portal? What if we should fall?"

"More's the pity for you," said Bryn. "Swimming would be the least of your concerns. Those rocks are treacherous."

"The answer is simple, my son," suggested Caradoc. "Don't fall."

As THE SUN began its final descent, Gwendolyn and Bryn made their way back through the gorge over to the knoll to spy on the barbican, leaving the rest of the warriors on the beach with Caradoc and Málik. Certain the *dawnsio* troop would have emerged onto the road by now, they approached from the northern woods, staying clear of the Old Road, climbing the knoll from the east side, and dropping to their bellies as they neared the top.

At this hour, with the sun shining in their direction, it would be easy to spy their silhouettes, so they remained close to the ground, hoping their heads would be mistaken for one of the boulders on the crown of the hill.

Simply being here gave Gwendolyn a twinge of sorrow, remembering wistfully how, as children, she and Bryn used to entertain themselves on this knoll, guarding the mound with make-do swords, only playing at the King of the Hill.

Of course, Bryn always let her win. But this was no longer fun and games.

If her plan did not work as she willed it, there would be no other option but to launch a full-scale attack, and even with greater numbers, that would not go in their favor.

Tonight, as yestereve, there were still a few traveling merchants encamped within the barbican—traders who likely had no allegiance to any beyond their bellies and purses. Gwendolyn did not blame them. Simply because the king was dead did not mean their families should be expected to suffer. Each man to his own in times such as these.

Many of the most sought-after merchants had homes within the city—the tailor, the cordwainer, the saddler and blacksmith, among others. But their supplies must still come from without. Unfortunately, they were too far away to see aught more than people and movement, so she couldn't tell who was there. For now, this was enough...

Waiting with bated breath as the *dawnsio* wagon ambled along the Old Road, Gwendolyn clenched her fist as they reached the bridge, where they were halted. Three guards approached at once, and Gwendolyn watched intently, her belly abuzz as they searched the cart.

Despite all her reassurances to Caradoc and Kelan, Gwendolyn was still worried, and she knew Bryn was as well. Silence was a third companion.

She hadn't wished for those dancers to be in that barbican for a single moment longer than necessary. The excitement of their arrival was bound to create even more of a distraction, but time was growing short, and there was still much to be done.

Fortunately, there were a few others waiting to cross the bridge—a farmer perhaps returning to his family. So Gwendolyn exhaled in relief as the guard waved the wagon by, and she and Bryn watched as they entered the barbican and found a place amidst the merchants to settle their cart. Giving them a few more moments, Gwendolyn waited until the last of the exiting merchants crossed King's Bridge, then wended their way north.

One veered south, taking the Small Road, passing directly below, but the woman never peered up. Even from this distance, Gwendolyn recognized her as the lady who sold morels. Tonight, she was without her daughter, walking alone, with a basket in hand. She ambled along till she became naught more than a speck against the winding road, then vanished.

Back in the barbican, the wagon was settled, drawing a crowd. All they needed now was for the diversion to begin—a dance for all dances...

In traditional *dawnsio* regalia, they would perform amidst the merchants in garments so revealing as to require leaving them with guards to keep the peace. There should be plenty of revelry, loud enough to divert any attention from disturbances near the postern.

"Almost time," she said, gauging the sun's waning light. "You have the glass?"

"Aye," Bryn said, then added, his blue eyes twinkling. "The Mester Alderman would be proud to see how you've applied his lessons."

Gwendolyn smiled, sad to consider the old man's demise. Far too many had perished because of Loc's betrayal. "I paid attention to more than that," she said, taking one last gander at Bryn's handsome, beloved face. She didn't know how this night would end, but Gwendolyn couldn't have accomplished any of this without him. When only some weeks ago he couldn't wait to leave her and ferret Ely away to safety, he'd been quick to support her plan. *The first to trust her. The last to question her.* In truth, she owed him some explanation, but daren't say too much, even now. "Do you recall how we used to play cat and mouse?"

He chuckled low. "*Gods.* How could I forget? You were a sore loser."

Gwendolyn laughed. "No doubt," she allowed. "But this is why I made it my mission to find every dark corner in that city. I warrant I know it better than any, including you."

He arched his brow. "Oh? And you think so?"

"I know so," Gwendolyn said, a smile unfurling, feeling, for the moment, much the same way she had when they were children. The two of them had been so fiercely competitive.

Alas for Bryn, she did have the advantage of being the King's heir. Gwendolyn only wished now that he had taken more of the glory for himself, and perhaps told her no more often, instead of allowing her to always have her way. Perhaps she mightn't have so thoughtlessly embroiled him in things he ought not be involved in, thinking herself above her father's law.

She was not, she now knew—no one was, not even her father.

This moment, there was so much she wished she had done differently—not simply for Bryn's sake, but for her own... for Trevena... for Pretania.

It wasn't too late—it mustn't be, not when she felt such a wellspring of hope. Not when she also spied that hope in Bryn's face...

His bright blue eyes glimmered, and his dark hair shone against the waning sun. This was the one way he most differed from his sister—his dark to Ely's light.

"Lest you forget," he said, turning away, perhaps moved by the moment, because she saw his throat bob. "They opened that portal for us that day we were stranded on the rocks." He sighed. "I hope you know some means to open it that I do not, since it cannot be done from the outside—lest you plan to have us mount each other and scale the wall?"

"And watch you all tumble down that cliff?" Gwendolyn scoffed. "I forget nothing," she assured.

"Magic perhaps?" he pressed, and Gwendolyn laughed softly, and said, "Not precisely."

It was time. The sun lowered to its final position before plummeting beneath the sea, and Gwendolyn gave him a nod. He flashed his bit of glass against the sun's dying rays and within moments, the distant sound of a lyre could be heard drifting up the hill.

This was their cue.

They slid down the hill on their bottoms for the first few yards, then bounded to their feet and ran to the beach. It was fully dark by the time they rejoined the crew.

Dressed in black-dyed leather to conceal them against the night, with Gwendolyn in her black mithril, they traversed the length of the beach, staying close to the cliff wall, then scaling the rocks where they must. The view onto this beach was far too good for anyone standing atop King's Bridge, but no one should be on that bridge after nightfall. Now seemed as good a time as any to test her mithril. At the most vulnerable spot, Gwendolyn went first simply to be sure, then waved them along when no alarm sounded. There was only another furlong or so before they reached the caverns below the city.

Naturally, Gwendolyn knew the tides as well as she knew her city. To know them, or not to know them, was a matter of life and death—particularly for an intrepid little girl.

For the time being, the tide was still low enough to traverse the lower cave and emerge onto the rocks below the hidden portal.

From there, it would be a steep path up one side of that cliff to the alcove, where the Dragon's fire was visible by night. Bryn knew the way there, so she tasked him with the ascent to lower the tarp. Once that was done, it would plunge the entire vicinity into darkness, and then her men faced another perilous climb up to the hidden portal with no room for mistakes.

But Gwendolyn must take yet another, more dangerous path—one she knew could be done, though no one except her father's engineers had ever attempted it before her.

This was the way up via the water screw—an ingenious feat of engineering designed by a generous, well-meaning Phoenician merchant, based on some design employed in the gardens of a city called Bāb-ilim.

The design comprised a lower chamber beneath the rocks, which made use of a natural cavern only accessible at low tide. Between that cavern and another reservoir above lay a conduit, with a rotating spiral, powered by a crank in the bathhouse. With that, the water was lifted to its highest elevation throughout a series of turns. It was a complicated process that must be done precisely—too slow, and the water would sluice down over the blades, straight back down into the cavern below. Rather, it must be turned at a precise speed. And because they could not use a pulley in that bathhouse, there were men who'd trained only for this purpose—strengthening their arms so they wouldn't tire and lose momentum. Essentially, as the shaft turned, the bottom end scooped up a volume of water, and the water was then lifted through the spiral until it poured into the reservoir above the salt bath. However, because of the design, lifting too much water was an impossibility—the greater the volume, the more labor involved in turning those cranks so the shaft was purposely narrow.

Within it, there would be scarcely enough space for a single, skinny engineer, but there was room, because, as all wood did when submerged in water, it eventually rotted and must be replaced. The stability of those blades was imperative to the workings of the *piscina*.

That was where Gwendolyn intended to go—alone.

She waited until Bryn started up the path to the Dragon's Lair, letting him believe she intended to wait for him before ascending to the gate. Once he was gone, she explained where she intended to go— down.

Through the rocks.
Under the surf.
Beneath the cliff.
Into the cavern below.

The narrow aperture was hidden amidst the rocks. Gwendolyn herself might never have known about it, except that, one day about five years ago, when the mechanism in the bathhouse malfunctioned, she'd followed the engineer down to watch him work.

She'd followed him straight here to these rocks, asking questions all the way, harassing him for answers that he gave readily for two reasons—one, because she was the King's own daughter; and two, because Gwendolyn had been fortunate enough to study those blueprints and he was the one who'd built the contraption and she was enamored of his work.

But this was the tricky part, and why she needed a swift tide: Once inside the cavern, with churning waters, she would have to wait until the water rose high enough so she could reach the conveyer. If she waited too long, she would drown. And worse, if she did not climb that conveyer in good time, there was every chance those dancers would lose the guards' attentions, and wander over the parapet, close enough to spy Gwendolyn's men.

"You are *not* going down there!" Málik demanded.

"Oh, I will," Gwendolyn said, undeterred.

There was nothing for it but to do it.

"You cannot!" he argued. "Let me go in your stead. Stay, lead as you should."

Gwendolyn shook her head. She was the only one who had ever seen those blueprints. She alone knew how to dismantle the tongue-and-groove blades.

At any rate, after so long traveling, hers was now the leanest body, and those conduits were scarcely wide enough to allow one person to ascend, particularly with only one side of the blades removed and she intended to use the other side to climb, like a ladder.

"For the love of the Divine, this is madness!" said Caradoc, blinking down into the dark, narrow crevice, filled with sea foam. The aperture was scarcely wide enough for a grown person to slip through, much less dive. "That is your mysterious plan?"

Gwendolyn didn't intend to wait about arguing. Having explored this chasm before, she knew it could be done. She would not be thwarted. Slipping past Málik, stepping down onto a small ledge closer to the aperture, she inhaled a breath and dove.

CHAPTER
FORTY

G wendolyn heard the splash behind her as she entered the water, but daren't linger to see who had followed. It didn't matter; she knew who it was.

Málik

Gods!

Even during the summer, the water was bitterly cold.

She turned and swam down into the churning waters, away from the muted light. It shouldn't be too far, so she wasn't worried—not about this part.

It was easy enough to feel her way into the cavern. It was only once inside that she must work quickly to find the opening to the conduit. It would be dark within, and she had only a vague memory of where it was. Always before, this had been done midday, when there was at least a sliver of sunlight pouring in through a crack higher in the stone.

But then, she realized... belatedly... with no light to guide her, she didn't even know which way was up, and for the first time since devising the plan, she panicked.

Blood and bones.

Which way to go?

Instinctively, her hands sought the stone walls, finding none now that she was in the cavern below the mountain. Even as she hesitated, trying to gain her bearings, her lungs began to ache, and her breath demanded to be freed. She coughed a bubble and tried to catch it, so she could follow where it led. It slipped through her fingers like quicksilver.

Gods, oh gods. Which way to go?

All at once, she felt a tug on her arm, and suddenly she was being dragged to the surface. Her face broke free of the foaming surf in time to exhale and suck in a breath. But then, as she treaded water, her feet searching for leverage, and found none—already the water was too deep.

"You're a hard-bitten woman," Málik complained. "What in the Goddess's name do you think you are doing?"

"Getting us into that city," she countered, spewing water, trying to calm the pounding of her heart. "Art planning to help, or did you come to harass me?"

Gwendolyn couldn't see his face, so she couldn't gauge Málik's expression, or his mood, but there was a note of *something* in his voice that could be mistaken for pride. And despite that, she felt his tension even as she felt the water warming around his body, tempting her close.

An instant later, the cavern lit with a familiar blue light, and then another. One flew toward her face so fiercely that she was forced to duck into the water to evade it.

"Your displeasure will not keep me from my

duty," she said when she re-emerged, but quickly, she realized he was not trying to prevent her from reaching the conduit.

He meant to help her.

Both Faerie flames soared through the pitch-black night, lighting the area in their immediate vicinity. Like battling blue stars, they crisscrossed the cavern, and then came to a halt before the conduit, which was still too far up to reach.

Gwendolyn swam beneath it, muttering a reluctant, "Thank you." No doubt she was grateful, but though some part of her wished she might have told him ahead of time so they could plan this together, she also knew Málik would never have willingly allowed her to subject herself to this danger. "We have to reach that conduit," she explained.

"I know what this is, Gwendolyn. Who do you think provided the design?"

"Not you!" she argued. "I distinctly remember the man who gave us the plans."

"And who do you believe provided the design for those gardens in Bāb-ilim?"

Gwendolyn's brows knit. "The Fae?"

"Precisely."

Treading water beneath the conduit, she tried to leap up to reach it, failing. Málik swam over to wrap his arms around her, and Gwendolyn didn't even realize how much she was shivering until the tremors ceased abruptly.

Merciful Mother! His warmth was magnificent!

"By the by, my people are Danann," he reminded her.

"Esme calls herself Fae," Gwendolyn argued. "Do you dislike the word so much?"

"No more than I do Elf or *Sidhe*, but these are your people's words, Gwendolyn. In my tongue, we are merely Danann. Though I do not care one way or the other, there is one person I know who concerns himself with the distinction, and you may do well to remember that."

"Who?"

"My father," he said darkly, and then fell silent.

Unfortunately, even once he held her aloft, Gwendolyn could still not reach the conduit, so she was forced to remain in his arms until the tide rose higher.

However, she could find no complaint in her current situation. The feel of Málik was delectable. Without realizing it, her nostrils flared and sought the crook of his neck, inhaling deeply of his scent... saltwater, sun, woods, male.

"I do care for you," he said, blowing out a sigh, the confession coming so reluctantly that Gwendolyn found herself slightly piqued.

"Do tell."

And yet, it shouldn't matter. She couldn't speak those three little words any more than he seemed able to. Nor would she so easily bare her heart—not when he already had all the proof he needed to glean how she felt, and as yet he'd not bothered to acknowledge this, nor to tell her more than *I do care for you.*

What did that mean, anyway?

What was she supposed to say?

Gwendolyn cared deeply for Bryn, but she did not love him, not the way she loved Málik. But for all she knew, this was all Málik felt for her—except she now knew better and she knew because of the gold he'd snipped from her hair. He did love her, even if he didn't want to confess as much.

"I'd never forgive myself if harm should come to you..." he said. "Let me lead."

Beneath the circle of his Faerie flame, Málik's sun-kissed face was lit with a bluish hue, his pale hair and *icebourne* eyes reflecting the flame.

Between them, the water grew warmer... and warmer still.

Gwendolyn shivered, but it wasn't from the cold. His heat was infectious, wending itself over her flesh and into her deepest self, teasing her cool skin.

"I will not bend to your will," she swore. "Never again will I do so because a man presumes I should."

"I do not expect you to," he said, his hands playing across the small of her back. "You are a queen, Gwendolyn. I am your servant to command, no matter how annoying you might be."

"*I* am annoying?"

Was he being serious?

Truly?

She was annoying?

"What about you? *You* are the one who fell silent, then marched away the instant proof of our destiny lay shining in my lap. Do you know how this made me feel, Málik?"

"I do," he said, lowering her, so her breasts nuzzled the warmth of his sinewy chest. His hands reached into her hair, his long fingers caressing her pate as his mouth came deliciously close to her own —so achingly close that she could scent the grass blades he so often chewed.

Gods. Oh, Gods. This was where she had so long desired to be—right here, in Málik's arms—but the timing was terrible. "I am sorry, Gwendolyn," he said. "For all the pain I have brought upon you. But you cannot possibly understand how wrong we are together. It cannot be."

By the eyes of Lugh! Gwendolyn's breasts pebbled against his solid warmth, and an ache coiled between her thighs. Never in her life had she been with a man. Only twice had she been kissed—once by Málik, the second time by Bryn, though she'd imagined that, too, as Málik, or she'd never have responded so wantonly. Even now, knowing she should not... knowing they were short of time, her hands found his neck, and she clung to him, still shivering, resting against his form, allowing him to support her. In some ridiculous part of her woman's brain, she considered that if death was inevitable, if all was truly lost, then this was the place she longed to take her final breath— right here, in his arms.

But those should not be the thoughts of a queen. She was more than a woman, and neither was Málik a man, simple or otherwise. Life was too complicated, and Gwendolyn could not allow herself to be distracted by his lips...

Bloody damn. She had wanted this too long.

"No, Gwendolyn," he whispered, as, of their own accord, her limbs found and wrapped themselves around his waist. She moaned softly as his lips descended upon hers—until suddenly, one of the Faerie flames shot down between their faces, blinding Gwendolyn unexpectedly.

"Blood and bloody bones!" she exclaimed.

Málik growled deep in his throat, flicking the wisp with a hand, but he sighed and disengaged, promising, "Later."

Something like joy threatened to possess Gwendolyn's heart at his promise, but she pushed it away, refocusing on her anger for Locrinus, too much diminished in the wake of Málik's confession. This was not the time to lose her head. Now was the time to keep her resolve.

As much as her father had loved her mother, it never kept him from his duty, nor did it keep her mother from doing hers.

Quickly, on the heels of Málik's confession, he'd spoken yet another truth—one she must not allow herself to forget, because it could well be the only truth she could afford to embrace.

You cannot possibly understand how wrong we are together.

It cannot be.

But that is not what his lips said, and despite that, Gwendolyn frowned because there was something else he was keeping from her—something Esme knew as well, but as yet had not shared.

The water rose to perilous levels.

Gwendolyn had never been here to watch it rise from this vantage, and she did not know how far it would go, nor if it would leave them air to breathe.

She suspected the only way to escape the rising tide was through the conduit itself. But once the lower conduit was filled, it would be virtually impossible to remove the blades.

Moreover, she had no way of knowing whether the lower blades were too waterlogged to displace. She wasn't too concerned with the higher ones, because it had doubtless been quite some time since the salt baths were filled, and they were probably brittle. But if she failed to enter the shaft, and the water in the cavern rose high enough—perhaps too high to give her time to sustain a breath to make it back down through the cavern and out—drowning was a distinct possibility. *Don't think about that right now,* she told herself.

Just swim.

Gwendolyn did, and when she was near enough, her fingers searched for and grasped the small ring built for this purpose—to steady the engineer whilst he worked on the first blade.

Without being asked, Málik's Faerie lights adjusted themselves so she could better see. One flew up the conduit and the other remained beside her, illuminating her workspace, while Málik held her steady below. All the while, the water grew more and more turbulent, bouncing off the far wall and returning to toss and tug at her.

Gwendolyn worked on the blades, even as the water rose high enough to slap the pipe extension that was constructed to begin the siphoning. Made of soft copper, easily welded and molded, the hollow structure was sadly warped from so much wear, encrusted with a layer of corrosion.

Intuitively, she understood the tide must rise at least high enough to submerge the first blade, or else the conduit would not have enough suction to begin. But she suspected it rose as high as the first few, in case one of the blades broke.

The water screw itself was made of wood. Naturally, there were provisions made so the blades could be removed and repaired because they, too, deteriorated.

All she had to do was remove one side of each blade, leaving the other.

It would not be a simple matter, but she could and would ascend via the blades like a ladder, making her way up through the conduit, until she reached the reservoir.

So long as the blades came free, the way should continue unobstructed.

There was another small opening above the reservoir, so the engineer could emerge there, rather than have to wait to descend through the cavern below.

Fortunately, there was a little more room within the shaft than she'd initially believed. The contact surface between the screw and pipe did not need to be watertight, so long as the amount of water being scooped with each turn was large enough compared to the water leaking out of each section of the screw per turn. If water from one section leaked into the lower one, it would be transferred upwards again by the next segment of the screw. It was a brilliant, yet simple invention, designed for easy repairs.

The first blade was swollen from continued contact with the water and stuck in its groove, but fortunately it cracked and broke away with the weight of Gwendolyn's body as she tugged.

Thereafter, she found it easy enough to remove each of the blades as she ascended, with Málik following close behind.

Before them, behind them, went his Faerie lights, and Gwendolyn was never more grateful for their help. Without them, she soon came to realize, the conduit may have been her tomb.

Scarcely had she released the second blade when the foaming sea water entered the shaft below, slapping vindictively at the sides of the copper pipe, lapping viciously at her hips.

Once Gwendolyn was free of the first blade and moved up to the next, she had to bend to take Málik's hand, pulling him up, so his head wouldn't be made into a bell clapper.

For another moment, his head was trapped between her thigh and the shaft.

"I know you don't wish to be commanded," he said. "But please hurry." He flashed a grin, and Gwendolyn had a sudden recollection of those sharp, pointy teeth skimming the flesh of her throat.

Gods. She told herself the shiver it gave her was because of the cold, frigid water, and blinked away the memory even as she moved on to the next blade... and then the next.... and the next... until the copper ended abruptly and the rest of the conduit was encased in solid granite. Meanwhile, as the water rose along the pipe, the sound of it rang like a death knell.

CHAPTER
FORTY-ONE

The interior of the shaft grew warm—in part, because Málik's body temperature was heating it. Gwendolyn wiped sweat out of her eyes with her arm as she climbed to the next blade, pulling off each in turn and dropping them below.

Clearly, it had been some time since these upper blades were exposed to water. They were drier, and easier to remove, but they were so fragile they were close to being worthless.

The ascent along the remaining blades was precarious. Should she slip and fall, they would both plummet into the water, and even if they could survive till the tide moved out again, her chance to retake this city would be lost. The blades could be repaired without a serious production. There would be no second chances.

Much had deteriorated as her father grew ill—far more than the land itself, and this was something she would need to address when she could.

Retaking the city was only the beginning of the work she must undertake.

Even now, despite that she still had doubts she could do it all, she was not about to be thwarted any more than she would allow a rotting piece of wood to stand in her way.

Tugging each in turn, she sighed with relief as they came undone.

"Make way for another," she warned Málik, and then smiled as she heard him curse when the wood clattered down, thwacking briefly against his head before tumbling down through the remainder of the tunnel beneath them.

"I told you not to come," she said, despite that he hadn't complained.

"At this rate, I should be covered by bruises before the battle is waged."

"Oh, really? Do you bruise?" Gwendolyn asked, sweat dripping from her forehead onto her nose.

"Everyone bruises," he said. "I bleed, too, while we're at it," he said. "Just in case you wondered."

"How should I know what flows through your veins?" Gwendolyn countered. "For all I know, 'tis molten lava, hot as you are making this tunnel."

"What do you expect? Without the heat of the sun, we are devoid of warmth in the Underworld. I have told you, Gwendolyn, the goddess arms her creatures accordingly."

"And your teeth? Will you tell me now what gives you sustenance?"

"What do you think? I eat what you eat. We simply do not need so much of it."

"So then, Esme lied? You do not eat babies or drink blood?"

"Well," he said, haltingly. "Some of us do. I do not.... not precisely. And yet, if in truth, if you offered me your throat to drink from, I could be tempted."

Gwendolyn stopped to consider that, perching herself onto the next blade, remembering the time he'd kissed her, pricking her lip, drawing blood. He'd lapped so greedily at her lips. The memory gave her a shiver—not of fear. Still, she didn't like his answer, so when the next blade dropped, she hoped it thumped his head.

"Ouch!" he said. "Something tells me you are enjoying this."

"Perhaps I am. What else have you not told me?"

"Quite a lot, I imagine," he said.

Gwendolyn encountered a few blades that were completely gone, disintegrated, and she imagined they'd broken off on their own. They were probably floating down there somewhere. In fact, there were three altogether that were entirely broken on both sides, and if it weren't for Málik, she couldn't have reached the next rung. As much as she loathed to admit it, they made a good team—particularly when he was actually being helpful.

If only he would tell her the truth—all of it. "You know, I could stop here, keep you confined indefinitely until you deign to tell me everything."

"Go on. Do it," he dared. "Your belly will grumble long before mine, and you will lose the chance to take your city. What else do you want to know? As I've already told you, Gwendolyn, I do not eat so much as you do. We simply do not have a vast supply of flora and fauna below since your kindred saw fit to cheat us of our lands."

"Cheat you?"

"Aye," he said. "When we agreed to cede the

choice of lands to the victor, we did not anticipate that you would banish us below, like rabbits and moles."

"You sound bitter over it," Gwendolyn suggested. "One would think that you were the very one swindled?"

He didn't respond for the longest time, and Gwendolyn's brows lifted. "Were you?"

But nay, it couldn't be. Because that would mean he was ancient—far, far older than she had ever supposed. His tone was embittered. "Let's leave that subject for another time," he said with a throaty sigh. "Keep your attention on the task at hand, Gwendolyn. In fact, we should be close enough now that perhaps it's best to end our discourse."

"How convenient for you," she grumbled.

But it was true. They were too close now—so close she could feel it in the sudden relief from Málik's heat, a cool draft that was also apparent by the feathering of his Faerie flame. It had behaved just that same way when it revealed the exit to her uncle's *fogous*.

Later, she told herself.

Later, she would make him tell her everything.

And then she would kiss him soundly, and the gods only knew what else she would do. Even now, her body tingled over the memory of his touch, and she didn't bloody care if she was still married to Locrinus. Her heart belonged to Málik.

After removing the final blade, Gwendolyn stood, then hauled herself into a mostly dry reservoir, crawling across only half an inch of stale, musty water.

She couldn't wait to be free of this contraption,

and no matter how brilliantly it was constructed, she was tempted to bury it when all was said and done. No man or woman should ever be expected to traverse this oxygen-deprived hole in the ground.

Spotting the exit at last, she crawled over, splaying her palm across the trapdoor. She pushed it, but the door came free with no help from her, clattering to the floor.

A pair of wide black eyes peered into the reservoir. "Yestin?"

"Majesty?"

The elder man froze, staring at Gwendolyn, blinking.

"You?" she whispered, her heart squeezing painfully, even as her mind raced with possibilities, none of them good.

Below her, she heard the hiss of metal as Málik's dagger left his scabbard.

Gwendolyn still had Borlewen's blade as well in case she needed it to pry loose the blades, but neither she nor Málik would have proper weapons until she opened the portal to admit Caradoc.

Her father's steward blinked at her, as though he could scarcely believe his eyes, then he gave her a nod. "Oh, gods! Yestin," Gwendolyn said, her tone filled with so much sorrow.... because suddenly, she understood how such a great deception could have been carried out so expertly—the *droguing* of so many guests, the allowance of weapons into their hall...

Her father's steward held the keys to their city. He, alone, had oversight over nearly every operation, every palace worker, every affair, and even the smallest of tasks.

Her father and mother had loved and trusted him without reservation, and Gwendolyn herself had looked to him first even before going to her parents.

Yestin had taught her to manage the household accounts. He'd planned her Promise Ceremony, and the only thing he wasn't in charge of was the palace security—a fact that left her feeling suddenly uneasy, because Yestin couldn't have managed alone.

The elder man swallowed, stepping back from the reservoir so Gwendolyn could no longer see his face. "Are we alone?" she dared to ask, but her voice lacked emotion. Bracing herself for battle, she inhaled a steadying breath.

"For now," Yestin said. "Who goes with you?"

"I do," growled Málik, his voice dark and menacing as he pushed Gwendolyn aside, emerging before her, landing like a cat on his feet, then flashing his blade.

Yestin did not speak again until Gwendolyn, too, emerged, and then he said, "I have regretted my part in this, Majesty... but... but... I... fear you'll never understand."

Gwendolyn swallowed her grief, making room for anger. "You are right, Yestin. I do not understand," she said. "Did we dis-serve you?"

The elder man shook his head. "I loved my King, but he was...so... ill... and so old... and..."

She guessed the rest before he could speak it. "And you did not believe I could lead my people?"

Gwendolyn saw the truth in his eyes. He had not believed in her. Given the choice to support a strong new king or wait to see if Gwendolyn could rise to the task, he had chosen Locrinus, and in his choice, he had sealed her father's fate, and hers as well.

"I did what I considered best for Trevena," explained Yestin. "I was made to see the advantage for our people. Brutus was unfit to rule!" he said, rambling now. "What hope can any man have to lead if his own sons will not respect him, and neither his bride?"

Gwendolyn swallowed with some difficulty, her spine snapping straight. With every word, she hardened her resolve.

"It was only a matter of time before your father succumbed to his illness—weeks, perhaps mere days —and then it would be Brutus or Locrinus with you by his side. I chose you," he said. "Don't you see, Majesty? My choice was you! He told me you would never be harmed?"

The last sounded more like a question, and this told her that even he had had some doubt. And still he'd left her to that viper. Her jaw worked as she listened to his confession. With tears stinging her eyes, she climbed out of the reservoir and bounded to the floor, her hand moving to Borlewen's dagger. And then, she focused on a single word... "He?"

Yestin took a defensive step backward, his gaze fixed upon Gwendolyn, not Málik, though Málik's blade flashed menacingly against a bit of torch light that slipped in through the open door. "I am sorry," he said. "*He* made me do it."

"He?" Gwendolyn said once more, certain that whoever *he* was, the man must have had great sway —not only with Yestin, but the palace at large.

"Yestin!" called a male voice, and then they were no longer alone. A red-cloaked figure came rushing through the door, discarding his cloak, and even as his fingers moved to his breeches, seeking his laces, he quickly assessed the situation and froze.

It happened so swiftly thereafter. Málik rushed across the chamber to dispatch the red-cloaked guard, slicing the man's throat before he had time to draw his sword. The gurgle he made as the blade withdrew from his flesh was amplified in the empty chamber.

The yowl that followed was Yestin's, imbued with sorrow. Her father's steward fell to his knees as Málik turned, wiping his dagger against his leather tunic, and said. "What should I do with him... Majesty?"

Gwendolyn could not allow herself to be moved by pity, and yet, she was. Clearly, these two men were lovers, but somehow, she did not sense that the *"he"* Yestin spoke of was this man who now lay in a puddle of red. This man was nobody.

Right now, she didn't have time to interrogate Yestin.

"Bind him here for now." It had been more than three months since news had left this city. Even so, she harbored some hope that he might know what became of her mother and Demelza.

"I have questions for later, but you may shut his mouth permanently if he doesn't cease sniveling. Just keep him quiet." She left Málik to do what he must, trusting him to know what that should be.

There was no time to lose.

Soon enough, the guards would grow bored with the dancers. They would find themselves a dark corner to satiate their lust, and thereafter, the dancers would hold little appeal—at least not until the morning, when they would be allowed entrance.

Hoping to the gods that her tunic would conceal her presence, she made short work of the distance to the hidden postern, feeling better when she raised no alarms. Once there, she climbed behind the stack of bricks, and then used Borlewen's blade to pry open the lock. Once it clicked, she drew open the door, relieved to see Caradoc's face.

"At last!" he said. "There's as much room on that cliff side as there is in the crack of my arse!" he complained.

Gwendolyn arched a brow as he entered, unwilling to discuss the dimensions of his arse crack. "All ascended without issue?" she asked, not immediately seeing Bryn's face.

"Aye," he confirmed, handing Gwendolyn her sword. "Your boy brings up the rear."

"Good," Gwendolyn said, turning. "Then remember your promise," she warned.

"And you remember yours," returned Caradoc, and without waiting for the men to file in after him, he went straight toward the courtyard, intending to secure the towers.

FORTY-THREE

H*e.*

Some inkling of suspicion reared, but Gwendolyn refused to believe it.

Eager to know if she was right, she didn't wait for Bryn or Málik.

Leaving Caradoc and his men to ascend to dispatch the sentries, knowing they could manage well enough without her, she made her way straight toward the palace.

The entire city was dark, with very few torches lit against the night. It was clear to Gwendolyn that Locrinus had already stripped this city of its stores, leaving them with so little and no impetus to replace what his armies consumed.

Selfish, self-serving boor.

Her blade thirsted for his blood, but she knew intuitively he wasn't here.

Someone else would pay in his stead... until she could find him and plunge Borlewen's dagger into his heart—not in his back, as he would do to her.

More than anything, Gwendolyn longed to watch the light leave his eyes as he died, and to have him know it was she who had taken his life—as he had stolen hers.

Her hand strangled the hilt of her sword, her feet moving quickly and with purpose, knowing the way better than she knew her palm.

Despite the faint lilt of music coming from the barbican, there was no air of festivity within the palace. If her father had been alive, this would be the hour when their hall would be filled with diners and dancers, and even during the quietest of evenings, there was still dancing and revelry.

Her mother's *dawnsio* was the pride of this city, and Queen Eseld never failed to seize the opportunity to display their talents, even without guests in attendance.

Tonight, however, she found the palace curiously vacant, with only a few guards trolling the halls. Despite her mithril, Gwendolyn intended to take no chances. Any time she heard the smallest noise, she hid, waiting to see what came. When nothing did, she continued.

The great hall was empty. Her father's throne still stood upon the dais, as though he'd only moments ago completed his audiences and wandered away. The sight of it grieved her, squeezing her heart painfully, but she did not linger to dwell on the past.

Continuing down the hall, she noted the stench of piss as she passed one dark corner and pressed the back of her hand to her nose as she hid there a moment to wait as two guards wandered by. *Godsblood.* Her mother would be horrified by this insult—her beautiful, polished granite floors were filthy after months of neglect. Trevena was well on its way to looking like Loegria. The thought of this disgusted

Gwendolyn, but it didn't surprise her, because Locrinus had never cared for this city. He only cared for his precious Troia Nova—a city that didn't even exist except as a thought in his greedy little mind. But those lands were not his to take.

It didn't matter whether Plowonida remained unclaimed, nor that the neighboring tribes were bitter enemies. No tribe—not even the Iceni—would stand by and allow another king to march in and take lands belonging to another. It was written in the Brothers' Pact, though that would not stop Locrinus. There was nothing sacred to him—not marriage, nor laws, nor life.

Eyes closed, with her back against the wall, she swore that, with her hand squeezing the dragon of Borlewen's blade.

Once the guards passed, she continued on her way.

Dressed as she was, with her hair completely shorn, she didn't believe anyone would immediately recognize her, but, just in case, she kept to the shadows.

She saw no one.

There were no young boys carrying towels for the *piscina*, no maids to convey messages betwixt apartments. The torches were not brightly lit, a few of the cressets were entirely empty, with black soot already creeping up the wall, where no maids had bothered to scrub in months.

Her rooms were now to the left, but Gwendolyn had no desire to return to her chambers, as so often she had done upon entering the palace. There was no telling who would be there tonight, and she was no longer a child to run and hide there. There was one place she sensed would not be empty, and this was where her feet led her now... to the king's chamber.

For years before his death, Gwendolyn had not entered her father's apartments. During his illness, he'd not encouraged it, and though he'd never forbidden it to her mother, he begrudged her entry as well. He did not enjoy being seen as frail, and, toward the end, there were many, many evenings he'd forgone the *dawnsio* and even his supper to rest alone in his rooms, save for the company of his Shadows.

Tonight, there were no guards in the king's antechamber, and Gwendolyn surmised Locrinus had conscripted every able body for his army. Inhaling a breath, she cracked the door and found... just as she'd expected... the room was *not* empty.

One man stood in the center of his room, his posture entirely too familiar.

"You?" she whispered.

Talwyn Durotriges spun to face her, his look of surprise quickly turning to one of annoyance, as though she were a cockroach he'd discovered in his bed. "Indeed," said her father's Mester at Arms. *Bryn's father.* "Who else could command such a feat?"

There were no words to explain the fury that ignited within her. The rumble that came from her lips was like that from of a wild beast. Gwendolyn lunged at him, not caring to hear his explanations, aching to carve the smirk from his face.

She was no longer his child prodigy. Thanks to Málik, she had moves her former tutor would never anticipate, and neither would she be squeamish about drawing his blood. She didn't care if he was Bryn's father. She would gut him and pull out his entrails—strangle him with them.

With two hands, she gripped her bastard sword, remembering every lesson Málik ever taught her. *Aim diagonally. Keep your eyes on the sword. Raise the pommel. Pull back as you thrust. Don't forget to step. Add your hip into the cut. Don't spin. Move your sword with your body.*

Bryn's father was a master swordsman.

Talwyn was never without his weapon.

He drew his sword easily, lifting it to meet Gwendolyn's strike. Feigning to parry, he spun, aiming toward Gwendolyn's ribs. She eluded the slice, resisting the urge to spin, having learned this tactic from none other than him. Instead, she kept her gaze on his sword, light on her feet, stalking him, backing him into a corner with her sword, two handed, adjusting it to be ready, mentally aware of every step she took and how it would affect her thrust.

Thrust don't swing. Light on your toes. Eyes on the sword.

"Why?" she demanded, the single word sharp as her blade.

"Why?" Talwyn's face screwed with hatred. "Why?" he asked again. "Because I gambled my life on your father and watched him grow feeble as a mouse!"

He lunged at Gwendolyn, but she was ready for him, blocking his strike. Now, instead of spinning as he'd taught her to do, she steadied herself, saving her energy for a more calculated strike.

"Why?" Talwyn continued. "Because I served my King well, I trained his men—I even trained you, a stupid, whiny little girl! I commanded this garrison, and when that filthy, faithless Elf came around, the King gave *my* duties to him, and left me to watch like a useless old bitch while that creature attempted to instruct me as well!"

"Why!" Talwyn shouted again. "Why? Why! Why!" He was livid now, red faced, the whites of his eyes entirely too visible. "Because, when my stupid son served the King's ill-begotten daughter so dutifully—so ignorantly! Only because he loved the stupid little turd! He was demoted and replaced with another. Discarded! Shame-faced! Bringing dishonor upon my name and house!"

Gwendolyn bided her time, refusing to take his bait, hoping his anger would lead to mistakes. She stalked him, listening, watching for the opportunity to strike. Once she was close enough, she shifted her feet and body into the proper position, and struck, grazing his wrist, drawing blood. But the man was too quick for his age, evading Gwendolyn's maneuver, then pivoting, stalking Gwendolyn instead.

"All for what? You?" he continued with loathing, spittle spraying from his lips. "A worthless bitch who no longer even honors your sex! Look at you!" Once again, he screwed his face with disgust. "You were never lovely, but now? You look like a man! No softness about you at all! You are a disgrace to your breed, and no matter. A woman should not command Pretania's throne!"

Gwendolyn's jaw ticked with fury, her fingers biting into cold steel, simmering with the desire to run this traitor through.

Bryn's father grinned with contempt. "Why? You ask why? Because the instant your father perished, we would have been left with nothing. Aligning with Brutus' elder born gave us the means to endure in this city that *I* helped to build!"

"You ungrateful whoreson!" Gwendolyn returned. "My father gave you everything, and I considered you among the noblest of men—particularly after turning your face from a dukedom to serve your king instead. Your brother is dead now—Adwen, did you know? Did he mean so little to you? And what of your son?"

He shrugged, unconcerned. "My brother and I were never of the same mind. His fate is not mine to lament. He had a chance and failed—as you will fail, you hideous, ill-favored creature. Locrinus is the wiser choice, and *he* will command this isle. My son will rise under his command!"

"Nay, he'll not," Gwendolyn assured. "I will see that the only thing Locrinus commands is a cell, and you will join him."

"Oh, no," Talwyn said hatefully. "You might prevail and you might even kill me. You might even keep your precious Trevena... for a while, but he has something you'll never have."

Gwendolyn's smile was cold. "Indeed, what is that?"

"A cock," he spat. "Butcher your hair all you wish, play at being a king, but you are not a man, and the thing you lack most is the one thing your *husband* has —the will to see this done."

"I may not have a cock," Gwendolyn returned. "But I intend to show you my balls!" She rushed at him, striking with all her might.

His sword met hers with a clang that reverberated through the palace halls.

Again and again, she struck, driving him back.

When she cornered him against the wall, he lifted a leg and pushed himself off, driving toward her so ferociously that his blade snicked the curve between her throat and shoulder, a fraction above where the mithril no longer protected. The sight of her blood seemed to arouse him, and he swung again, then turned so his back was to the door. Gwendolyn noted the entryway darken, but daren't look away from his sword. If she was outnumbered, she couldn't afford to acknowledge it. Blood trickled down her arm, seeping down between her palm and her sword, oiling the metal. She had not yet had much of a chance to practice left-handed, despite that the sword could be wielded either way. Right now, she couldn't afford to switch hands, nor could she take a moment to brush the blood from her palm.

The next time he came at her, she met his blade with hers, but the impact of it knocked her sword from her hand. It clattered across the floor. Instinctively, Gwendolyn reached for Borlewen's blade, but froze at the sound of a familiar voice, the timber of it sending a shiver down her spine. "Gwendolyn is too trusting."

Bryn?

For a terrible, heart-rending moment, Gwendolyn feared she had been betrayed by her closest of friends —her beloved Bryn.

"So... it was you who aided Locrinus?"

She heard him approach but couldn't turn to face him. The very possibility of his betrayal left her momentarily undone.

Talwyn grinned at his son. "Yes! Don't you see? I did it for you, Bryn! For our good name! Only I could have convinced Yestin to go along."

"Yestin?" Bryn asked calmly, his hand moving to his sword as he passed Gwendolyn, briefly meeting her eyes. Gone now was all trace of the boy he'd once been. In his place was a man, his expression hard and cold. He came sauntering into the room, his gait so much like his father's—the glint in his eyes, too. Gwendolyn had never heard him speak so coldly.

"Trevena will be ours," his father continued, his eyes avid, gleeful. "Ours, son! Only imagine! Did you never consider that this would be your fate? To some day sit upon our Cornish throne?"

"After you?" Bryn asked carefully, and Gwendolyn still could not tell whose side he was on. Her gaze slid to her fallen sword, uncertain whether to dive for it. But if she did, and Bryn intended to take his father's side, he could easily turn and smite her. He was standing right beside her.

"Where is my mother?" Bryn asked.

"Fled," Talwyn revealed. "I knew she'd not have the stomach for any of this, so I let her go."

"As you *let* me go?" Bryn asked.

"Of course."

"I did wonder... even when Ely and Gwendolyn did not... why my sister and I were both allowed to leave Trevena after the wedding, when before you both forbade it. For so many years, you denied us service to Gwendolyn together, with the argument that you required one child to remain in Trevena." He cocked his head the other way. "I then wondered why Locrinus seemed so willing to pardon me even as he tormented me—do you have any clue what I endured by his hand?"

Bryn's father shook his head.

"And then, father... I wondered why every time I mentioned your name, the topic was turned, and no news of your death ever arrived, even after I sent men to investigate."

His father answered with silence, and Bryn continued. "I also wondered why Queen Innogen—indeed, even her son—would be so willing to believe my uncle would so readily bend the knee that they would invite him to feast."

"My brother—"

"Shut up!" Bryn exploded, and it was only in that moment that Gwendolyn was reassured... He was on her side. The hatred she spied in his countenance as he regarded his father grew palpable, but quickly, on the heels of that thought, came another... if she allowed Bryn to kill his father, he would never be the same thereafter.

"Even when Adwen *told* me he suspected your part in the coup, I refused to believe it."

"You knew?" Gwendolyn asked, stunned, her hand automatically reaching for Borlewen's blade, her thumb pressing against the dragon's eye. But Bryn did not look at her and neither did his father. Father and son continued to glare at one another.

Bryn walked about his father, and with Gwendolyn swordless, he mistook her to be the lesser threat, following his son as Bryn turned him in a circle. "Why, Father? Why, when you could have had Durotriges?"

"You fool! I did not want Durotriges!" replied Talwyn. "I wanted Trevena and Cornwall. What is a sad little village in comparison?"

Rage burned through Gwendolyn's veins—more intense by far than her outrage over Bryn's closely kept secret. There were far too many secrets being kept, but she wanted this man dead.

Faces flashed before her—her father, her mother,

Demelza, Cunnedda, Beryan, her sweet cousins, Lowenna...

She wanted to cut out Talwyn's heart and hold it in her hand, crush it as he had crushed hers. But if she did this, Bryn would never forgive her...

Unbidden, Málik's voice whispered into her ear—an echo from the past... *Notice where the point is... Do not aim for the heart. 'Tis difficult to hit anything of consequence when you stab a man in the back. Here, you will pierce the reins. The pain will be excruciating, and your opponent will drop like a stone.*

No longer would she allow others to fight her battles. If she would be queen, it must come at the cost of blood... beginning with Talwyn's.

Gwendolyn moved close enough to kick her fallen sword to across the room. When Talwyn turned toward the sound, that's when she moved. The blade in her hand was long enough to slip between a rib and stab a heart. But she sought the place Málik once directed her. *His Liver.* Unerringly, Borlewen's blade pierced his reins, and her traitor—Bryn's father—dropped like a stone.

FORTY-FOUR

Gwendolyn sent messengers into the Cod's Wold to retrieve any who would return to the city. A few would remain with their flocks. The rolling hills were ideal for grazing sheep, and Málik suggested their presence would be gladly received, for the weavers in the Eastwalas temple were sorely in need of a good supply of wool—some for their death shrouds, some for their scholarly robes.

Here in Trevena, Caradoc immediately settled himself in the king's chamber, and despite that Gwendolyn had some trepidation over leaving him with the keys to her city, she knew she must. She had spoken truthfully when she'd said she could not cower behind Trevena's gates. As it stood, she had but a handful of castaways amidst her numbers, and if she did not seek an alliance with the rest of Pretania's tribes, they would wither away in this corner of the isle and die. Indeed, for all the reasons she'd previously disclosed, one prolonged siege might finish them, and if they did not drive each other mad, or die of starvation, they would eventually take their final breaths in a city where no one could be interred and their bodies must be cast into the sea.

Under a crescent moon, she stood musing atop the ramparts, arms crossed against a cool evening breeze, staring out over the darkened city. There were but a few discernible lights in the barbican and beyond, but the city itself lay at rest, all lights extinguished so that only the stars and moon lit the night. But Gwendolyn could not rest—not yet. There was too much to be done to restore the city to its former glory. Their stores were entirely depleted, and except for the men she'd brought with her, the garrison lay unmanned. So many of her father's loyal warriors fled after Talwyn's betrayal.

Already, she'd dispatched messengers to nearby villages to see what could be spared—be it men, or supplies. Now, with the tarp once again lifted to bare the Dragon's Flame, the port was preparing to receive ships, although it would take time for the return to normal business, and some manner of practicable defense for the harbor must be established to guard against raiders.

No longer could they adhere to her father's open-door practice. They must now find some compromise that would allow for the import of goods without leaving them quite so vulnerable.

As for Yestin. She hadn't yet decided what to do about him. The poor man was heartbroken, and he had done no more than listen to the wrong person. He had believed with all his might that Gwendolyn would never be harmed. His worst offense was the betrayal of her father, but he had also believed the King was dying, and he'd considered her father's death a mercy. But, as influential as he always was,

Talwyn was even more so, and Talwyn wasn't merely his brother by law, he was the Mester at Arms. As such, he should have known best how to defend the city. That Yestin later discovered a lover amidst the enemy hadn't helped her father's cause, but the death of his lover was, perhaps, punishment enough. His remorse over his part in the coup was more than apparent. He himself had insisted upon being held in a gaol cell, and refused to eat or drink. Tonight, Gwendolyn had insisted he be removed, and detained in his own quarters and before she left, she must attend him to see what more she could discover about Loc and his defenses.

And yet, what irony there was in that the most impenetrable city on the isles was so easily infiltrated by a handful of men, and one woman.

Unfortunately, now that so many knew about the city's one vulnerability in terms of accessibility, she must order the destruction of her father's *piscina*. Even now, the long shaft housing the water screw was being prepared to be dismantled and sealed.

Later, if perchance Caradoc intended to betray her, Gwendolyn would have no way back into the city. But that could not prevent her from pursuing justice.

Sadly, after all she had endured, trust would not come easily, but she must begin somewhere or she'd accomplish little, and Locrinus would prevail.

But for Talwyn...

She shook her head, remembering the hatred that gushed from him. She had never had a clue—not one inkling—that he'd felt this way about Gwendolyn and her family.

Gods. The look on Bryn's face when she slew his

father was one Gwendolyn would not soon forget—such torment, such pain, and grief... Yet he seemed to understand she'd had to do it.

Poor Ely... the tears she'd wept would fill the *piscina*.

And still there was no word of Lady Ruan. Moreover, no one could say whether Queen Eseld and Demelza had followed her. In truth, there was no proof anyone had escaped. For all Gwendolyn knew, Talwyn was lying and perhaps he'd murdered his own wife, disposing of her along with the rest of the dissenters?

Gwendolyn's hope was that Yestin had insisted his sister fled with her maid, and if Lady Ruan found a way out of this city, perhaps Gwendolyn's mother had as well?

It would be impossible to inventory the dead. Even if their bodies could still be recognizable after so many weeks, all the cadavers were cast into the bay, to be consumed by porbeagles and threshers.

As for the alderman who'd murdered Bryok, there was no sign of him here, and Gwendolyn was certain he, too, had fled. Perhaps he'd outlived his usefulness?

She heard footfalls behind her, but didn't bother to turn, recognizing the gait.

After a moment, Málik sidled up beside her, lifting an arm over her shoulders, though for the longest moment, he said nothing, daring to enjoy the quiet before the coming storm...

For truly, that's what this was.

A maelstrom raging on the horizon—a rain of blood and ash.

Indeed, all that had transpired here would be nothing compared to what was still to come...

"Your mother's chambers are being prepared for you," Málik said. "I should sleep in your antechamber."

Gwendolyn wanted him to be closer, but couldn't demand it. So much as she loathed the thought, she was still Locrinus' wife, and so, much as she knew the Lifer Pol Druids would favor her, there was still the Llanrhos Order to consider, and the *Awenydds and Gwyddons* as well. None of these were factions Gwendolyn could afford to alienate if she wanted their support in her bid for the crown, and, truly, it wouldn't matter that her marriage to Locrinus was not consummated, she stood in front of those authorities, not once, but twice to give her assent. They would expect her to honor her vows until Locrinus was dead—but how inane that they would not have cared if she'd taken lovers discreetly as she ruled by his side... Or that Loc himself could share his quarters with a mistress and her child. But still they would judge Gwendolyn by her every action merely because she was a woman who dared to seize the crown for herself. This was a man's world... yet not for long, she vowed.

"I suppose Caradoc gave my bower to his daughters?" she asked.

"So I'm told," Málik confirmed.

Gwendolyn sighed, hugging herself tighter, cupping her elbows.

Málik perhaps mistook her sigh. "As you have said, 'tis but a temporary measure. Caradoc will surely keep his word."

Gwendolyn was certain of it as well—in part because Taryn would see to it. In her absence, she had insisted Taryn must share in Trevena's governance. It was the least she could do to ensure that the Durotrigan refugees' needs were met. Not all of them had agreed to be ruled by Caradoc, and Gwendolyn would not force them to return to their homesteads if they preferred to remain in Trevena.

Before traveling north, she also intended to award her mother's chamber to Ely and to Kelan. But, in fact, aside from making certain her most beloved were cared for, Gwendolyn wasn't too concerned about who made use of what, nor what remained upon her return. However, there was something bothering her...

She turned to look into Málik's face... his silvery eyes darker in the shadows. He slid a hand to her shoulder, and for a moment, there it remained, the gesture sweet and tender. "Did you speak to Bryn?" she asked.

He nodded, dropping the hand to his side. "He means to ride north with us. Lir as well... but..."

"But?"

"I have concerns..."

"I know," she said, anticipating his words, because it was on her mind as well. "You fear we'll not be able to convince Baugh to ride south under our banners despite that we have promised as much to Caradoc?"

Málik nodded again. "He might be your grandsire, but too long he has divorced himself from these southern tribes. He'll not be swayed to your cause merely because his blood flows through your veins. And yet I'm certain you knew that."

It was Gwendolyn's turn to nod, and she cast her

eyes down, worried. "I did fear as much," she confessed. "And yet I mean to give him another consideration. Innogen confessed his brother intends to ride north again. I mean to promise our support."

"Even so, he may not be swayed," Málik warned, and Gwendolyn knew he spoke true. Baugh was a man unto himself. He had repeatedly rejected even the notion of a Prydein confederacy, and had accepted his role as their leader with much reluctance, preferring to remain unencumbered by duty to any but his own tribe. He'd agreed to give a daughter to Cornwall only grudgingly—grudgingly enough so that in all of Gwendolyn's nineteen years, he'd never once cared to inquire over his granddaughter, even despite honoring the treaties he'd made with her father. Nor had he once sought news of his own daughter, leaving her to live her life alone amidst strangers.

He might be king in the north, but he was a mystery as well—one that her father and her mother had discouraged Gwendolyn from ever resolving—why she did not know.

Crickets chirped. An owl hooted. Somewhere in the distance, a fox screamed, seeking his mate.

Gwendolyn could tell there was something more Málik wished to say, but he was oddly reluctant to speak.

Foreboding hovered like a storm cloud between them, and the silence continued to stretch, leaving Gwendolyn with a sick feeling in the pit of her belly. "Speak," she begged, and he blew out a sigh fraught with tension.

"There is more I must tell you... but... I do not know how you will receive it."

Gwendolyn gave him a wan smile. "There's one

way to find out, though if you mean to tell me you intend to leave again, I'll not allow it."

His lips turned slightly at one corner. "How will you stop me?"

Gwendolyn lifted a shoulder. "I'll think of a way," she answered coyly, and her woman's intuition said it was true.

A mirthful sound escaped him, but that laughter died abruptly on his lips. "I will not leave," he promised. "But you may demand it if I tell you the truth..."

"Say it and be done," Gwendolyn told him. Her playful tone vanished as he crossed his arms and took a step back.

"Very well. To begin with, you must know the northern tribes are much akin to the Fomorians. As it was with Balor, loyalties go only so far."

Fomorians? Gwendolyn blinked up at him, confused. "I thought the northern tribes were kindred to the sons of Míl?"

"They are... but... as it is with all mortals, blood ties are not always so pure. Fomorians are Danann, only mated with the sons of Míl."

Gwendolyn lifted a brow. "So..." She blinked. "*I* am part Fomorian?"

His eyes glinted against the night. "In part, their legacy makes you fearless, Gwendolyn. But lamentably, you'll find your Prydein kin are equally so. They are not to be trifled with, and if you've never met one, the size and breadth of them will astound you."

Gwendolyn blinked. How could so much of this have escaped her? "I don't understand." She shook her head. "My mother was Prydein. She was no taller than my father?"

"Your mother was not typical," he said. "Why do you think Baugh took so long to offer a daughter to the southern tribes? If she had been another, your father may have denied her." His eyes slanted sadly as he reached out to touch a finger to Gwendolyn's cheek. "Make no mistake, Gwendolyn... Eseld was beautiful. As are you—the loveliest creature I've ever beheld. And despite this, you will not find your grandsire so eager to lay down arms simply because you ask."

His revelations were all so confusing—everything, from his claim of her beauty to the lessons of her bloodline. She had never considered herself to be beautiful, and it was not something she was comfortable hearing. She turned away, a thousand questions dancing on her tongue. "What should I do?" She hardened her heart against the prospect of war. "I'll not raise my sword against my mother's own kin and the people I hope to rally to my cause."

"No," said Málik. "But there's another way..."

He pulled her close now, reaching out to mold one hand into the curve of her neck, with two fingers resting against the pulse behind her ear. The heat of his touch left Gwendolyn breathless, and for the longest moment, she could think of nothing but him —not Baugh, nor Locrinus, not the possibility of war...

There was only here, now.

"Gwendolyn," he whispered, bending to brush his mouth against her trembling lips, grazing her tender flesh with the sharp points of his teeth...

Gods. At this instant, Gwendolyn was neither a queen, nor a warrior, simply a woman, and the warmth of his hand on her cool skin stole away her breath.

She didn't stop him when he covered her mouth, the heat of his lips blistering hers, his hot tongue seeking entrance, his fangs nipping ever so gently. In response, Málik deepened the kiss, and Gwendolyn forgot to breathe.

She forgot to be timid or refined.

She forgot, too, that she had no experience with loving a man.

All she knew... all she understood was this undeniable hunger... and it drove her to mimic the way his lips and tongue tangled with her own. All those reasons she'd given herself for not allowing herself to form a physical bond... much having to do with the approval of others... flew from her head.

Craving more, her fingers dug into his leathers, clinging to him desperately, plundering his mouth, adoring the taste of him, wanting more... and more... and more... until...

A growl erupted from the depths of his throat, and he broke free of the kiss, extricating himself from their embrace, and then returning to rest his forehead against her own, trembling with the effort to restrain himself. Gwendolyn sensed more than saw that he closed his eyes, his long, soft lashes tickling her skin.

"If all were as it should be... I would make you a widow," he said. "And then I would make you my own."

As though to emphasize the truth of his words, his body hardened against her, and she could feel the length of his arousal—unmistakable despite that she had never once had the occasion to know a man's body.

Her own body responded like a wanton, her breasts pebbling against his leathered chest, her arms aching to embrace him more fully... wanting so wretchedly, to lie down on these ramparts, in full view of everyone, including the gods... to experience the deliciousness of his weight atop her.

Desperate for this experience, Gwendolyn tried to make him kiss her again, pulling him close, begging without words, and once again, he pulled away, seizing her by the wrists, and said, "No."

"Why?" Gwendolyn cried. "Why! It cannot be because I am wed? My heart does not belong to Loc!" And yet, despite that, even now, she could not admit that it already belonged to Málik—not when she had such a terrible, awful feeling that, despite his promise, he meant to go again.

For a moment, he ignored Gwendolyn's question, answering another. "The way to convince Baugh to follow you, Gwendolyn, is to ask my father for *Claímh Solais*. That sword will burn for you, and no other. If you wield it, Baugh will not refuse you."

Gwendolyn's brow furrowed, focusing not on the promise of *Claímh Solais*, but on the *other* thing he'd said. "Your father?"

He nodded again. "The King Below."

"But... that would make you—"

His eyes remained shadowed with something like regret. "Not as it would appear, Gwendolyn... I was his foster son, and despite so, it matters not if that sword should be yours by right. He'll not return it to you if you come to him as my heart-mate. Instead, he'll lock you away as he did my true father... Or he'll send you back here. Nameless and faceless... only to torment me again, and again, and again..." He cupped her face with both hands, shaking her gently, his bright silver eyes begging her to understand. "It is not because you are part Fomorian he'll decide against you, Gwendolyn. He, himself, is a son of Milesius. What will be the end of you is..." He inhaled sharply, closing his eyes. When he reopened them again, the blue in his irises had brightened to the hottest shade of a flame. "*Me,*" he said, his pupils elongating, then thinning, like that of a viper's. Even with the barest hint of moonlight, his translucent skin began to shimmer and two small horns appeared on his head. "You see... I am the son of the Dark One," he explained. "The Banished Wyrm. The last true-blood heir to the Tuatha'an throne... and you... you... have been my weakness for a hundred thousand years."

Confused, Gwendolyn's arms dropped to her sides.

Only then did it occur to her that the prophecy suddenly made sense with this revelation. The union she was born to make was *not* to the serpent of Loegria... It was to... *Málik.*

Gooseflesh erupted on her skin. "*You...* are... the Dragon Prince," she said, her voice barely above a whisper.

He nodded. "Indeed," he said. "It was my sire who lost the battle against the Milesians. When trickery found him banished behind the veil, Aengus seized his throne and imprisoned him, called him a demon. He then took me as his ward... for my own good, he said. Esme is his daughter, and this is why he would like to see us wed... to validate his half-blood lineage, even as Locrinus wishes to do with you."

"And... your true father?"

Málik shrugged. "All that remains of him lies in

the power he bestowed upon your sword... and in your Dragon's Lair. And... in me."

Gwendolyn opened her mouth to speak, then closed it again, bereft of words. She understood now that Esme had attempted to prepare her for this revelation, but there was nothing that could have done so.

"You asked me why I came to Trevena... I told you I was both summoned and sent. Your father called me to service, and mine sent me to retrieve that sword... but the true reason is neither. I came to see about your Dragon's Lair—to discover if there was anything left of my father, some echo that would provide a clue to his end."

Gwendolyn could find no words. She stared, blinking, and he continued. "I took the sword, not for safe-keeping," he confessed. "But because Aengus promised that if I returned it, he would—"

He suddenly paused, and whatever it was he was about to say seemed to think better of it and close his mouth. "There is more," he admitted with a sigh, cupping her cheek. "But it must be told another time. What you most need to understand right now is that *Claímh Solais* is your best chance to unite these tribes. But you must make a choice, Gwendolyn."

"Choice?"

"I can take you to my father. But you must be absolutely certain it is what you wish, because if you are not, and your will is weak..."

The thing you lack most is the one thing your husband has.... the will to see this done. But she was not weak, and she could and must see this through. She must have that sword to save her people. Intuitively, Gwendolyn knew he was right: That sword was the key to uniting the tribes. "What must I prove to reclaim my sword?"

His brow lifted, and he tilted his head with a mirthless laugh. "In the end, you may have to seize it from him. But I promise you that if you believe what you endured by Loc's hands was too much, you'll not be prepared for the trial to come. My father does not favor me, Gwendolyn, nor will he favor you. So I ask you once more... would you come away with me and allow me to keep you safe... or will you face my father and demand the sword to champion your people?"

One, two, three heartbeats passed...

There was only one true response.

More than anything, Gwendolyn wanted to choose Málik.

She had a sudden, inexplicable vision of the two of them lying in a field of sunflowers... under a brilliant, golden sun...

But she understood how she must answer...

And so did he.

There was a reason her people had been given stewardship of these lands and knowing what Málik had confessed only strengthened her resolve. "I must... have the sword," she said, knowing it was, in truth, the *only* choice to be made.

He nodded. "As you will," he said ruefully, then bent to his knee, and peering up at her, he took her by the hand. "You inquired once if I would bend my knee to you, and here I will... I am a prince, in truth, but I would rather be your huntsman, your Shadow, and if you will allow me, Gwendolyn, I will defend you with my dying breath. I will put no one before you—not even my blood."

Gwendolyn peered down at her hand in his, his

shimmering flesh revealing what appeared to be shimmering scales beneath the moonlight... his upturned face so darkly beautiful.

She lifted a hand to one of his ivory horns, marveling at the transformation... so soft, but hard beneath her palm, and she felt her skin flush with desire.

A slow smile spread across his face, his lips pulling back over the sharp points of his teeth. "I can smell you," he whispered. "And one day I will taste you as well, but not yet," he said. "Not yet."

ESME

I was there... by her cradle when the gifts were bestowed.

I gave her mine with such prudence—two faces that would reveal a lover's true intentions. And, in truth, I want her to win.

I need her to face my father.

I will her to face him with Málik by her side—but why? Do I hope he'll smell their bond and smite them? Do I need him to end her because I cannot?

I loved him once. That is true, but he gave his heart to *her*.

I love her, and I loathe her, too.

I love her because she is brave and bold.

I loathe her because she wins. *Every. Time.*

I love her because she rises against all odds.

I loathe her because I try to do the same. *And fail.*

I love her because no matter what face and name my father gives her, she returns like a filthy cat, triumphant and smiling.

I loathe her because... in the end, she will take from me not only *him*, but my father, and my crown, my legacy, and future.

Yet I love her.
Mostly because...
She is my sister.
The Fallen Child.

AFTERWORD

Dearest reader,

If you've come this far with me, you know this book is a book of my heart. It was perhaps the story I was born to write, and I've loved every moment of my time in this world.

When I began its telling, I was certain I could write it in three parts, but it soon became clear that's not so. Now, I think it will be told in four books, although I intend to be true to this story and take my time with it, rolling out as rich a tapestry as I can. What I can promise you is that the end of this tale will be worth the wait, and the journey will be thrilling.

By now you also know that Gwendolyn's story is not entirely fiction. As I've already said, hers is the first account I ever read, historically speaking, of a strong woman, who kicked a cheating husband to the curb. She then raised an army to defeat him, taking the crown and throne. Technically, she is Briton's first Queen Regnant, but there wasn't a united Briton at the time of her reign.

I do make every attempt to stick to the historical

record, but I've also incorporated many of the Celtic legends, including the advent and eventual defeat of the Tuatha Dé Danann. If you've read The Irish Chronicles or Mabinogion, you'll find many, many familiar characters, only re-imagined. Despite that it's based on a true story, this is not meant to be a history lesson, but I hope you'll enjoy the many hours of research I've invested to enrich the setting, and to include the politics of the age, as well as some of the finer details (even if some of it is a bit fantastical).

For example, the water screw is very much a product of the age, and it dates back to ancient times. It is believed to have been the source of water for the Hanging Gardens of Bāb-ilim. However, the "Stone Isle" is in fact the historical setting of Tintagel (or initially Tre war Venydh, pronounced as Trevena) and there is no water screw there, nor is there any proof that any sophisticated fortress ever existed there. There is, however, evidence of an ancient settlement[1] that may have been the seat for the ancient kings of Dumnonia.

This site was also believed to be a thriving port, and pieces of imported Mediterranean pottery were discovered there, including table- and glassware. Merchants may have come from all over, looking to trade for copper and tin. I found it utterly fascinating to consider that Cornwall and Wales may have had far, far deeper roots, and a richer culture than I ever suspected, and perhaps more so than London itself. Like the princess in this story, its history defies everything I ever came to believe about its place in Britain's history.

But all this said, let me tell you what it is about this story—aside from the rich historical setting, and the mountain of possibilities after discovering Cornwall's history—that drew me.

Very simply, this is a story we women have lived for millennia. We know Gwendolyn's tale because we are still striving to overcome the pitfalls of life in a man's world. Her struggles are *our* struggles, and in the end, she prevailed, and this is not merely symbolic to me, but it gives me a wealth of hope that, in the end, we, too, will overcome. We are *all* queens in our own rights—all worth far more than even we, ourselves, are willing to accept. Gwendolyn's journey, from a child—sometimes precocious and innocent— to a mature and accomplished woman is intrinsically familiar. She is me, and she is you. I intend to give her one-helluva journey and I hope you'll join me in cheering for her and then sit back with a smile at the end, because no matter what hardships she may endure, she'll win in the end.

Here's to us. To me. To you.

Happy reading!

---

1. https://www.english-heritage.org.uk/visit/places/tintagel-cas
   tle/history-and-legend/history/

READER'S GUIDE

Main Characters

    Adwen Bryn's uncle, Duke of Durotriges

    Albanactus Brother of Locrinus; "founder" of Alba

    Baugh Prydein thane, king in the north

    Brutus King Brutus; Trojan by birth, "founder" of Britain

    Bryn Durotriges Shadow Guard to Gwendolyn

    Caradoc Chieftain of the Catuvellauni

    King Corineus *[cor-en-ee-us]* vassal of Brutus

    Gwendolyn Daughter of King Corineus and Queen Eseld

    Queen Eseld Queen consort and princess of Prydein

    Kamber Brother of Locrinus; "founder" of Cumbria

    Locrinus *[lock-ren-us]* Son of King Brutus of Troy

    Málik Danann *[mah-lick dah-nuhn]*

    Elowyn Durotriges *[El-oh-win]* Bryn's sister, and Gwendolyn's dearest friend

    Esme Faerie

    Estrildis Loc's mistress

    Habren Loc's son by Estrildis

    Queen Innogen Loc's mother, wife of Brutus

    Talwyn Trevena Mester at Arms

    Yestin Steward, Trevena

Caledonia (n) Scotland/Scottish

Cymru "Land of friends"

Dryad/Drus Faerie oak spirit

Dumnonia Ancient Cornwall

Ériu *[eh-ru]* Ancient Ireland

Hyperborea Fabled land whence the Tuatha Dé Danann may have come

Loegria Essentially Wales. Old English, meaning "land of foreigners"

Plowonida Ancient London

Pretania Ancient Britain

Prydein Welsh term for the isle of Britain; for The Cornish Princess, specifically Caledonia/Scotland

Sons of Míl Hiberians who conquered the Tuatha Dé Danann and settled Ireland

Tuatha Dé Danann *[too-uh-huh dey -dah-nuhn]* - "Tribe of the gods," ancient race in Irish mythology. Also, *Sidhe [*shē*], Elf, Fae*

Wheals Mines

ysbryd y byd Spirit of the world.

The Four Talismans of the Tuatha Dé Danann

Claímh Solais *[Klau-Solas] The sword of light*

Lúin of Celtchar Lugh's spear

Dagda's Cauldron *[DAW-dYAW's Cauldron]*

Lia Fáil *[lee-ah-foyl] - The stone of destiny, upon which even Britain's current kings are crowned.*

Awenydds Philosophers, seeking inspiration through bardic arts

Gwyddons/Gwiddons Priest-scientist, believe in divinity of and for all: *gwyddon, male*; *gwiddon, female*

Druids Priests, teachers, judges

Llanrhos Druids The most ancient order of Druids occupying the area now known as Anglesey

dewinefolk *Witches, faekind*

The seven Prydein tribes

Caledonii Scotland during the Iron Age and Roman eras

Novantae Far northeast of Scotland, including the offshore isles

Selgovae Kirkcudbright and Dumfriesshire, on the southern coast of Scotland

Votadini Southeast Scotland and northeast England

Venicones Fife (now in Scotland) and on both banks of the Tay

Vacomagi Region of Strathspey

Taexali Grampian, small undefended farms and hamlets

Four Tribes of Ancient Wales

Deceangli Far northern Wales

Silures Southeast of Wales; "people of the rocks"

Ordovices Central Wales; area now known as Gwynedd and south Clwyd

Demetae Southeast coast of Wales

Three Tribes of Ancient Cornwall

Dumnonii British Celtic tribe who inhabited Dumnonia, the area now known as Devon and Cornwall

Durotriges Devon and parts of Dorset and Somerset

Dobunni West of England

Remaining tribes of Ancient Britain

Atrebates Far south of England, along what is now the Hampshire and Sussex coastline.

Brigantes Northwest of England; Manchester, Lancashire and part of Yorkshire

Iceni East coast of England; Norfolk

Catuvellauni London, Hertfordshire, Bedfordshire, Buckinghamshire, Cambridgeshire, Oxfordshire, parts of Essex, Northamptonshire

Cantium Far Southeast England, Kent and a small part of Sussex

Parisi North and east Yorkshire

Trinovantes Essex and part of Suffolk

ALSO BY TANYA ANNE CROSBY

Lion Heart

Highland Song

MacKinnon's Hope

GUARDIANS OF THE STONE

Once Upon a Highland Legend

Highland Fire

Highland Steel

Highland Storm

Maiden of the Mist

THE MEDIEVALS HEROES

Once Upon a Kiss

Angel of Fire

Viking's Prize

REDEEMABLE ROGUES

Happily Ever After

Perfect In My Sight

McKenzie's Bride

Kissed by a Rogue

Thirty Ways to Leave a Duke

A Perfectly Scandalous Proposal

ANTHOLOGIES & NOVELLAS

Lady's Man

Married at Midnight

The Winter Stone

ROMANTIC SUSPENSE

Leave No Trace

Speak No Evil

Tell No Lies

MAINSTREAM FICTION

The Girl Who Stayed

The Things We Leave Behind

Redemption Song

Reprisal

Everyday Lies

ABOUT THE AUTHOR

Tanya Anne Crosby is the New York Times and USA Today bestselling author of thirty novels. She has been featured in magazines, such as People, Romantic Times and Publisher's Weekly, and her books have been translated into eight languages. Her first novel was published in 1992 by Avon Books, where Tanya was hailed as "one of Avon's fastest rising stars." Her fourth book was chosen to launch the company's Avon Romantic Treasure imprint.

Known for stories charged with emotion and humor and filled with flawed characters Tanya is an award-winning author, journalist, and editor, and her novels have garnered reader praise and glowing critical reviews. She and her writer husband split their time between Charleston, SC, where she was raised, and northern Michigan, where the couple make their home.

For more information
Website

Email
Newsletter